FRAGRANT BOOKS
## *The Orchid Tree*

Siobhan Daiko was born in Hong Kong, went to school in
Perth, Western Australia, and moved to the UK in 1981.
She has worked in the City of London, once ran a post
office/B&B in Herefordshire, and, more recently, taught
Modern Foreign Languages in a Welsh high school.
Siobhan now lives with her husband in the Veneto region
of Northern Italy, where she spends her time writing,
researching historical characters, and enjoying the *dolce vita*.
*The Orchid Tree* is her second novel to be published.

ALSO BY SIOBHAN DAIKO

*Lady of Asolo*
*Veronica* **COURTESAN**

# The Orchid Tree

### SIOBHAN DAIKO

Fragrant Books

Published by FRAGRANT BOOKS

First Edition 2015

The English used in this publication follows the spelling and
idiomatic conventions of the United Kingdom.

ISBN-13:978-1507525845

ISBN-10:1507525842

All enquiries to info@fragrantpublishing.com

Edited by John Hudspith

Cover painting "Junks" by Douglas Bland (courtesy of the Bland
Family Collection)

Cover design J.D. Smith

In memory of my parents and grandparents.

# ACKNOWLEDGEMENTS

I would like to thank the following people:

Members and professional reviewers of YouWriteOn, the peer review site, for their feedback on the early chapters.

Ann Bennett, Tony Fyler, Safia Moore and Judith Ozkan, my talented fellow writers, for their helpful comments on early drafts.

John Hudspith, my inspiring editor, for his highly professional, prompt, and precise editing.

Jane Dixon-Smith for her wonderful work on the cover design.

My family: my late parents and grandparents, Veronica, Douglas, Doris and Vernon, whose lives inspired this novel; my brother, Diarmuid, and my sister, Clodagh, for their encouragement.

Victor, my husband, for his love and support. Our son, Paul, and his girlfriend, Lili, for their help with technology.

Last, but not least, I thank you, dear reader, for buying this book and reading it.

# HONG KONG, DECEMBER 1948

Another deep blast reverberated from the ship's horn. The deck vibrated beneath my feet, my toes tingling as the engines grumbled to a stop. Hong Kong Island loomed, like an enormous whale rising into the morning mist. The salty tang of the sea filled my nostrils. Was I doing the right thing? On the water, the dark shapes had turned into ships, junks and sampans. I was home and there'd be no going back now.

My wrist touched the metal rail, cold as the Japanese executioner's sword, and my breath caught. A blade, glinting in the sun. A streak of silver. Shining. Silent. Deadly. Choking back a sob, I raked my nails across the scabs on my hands, scratching harder and harder until I could bear the pain no more.

The clatter of the anchor chain, then the chug-chug of a motor-boat, and I leaned over the barrier. Where was Papa?

A young man in a navy blue jacket strode up the gangway. 'Miss Wolseley?' He swept off his peaked cap. 'Lieutenant James Stevens,' he introduced himself. 'I'm here to take you ashore. Your father sent me.'

I forced a brief smile. Lieutenant Stevens was taller

than me by a couple of inches, and his bronze-coloured hair had curled in the moisture-laden air; he was patting it down as if he wanted to draw attention to himself.

'There aren't any liners direct from Sydney. I'm sorry you had to come all the way out to the middle of the harbour,' I said.

'Not a problem. How long were you away?

'Over three years. Since September 1945.'

'You were in Hong Kong during the occupation?'

'In the internment camp at Stanley.'

'I've heard about that place,' he said, frowning.

I flinched. I'd grown up in "that place", behind barbed wire, suffering cruelty and starvation at the hands of the occupying Japanese, my heart frozen ever since.

*So why come back?*

# PART ONE
# 1941-1945

# 1
# HONG KONG
# DECEMBER 1941

Bamboo by the side of the path rustles in the breeze, and a waterfall gurgles into a natural pond. My pony bends his head to crop the grass. I let go of the reins and slip off my riding hat. It's time for a rest now. Papa and I set out from the stables at Jardine's Lookout an hour ago and have ridden right round Happy Valley.

I dismount and run my hands over the smooth leather of my saddle. It's too small since my recent growth spurt; I'm such a beanpole.

'Papa, do you think I can have a new one for Christmas?' I give him my best smile.

'Maybe.' He winks and reaches into his pocket for his pipe. Papa is tall with wavy dark-brown hair, amber-coloured eyes and a high forehead. I adore him, of course, but hate taking after him. I wish I'd been born blonde and blue-eyed like my beautiful mama.

Rubbing Merry's dusty chestnut neck, I breathe in the sweet scent of equine sweat, one of my favourite smells. Of course Papa will get me the saddle. Mama says I'm spoilt rotten and it's true. Only Papa does the spoiling, though . . .

'Come on, Kate,' he says. 'I need to change my breath.' Papa says that every week and it's become a joke between us. All he really wants is a change of scene. We remount and trot back to the stables, then stop off at the Yacht Club on the way home.

Papa goes to the bar, but I'm not allowed in there as I'm not sixteen yet. So I wait outside the clubhouse, soaking up the winter sunshine and watching the junks in the harbour, their sails open like giant butterfly wings. The creak of an oar, and the boatwoman selling orchids from her sampan ties up at the jetty. She steps ashore with a bouquet in her hands. There's a baby, head lolling but fast asleep, in a sling on her back. I pay the woman and clutch the purple flowers. I'll give them to Mama, like I do every Sunday. And Mama will nod, smile, and hand them to one of the servants as usual.

The sound of footsteps, and Papa arrives. 'All the chaps have been called up for manoeuvres,' he says in a false jaunty tone. 'I was practically the only one in there.'

A prickle of anxiety creeps up my spine, and I grasp his hand.

'Nothing to worry about, dear girl.'

I relax my shoulders and walk with him towards the pier.

\*\*\*

The next morning air-raid sirens wail from Victoria City far below. I stifle a yawn; it's only another drill. Pulling at my maroon school jumper, I lean back at the breakfast table opposite Mama and Papa. There's a geography test this afternoon. Have I done enough revision?

A pang of disquiet. Something's different. The sirens are wailing longer than usual and a droning sound echoes. The door bursts open and my amah erupts into the room.

I eye the chopping knife in my old nanny's hand. Ah Ho has been a constant presence for as long as I can remember, yet never before have I seen her take a knife from the kitchen.

Rocking from one foot to the other, Ah Ho drops the blade onto the table and wraps her arms around her starched white tunic. 'Too much air-plane,' she shrills. 'Too much air-plane.'

Leaping up, I send my chair crashing to the floor. Hong Kong only has a few aeroplanes. Are these American? Or even Chinese? Not Japanese, though. That would be unthinkable. Besides, everyone knows how hopeless their pilots are . . .

I rush through the wide doors and onto the veranda skirting the front of the house. Planes soar in a V-shaped formation above the harbour almost level with my eyes. Grey planes with a red sun under their wings. Something, I'm not sure what, spills from their bellies.

The echoes of explosions ricochet off the distant hills. Papa comes up and pulls me towards him. 'Bally hell!' His grip is so firm that it hurts.

My gut twists and the orange juice I drank at breakfast comes back up my throat, the sourness stinging my tongue. A flying boat is on fire. Coils of smoke rise from the airport. I clamp my hands to my ears, a sick feeling spreading through me.

Papa's hold tightens. I push my head into his shirt; I've recently turned fifteen and haven't done that for years. I lift my gaze. One by one, the planes tilt their wings and peel off in the direction of China. 'Is it over?'

Papa shields his eyes with a hand, his knuckles white. 'I hope so.' He leads me back into the house.

In the dining room I run to Mama. She stands at the picture window, her lower lip trembling. I squeeze her icy fingers. 'They've gone.'

Mama blinks, takes her hands away and shakes her bobbed hair. 'Why on earth did you run outside?'

'I don't know. I just had to see. Where's Ah Ho?'

'She went to find Jimmy.'

He's Ah Ho's son, one year older than me and a close friend. Breathing in short, sharp bursts, I run after my amah.

*Pray God Jimmy hasn't left for school yet!*

\*\*\*

The planes come back again and again.

I bite my nails. This can't be happening. Things like this don't happen. Yet, it *is* happening and nothing will ever be the same again. I should be at school, not crouching in the sitting room with Jimmy, Ah Ho and my parents, in near darkness, as Papa has ordered the typhoon shutters to be put up on all the windows.

I can't stop thinking about the people I know who might be caught in the bombing: the flower seller at the Yacht Club; the grizzly old newspaper vendor on the ferry concourse.

Are they still alive? My heart thuds against my ribs. Are we all going to die?

'I'm frightened,' I whisper.

Ah Ho strokes my hair like she used to when I was little. 'Everything be all right.'

Jimmy pulls a pack of cards from his pocket. 'Let's have a game of Canasta to keep our minds off things.' He smiles his crooked-toothed grin. It's too dark to see, though, and impossible to concentrate. Jimmy puts the cards away and we sit in silence, arms drooping.

Every now and then Papa turns on the radio. The same announcement each time. There haven't been any sightings of the Japanese Navy steaming towards Hong Kong. 'The raids are probably just a show of force,' he says.

Towards evening the all-clear is sounded. But the typhoon shutters stay up.

\*\*\*

That night I toss about in bed, the sheets wrapping themselves around my body. I can't rid the image of the bombs dropping from my mind. If the planes come back tomorrow there won't be anything left of Hong Kong.

The sound of a radio wakes me; it must be morning. I pad across the corridor and push open the door to my parents' room. My feet sink into the deep pile carpet as I stare at the untouched tea tray on Mama's bedside table. My gaze passes to Papa. Why is he still in his dressing-gown?

'The Japanese have bombed Singapore and the American base at Pearl Harbor in Hawaii,' Papa says in a shocked tone. 'And their bally troops marched across our border last night. Not to worry, dear girl, our chaps will soon see them off. But in the meantime, we have to be brave.'

I sit down heavily on my parents' bed. I will be brave. Of course I will. Just like the Hong Kong Volunteers and the garrison soldiers are being brave. They'll defeat the enemy and life will return to normal, won't it? The alternative doesn't bear thinking about . . .

# 2

In Happy Valley, standing on the front drive of a large house overlooking the Jockey Club, Charles Pearce is helping his father load up their old Austin. He spent the whole of yesterday crouched with Ma and his little sister under the dining room table, ears ringing with the boom of explosions, the crash of falling masonry and glass, his stomach twisted into knots by the terror, the indescribable terror. Either the Japanese pilots thought the racecourse was a strategic target, or they were useless at aiming for the oil tanks at North Point. This morning there's a lull in the bombing. Good thing Pa has decided they must leave.

Charles turns round for one last look at his home, perched on the side of the hill with a gap next to it like a missing tooth. His neighbours' mansion has been reduced to a pile of rubble, the fate of its occupants unknown.

*Hope we'll find shelter on the other side of the island . . .*

After checking his shortwave radio is carefully stowed, Charles lifts his knapsack onto his shoulder and piles into the car with his little sister. Ruth's light brown curls are tied in bunches, the red ribbons unravelling, and fear is in her eyes. He gives her a hug. 'We'll be safe now.'

Pa gets behind the wheel and pushes back his thatch of

white-blond hair. Ma sits next to him, dressed as ever in a *cheongsam,* her delicate face pinched with worry.

They take the road that cuts through the hills and leads to the south. Cresting the rise, they come to a roadblock. A European soldier points his rifle at the car and Pa winds down the window. 'Let us pass! We're British!'

'Japs are on the island. Didn't you know?'

Pa jerks his head back so fast his glasses fly off the end of his nose.

'We'll stop them here,' the soldier says as Pa contorts downwards to retrieve his specs.

Charles slumps in his seat. No point in worrying Ma and Ruth, but the European was being a tad optimistic, given the fact that the British couldn't halt the Japanese advance on the mainland. How wrong of them to have expected that an attack, if it had to happen, would have come from the sea . . .

The road levels out by the Repulse Bay, and Pa says they should wait in the car while he goes and sees if they can stay here. The hotel faces the beach, its main section and two right-angled wings come forward towards the ocean and form three sides of a square, with the road, sands, and South China Sea making up the fourth side. Behind are steep slopes covered with trees and scrub undergrowth where Japanese soldiers might well be hiding.

Charles puts his arm around his sister again. Mustn't let her see he's scared. She's only eight and a half and he's twice her age.

Pa emerges from the front of the hotel. 'There's lots of food, apparently. But not many staff. Just a group of Naval Volunteer officers and a few British families. I think this'll make a good bolt-hole. The senior pageboy is doubling up as receptionist and he's sorting out a couple of rooms for us.'

Moments later, Charles steers Ruth across the lobby behind his parents. The scent of polish from the parquet floor mixes with the aroma of freshly baked scones. It's just like he remembers from his last visit and hard to believe there's a war on.

A British woman, slumped in a rattan chair at the far end of the room, calls out in a braying voice, 'What're those Chinese doing? They've got no right to be here.'

Ma rolls her eyes and keeps walking. Charles swallows the bitterness in his throat. He carries both suitcases and shields Ruth from the woman's stare. Luckily Pa is half-deaf as well as being short-sighted, otherwise there'd be hell to pay. It's obvious that his father is English, just as it's obvious that Ruth and he don't look anything like the locals. Ma's Chinese, but she has finer features than the Cantonese, because she's from the north. Charles mutters to himself. Shame they couldn't find refuge with their family in Macau . . .

***

The following morning, he sits by the open French windows in his bedroom. Ma has gone with Pa and Ruth to the lobby, saying they need to establish themselves.

*Fat chance of that!*

Charles picks up the Steinbeck novel someone's left on the desk. Sunlight filters through the window and he catches movement on the road.

*What?*

He shades his eyes. Short, stocky men with black hair. Fully armed and camouflaged with bits of leaf and grass. Slouching in front of a garage.

Charles takes off his shoes, lets himself out onto the veranda, then down to a small lawn. *Better find out who they are.* He crawls for a short distance, rough prickly grass scratching his stomach, then freezes. *Damn!* The men are wearing peaked caps with red bands. Japanese uniforms.

He hides behind a low wall, his palms sweaty, and peers over the top. An enemy soldier is pointing a bayonet at six British men dressed in uniform. Another man, an officer

18

as he's wearing a sword, starts yelling and repeatedly slapping one of the Europeans on the face.

Heart pounding, Charles wriggles his way back across the lawn then runs to the dining room, where the British commander is taking tea with his men.

'There're Japs. On the main road,' Charles yells. 'They've got some of our chaps. I think they're going to kill them.'

'Stay here,' a Volunteer shouts, grabbing his rifle and charging off down the corridor.

Charles sneaks back to the veranda, and flattens himself against the wall. On the other side of the lawn, the Japanese officer is still slapping the British soldier. The man stands taking the blows and doesn't even seem to notice them.

The Volunteer takes aim. Cold sweat spreads over Charles' body. He holds his breath. Bullets catch the Japanese officer on the side of his face and neck, spinning him around. His body crumples to the ground. Charles has never seen anyone killed before and nausea swells his gullet. He retches, and half-digested porridge spews down his chin.

The rest of the Volunteers form a group at the windows above. They open fire, aiming wide of the British. The unarmed prisoners scramble headlong into the garage with the enemy behind them, colliding and tripping each other up. Five of the Japanese fall in twisted heaps.

The surviving Japanese soldiers poke their rifles out of the garage. Charles hides behind a pillar. A bullet whizzes past his left ear and his bowels become water. Shaking like a dog with distemper, he runs back to the lobby.

\*\*\*

Three days later, he sits on a brick in a drainage tunnel behind the hotel, hiding with the rest of the civilians to avoid catching a stray bullet from the continuing battle.

The chill seeps into his bones and the stench of rotting vegetation comes through the dank walls.

Ruth pulls at his trousers with one hand and points with the other towards the shadows, her eyes enormous. A huge rat is watching them, whiskers twitching.

'You're being so brave,' Charles whispers to her. The rodent scuttles away. He touches Ruth's arm and looks at the collection of people around them, English men and women, for the most part, and a handful of children.

'The Volunteers have decided to leave tonight,' one of the men murmurs. 'They're heading for Stanley Fort.'

Charles' stomach clenches. The soldiers are abandoning them; they probably realise this is a lost cause. Or maybe they think by staying they're putting the civilians in more danger.

The trapdoor crashes open. He jumps, but it's only the junior pageboy. The boy drops down, balancing a tray with water, coffee and food. *How has he managed to avoid getting shot?* Shrugging, Charles reaches for a sandwich and passes it to his sister.

They munch in silence. It's been easy to keep quiet for the twelve hours a day they've hidden in the darkness. The periodic sound of gunfire above their heads would quieten anyone. Unless help comes soon, however, capture is certain. Fear gnaws at Charles and grows stronger by the minute.

Night comes; it's too dark for the snipers to see their mark. He creeps back into the hotel with the others. They wait in tense silence on the first-floor corridor; anything could happen at any moment . . .

The hotel staff, or rather the senior pageboy and his assistant, arrive with trays of supper. A sudden flicker on the window panes. Lights are flashing in the north wing. Charles can hardly breathe. Japanese voices and the echo of footsteps. A patrol going from room to room. The enemy forces are battle-stained and most likely battle-maddened; they'll shoot everyone on sight. *Best to let them know that only civilians remain.*

Charles leaps up and calls out, 'There aren't any soldiers here!'

The door crashes open. Two Japanese men come in and point their bayonets directly at him. Everyone puts their hands up. The women let out muffled sobs. Charles stands still.

*Keep calm! Don't let the side down!*

The soldiers glare at him then spin on their heels. There's a stunned hush.

Within minutes, the heavy tread of more soldiers from the other side of the door. The senior pageboy, eyes wide and jaw set, bars their entrance.

Pa rushes to stop him. Too late. An enemy soldier knocks the pageboy back against the wall. With a flash of steel, his commanding officer makes a jabbing motion and sticks a bayonet into the pageboy's chest. Blood spurts, the pageboy twitches and his eyes glaze over.

Charles glances at Ruth. She's still asleep on her mattress, thank God. But how will he ever forget what he's just witnessed? There's no time even to think about it; the officer is barking orders to the civilians to line up. 'You must get ready. Tomorrow very early you go North Point.' Charles gives his sister a gentle shake.

\*\*\*

After packing what bags they can carry and snatching a few hours' sleep, Charles and his family troop outside with the other prisoners. He blinks in the early morning sunlight. A foul stench hits the back of his throat, like nothing he's ever smelt before: much worse than the stink of the drainage tunnel or even the raw liver their cook had once forgotten to put in the fridge. It fills the air, lodging in Charles's mouth, clinging to his taste buds and coating his tongue. He gags. The smell is coming from something or someone who's died, and he shouldn't look. A force beyond him, an intense curiosity, turns his head with an invisible hand.

He eyes the building opposite. Eucliffe mansion, property of a Chinese millionaire. Piles of bodies lie by the balustrade overlooking the sea. British prisoners. Tied together. Shot and left to rot. Ma snatches a couple of handkerchiefs from her bag. 'Cover your nose!'

During the long, dreary trudge up the hill they pass the bodies of numerous soldiers, left unburied by the side of the road. Each time, Charles places himself between Ruth and the dead men. Each time, his stomach lurches. Each time, his anxiety grows.

At the top of the hill, he sets off with Pa and the other men; they'll march the rest of the way. Except, a Japanese soldier points his rifle and indicates his place is with the women and children in some lorries that take them down to Happy Valley.

*How old do they think I am? I'm in my second last year at school, for God's sake . . .*

The roads are empty, but the sound of mortar-bombing reverberates in the distance. Hong Kong hasn't surrendered yet.

At an abandoned factory, the Japanese herd the prisoners into a wide ground-floor storage area lined with cans of paint. They give them water and sugar, the only food they've had all day.

'I'm hungry,' Ruth whines.

'Hush.' Ma opens her bag and rummages around. 'I wish we'd thought to pack something to eat.'

Pa and the rest of the men arrive. 'Let's spread our overcoats on the floor and make ourselves a den,' Pa says.

Even sitting on his coat, the concrete chills Charles' bones. 'It's Christmas Eve. Why don't we sing some carols?' he suggests. Tentatively, he starts on the first verse of *O Come All Ye Faithful*.

A middle-aged couple, who've copied them and are sitting on their jackets, put their thumbs up and add their voices. 'Sing choirs of angels.'

The groups of internees around them join in, one after the other. 'O Come let us adore Him.'

Charles progresses to *Hark the Herald Angels Sing* and they all chorus, 'Peace on earth and mercy mild, God and sinners reconciled.'

The Japanese soldiers shout and wave their rifles. The singing stops. Have they understood the words? With the carols, unity of a sort has developed among the prisoners; more likely, their captors wanted to spoil it.

\*\*\*

The next night, Charles sits with Ma, Pa and Ruth, clumped on the  damp deck of an old ferry. God only knows where the Japanese are taking them . . .

The skyline is dark, yet he can make out the stately old colonial buildings lining the waterfront. He tucks his hands under his armpits. Waves slap against the side of the boat and the breeze feels as if it will pass straight through him.

At Kowloon pier, the gangplanks wobble under his feet as he takes Ruth's hand. Ma and Pa line up next to him on the concourse. Japanese soldiers wave their bayonets and march them in the direction of Nathan Road.

Ruth nudges him and makes a face. 'I hope they give us something proper to eat. I didn't like that nasty cold rice and those turnips this morning.'

The streets, normally bustling with people, cars and rickshaws, are quiet. In five minutes they arrive at the back of the Peninsula Hotel, and a soldier ushers them into a hostel. On the fifth-floor they move into a pokey room with only one bed, which they'll have to share with another family.

'This isn't the worst of it,' Pa says, his mouth twisting. 'I've just heard that the governor has surrendered to the Japanese.' He pauses. 'Happy Christmas!'

Charles laughs. 'A *Very* Happy Christmas.'

# 3

I turn the last page of *Rebecca*. Maxim de Winter is so romantic, even if he has committed murder. How odd that his second wife doesn't have a name. And Mrs Danvers! Altogether too creepy for words . . .

My parents and I have been confined to our house on the Peak since the surrender. Thank God I'm an avid reader, and Mama has said I can read my way through her collection of books, otherwise I'd be terribly bored. We've been waiting for the Americans to come and liberate Hong Kong for ever, it seems.

Papa's pipe smoke wafts across the room, making me sneeze. Gravel crunches in the front courtyard, then footsteps scuffle in the hall. Strange at this time of the day, given that it's nearly lunchtime. My pulse hammers. A Japanese officer is standing in the doorway.

Mama's face has frozen: eyes wide, lips pressed together, cheeks colourless. Our first encounter with the enemy face to face and certainly not unexpected, yet terrifying all the same.

Papa puts down his pipe, gets up from his armchair, and glares at the officer. 'What can I do for you?'

'You go Stanley Internment Camp tomorrow,' the

Japanese man says, saliva spraying from his mouth as his tongue trips over the English words. 'All things will be good. Plenty food.' He fingers the sword hanging from his hip and smirks, his thin lips curling but his eyes expressionless.

I gape at him, trying to take in what he's just said. Stanley is a prison on the other side of the island where they usually send murderers. Why are they putting us there?

The officer puffs himself up, thrusts his chest forward, and points at Papa. 'Bow!'

Papa stands immobile and fixes his gaze on the opposite wall. Should I go up to him and whisper that he must bow if he doesn't want to get into trouble? But my feet are rooted to the floor. The second hand on the grandfather clock ticks through half a minute, and I hold my breath.

The officer shrugs, marches up to Papa, and slaps his face with a front-hand-back-hand motion. Slap. Slap. Slap. The sound plays in my head again and again like a stuck gramophone record. A trickle of urine wets my knickers; I put a hand to my mouth, my cheeks burning.

I shake myself. Finally my legs obey me and I run to Papa. He wipes his moustache, grimaces and bows his head to waist-level. His eyes hold mine and he mouths the words, 'Steady, dear girl!'

The officer struts out through the open door, his long sword trailing behind him. Gravel crunches outside again and an engine races. Then silence. Even Mama, normally unafraid to have an opinion on everything, has been struck speechless.

I hug my father. 'Poor Papa, look what he's done to you.'

'Stings a bit, but not to worry. I'll be all right,' he says, although a red blotch has formed on his cheek.

Mama moves from the sofa, as if in a trance, and dabs at his cut with her handkerchief. 'Did he say there'll be lots of food in Stanley? We've almost run out here.'

'We've run out of more than food.' Papa's voice is quiet. 'Japs have locked up practically all the British. They only let us stay up here on the Peak this past month while they sorted out where to put us all.' He shakes his head. 'I suppose we'd better start packing.' He turns to the crystal decanters on the mahogany sideboard, pours himself a large whisky, and swallows it in one gulp.

I don't want to pack; I don't want to leave my home and go to a prison. Yet there's no getting out of it. I walk from the room, my feet dragging. 'I'm going to see Ah Ho.'

After changing my underwear, I cross the small courtyard dividing the staff quarters from our two-storey house. My mouth trembles, but I clamp my jaw firm. It's the way things are done in our family.

*Mama and Papa are keeping calm, so I'll do the same and not think about what might happen.*

I run up the steps and pull open the door to Ah Ho's room, breathing in the comforting scent of camphor from the White Flower Oil she rubs into her knees to ease their stiffness. 'Where will you both go after we've gone?'

'Back to China,' Jimmy says from his chair by the window.

'But the war's there too, isn't it?' I tug at my hair and tuck it behind my ears.

'Our village won't interest the *Law Pak Tau.*'

'What?'

'Turnip heads,' Jimmy giggles. 'That's what we call the Japanese because they're always eating turnips.'

I pick up a handful of rice from the sack in the corner, and let the starchy grains trickle like tiny pebbles through my fingers. 'Where will you live?'

Jimmy sits forward and places his elbows on his knees. 'Uncle will take us in.'

Ah Ho perches dejectedly on a stool; she must be dreading going back to the subsistence life of a peasant.

I take the seat opposite Jimmy. 'Will you be able to go to school?' Papa has paid for him to attend an English-speaking school since he turned six.

'I'll need to work in the fields with my cousins.'

A picture comes into my mind of farmers in the New Territories, near the border with China, planting rice in the paddy fields, their wide-brimmed straw hats shaped like giant toadstools, backs bent double as they push the seedlings one after the other into the water-sodden soil. I make fists of my hands. Jimmy is a brilliant student; he shouldn't have to give up his studies.

'It won't be for long, you know.' I try to inject a note of optimism into my voice. 'The Americans will rescue us.'

His lips have formed a straight line; it's clear he doesn't believe me. 'I heard my parents talking about it,' I say. 'My father said the American Air Force is the best in the world and they'll help us. Once they've recovered from Pearl Harbor, of course.'

Ah Ho gets up from her stool and pulls a metal comb through her long, thin, black hair before fastening it in a bun. She strikes a match and lights a joss stick. The fragrance is so familiar that my breathing slows. If only I could stay here with the people I love, where I've grown up, where I feel safe.

I get to my feet and face the small statue of the Bodhisattva of Compassion by the door, running my palms up and down the smooth white soapstone. *The Japanese will be defeated quickly. They have to be.*

Ah Ho puts her hands together and bows three times. With a sigh, she reaches under her bed for a battered leather suitcase.

'Let's go out to the garden,' I say to Jimmy. 'Some fresh air will cheer us up.'

On the other side of the terrace, Papa and Ah Woo the houseman are digging a large hole. 'What are you doing?'

'Burying the family silver. We can't let the Japs get their hands on it.'

'We're just heading down there.' I point to the path leading to the tennis courts.

The oleander bushes sway in the breeze, and a gecko scuttles back into its hole in the hedge. I pluck a heart-shaped leaf from the orchid tree and crush it between my fingers; the dried-pea scent teases my nostrils and the garden walls enclose me as if I were already imprisoned.

'Jimmy, let's have one last walk around the Peak.' I pull him gently towards the front gate and meet with little resistance. He probably wants to escape for a while as well. I look behind to check we haven't been seen. Papa would have my guts for garters if he knew I was leaving the compound. 'Why are the Japanese going to lock us up?' I ask Jimmy. 'We could stay up here and not be any trouble.'

'They won't allow white people to look down on them.'

His dark eyes briefly meet mine before he looks away. I throw my arms around him, but he's so unyielding I might as well be hugging a rock.

I let him go, and he follows me along the pathway circling the summit of the Peak. The pungent sweaty-socks smell of the sub-tropical forest wafts into my nose. Brushing past a plant with leaves as large as elephants' ears, I peer through dense clumps of vegetation hanging like interwoven ropes.

The houses, apartments and office blocks below are so small they could be mistaken for children's toys. Where are the junks and sampans usually clogging the harbour? Only Japanese ships have anchored in its depths. Kowloon Peninsula, a narrow piece of flat land, juts out into the deep blue-green water. Bare hills, with ridges like dragons' backs, form a framework to the scene. When will I see it again?

A British anti-aircraft gun battery nestles halfway down the western flank. I grab Jimmy's wrist. 'Come on. There's no one about. Let's see if we can find any mementos.'

Slabs of concrete and metal bolts stick up from the ground, and there are gaping holes blasted through the thick walls of the brown and green camouflage-striped buildings. Shards of broken glass shimmer in the sunlight. I pick up a spent bullet. A cold gust comes from nowhere and I shiver. Someone or something is moving in the azalea bushes below . . .

'A soldier died when this place came under heavy artillery fire,' Jimmy says, glancing from left to right. 'He's probably a ghost now.'

My scalp prickles. A spirit is definitely lurking in the untamed vegetation, ready to cause chaos. We'd better get out of here . . .

'Come on!' Jimmy breaks into a run and heads back up the hill.

I follow his zigzag footsteps. The soldier's ghost will be hungry for revenge, but Jimmy once told me that spirits can only travel in straight lines. Jimmy and I will be safe enough.

Our feet pound the dusty track, and scores of butterflies rise from the feathery fronds of the wild banana trees. We sprint past the high broken-glass-topped walls of the mansions of the wealthy, and into our own open gateway at number eight. We barge through the front door, still uselessly guarded by stone lions, then turn right into the kitchen.

Ah Ho looks up from chopping vegetables. 'Wah! Missy angry no can find you.'

'Sorry, Ah Ho.' I peck my amah on the cheek.

Jimmy goes to his room, and I head for the sitting room, sliding across the polished parquet floor to where my mother sits at her antique rosewood desk.

I shift my weight from one foot to the other. 'What are you doing, Mama?'

'Making lists of the items we won't be taking into the camp. So we can check they're still here when this nightmare is over.' She puts her pen down. 'Where have you been?'

'Jimmy and I went for a walk.'

'What were you thinking of?' Mama's voice is sharp. 'Don't you realise how dangerous that is? I've just heard from Ah Ho that Jap soldiers have been doing unspeakable things to women, and even girls of your age. Jimmy wouldn't have been able to protect you.'

'I'm sorry. I didn't think.' And it's true; I never thought for a moment I might be in danger.

'Well, you'd better start thinking. Do something useful and take the silver-framed photos to the garden!'

Outside, the trench full of silver opens up like a grave and there's the cup I won last year in a show-jumping competition. My eyes sting. It's been fifty days since I've seen Merry. Fifty days since the enemy came across the border. Fifty days waiting to be rescued.

I wince, no longer able to keep what Mama said about the Japanese out of my mind. I can guess the unspeakable things they are doing to women. A shiver of fear. Will they do unspeakable things to me in Stanley?

# 4

'I've come to say goodbye.' I'm standing in the doorway of Ah Ho and Jimmy's room. It's the morning after the Japanese officer's visit and my voice, clogged with emotion, sounds almost strangled to my ears. I stare through the window at a bank of fog obscuring the view of the garden. Chilly, damp and miserable, it fits my mood.

Ah Ho perches on her stool, her bottom spilling over the edges. 'You sit down.' She pats the seat of the rattan chair next to her.

I lower myself and give Jimmy a half smile. 'All packed?'

He nods and hands me a small package. I tear it open to reveal a jade bangle. 'To bring you luck,' he says.

I slip it onto my wrist, the emerald green stone cool against my skin. 'It's beautiful. Thank you. I've got this for you.' My words are even more choked now. I give him my treasured copy of *Murder on the Orient Express*. 'My mother will help you out with some of her jewellery, too.' I squeeze Jimmy's hand. 'You can sell it.'

Ah Ho sobs, open-mouthed, and enfolds me in a warm embrace. I rub my cheek against the starched white tunic. My throat tight, I swallow hard. I won't let myself cry.

Instead, I give my amah a hug and say, in my brightest voice, 'I expect we'll be together again before too long.'

An hour later, I stand on the forecourt with my parents and Ah Ho. The houseboys are loading up an open-topped lorry: mattresses, an electric hot plate, three suitcases full of clothes, my mother's jewellery, and a large hat box. The Japanese officer ordered Papa to arrange our own transport to the camp.

Mama, dressed in her mink coat, hands Ah Ho a gold necklace. 'To be sold. Divide the money between you all.'

I fling myself into my amah's arms. 'I'll miss you,' I sob. The tears run freely; I can't stop them.

Ah Ho kisses me noisily on the cheek. 'I come back by and by.'

My lower lip wobbles, but I stiffen it.

\*\*\*

Heading south, the lorry trundles its way around the craters and pot-holes left by the shelling. Soon we reach the Repulse Bay Hotel, where I would have Earl Grey and cake as a special treat with Mama before the war came. The fountain at the front of the building is dry and the palm trees gracing the gardens have a downhearted look, as if they've seen things they'd rather forget. At the check-point, a Japanese soldier barks questions to our driver. My heartbeat races, but the soldier waves us on.

We pass the resort where I used to spend lazy summer days swimming, and paddling a canoe from the rocks with my best friend Mary. Mama and Papa would play bridge with Mary's parents and drink gin slings in their beach hut, only occasionally venturing into the warm waters of the South China Sea. Mary left for Australia with her mother last year. We've been writing to each other faithfully. How will I keep in touch with her now?

There's the lido! It's boarded up. What did I expect? Hardly likely the Japanese would keep it open for Sunday afternoon tea dances . . .

Gears grinding, the lorry climbs the headland then follows the road down to Stanley Village. Fishing boats line the beach like deck-chairs. Old men sit in doorways smoking their long pipes; dogs and children play in the dust; washing hangs from bamboo poles.

*Such a different world to the Peak . . .*

On the other side of the police station, we cross a short strip of land leading to a small peninsula. Barbed wire blocks the road. Japanese guards verify our names and let us through.

'Out you hop,' Papa says in a false bright voice. 'I'll go and find out where we're to be billeted.'

A cold wind whips my coat. I shiver and stare at a queue of people waiting by a building. Papa returns with a short bald man. 'This is Mr Davies from the Housing Committee.' His voice is still chirpy. 'We're in the Indian Quarters.'

'What are the Indian Quarters?'

'Where the Indian prison wardens used to live. The Japs've kept some of them on as guards, but they're living in the village now.' He smiles briefly. 'I don't think it's going to be too bad here, after all. The camp is governed by the internees. Housing, food distribution and medical care are all run by our chaps. Apparently, the Japanese just oversee things and send in supplies.'

Papa folds his gangly frame into the lorry. I heave myself back into the cab with Mama and the bald man, all squashed in together. We pass a school and stop by a block of garages. The last two hundred yards we struggle on foot, carrying our luggage down a few steps, past a small mosque, and along a stony path.

'How can you put us here?' Mama drops her hatbox. 'These buildings have been bombed to bits.'

'Not all. Follow me!' Mr Davies leads us up a narrow stairwell. 'I've managed to get you a room to yourselves.'

'A room?' Mama echoes.

We enter a two-storey block facing the sea and climb the stairs to the first floor. 'Our youngest amah has a room bigger than this. And she has the room all to herself.' Mama places her hands on her hips and, with a shudder, eyes the grubby grey walls. Her face looks as if she's swallowed a mouthful of sour milk. 'Is there a bathroom?'

'A washroom with a tap,' Mr Davies says apologetically.

I glance at the lavatory. We have similar loos at home for the staff, and Jimmy calls them "couchers on account of having to squat over a hole. If Jimmy can manage I'll manage too. But Mama must be beside herself with disgust.

Mr Davies waves his arm to the left. 'There's a sort of kitchen as well.' A single tap graces a small annex; it's like no kitchen I've ever seen. Filthy stone benches line the sides; there's neither a stove nor any cooking utensils. A balcony runs along the front of the flat, and an open passage through the back.

I peer into the adjacent room. 'Who lives there?'

'The Chambers and the Morrises. They seem to be out at the moment.'

'Two couples sharing?' Papa stands on the tiny floor space next to the mattresses, our suitcases piled on top. He frowns. 'For God's sake, my dear chap. That's a bit poor.'

'This is the best I can do for you. You've no idea what things have been like. In other parts of the camp, where the rooms are bigger, we've had to pack even more people in. Some of the apartments and bungalows have between thirty-five and forty-five souls with only one bathroom.' Mr Davies sighs. 'There's no water for the toilets either, so they're overflowing with sewage. And there aren't any beds. People have been reduced to sleeping on the floors. No provision has been made whatsoever. It seems the Japs had no idea there'd be so many of us to deal with.'

'We should've been rescued before now,' Mama says, opening a suitcase. 'What *are* the Americans doing?'

'We've discussed this, Flora.' Papa puts his arm around

her. 'They've got other fish to fry. I shouldn't think it will take them too long to defeat the Japs, though. We must have faith, that's all.' He turns to me. 'Stay and help your mother unpack, dear girl, and I'll go back up the hill with Mr Davies to fetch our other stuff.'

Papa returns, and I hover by the cases. This room is far too small. How will we cope all cooped up together? I've never spent more than an hour a day in both my parents' company before now . . .

'Thank God we've brought a few basics.' Papa takes a hot plate into the so-called kitchen. 'I presume the electricity is working.'

'The only thing that does,' Mr Davies says.

Mama trips over one of the mattresses and falls against me. 'Must you get underfoot, Kate?'

I step out of the way. 'Can I explore outside?'

'If you're careful,' Papa says. 'But don't go near any Japanese!'

\*\*\*

I stroll along a narrow trail leading away from our quarters and around the headland. Waves smash against the shingle below and the scent of the sea fills the air. Sunlight sends a gleam of gold across the turquoise swell of the ocean. I contemplate the stark beauty of the hills on the other side of the bay; the vegetation slopes down like the wing of a bird to rocks hugging the shore. A long coil of barbed wire hangs half way down the cliff like a hedge of thorns. Despondency washes over me. I'm imprisoned, and no amount of beautiful scenery will compensate for my loss of freedom.

I walk until I reach an asphalt road. White-washed prison ramparts rise up, cut by massive black gates. A glint of steel. A Japanese sentry is standing straight-backed, his rifle pointing skywards. Heart thudding, I duck from view.

A path edges the jail gardens and I follow it, the grass

soft and springy under my shoes. I climb through a thicket of conifers. A clearing opens up ahead, dotted with old tombs spread out as if they were on a plate of enormous Swiss rolls and up-ended biscuits. I sit on one and recover my breath. Twiddling my plaits, I take in my surroundings. Then stop and listen. Someone's coming up the hill, swinging his arms and heading straight for me . . .

I scramble down from the tomb, crouch behind it, and peer over the top. A tall boy, dressed in a light blue jersey and beige slacks. He's definitely not a Japanese soldier; he's wearing civilian clothing. Getting to my feet, I study his dark brown hair and European features. The boy has oriental eyes, though, and they widen with surprise as he catches sight of me.

'Oh! You made me jump,' he says. 'What are you doing here all by yourself?'

'Exploring. I'm Kate Wolseley. Who are you?'

'Charles Pearce. You're a bit young to be wandering around on your own, aren't you?'

'No, I'm not. I'm fifteen,' I say, indignant. 'How old are you?'

'Seventeen. I'm sorry. You look younger.'

Heat whooshes up to my face. If only I'd worn my hair loose around my shoulders, instead of tied up in the schoolgirl plaits that make me appear like a twelve year-old child . . .

Charles sits cross legged beneath a tree and I lower myself down next to him, the ground hard and dry. I gaze in silence at a junk tacking its way across the bay, sails flapping, then take a quick peek at him. He's terribly good-looking, like a young Clark Gable minus the moustache. I smile, but he only gives me a brief glance before looking away again.

*He seems a bit standoffish.*

'How long have you been in Stanley?' *Might as well be friendly.*

'Three weeks. We were interned in a hotel before that.

Where were you?'

'The Peak. We only got here an hour or so ago.' I stare at the crumbling tombs. 'How old is this cemetery, do you think?'

Charles hugs his knees. 'I went to St Stephen's, the school here,' he says in a proud tone. 'So I know the history. It's where they buried the soldiers killed by pirates, or those who died of typhoid fever and malaria in the last century.' A spark of warmth flashes in his eyes. 'I'll show you around the camp, if you like.' He pushes himself to his feet. 'It won't take long and you'll be able to get your bearings.'

I follow him down the hill, past a mound of freshly-dug earth. 'What's that?'

'A communal grave, I'm afraid.'

I let out a gasp. 'What happened?'

'St Stephen's became a hospital towards the end of the battle. Stanley held out until Christmas morning, you know, shortly before the Governor surrendered.' Charles falls silent; he seems to be considering what to say next. 'Some drunken Japanese soldiers went on a rampage and did terrible things . . . and afterwards the survivors buried the dead here in this cemetery.'

A chill slices through me. 'Have the Japanese killed anyone else since you arrived?'

'No, we've been left alone and the Camp Commandant isn't even Japanese. He's Chinese.'

'I thought Japan was at war with China.'

'My father said a group of Chinese spies had wanted to get the British out of Hong Kong and they're in the pay of the Japs. It's one of the reasons they defeated us so quickly.'

'Oh.' *How strange! I've always thought of China and the colony as separate entities, not part of the same country at all.*

We pass the building where I saw people queuing earlier. 'This used to be the Prison Officers' Club,' Charles says. 'Now it's a canteen where you can buy expensive groceries. Problem is, there isn't much available.' He pauses. 'I say, would you like to meet my parents and sister?'

Without waiting for a reply, he sets off towards the sinister-looking gates of the prison, then down a short road on the left, and I practically have to run to keep up with him. 'They call these the Married Quarters.' He indicates with his hand. 'It's where the married British prison warders used to live. Our "mess" is very over-crowded, unfortunately, and we're sharing with another family.'

In the front room of the first-floor flat, a European man sits on a camp-bed and squints at me through the thick lenses of his glasses. 'Hello,' he says, running a hand through his hair. 'Welcome to Stanley! Have you just got here?'

'We were allowed to stay on the Peak for the past month. But now we're in the Indian Quarters.'

A petite Chinese woman with porcelain skin and a chignon appears at my elbow. 'I'm Charles' mother. So sorry they've put you in those awful flats. They seem to have reserved the worst billets for people from the Peak.'

A girl, sitting with a book in her hands, looks up from a camp-bed. Her curls are tied in neat bunches, and her eyes tilt attractively in her oval face.

'This is my sister, Ruth,' Charles says.

I smile at the girl then gaze around the room. On the far side, an Englishman, a Chinese woman, and three children of junior school age sit despondently on camp-beds pushed against each other on the bare parquet floor. 'This place is bigger than ours. But at least we've got it to ourselves.'

'Well, that's a blessing.' Mrs Pearce lets out a short laugh. 'Please can you ask your mother if she has any clothes to spare? The nights are freezing and we can't get warm, although we all huddle together. We weren't able to bring much with us.'

'Yes, of course.' Mrs Pearce's dress is hanging off her and her husband's face has a sunken look. 'I'd better be off. I'll see what my mother can find.'

Charles is sitting with his sister on the camp-bed and isn't looking in my direction. What to make of him? He was pleasant enough while showing me around the camp, but now I feel like a stray puppy he's found and handed over to his parents. Picking my way between the beds, I head out of the door. I've been exploring for at least an hour and my parents are probably worried.

I stroll along the path overlooking the shore. A Sikh guard stands with a rifle in his hands, ignoring me as I edge past him. Below, the sea has turned choppy in the breeze. I knuckle the hot tears from my cheeks; I've held them back all day. Now I'm alone I let them flow.

*I'm so afraid.*

'But I will be brave,' I repeat like a mantra all the way back to the Indian Quarters.

# 5

Sofia Rodrigues gazes out of the back window of her father's limousine. There're definitely more beggars out on the streets of Macau since Hong Kong surrendered to the Japanese. She reaches into her pocket for a coin. It's the last of her pocket money, but she doesn't mind. Father will give her more when she asks for it. The car slows at the pedestrian crossing, and she tosses the money into the tin held out by a thin Chinese man dressed in filthy grey rags.

She eyes Natalia, sitting next to her, and smiles to herself. Her governess isn't what you'd consider a beauty, with her beaky nose and cropped grey hair. No man would have wanted to take Natalia for a concubine, like Father took Mother a year before Sofia was born. Poor Mother. If only she'd had the chance to know her. But then she wouldn't have Natalia, would she?

Sofia grasps her governess' hand. 'I can't wait to get to Uncle's. He promised he'll take me out on his biggest junk.' Uncle's junk-master taught her how to handle the sails on her own last autumn, the day after she turned thirteen. She hugs herself, excitement sparking in her chest. That sense of freedom she gets running before the wind is so intoxicating . . .

Natalia squeezes her fingers. 'You worked hard on your studies this morning, my Sofichka. I hope you enjoy the sail.'

'French verbs, English translations, Algebra. I feel as if my head is about to explode. I need some fresh air.'

The car pulls up in front of Uncle's mansion, a two storey structure with a balcony running along the side. She's seen pictures of the buildings in Portugal, and Uncle's house wouldn't look out-of-place there.

She's never been to Portugal; she's only ever visited China, Hong Kong and the Philippines. The British colony is her favourite. She can speak perfect English, albeit with a slight Russian accent, thanks to Natalia, and she loves to go to the cinema in Hong Kong to watch British and American films. She and Natalia always stay in the Peninsula Hotel. Unfortunately, they won't be able to do that anymore.

Sofia huffs to herself. *I wish the Japanese hadn't come and spoilt everything.*

The Japanese seem to be everywhere, in spite of Macau, like Portugal, being neutral in this war. She's seen Japanese soldiers and the *Kempetai*, their secret police, parading openly in the streets. Sofia doesn't know any Japanese and she doesn't want to, either; she's heard stories about what they've done to people in China . . .

She clambers out of the car. Natalia has some errands to run in the old town, where she'll stock up on necessities before the shops sell out of everything. 'See you later, darlink,' her governess says.

Uncle's houseman opens the front door, and Sofia strides across the marble-tiled hall to the sitting room. She stops dead. Why is Uncle still in his long robe? He should be in the trousers and jacket he normally wears sailing.

'Ah, my child,' Uncle says in the Chiu Chow dialect he has taught her to speak with him. He pushes up his sleeves, his fat cheeks wobbling. 'I tried to telephone earlier, but the lines are down. I'm afraid we can't set out for the open sea. Those turnip heads have put a blockade around Macau and it's too dangerous to try and slip through in broad daylight.'

'I was really looking forward to it.' She must keep her voice from sounding sulky, though. She can't stand sulkiness; she stopped being friends with Jennifer Kwok last year because the girl was so moody. 'What can we do instead?'

'Well. I can take you to lunch at the Solmar, if you like.'

Sofia claps her hands. 'My favourite restaurant.'

Uncle is good to her, but then, most people are. There're only a couple of people she can think of who aren't, and one of those is Leo, her half-brother. She can guess why that is, and there's nothing she can do about it.

***

She gets home early to the white villa overlooking the old town of Macau. The afternoon stretches before her with no lessons and the prospect of boredom. Sofia hates being bored almost as much as she despises moodiness.

*I'll go and find Father.*

The walls of his study are panelled in teak, and a Tientsin carpet, decorated with a floral medallion surrounded by blue and purple birds and animals, covers the centre of the room. She feels the thickness of the pile through the thin soles of her house shoes and inhales the scent of beeswax. Father is sitting at his mahogany desk. She crosses the room, and he looks up from his papers.

'*Querida!*' Father likes to use the Portuguese term for beloved, although they usually speak Macanese with each other. 'You're back early.'

'Uncle says sailing is too dangerous because of the Japanese. I wish they'd just go and leave us alone.'

'Not much chance of that, I'm afraid. Your uncle is quite right not to put you in danger and I'm glad you're back in time. We have visitors this evening. Japanese visitors.'

'Father! How can you invite the enemy here? We should have nothing to do with them.'

'Hush, *querida*. All is not as it seems. We must be polite to them, that's all. They've children of thirteen and twenty like you and your brother. In import-export like we are. Be nice to them!'

'All right. But what about Leo?'

'Oh, he's very enthusiastic. He's been telling me we should side with the Japanese. He says European civilisation has come to an end and it's the turn of the East now.'

'Typical of Leo to say that.'

'Now, now, I want you two to get along this evening for once.'

'I'll try.' And she will. She always tries to get along with Leo . . .

'Is your wife going to be there?'

'I wish you'd call her Mother.'

'Siu Yin isn't my real mother.' Sofia moves to his side. 'My real mother wouldn't look down her nose at me all the time.'

Father puts his arm around her shoulder. 'Just ignore her. She's quite harmless, really.'

Sofia wriggles out of his embrace. She won't tell him of the snide remarks about her illegitimacy, or the surreptitious pinches that really hurt. She hates tale-tale-tits even more than she despises moodiness and boredom.

'Shall we have a game of chess before getting ready for dinner?'

'And have you thrash the living daylights out of me,' Father says in an indulgent tone. 'Why the devil not?'

\*\*\*

A large rosewood table dominates the centre of the dining room. Sofia shoots a glance at Leo, placed opposite, and eyes his tall muscular frame. He has the physique of a grown man and appears far more Portuguese than Eurasian. A throw-back, everyone says, despite Siu Yin being half English on her father's side and Chinese on her mother's.

Chinese blood. That's what links them. But they're a hotchpotch, really. Sofia has the light skin and dark brown hair Father inherited from his Dutch great-grandmother. Would she like to be just one nationality? No. That would be so boring . . .

Leo's voice cuts into her thoughts. He's preaching about Asian nations achieving independence from the Western powers - one of his favourite topics. There's an arrogance to Leo's nature that simmers beneath the surface. Being the legitimate son of the head of the Macau Consortium must give him a sense of power in the territory. She's seen how he behaves towards others – lording it over them like a big-headed prince – but she's also seen a side to him that few have.

When she was small, he used to carry her around on his shoulders, and he taught her how to swim almost before she could walk. Yet something happened as she grew older, and it turned him against her. Shrugging to herself, Sofia gives her attention to the Japanese girl on her left. Her name is Michiko, and she's delicate-looking, with an oval face, straight nose, and bow-shaped mouth. 'What a pretty Kimono,' Sofia says in English. She doesn't speak Japanese, and neither do Father, Siu Yin or Leo. That doesn't matter - the Kimuras speak fluent American English. Apparently they used to live in San Francisco . . .

Michiko thanks her politely, then remains silent. Sofia gives up trying to draw the girl out and, suppressing a yawn, studies the boy opposite her. Supposedly her age, he's shorter than she is and uglier than his sister, who's actually quite pretty. The boy is shovelling rice into his mouth as if he hasn't had a square meal in weeks. But from his general chubbiness, it's probably only been a couple of hours . . .

Sofia fidgets and turns her gaze towards the mother. Mrs Kimura is an adult version of her daughter, and Father is having more success at drawing her out than Sofia is with Michiko. The older woman giggles at something Father has said, and hides her mouth behind her hand.

Siu Yin's chatter drifts across the table, and Sofia peers at her step-mother. Siu Yin sits at the far end between Mr Kimura and Leo, tossing her glossy black hair and pouting her lips like some Hollywood actress. They're discussing pearls, of all things. *Pearls!* Father's business is in gold. Sofia glances back at the Japanese woman. Mrs Kimura is wearing a long string of the largest pearls she's ever seen. Could that be the import-export business Father was talking about? Why else would he invite a Japanese family to dinner?

Sofia picks at the grouper fish on the plate in front of her; she's not hungry. One large meal a day is enough, and she ate more than enough at lunch with Uncle. Boredom nudges at her. Threading her fingers through the lace at the edge of the tablecloth, she lets her mind wander.

Father said all was not as it seemed. What if Mr Kimura wasn't really a businessman? She's been reading about spies in the Helen MacInnes novel Natalia got for her to improve her English. It would be fascinating if Mr Kimura was a spy. Natalia said Macau is full of Japanese spies . . .

# 6

An acrid stench of overflowing latrines hangs in the air, contrasting with the loveliness of sunbeams dappling the leaves on the orchid trees beside the main road as I stroll towards the canteen. Cramped in our shabby room, Mama has all but pushed me outdoors this morning.

We've been in Stanley for over a week now, and I've already found out that the few classmates I had are here too. Classmates, not friends. My friends left Hong Kong at the same time as Mary.

My step lightens. Ruth and Charles are crouching behind a shrub up ahead. They're staring at a group of European men loading tins onto trucks, parked by warehouses everyone calls godowns. Japanese and Indian guards sit on the side, smoking.

'What's in those cans?' I whisper to Charles.

'Food.'

'If they've got all that food, why can't we have some?'

'It's *our* food. The Government stashed it here before the invasion so we'd have enough to last through a blockade. The Japs've stolen it just like they've stolen Hong Kong.'

I shade my eyes. Each time a guard looks the other

way, one or other of the European men drops a couple of tins into a ditch. A man with sandy coloured hair has even tied his trousers at the ankles, and is filling the improvised bags with sugar from some torn sacks. The man motions to the guards, goes behind a bush not far away (probably pretending to go for a wee), and empties the sugar into a sack he must have hidden earlier.

Moments later, the working party moves off and Charles beckons.

I scramble down to the trench after him and collect as many cans as I can squirrel up my jumper: a jar of strawberry jam, a tin of potatoes, and a can of bully beef.

Charles does the same, and Ruth shoves a packet of biscuits into her pocket.

I follow them up to the road, but a blond boy jumps out from behind the godowns and blocks my way. 'Hand that over,' he barks.

I stand firm. 'Finders keepers!'

'Those men are in the Hong Kong Police,' the boy says with a sneer. 'You've pinched some of their loot.'

'Rubbish!' Charles glares at him and plants his feet wide apart. 'It's the police who've done the stealing. By rights they should share everything. Anyway, there's plenty left down there. We've only helped ourselves to what we can carry.'

The boy raises his fist and aims a punch at Charles. Before the blow can land, Charles moves to the side and leaps into the air, floating for an instant. His whole body twists and he kicks the boy's fist away.

My mouth opens like a goldfish at feeding time. I've heard about Chinese fighting skills, but I've never seen them in action before now.

'I'll get you later,' the boy shouts, backing away. He scrambles down the bank towards the gully and disappears behind the warehouses.

Charles stares after him. 'I've seen him hanging around with some rough-looking boys. I wonder who he is?'

I shrug. Charles looks at me and shrugs back. He turns and I fall into step beside him, eager to take my pickings back to the Indian Quarters.

***

The chill of winter has given way to the mugginess of spring. I stretch as early morning sunshine slants through the curtain-less windows and moisture fills the air. Running my tongue over the beads of perspiration on my upper lip, I taste the salt. It's late May now, and in a fortnight or so the heat and humidity will be ten times worse.

If only I could be back in my comfortable room at home where I used to sleep below a ceiling fan, its whirring lulling me on hot summer nights. Beneath my mosquito net, I'd imagine I'd been cast adrift on the ocean under a transparent sail. In Stanley, though, I'll soon be melting in a pool of sweat and covered in mosquito bites. I give a shudder; those mosquitoes might carry malaria.

Rolling over, I feel my bones rubbing the stone floor through my lumpy mattress. I was dreaming of breakfast: bacon and eggs, toast and marmalade and a cup of steaming hot tea. I'm fed up with congee; I always gobble the rice and water porridge too quickly and am left desperate for more. The last time I had an egg was at Easter, when the guards gave us one duck egg each. Far from doing unspeakable things, the Japanese officers keep their distance and, when we first arrived, the guards even gave the kids sweets from time to time.

That was ages ago, though, and now they don't give us anything. Hunger knots my belly and I glance at my parents snoring on their mattresses. They've both lost so much weight; their bodies have shrunk inside their clothes.

I creep out of bed and pull on a cotton dress. It hangs off my skinny shoulders, but feels cool and comfortable. Outside the early morning queues for hot water have already formed, and the blond boy from the godown raid has staked a place at the front of the line. Yesterday I discovered his name - Derek Higgins - when a teacher called it out. There are lots of teachers among the internees, and the adults say we children are running wild, so, a week ago, a group of parents decided to organise classes. A good thing too, otherwise I'd be terribly bored.

Derek is fluent in Chinese, and I've seen him spending his time with the Eurasian boys whose mothers married English policemen. He shuffles up to me barefoot. Like most of the kids, I discarded my shoes weeks ago. I rub my feet on the gravely soil; they've grown as tough as leather.

Derek runs his hand through his wispy blond hair and glowers at me. 'Where're you going?'

'None of your business!'

I head up to the cemetery, sit behind a headstone, and think about Charles. I've got into the habit of standing close to him in the supper queues, yet he hardly talks to me and I'm too shy to start a conversation. Whenever I see him my heart rate flutters, and I want him to like me as much as I like him.

My experience with boys has been limited to those spotty English youths who fumbled the odd kiss at school dances and Jimmy, of course. He used to call me his *mui mui*, little sister. I didn't mind Jimmy thinking of me like that; he was like a brother to me. But I want Charles to think of me differently. How differently? Not like a sister, that's for sure . . .

I peer around the gravestone. Derek Higgins is coming up the hill, looking from left to right. What's he up to? *Ha!* If he thinks he'll find me he's got no chance. I gather up my dress and prepare to run. The chorus of birds in the thicket falls silent and the hairs on the back of my legs tingle. There's a presence behind me. A ghost? The cemetery is probably full of them . . .

I spin around. A huge cat crouches in the undergrowth.

Two eyes burn bright in a striped face. Enormous whiskers quiver.

*Oh my God! It's about to spring.*

I leap to my feet. 'Tiger! Tiger!'

'Don't be stupid,' Derek shouts, chasing after me. 'There aren't any tigers in Hong Kong.'

I reach the main road. Charles is carrying a pail of water in my path, and I run full pelt into him.

'Steady.' He drops the bucket. 'This is hot.'

I suppress a smile as Derek runs off.

Charles rubs his hands on his shorts. 'Why was he chasing you?'

'I told him I saw a tiger and he didn't believe me.'

'Are you sure the light wasn't playing tricks with your imagination?'

'I saw a real tiger. I'm positive.'

'Right.' He picks up the bucket and, balancing his weight carefully, looks at me. Our eyes meet, and my heart beats so loudly I'm sure he can hear it.

A shout, and Papa arrives, his lips pinched together. He wipes his forehead and puffs. 'Where have you been? I've just found out one of the guards has been mauled by a tiger.'

Should I run after Charles and warn him? But Papa grabs my hand and leads me away.

Scooping the last of the watery rice from my breakfast bowl, I get to my feet. The sooner I get my chores done, the sooner I'll get away from the claustrophobia of this room.

I pick up my parents' bowls and take them through to the kitchen. Papa has bought lye soap from an enterprising man in the flat below. It's made of wood-ash and lard. The trouble is, the man used too much wood-ash in the recipe. The soap is caustic and irritates my skin, but it's all that's available to clean my teeth, wash my body and do the dishes.

I pour the water I queued for at daybreak into a pan and scrape off a few flakes of soap with a knife. After immersing the breakfast bowls in the suds, I rub them with a threadbare cloth, then take them back to the room. The soapy water will be used to flush the stinking toilet later.

'A rumour's going round some people have managed to escape,' Papa says, wiping his moustache and looking up at me.

'I thought Stanley was escape-proof?' Mama mutters from her mattress. 'I mean, we're surrounded by barbed wire and sea on three sides. And the road to the village is always guarded.'

'It appears two or maybe even three groups of people have managed to sneak out, my dear. They're going to find it difficult, for it's a long way to unoccupied China.'

'The Japanese would be punishing the rest of us if it were true. Just like they made those policemen they caught after the raid march up and down the main road for hours.'

'Not necessarily. They can't be seen to lose face.'

'I'm surprised no one's formed an escape committee.'

'We've enough wretched committees in this place, Flora,' Papa retorts with a huff.

'Has anyone formed a committee to catch the tiger?' I haven't told my parents about how near I came to ending up the animal's supper.

'No, and you're not to go anywhere near the thickets, Kate,' Papa says.

'I promise.' *Drat! I won't be able to wonder around so freely on the off-chance of bumping into Charles.*

***

A week later, I stroll along the path leading to the old football field in front of the Indian Quarters. The village green, as everyone calls it, bears little resemblance to those traditional village greens in my childhood picture books. A scrappy piece of land, parched and forlorn in the dry weather when we first arrived, is now a soggy mess in the wet of summer. But at least it's somewhere for the children to play.

I've been cooped up with my parents all morning. They've been bickering over which piece of Mama's jewellery they'll sell next to buy some food. I press my lips together. What does the jewellery matter if we starve to death? All we get at every meal are a few tiny pieces of bad fish or a couple of teaspoons of stringy, watered-down buffalo stew. And the rice is contaminated with particles of grit, cockroach droppings and the occasional weevil. *Disgusting!*

A ginger-haired man is approaching from the opposite direction. The sun has turned his skin a fierce shade of pink and his legs, poking out of his baggy shorts, remind me of a couple of raw sausages.

'*Aalreet*, little lass?'

'Sorry?'

'Forgetting me manners,' he says in a thick accent. 'Name's Bob.'

'I'm Kate. How do you do?' I offer my hand.

'Well as can be expected,' he says, smiling.

'Where are you from in England?'

'Newcastle. What are you up to?'

'Nothing much. In fact, I'm terribly bored.'

'You don't need to be bored. I'll show you a game I used to play when I was a lad. We called it *cannon*.'

Bob takes an empty can from his pocket. There's a picture of pears on the label; he must have been involved in the police raid on the godowns. After setting the can down in the middle of the field, he scrabbles around for a couple of sticks. Then he takes a tennis ball from his other pocket. 'It's a competition, you see,' he says. 'The person who throws the ball and knocks the tin and the sticks over with the fewest tries is the winner.'

I have three turns before I manage it, then I give the ball back to Bob. 'Your go.'

A shout rings from the entrance to the Indian Quarters. 'Kate, come back this instant!'

'Sorry. I've got to rush. Can we play again another time?'

'Aye, whenever you like, pet.'

At the bottom of the staircase, Mama grabs me by the arm and marches me inside. 'Stay away from him! He's not our sort of person.'

My jaw drops. 'What do you mean?'

'He's one of those rough Northern policemen.'

'I thought he had a different accent. I couldn't understand him at first.'

'I don't want you mixing with the likes of him. Why they had to move those policemen over here from the college is beyond me.'

'They repaired those blocks on the other side of the village green, and I expect they were very crowded in St Stephen's.'

'The committee could have installed families. That would have been much more suitable.'

'I think you should be glad the policemen have moved here.'

'Really? And why's that, young lady?'

'Well, they've taken over all the heavy jobs for a start.'

Mama watches me with raised eyebrows, but I carry on. 'Everything's much better organised. We don't have such long queues for food.'

My mother sniffs.

'And they've pasted V for Victory signs on the glass doors,' I say. 'I think we should be grateful to them.'

'Are you answering me back, Kate?' Mama taps a foot. 'Because, if you are, I want you to stop right away.'

'Well, I think you're being a snob.'

I run from the room. On the stairwell I career into Papa, nearly knocking him over. I don't stop to apologise. Glancing at him, I find I have nothing to say. If I told him about Bob, he'd back Mama up. He gives in to her more than ever these days.

I stomp along the pathway that edges the coastline, then slow down and listen to the sound of the sea. Shutting my eyes, I imagine the waves washing through me, rinsing away the squalor of Stanley, and carrying me back home to the Peak.

\*\*\*

Two nights before the bombs started falling, Papa and

Mama went out to what was called "the tin hat ball" at the Peninsula Hotel, organised to raise money to buy a bomber for Britain. Freed from my mother's strict rules about what I could and couldn't eat, I squatted at the staff table for some *chow fan*.

Whenever Papa and Mama went out to socialise, which happened often, I would have supper with the servants and my parents never found out. They didn't like Chinese food, but I loved it.

I picked up a piece of crunchy *pak choi* with my chopsticks from the communal dish. The oyster sauce dribbled down my chin and I put the bowl to my teeth and shovelled the steamed rice in, coolie style, letting out a burp like the locals to show how much I'd enjoyed my food. (Only once did I ever make the mistake of belching in front of Mama - a topic of scorn for days.)

Ah Ho was sitting on a low stool. Her bottom, as ever, overflowed the edges. She smiled and her gold teeth shone in the low light. '*Bo*,' she said as she always did. 'Full up.'

The staff gossiped about the other families on the Peak. I wanted to join in, but would have needed to sing different tones in their tricky language, which changed the meaning of words, and I usually sang them wrong – even though I understood most of them.

Anyway, Papa and Mama didn't like me to speak Cantonese. *Not the done thing*, they said, which was one of their favourite expressions. And Jimmy always laughed when I made mistakes; his command of my own language was perfect.

Later on, upstairs, I slipped into my mother's dressing room. The wardrobe overflowed with the latest fashions, copied from Vogue by expert tailors. I tried on one of Mama's ball gowns and sprayed behind my ears with Chanel No. 5. Preening in front of the mirror, I smoothed the silk against my skin then smeared my lips with a bright red lipstick. Ah Ho came through the door, scolded me and sent me to bed. I bridled and thought Ah Ho still treated me like a child.

***

I'd give anything to be treated like a child by my amah now. I stare towards the horizon. Where is Ah Ho? Have she and Jimmy managed to get to their family in China? There's no way of knowing. I've visited that huge country beyond the Kowloon hills only once. When I was nine, my parents took me with them on a trip to Shanghai. It was a cultured vibrant city in comparison with sleepy provincial Hong Kong. After I returned to the colony, though, I was relieved to get back to my routine of school from Mondays to Fridays and weekends at the riding school.

Thinking about my favourite pony, I twirl my jade bangle and taste the salt of my tears. Did Merry survive the bombing? Who's looking after him now? Sniffing, I brush my cheeks with my hands and make my way down the path. Crying for my old life is a sign of weakness I won't allow myself.

Back at the Indian Quarters, Papa gets me to clean out the foul-smelling lavatory as a punishment for being rude to my mother. The smell of the backed-up sewage makes me retch, and I have to force down the usual revolting lunch.

I set off for school in the afternoon. On the village green, my foot knocks against a pebble. Only it isn't a pebble; it's a boiled sweet. Sneakily, I take off the cellophane wrapper and pop it into my mouth.

The sugar has an immediate effect, making me quicken my step and run up the road. By the time I arrive at the school hall, my energy has gone and guilt has taken its place. It was selfish of me to keep the sweet for myself instead of sharing it; I'll never be able to admit what I've done.

Later, after Professor Morris has set our Latin homework, I sit next to Charles. He'll ignore me as usual.

But he smiles and says, 'I'm sorry I didn't believe you about that tiger. It's just that normally we don't have them roaming the countryside.'

'That's all right. I wouldn't have believed it either if I hadn't seen it.' His eyes meet mine and a thrill of pleasure courses through me. 'This morning,' I say, 'I met one of those policemen who've moved into the block next door to ours. He was showing me how to play a game called "cannon". Only my mother won't let me talk to him again.'

'Well, that's easily fixed.' Charles appears thoughtful for a moment before smiling his lovely smile, the smile that makes my heart rate flutter. 'I'll ask him to teach me the game and show it to the rest of the children. If everyone's out there playing with this man, your mother won't have a leg to stand on, will she?'

'Mama never does anything but complain and get my father to run around after her. She's impossible.'

'I suppose she's finding it hard to get used to how things are here.'

'I suppose.' I giggle, grab his hand, and pull him to his feet. 'Come on! School's finished. Let's take Ruth along to find Bob and we can put your plan into action!'

# 8

'They've caught that tiger,' Papa says at supper three days later. 'An Indian guard shot it.'

I put down my spoonful of cold gritty rice. *Thank God.* 'Do you know where it came from?'

'Apparently, it escaped from a circus. A fellow who used to be a butcher at the Dairy Farm will skin it. I wonder what tiger meat tastes like? No doubt only the Japanese will get any.'

Papa said the Japanese rations were almost as poor as ours; of course they'll get first sniff of the tiger meat. Mama must be shuddering on her mattress at the very thought of being interned with a butcher. In Hong Kong society she wouldn't have dreamt of mixing with a tradesman.

'How many of us are here in this camp, do you reckon?' I ask my father.

'At the latest count, two and a half thousand British, sixty Dutch and nearly four hundred Americans, but the Yanks are due to be repatriated any day now.'

'Lucky them.'

'They're about to be exchanged with some Japanese nationals in the United States.' Papa stands and makes a move to gather our empty plates, then quickly sits down again. 'Bugger! All the strength's gone in my legs.'

'It must be the bad diet,' Mama says from the other side of the mattress. 'Too much polished rice and no greens. The hot weather doesn't help.'

'We'll be able to cool down a bit this morning.' I deliberately insert cheerfulness into my voice. 'Don't forget we've been given permission to swim!'

Papa's mouth twists grimly. 'You go with the young ones, dear girl. It's too much of an effort for your mother and me.'

***

After doing the washing up, I line up with the rest of the children. Two guards march us down a path edging the bleak white walls of the prison. Dense scrub hides the beach from sight until we walk through a clearing in the canopy. 'Last one in's a rotten tomato,' I call out, the sand hot between my toes.

I pull off my shorts, and wade into the ocean in my knickers and a thin cotton vest. Charles and Ruth come up behind me, laughing and splashing. Treading water warm as a bath, I gaze at starfish splayed on the sandy seabed. 'Why don't we swim over to those rocks and look for sea urchins? My father told me we can eat them.'

Charles sets off at a crawl and I follow, swimming at a slower pace. Light-headed from the exercise, I clamber onto the sun-warmed rocks, then stretch out and half-close my eyes.

Low clouds of humidity cover the tops of the distant islands. The sun beats down through the haze and dries me in minutes. The pungent smell of seaweed, left by the retreating tide, tickles the back of my throat. The gentle waves make a sucking sound as they slosh against the barnacles. I brush salt from my arms and stare out to sea, picking at the mosquito bites on my legs. 'I wish we could swim like fish and get away.'

'My mother saw four of the men who escaped. They've been caught.' Charles squints in the sunshine. 'They were in an open lorry being driven into the prison. We have a good view from our balcony and Ma hardly recognised them. She said they were like walking skeletons.'

'How terrible!'

'Ma was angry. She thought the men had been starved.'

The sound of splashing, and Derek Higgins swims towards us with two of his friends.

Charles pushes himself to his feet. 'Go away! We were here first.'

Derek heaves himself onto the rocks. 'We've got as much right to be here as you,'

He leers at me and I look down. My breasts are visible through my damp vest. How humiliating! Derek speaks in Cantonese to the other boys; they snigger and make a lewd remark about my nipples.

Charles lets fly a stream of Chinese insults, calling them stupid pigs. My cheeks burn as he turns to me. 'I'll race you back to the beach,' he says quickly. 'It's too late to look for sea urchins. I can see the guards waving their rifles. They want us to go.'

On our way back up the hill, I keep my arms folded in front of me. I should have packed a swimming costume when we left the Peak. But I never thought I'd need one; the Japanese were supposed to have been defeated before now. Worst of all, Charles must have seen me semi-naked and realised what a kid I am . . .

\*\*\*

After school, I hurry home, finish my Latin translation, and queue for supper. The adults have organised a concert on the lawn in front of the canteen. Everyone says it's a sham. A team of Japanese press and cameramen are making a propaganda film about the supposedly cheerful, contented detainees enjoying their treats.

I sit next to Ruth on the grass in the front row. Charles is on the other side of his sister. Best to ignore him; I'm still too mortified about what happened earlier. Frogs croak and crickets screech in the thickets that separate the canteen from the Indian Quarters, almost drowning out the crash of waves on the rocks below. There's a tang of fresh vegetation in the air. Rain in the early evening threatened to cancel the performance and the ground is still moist. The new moon cuts a thin sliver of silver in a sky that billows with stars.

Leaning back on my arms, I watch the show. The Japanese have commandeered a floodlight from somewhere to illuminate the stage; mosquitoes and moths flutter in the beam. A group of internees are singing and dancing to music performed by the orchestra, a collection of people who've managed to bring their instruments into the camp. They play discordantly, but no matter; the tunes distract us from the filming.

'This is stupid,' I mutter. 'How can those cameramen and journalists think we're happy to be locked up here?'

'Let's show them!' Charles says, giving the V for Victory signal.

'Yes,' Ruth joins in.

Impossible to ignore Charles now. I giggle and make the sign with my fingers. The other children swiftly catch on, even Derek Higgins. Seconds later, most of the adults lift their hands in the air as well.

The photographers stop filming and Yamashita, the newly arrived Japanese Commandant, jumps up from his seat. 'No more entertainment for one month,' he spits, hopping from one foot to the other like a manic tap dancer.

A heavy crunch of boots on the path behind, and I twist around. Where's Charles? I hold back a scream. A squat Japanese guard is pointing his bayonet straight at him. 'You! Boy! Very bad!'

# 9

It's late August, and I wake up after a hot, mosquito-infested night. I think about Charles. Something changed in him when he spent twenty-four hours in the prison. He's been avoiding me, and doesn't even come swimming these days . . .

I crawl off my mattress. There's a small black spot, marooned in the middle of my sheet. 'What's that?'

'A bed bug, I think.' Papa squashes the speck between his thumb and forefinger. 'What a stink!'

I wrinkle my nose and inhale a whiff of bitter almonds.

Papa fetches a knife from the kitchen, turns the mattress over and cuts a hole. Thousands of slimy, shiny, black insects squirm as if irritated at being disturbed.

I back away, revolted. I stare at the spots on my legs and my stomach heaves. 'I thought these were mosquito bites. Do you think they're in your beds as well?'

'More than likely,' Papa says.

Mama pulls up her nightdress and examines the angry, red wheals on her thighs. Her face blanches. 'I can't take any more,' she sobs.

'There, there.' Papa pats Mama on the back. 'I'll find something to get rid of them and, in future, we'll make sure we do spot checks.'

I clutch my sides as hysteria builds up. 'Ha, ha, ha spot checks!'

'Be quiet, you silly girl!' Mama slaps me on the arm. 'We can't let the neighbours know we've got bed bugs. Whatever will they think?'

'If we've got them they've probably got them too. Stay here with your mother, Kate, while I look for a container.'

He manages to find an old kerosene tin, which he trundles over to the Police Block. I strip the beds as my mother looks on helplessly.

Half an hour later, Papa returns with Bob.

'Aalreet, pet?'

Bob pours carbolic acid from the tin into our only pan, then mixes it with the water I collected in a bucket from yesterday's rainfall. 'This is how we deal with the little beasties,' he says, setting the pan on their hotplate.

The water boils, and Papa soaks all three mattresses with the liquid. Then Bob and I haul everything over to the balcony. Mama stands to the side and fixes the policeman with a frosty stare.

'I'll be off now,' Bob says. 'Got to get back to me rice cooking shift. Did you hear the good news?' He smiles. 'There's been a delivery of pork today. Disease has struck a pig farm in the New Territories and they've killed the whole herd. We'll have some meat with our dinners for once.'

Papa shakes Bob's hand and thanks him for his help. I go with my friend to the bottom of the stairwell, and watch him saunter across the village green. He stops and throws a "cannon ball" with a group of children. *Such a nice man.*

Back indoors, I help Papa scrub our sheets in lye soap, wishing my mother had shown more gratitude to Bob.

'How low we've sunk that we can even contemplate eating diseased food,' she says.

Papa heaves a sigh. 'I'm sure the Colonial Vet will

check to make sure it's safe.'

Mama glowers at him. 'We'd have been able to buy more bully beef from the canteen if you hadn't used up our spare cash for your wretched tobacco.'

'There hasn't been any tinned meat available for ages, my dear. Do you think I'd put my pipe before your needs?'

'I can't understand why you still insist on smoking it when it's so difficult to get hold of tobacco. I've managed to give up my cigarettes. You should give up your pipe too.'

'Having a smoke clears my airways. You don't want me catching TB again, do you?'

Papa's TB was the reason my mother and I were still in Hong Kong when the Japanese came. Most of the British women and children, including Mary and my other school friends, had been evacuated eighteen months before then, as the authorities must have thought war was on the cards. If it weren't for that TB scare, Mama wouldn't have had the excuse to stay and nurse him back to health.

Papa never believed the Japanese would attack, so he was happy for her to remain, and I didn't want to go without her. Mama fed him huge amounts of protein and moved his bed onto the veranda so that he could breathe plenty of fresh air. When fog came to the Peak, she bundled him into the car and drove him to Repulse Bay with the window down. Gradually he recovered, but his poor health kept him out of the Volunteers.

*Thank God for that. If he'd survived the battle he'd be in the POW camp in Kowloon instead of with the civilians in Stanley.*

I put the sheets in the sun. The mattresses are still airing on the balcony, so I sit on the concrete floor. A sudden rumble of thunder, and I run outside. Rain peels across the village green and people scurry for cover. Everything is soaked.

Mama bursts into tears. 'I can't bear it.'

'Maybe tonight we'll sleep in soggy sheets stinking of carbolic acid,' I say. 'But it's better than being eaten alive by bed bugs, don't you think?'

'Cheer up!' Papa puts his arm around Mama and gives me a disapproving look.

'I'm sorry,' I stutter. 'I didn't mean to be rude.'

\*\*\*

From then onwards, Papa's pipe makes rare appearances. Often, I see him stooping and picking up cigarette butts discarded on the roadside. He retrieves the small amount of tobacco then mixes it with dried sweet potato leaves and toilet paper, which is really just a piece cut up from *The Hong Kong News*.

Our neighbours soon give every indication that they're struggling with the over-crowded conditions as well. They've divided their room in two by hanging a curtain made from old sheets stitched together. It's difficult sharing the kitchen and bathroom with the Chambers and the Morrises. Squabbles often break out between us about who's responsible for cleaning the communal areas.

I remember the first time I met the two couples last February. After an awful meal on our first night, I stood with my parents at the door dividing our rooms. A grey-haired man staggered to his feet. 'Professor Stuart Morris, Hong Kong University,' he said.

A mousy-looking woman got up from her camp bed. 'And I'm his wife, Diana.'

I spotted another woman, fast asleep under a large, brown overcoat. A tousle of wavy red hair spread over the pillow.

'You'll excuse my wife if she doesn't get up?' A burly man with a dark beard stepped forward. 'She's suffering from a nasty cold. Bloody freezing here at night. We're the Chambers by the way. Tony and Jessica. Welcome to Stanley!'

'We've met before, haven't we?' Mama held out her hand. 'Weren't you at the Boxing Day Meet last year?'

'Of course. How could I forget?' Tony Chambers clapped his hand to his forehead.

His brown eyes smiled at me. 'You're something of a horsewoman, young lady, aren't you?'

'I can't stand the creatures myself,' my mother chipped in. 'They make me sneeze. Well, we'd better get on. Things to do. No doubt we'll meet again.' She laughed in an almost hysterical way and I followed her through the door, wishing I could have shrunk to a speck of dust on the floor, I was so embarrassed.

Since then, I've seen a lot of Professor Morris at school as he's my Latin teacher, and his wife helps out with French. But the Chambers keep themselves to themselves.

\*\*\*

After the discovery of the bed bugs, Mama has become obsessed with getting me to do the cleaning. She makes me scrub our room from wall to wall every day then wash the clothes. I rub them with lye soap until my hands bleed.

'Off you go,' Mama says to me one morning after I've done my chores. 'I can't be doing with you getting in my way any longer.'

'I haven't been getting in the way. I've been slaving over a scrubbing board. Why can't you do more of the work?'

Mama lifts her hand. I duck, and before my mother's palm can reach its target, Jessica Chambers pokes her head around the door. 'Your daughter has stolen my lipstick.'

Mama's eyes widen. 'I beg your pardon?'

'Well, who else? The children are out of control, thieving left, right and centre.'

Mama gives me a stern look. 'Did you take Mrs Chambers' lipstick?'

I cross my fingers behind my back. 'Of course not.'

'Let this be a warning to you, Little Miss Butter-Wouldn't-Melt-In-Her-Mouth,' Jessica spits. 'If ever I catch you in our room, you'll receive the severest of punishments.'

'Please don't threaten my daughter!' Mama holds up her hands. 'I know my Kate's mixing with all *sorts* of people in this place, but she wouldn't steal.'

I slip out of the room, pretending that I'm leaving. But I hide behind the door instead, peer through a crack, and listen.

'Perhaps it wasn't her. The lipstick went missing yesterday. Not the first thing that's been taken,' Jessica says, the colour rising in her cheeks.

Jessica Chambers has red hair. Not auburn, but deep red. Bob's hair is distinctly carroty by comparison. Jessica is probably only in her mid-twenties, no more than a decade older than me, yet in spite of the months of living in close proximity, Jessica hasn't spoken a word to me until this morning, which makes her fair game. Jessica left the lipstick in the kitchen, so what did she expect? She should have looked after it. I turn around and march out of the flat.

On my way down the stairs, guilt ties my stomach up in knots. Maybe Mama is right and Stanley is changing me? I wouldn't have dreamt of stealing anything when I lived on the Peak. I put my hand into the pocket of the shorts I stitched together from an old rice sack, and clasp the tube. I'd wanted to make myself look pretty for Charles. Now I'll have to bury the lipstick on the hillside behind the cemetery, so no one will discover I took it.

I reach the village green and stop dead. Derek Higgins is bent double, surrounded by a circle of European men, his white buttocks bared and receiving six of the best from a thin bamboo cane.

The cane comes down with a thwack, and I wince. Thwack, thwack, thwack. I screw my eyes shut. *Poor Derek!*

Finally, the men leave and Derek comes up to me. 'Why were you watching? I suppose it seemed funny to you.'

'Not it didn't. Not at all. I just wanted to make sure you're all right. Who were they and why were they beating you?'

'From the camp tribunal. They caught me with some cans of bully beef I took from the canteen a few weeks ago. I only took them because my dad is sick.'

'Gosh! I wouldn't like that to happen to me. Do you think they'd beat girls as well?'

'More than likely. Better than the Japanese Gendarmerie, I suppose. Well, I'd better get back to my parents. Dad's ill with beriberi because he's not getting enough vitamins. That's why I took the cans.'

'Oh. I'm sorry. Did you know the Red Cross are sending comfort parcels? Hopefully they'll arrive soon and we'll have some extra food.'

I wave Derek off and go up to the cemetery. Burying the lipstick, I promise myself I won't take anything that belongs to someone else ever again. What was I thinking of?

\*\*\*

Three weeks before my sixteenth birthday, in early September, Papa rushes into the flat and exclaims with a wide grin, 'The parcels are here. Come on, we're to line up at the canteen.'

We wait for an hour in the queue, Mama complaining all the while that she has things to do. What these things might be, I can't imagine. After all, I'm the one doing all the washing and cleaning . . .

'Flora, my dear, you don't want to be shut up indoors on such a lovely morning,' Papa says, laughing. 'It'll do you good to get some fresh air.'

I look up at the sky, so blue and cloudless it seems to go on forever. For once, the high hills separating Stanley from the other side of the island are clearly visible, not hidden by warm mist.

Finally the Red Cross representative hands us two packages each. Back in the Indian Quarters, Mama says we don't have enough storage containers so we can indulge in an instant feast. I open my parcel. *Chocolate tablets, biscuits and packets of sugar!* I tear the wrapping off a Dairy Milk bar and stuff every morsel into my mouth, savouring the sticky sweetness. A sensation of fullness settles in my belly, which lasts the rest of the day. For the first time in months I go to bed without feeling hungry.

The sound of screaming wakes me, and I blink in the morning sunshine. What's wrong with Mama?

'There are ants crawling on everything,' she wails.

'I'll boil up some water and pour it over them,' Papa says in his keep calm voice.

Mama eyes the soaked sugar. 'All ruined now. What a mess!'

I help Papa scoop up the soggy packets then glance at my mother. *Oh, no!* Her face has a yellowish tinge.

***

That night, a moan comes from Mama's mattress. 'I feel terrible. I've got the shakes and my head is killing me.'

Papa grabs a thermometer and takes her temperature. 'Good God! It's one hundred and three,' he says, shaking the glass tube. 'I'll fetch some water, my dear.'

I hold Mama's hand as she groans and thrashes about, then I help Papa sponge her down. Finally, Mama slips into a fitful sleep, but neither Papa nor I can bear to leave her side.

'I'll take your mother to the camp hospital,' he says at daylight. 'They'll be able to help her. She's probably got malaria and they must have some quinine.'

Regret surges through me as I remember my harsh words to my mother. I stay in and do my chores. How long has Mama had malaria? No wonder she's been even colder than usual these past weeks. I scrub the toilet. How to make sense of things? Mama doesn't resent me. She's just ill, that's all . . .

Papa returns at lunch-time. 'They'll keep her in there for a few days,' he says, his expression grim. 'Your mother would like you to visit.'

I follow the path around the headland to arrive at a three-storey red-brick building. Mama is in a ward on the second floor with four women and their new-born babies. I perch beside her on the bed.

'Oh, darling,' she says. 'It's dreadful. I can't sleep with all the noise. Can you read to me, please? I need distracting.'

There's a bookshelf in the corner of the room where I find a well-thumbed copy of *Gone with the Wind*. I read aloud as my mother dozes.

*"Let's don't be too hot-headed and let's don't have any war. Most of the misery of the world has been caused by wars. And when the wars were over, no one ever knew what they were all about."*

Then, later.

*"Hunger gnawed at her empty stomach again and she said aloud: As God is my witness, and God is my witness, the Yankees aren't going to lick me. I'm going to live through this, and when it's over, I'm never going to be hungry again. No, nor any of my folks. If I have to steal or kill - as God is my witness, I'm never going to be hungry again."*

I put the book down and wipe her forehead with a damp cloth. Mama has to survive this. She has to . . .

At the end of the week, Mama comes out of hospital. Her fever peaks and troughs, but Papa says she's out of danger. Even so, my chest aches with worry.

*I hope he's right; he has a tendency to be over-optimistic.*

\*\*\*

On the morning of my birthday, I roll out of bed onto Mama's mattress. She pulls an item from under her pillow. 'I made it myself.' Two of Papa's silk handkerchiefs have been stitched together to make a halter-neck top. 'I hope you like it.'

I take the gift and hold it against my chest. With joyful tears, I hug her and receive a peck on the cheek in return.

'And I've got this for you.' Papa hands me a bar of chocolate. 'It's the last one from my comfort parcel. I managed to save it from the ants.'

If anyone had told me a year ago I'd be happy to receive such gifts, I'd have thought they were mad. My usual presents are cashmere cardigans, Yardley's toiletries, riding accessories and books. When the war is over and life returns to normal, I'll appreciate every single thing I used to take for granted. It's a firm promise I make to myself.

Once dressed, I go to queue for hot water. I took over the duty months ago, supposedly to give Papa some respite. But, actually, it's a way for me to see Charles, even though he usually ignores me. This morning, though, he waves and I go up to him. 'Happy Birthday,' he says, touching my arm.

My heart dances. I've known him for about eight months now, but never tire of looking at him. I've such a crush. If only I were more gown-up and knew what to do where boys were concerned . . .

*How can I tell if he likes me as much as I like him?*

\*\*\*

On the 30th of October, I'm at an informal celebration for Charles' eighteenth birthday on the village green. Even though the weather is still hot, the air has turned dry and we no longer drip with sweat. Mrs Pearce has saved her flour rations and has baked a sponge cake in one of the communal ovens. I've contributed the few biscuits I kept from my comfort parcel.

The Red Cross deliveries indeed included some desperately needed medicines. Only a small amount of quinine, though, which has to be shared among countless others. Mama sits on the edge of the group, sipping watered-down tea. She's receiving treatment, but she's still weak.

I bite into the unaccustomed floury texture of the cake and lick my fingers. There were tears as I struggled to find something pretty to wear. In the end, I put on one of Mama's blouses. It's too big for me and looks funny worn over my shorts.

I giggle at Charles; he's doing an impression of Professor Morris, and has got his "now for your Latin homework" saying spot-on. A loud drumming noise echoes. A flock of silver planes soars above. I can just make out the stars of the US Air Force under their wings. 'Look! They've come to rescue us!'

'They're probably headed towards Canton,' Charles says calmly.

Gunshots ring through the air. The Japanese soldiers at the fort on the other side of the camp have started firing at the planes, even though they're a mile high. 'Ha,' Charles laughs. 'They'll never hit them.'

'Come indoors,' Mama says briskly. 'We don't want to catch a stray bullet.'

In our tiny room I huddle with my parents, Charles and his family. Explosions boom in the distance and, through the window, a cloud of black smoke rises behind the mountains.

'They're bombing the airport,' Papa says in a loud voice.

Charles leaps up. 'It's begun.'

'At last,' Mama murmurs.

'The Americans are going to set us free,' I squeal, excitement making me dizzy.

*** 

The next afternoon, I set off for school as usual. There hasn't been a repeat of the bombing raid. Surely there'll be another one soon? Then the Japanese will be so badly hit they won't be able to do anything but surrender Hong Kong.

I sit on a mat spread on the floor. Charles lowers himself down next to me, and I give him a surprised glance before going back to the algebra problem scribbled on the back of an old piece of card. There aren't any exercise books available for school. I chew the end of my pencil; I haven't got the faintest idea how to do the sum.

'Here, let me help you.' Charles talks me through the working-out step by step.

'I've think I've got it.'

'Are you sure?'

'No. Not really. I hate maths. I'm much better at geography.'

'Then, when we do geography, you can help me.'

I'm sure he's good at geography too, but the lie doesn't matter. He fixes his gaze on me and our eyes lock. I glance away then back again, not knowing what to say. *Idiot! Ask him something about himself!* 'Is it strange for you to be in your old school?'

'A bit. I keep expecting to bump into one of my old teachers. Which school did you go to?'

There's only one school considered suitable for expatriates. 'The Central British School in Kowloon. It took me ages to get there and back every day. I would have gone to boarding school if it hadn't been for the war.'

'I'm hoping to go to university in London. When the war ends.'

'I sometimes wish my mother and I had been evacuated. Papa was ill so we stayed on. My parents never believed the Japanese would dare attack.'

'My mother tried to get us evacuated, you know.'

'Did she?'

'She thought we'd be eligible as we've got British passports. She was told by the authorities they didn't know what to do with the likes of us.'

'That's terrible,' I say, shocked.

A shuffling sound, and Derek Higgins sits down behind us. 'Stop talking or I'll tell the teacher.'

'Don't be a snitch!' Charles glowers at him. He turns to me and gives me a smile that makes my heart miss a beat.

After class, he walks me back to the Indian Quarters. At the bottom of the stairwell, he turns to me as if about to say something. Then he takes my hand and gives it a brief squeeze. 'See you tomorrow.'

Smiling, I run up the stairs and into our room. Papa is sitting on his own. 'Thank God you're back, Kate. I've just taken your mother to the hospital. The fever's returned and her temperature is sky high.'

\*\*\*

Mama is in a side room, apparently fast asleep. A nurse leads Papa and me to one side. 'Mrs Wolseley has slipped into a coma. There's very little we can do, I'm afraid.'

'Nooo!' All the saliva drains from my mouth. 'She can't die.'

Papa grabs me to him and whispers, 'Be brave, my dear girl. Your mother might be able to hear and you wouldn't want to upset her.'

I pull out a chair for him, and we sit in silence, giving each other worried glances until the nurse makes signs that visiting hour is over. For the next three days we visit and watch helplessly as Mama slips away. Each day, I feel it's like being in a living nightmare. Each day, the sense of unreality grows. Each day I ask myself, *how can my beautiful vibrant Mama have been reduced to this inert creature lying wraith-like on a bed?*

# 10

Sofia stands at her bedroom window peering at two coolies pulling a cart up the road. *It's laden with dead bodies!* She shudders. People have literally been freezing to death on the streets. A year now since the fall of Hong Kong, and Natalia has told her about rumours of the terrible conditions in the old British colony: food shortages, massacres, atrocities against women, starvation of prisoners and the rampant spread of typhoid and cholera. The misery goes on and on . . .

Here in Macau, things aren't much better. Thousands of homeless beggars and this winter has been so cold. Even if the poor had any money, they wouldn't be able to buy much to eat. When did she last have any meat? Sofia can't remember. And she's fed-up with fish, in spite of it keeping her from feeling hungry all the time.

She leaves her room and marches down the corridor to the front stairs. Leo is in the hallway. 'I'm just going to see Uncle,' she says. There's something she needs to tell him, and she'd better get on with it before he finds out from someone else.

'Give him my regards, won't you?'

Sofia opens her mouth in surprise. Leo has never

expressed anything other than disdain for Uncle in the past. Come to think of it, he hasn't been nasty to her for ages, either. 'When you get back,' Leo says, 'I'll show you those kung fu moves you keep asking about.'

She's been dying to learn from him. She's watched him practising - kicking and punching the air as he fights imaginary enemies. She's begged Father for lessons, but he says it isn't seemly for a girl. 'You could show me now.' She can barely contain the eagerness in her voice.

Leo's brow creases. 'Later. I'll be on the front terrace at four o'clock.'

Her shoulders sag, but then she remembers her mission to visit Uncle.

The iron gate clangs shut as she steps onto the pavement. It's Natalia's afternoon off, otherwise she'd be with her like she always is. Normally, Sofia wouldn't go out on her own. There are too many desperate people on the streets. Starving people who'd rob her and throw her body into a ditch. Is she being rash? No, what she has to tell Uncle is far too important to wait. The risk isn't that great, anyway. Not in broad daylight. Perhaps she should have telephoned him to say she was coming? It's too late now. She'll just have to surprise him . . .

She hails a passing rickshaw and jumps in. The rickshaw puller is so, so thin. How can he stand on his own two feet, let alone pull this cart? Thankfully, she doesn't weigh much. They get to the last, steep part of the road. She climbs out, pays the man his full fare plus a generous tip, and walks on. At Uncle's door, she knocks. No answer. *Where can he be?* He's usually at home in the early afternoon and, in any case, his houseboy should have opened.

Sofia goes down the alleyway at the side of the house. The gate might be unlocked. She lifts the latch and lets herself in. *Rather careless of Uncle's staff not to have bolted it.* Tall bamboo shades the small patch of land. There's a smell of damp vegetation, and the path is mossy beneath her feet.

*There's Uncle!* He's on the patio with two Chinese men, surrounded by boxes. Sofia stomps up to him. 'What are you doing?'

Uncle gives a start and drops a lumpy-looking package. 'How did you get in here?'

'Someone left the gate open,' she says, surprised at his tone. She points at a packet of white pills. 'Who are those for?'

'Nobody with whom you should be concerned.' Uncle takes her arm and practically drags her indoors. She glances around for his servants. 'Where is everyone?'

'Cook and amah have gone to the market.'

'But I'm here,' says a voice from the pantry.

Sofia lets out a gasp. What's her governess doing spending her afternoon off at Uncle's? 'Why?' Sofia asks, in English.

Uncle's English is heavily accented, but Natalia doesn't speak Chiu Chow and Uncle doesn't know any Russian. They continue in the language of Perfidious Albion, as Natalia likes to refer to it. 'I'll tell you why I'm here later. First of all you've got some explaining to do. You know you're not allowed out on your own. It's far too dangerous.'

'I wanted to let Uncle know about Leo.' Sofia crosses her arms. 'But I suppose you've already told him.'

'Told me what?'

'That he's getting married to Michiko.'

There, she's said it. She plants her feet firmly apart. Uncle slams his fist down on the kitchen table, his face puce, and his fat cheeks wobbling. 'Collaborating with the enemy, I'd call that.'

'Actually, I really do believe he loves her. He's been different lately.'

'How can your father agree to this?'

'You'll have to ask him that yourself. He won't say anything to me on the subject. He says I shouldn't concern myself. I'm fed up with being told I shouldn't concern myself. It's all you and Father say to me these days.' She's so annoyed, she's in danger of sulking.

Uncle blows out a sigh. 'Natalia, take the child home. I'll leave it up to you to fill her in with what she needs to know. I trust your discretion, but you should have told me yourself.'

'We only found out this morning,' Natalia says quickly. 'I was about to tell you. You know I tell you everything . . .'

'Tell him everything?' Sofia grabs her governess' hand. 'What do you mean?'

'Come along,' Natalia says in a brusque tone. 'We'll let ourselves out.'

They walk down the hill towards the *Avenida*. There's a bench underneath one of the banyan trees and Natalia sits, motioning that Sofia should do the same. 'You know your uncle is a communist, don't you? He was recruited to spread Anti-Japan and Save the Chinese Nation propaganda years ago.'

Sofia bats away a fly, buzzing by her ear. 'So?'

'I met him when he visited Shanghai shortly after your mother died. I was working for the Party too, in a very minor capacity, mostly distributing leaflets when I was a freelance translator.'

'You? A communist? I thought you left Russia because of the revolution . . .'

'That's the story I let people believe, not the real one. I was regretting my decision to leave the mother country, thinking I could have done more at home. Then I met your uncle, who suggested I come here to keep an eye on your stepmother and her nationalist connections.'

'Then you're a spy?'

'Not really. I'm your governess first and foremost. In fact, I hardly tell your uncle anything, as there hasn't been that much to tell. I merely let him know when Siu Yin's family visits. You're my main priority these days, Sofichka.' Natalia strokes her hand. 'The Party has taken second place in my heart for years.' Natalia has called her by her pet name, and Sofia feels her governess' warmth through her fingers. But all this subterfuge? It's the stuff of espionage novels, not everyday life. And there she was, thinking Mr Kimura was a spy when all along it was Natalia. 'Who're all those boxes for?' She's fighting another attack of the sulks. How can her beloved Natalia have been deceiving her all these years?

'Your uncle is helping the anti-Japanese guerrillas smuggle medicines into the POW camps in Hong Kong. It's a wonderful thing he's doing. You should be proud of him. And you must never, ever breathe a word of this to anyone.'

'I won't.' And she definitely won't. Father would be upset. And Leo? Leo would go back to being horrible to her and that's the last thing she wants.

\*\*\*

A month later, Sofia is standing at the entrance of Macau cathedral. She runs a hand down the white silk of her bridesmaid dress and clutches a posy of pink roses. Leo is waiting by the altar with Father. Michiko is due to arrive at any minute now. Sofia glances at Natalia. Her governess is standing next to her, dressed in a dark red suit. Red like her political affiliations.

Sofia remembers the story of how her parents met. Father had fallen for Uncle's favourite sister, Sofia's mother, on a visit to China, and brought her back with him to Macau. He provided Uncle with a fleet of junks in compensation. Uncle more or less sold Mother to Father, but that's the way things are done in China. For the past month, ever since she found out about her governess, she's wondered if Mother was the intended spy in Father's household, substituted by Natalia after Mother's untimely death. Then she's told herself not to be silly. Uncle wouldn't have used his own sister like that.

Leo is standing tall and handsome, his thick black hair styled like Cary Grant's, her favourite film star. Will Leo stop teaching her martial arts after he's married? There's still so much she wants to learn. Leo has been patient with her, just like he used to be while he taught her to swim. The old Leo back again. It was Siu Yin who poisoned him against her. Her step-mother was furious when Father decided to give Sofia equal status to his legitimate son, in spite of the fact he never married Mother. Sofia can feel eyes burning a hole in the back of her neck. Siu Yin is glaring at her, hatred in her expression.

A limousine pulls up in front of the church. Sofia grips her flowers and goes to help the bride. Father insisted the Japanese girl converted to Catholicism. He likes to be seen as a good Catholic and benefactor of the various religious orders in Macau. Sofia has been brought up in the faith, but for her it's more a tradition than a conviction. What does Michiko make of the sudden change in her life? Sofia studies the girl and she's reminded of one of the pawns on her chessboard. She pushes the thought away.

Michiko is wearing a traditional white gown, on Siu Yin's insistence. It's the way all Catholic women get married in Macau. The Japanese girl resembles one of those figures on top of a wedding cake. She places her hand on her father's arm, and Sofia falls in behind them. They progress down the aisle. Mr Kimura looks from left to right, and smiles at the congregation. His daughter keeps her eyes downcast.

At the altar, the Japanese man bows to Leo, and he returns the bow. Hysteria bubbles up inside Sofia. She claps a hand to her mouth; she must keep quiet. Her eyes water with the effort, her shoulders shake, and a muffled giggle escapes. Why is she laughing? She should be crying. She'll have a Japanese sister-in-law and Japan is the enemy. Leo, towering over his future father-in-law, shoots her a thunderous look. She's really ruined things now . . .

# 11

Charles is staring at a plate of cold rice and turnips, practically all he's been given to eat for the past six months. The American air-raid last October raised such false hopes of freedom. Conditions in the camp are worsening by the day. The pets people brought in with them have all disappeared; the dogs and cats have either died from starvation, or they finished up in someone's cooking pot. Another thing, and it's odd, but he doesn't hear the croaking of frogs anymore.

He thinks about Kate. She's not the giggly, sparkly Kate of before. Will he ever hear her laugh again? As a form of self-preservation, he's become almost immune to the awfulness of everything and, by the dull look in her eyes every time he sees her, numbness has seeped into her soul as well. Her mother's death has crushed her.

Charles glances at Pa, sitting opposite him and so thin his rib bones jut out over his concave stomach. Pa fiddles in the back of his mouth and pulls out a piece of molar. 'Blast! I've broken a tooth. Must have been a bit of gravel left in the rice. Bugger! I thought I'd rinsed it all out before we cooked it. And here's a black too.' He gingerly picks up a piece of cockroach dung. 'What a pong!' Pa opens his mouth.

Charles staggers to his feet. 'Don't eat it!'

'Might as well.' Almost jauntily, Pa crunches on the offending morsel. 'It's the only protein I'm likely to get.'

Half-digested rice rises up in Charles' gullet. He rushes out of the room and onto the balcony. Although he's starving, he can't make himself eat such things. His guts twist. Last week, Pa caught a rat behind their quarters. Ma cut it up and pan-fried it for their supper. She lied to him and Ruth, saying it was chicken.

*Chicken, ha!* Charles found out later. A long, grey tail was left at the bottom of the rubbish bucket and he'd rushed out of the room then too.

A shout echoes, and he eyes the path below. Bob is waving at him; he waves back. 'Just a minute. I'll come down,' Charles calls out, glad of the distraction.

'Japs are looking for someone ta' repair their radio in the prison.' Bob's voice is barely above a whisper. 'I remember you saying you're a radio ham. Do you think you can manage it?'

Charles built his set himself. Of course he can manage it, but does he want to? He's been in that prison once before and doesn't fancy setting foot in the place again.

'Might be useful to have a contact,' Bob says. 'Someone neutral like you who can speak the lingo.'

'I'm not sure I'm the right person for the job. Why should we help the Japs?'

'The men who escaped and were captured last summer are from the police. We need ta' find out how they are.'

'The problem is I've already had a run-in with the guards.'

'When was that?'

'Over a year ago.'

'The guards in the prison are a new lot.'

Charles thinks for a moment. *Might as well.* It would distract him from constantly fretting over his next meal and worrying about Kate. 'I'll do it.'

\*\*\*

The following morning, Charles presents himself at the prison gates. A bandy-legged sentry looks at him with a narrowed gaze. Charles explains the purpose of his visit, and the guard takes him to an office at the side of the main building. He introduces him to a Chinese man, Fung, an electrician, who is tinkering with the radio.

'You show him how to repair set,' the guard barks, turning on his heel and striding out of the door.

Fung has a box of spare valves and Charles explains how to replace the faulty one. He chats with Fung in Cantonese. Fung is probably in his mid-thirties, is balding, and has a mole on his cheek with a long hair growing out of it. He keeps referring to the Japanese as *Law Pak Tau*, and says he's allowed out of the prison every Friday morning to go into town and visit his wife. He also tells Charles he's seen the police officer prisoners; they're so emaciated they're probably dying.

The guard comes back and escorts Charles to the prison gate. Bob is waiting at the top of the main road. 'Alreet?'

'I got on well with the electrician,' Charles says, then explains about Fung's weekly visits into town.

'I wonder if he'll agree ta' smuggle some food in for us.'

'I could wait for him on the main road the next time he comes out and ask him.'

\*\*\*

On Friday, Charles spends the whole morning meandering up and down the road, on the off-chance he'll bump into Fung. One of Bob's contacts has written a note in Chinese, which Charles will pass to Fung. It's highly dangerous, as Fung might well be a Japanese spy, but a feeling in his gut tells Charles that Fung is anti-Japanese.

At about eleven, Fung comes out of the prison gates. Charles walks up to him and deliberately stumbles. Fung bends down and helps Charles up, his mole hair quivering. Charles quickly slips him the note.

The following week Charles bumps into him again, praying the Japanese on the hill are looking the other way. It might be considered one stumble too many. Fung passes Charles a slip of paper.

Bob is waiting for him on the village green and Charles gives him the message. Although he speaks fluent Cantonese, he can't read or write it. But one of Bob's fellow policemen can.

'Fung agreed,' Bob says the next day in the supper queue. 'He'll hang a towel out of his window in the prison just before he leaves on Fridays. You'll be able ta' see it from your balcony and get down ta' the main road in time ta' meet him.'

'Right.'

'I've managed ta' arrange chocolate fortified with vitamins sent in from outside. It'll be packed in small flat tins you can easily give ta' Fung.'

\*\*\*

For three months, every Friday, Charles casually passes Fung on the main road. He pulls a couple of tins from his pocket and drops them into a bucket carried by the Chinese man. Clammy sweat breaks out over Charles' body. At the same time, he finds himself becoming increasingly addicted to the adrenalin rush.

In late July, Fung announces that he's leaving for Macau. Will his replacement carry on with the ruse? The new electrician, a man called Lai, meets Charles following Friday. 'How much money you give me?' the man asks.

'Sorry?' There's something fishy about Lai. Fung never asked for payment. Charles shoves his hands into his pockets and shakes his head. 'No money.'

'Then no can do,' Lai says, skulking off.

Charles shrugs. *Good riddance, but what about those poor policemen?*

\*\*\*

Charles' summer task is to help with the gardening. Fortunately, they're now able to grow their own vegetables; otherwise all they would eat would be rice, rice and more rice.

Last winter, Pa cleared a small patch in the scrub on the other side of the pathway from the Indian Quarters and planted tomatoes, lettuces, carrots, peas, and even celery. Others in the camp have done the same and these days everyone participates in a thriving seeds trade. The adults exchange them for food and cigarettes and give the rest to friends. Pa grew his first crops from the pips saved from early fruit and vegetable rations.

Now the plants produce their own seeds, and Charles spends the evenings with Ruth helping sort them into old envelopes. Instead of proper gardening equipment, they use sticks and improvise hoes and rakes by hammering what nails they can find into them.

'The tomatoes are nearly ready for picking,' Pa says.

Charles collects a rake. 'I don't need to queue for any fertilizer, do I?' Whenever the septic tanks are cleaned out, long lines form of people wanting the excrement for their allotments. Those who are first get the best bits - the ones that are firmest.

'No, son. We don't need any at present.'

Pulling up the weeds, Charles grumbles to himself. Sweat runs down the back of his neck and he's dizzy with tiredness; he should be taking a nap like Ma and Ruth.

He lets out a heavy, pent-up breath. He hardly sees Kate now that school has broken up for the summer. And in the autumn he won't be going back to class, as

Professor Morris said he's taught him everything he can. Soon he'll have to join one of the working parties with the other men in order to earn more rations for his family. He'll never get the chance to spend time with Kate then.

*I'll miss her.*

She's become important to him. If a day goes by without seeing her, the relentless drudgery of the camp becomes a hundred times more unbearable.

Footsteps sound on the stony path. Bob arrives, perspiration running down his face.

'I had to send Lai packing,' Charles whispers. 'He wanted money. I hope he doesn't spill the beans.'

'That would implicate him as well. I'll let you in on a secret. I've been in touch with the BAAG on me radio. They might be able ta' help me mates in the prison.'

'What's the BAAG?'

'The British Army Aid Group. They smuggle medicines and other supplies in and out of the camps and gather intelligence for the Allied Forces. They're in cahoots with the anti-Japanese guerrillas and even manage ta' get escapees from the POW camps into Free China.' Bob glances around and lowers his voice even further. 'Have ta' be careful, though. There're spies in our midst.'

'Right.'

'I'm telling you because you've helped us out. And you never know when the information might come in handy.'

Charles puts a finger to his lips.

\*\*\*

It's roll-call, and Charles is standing next to Kate, surrounded by the sullen faces of their fellow prisoners. 'Come on, Japs have finished registering us.' He takes hold of her hand. 'Let's get away from here!'

'Shouldn't we wait for Ruth?'

'I'd rather it were just the two of us.'

People mill around and he leads her away. Where to

take her but the hill above the cemetery? Even though her mother is buried below a rough-hewn headstone, there's nowhere else they can be alone. He leads Kate past the graves, and she keeps her eyes fixed on the path ahead.

He finds a patch of dry grass under an orchid tree and gently pulls her down. Kate leans back on her arms and looks at him. He averts his gaze from the hip bones jutting through the thin material of her shorts, and focuses his attention on two men sculling their sampans across the bay. A tanker has lain half-sunken in the water for as long as they've been in the camp, and its dark hulk floats like a surfaced whale. The tide is out and the reek of seaweed fills the air. 'God, I can't wait for this war to end,' he groans. 'I'm fed up with being hungry all the time.'

'Me too. I sometimes think it will never end. We've been here forever. No one cares about us. No one has come to rescue us. The whole world has forgotten us.'

Her hand is close to his; he could move his little finger and touch it if he let himself. He looks at her profile; she has the prettiest nose: narrow and just the right length for her face. The corners of her bow-shaped mouth, which always used to be upturned as if she was about to explode into one of her irrepressible giggles, are now turned downwards. *How to cheer her up?*

'The Japs are suffering a real hiding at the moment.'

Kate tucks a curl behind her ear. 'What makes you say that?'

'I've got a radio hidden in the wall of our room.'

'Charles!' She frowns. 'That's terribly risky.'

'Pa and I listen to the overseas news when we can manage it. We're very careful. No one else knows.'

'Even so. I think you should get rid of it.'

'But how else would we know what's going on in the outside world? *The Hong Kong News* is full of lies.' He takes a breath. 'I found out that the Allies have practically defeated the Japs in New Guinea.'

'That's miles away from us.'

'I expect they'll go from island to island until they eventually get here.'

'It could take years. In the meantime, if the guards catch you with that radio, they'll put you in the prison.' She blinks. 'Or worse.'

'Bob has a transmitter. He receives messages in Morse from people who've escaped to China.'

'Gosh! What he's doing is even more dangerous. We must tell him to stop.'

'Don't worry!' Kate's amber eyes fix on his, the golden lights in them distracting him. *Best change the subject.* 'What are your plans for when we get out of here?'

'Boarding school, I suppose. My father would like to go to Australia. He thinks it's a better place than England to recover his health. What about you?'

'We'll probably end up in London. An uncle on Pa's side of the family will take us in. A letter came from him via the Red Cross. I fancy studying law.'

'I think you'll make a wonderful lawyer. You're good with people and you're terribly clever.'

'Not true. I didn't realise you'd be going to Australia. Somehow I imagined you'd end up in England like me. I'll miss you.'

'And I'll miss you too.'

He moves closer to her, lifts his hand, and strokes her cheek. He can't help himself; it's so warm and lovely. Then he leans in and kisses her gently on the mouth. She pulls back, clearly surprised.

'Sorry,' he murmurs, appalled at himself.

'It was nice.'

'Nice?'

'I mean, wonderful.'

He takes her hand. 'Shall we do it again?'

'Please.'

He inclines his head towards hers and meets her lips. So soft and sweet. A rustling sound, and Ruth skips towards them. 'There you are,' he says with false enthusiasm. 'We couldn't find you earlier.'

# 12

It's a week after Charles kissed me, and I'm sitting on a rock next to the path leading around the headland. I've only seen him briefly at roll-call or in the supper queue since, and we've exchanged shy smiles but haven't managed to be alone together. Stanley is over-crowded; even married couples have few private moments. I wish we could be together more; I'm torn between wanting to shout my feelings to the world and the need to find out if Charles feels the same.

Dejection washes through me. The Japanese have just broken the promise they made a few weeks ago when they said they'd repatriate all the women, children, old people and those who are ill as an act of goodwill. Instead, they only repatriated the Canadians, and those lucky people left yesterday. Papa explained repatriation meant you had to have an exchange of prisoners. The only Japanese available to be exchanged with the British are some pearl fishermen caught in Australia, and the Aussies have turned their noses up at a bunch of half-starved, malaria-ridden people from Hong Kong. Someone said it was because the fishermen are familiar with the Australian coastline and they don't want them reporting back to Japan. Hopefully, that's the real reason. And I bet the internment camp in Australia is nicer than Stanley . . .

I hug my knees and stroke the cool stone of my jade bangle. Nearly a week ago, the American bombers returned and now they come back every day to bombard the harbour. I was filled with hope, thinking the war was bound to end and I'd be able to go home. Yet the days have worn on and now I feel even lower than before.

I've tried to keep cheerful. The adults hold regular concerts and perform plays, but the good times are few and far between. Sometimes, I take a pin and push it into the back of my leg to keep the guilt for Mama's death at bay. If I'd realised how ill she was, I wouldn't have resented having to do all the washing and cleaning. I would have been nicer to her and not have answered back all the time.

Shutting my eyes, I think about that terrible night when I held Mama's hand and said goodbye to her. The pain of the loss is as strong as if it happened yesterday. I can't bear to remember Mama's face, so still and white. I can't bear to visit her grave. I can't bear to think of my mother's body rotting in the earth.

Getting up from the rock, I dust down my shorts then traipse towards the Indian Quarters. There's Charles, standing in the middle of the village green, surrounded by a group of children, Ruth's friends, playing cowboys and Indians. I wave at him. 'Shall we go for a walk?'

Charles spreads his arms out wide. 'Sorry. Later maybe. Why don't you give me a hand?'

I glance at the kids. Generally, they run around playing games and I don't have much to do with them except when they dive-bomb me and shout, 'Ratatata!' Charles has become a sort of stand-in uncle and seems to enjoy supervising them, but I prefer to stay detached. I have no experience with young children.

Once, I spied Ruth doing her business behind a bush. It was revolting: worms wiggled among the turds. 'Make sure she washes her hands before eating,' I said to Charles. Then I told myself off for sounding like a prig.

I smile at him now; it would be rude to refuse. And, anyway, I'd do anything for him. 'All right.'

'We've captured Charles and we're about to scalp him,' Ruth shouts; she turns to her brother. 'Surrender, paleface!'

Charles gives me a helpless glance. 'Rescue me, please!'

I march towards him, children hanging onto me. By the time I reach him, I've started to laugh. I've been wading through a sea of infants and he looks so out of place stranded in the middle, his hands tied behind his back, his face anxious.

Collapsing on the ground, I clutch my belly as the giggles escape. 'I have you in my power. Yield!'

'All right, I give up.' Charles grins and shakes his head.

I want to push back the hair flopping across his forehead, and kiss him right here in front of everyone. I untie him and our eyes meet. But the children pile on top of us in a scrum and spoil the moment. 'Come on! We can go for that walk now.'

On the path leading up from the Indian Quarters, I wrap my arms around his waist and breathe in his musky citrus smell. I lift my head and his mouth covers mine. I kiss him until the numbness goes. I drink him in, love for him flooding through me.

A new sensation takes hold. His hand moves slowly down my body. My heart hammers, but I don't stop him. I want his touch.

Footsteps echo. 'Hello, you two,' Jessica Chambers says brightly. 'That's a shamefaced look if ever I saw one.' Laughing, she makes her way towards the blocks of flats.

I give her back a withering look. 'Let's go to the cemetery, Charles. We can find a spot where no one will see us.'

Under the orchid tree, well away from Mama's grave, he gathers me to him. Gently, his hands explore the hollows of my back. Our kisses become more urgent and our breathing deepens.

A sudden cry from below. 'Kate, your father wants you to go home straight away,' Jessica shrills. 'He's been coughing blood.'

'Oh, my God!' I leap up and run down the hill.

\*\*\*

'Have you been with that Eurasian boy?' Papa asks.

I nod.

'You're spending far too much time with him. It can't continue. People will talk.'

'Never mind about that. I've been begging you to see a doctor about that cough, but you've been too stubborn to do anything about it.'

'You know how much I hate quacks. Ever since my TB.'

'I hope it hasn't come back. What am I going to do with you?'

I wipe my sweaty hands on my shorts. There're other cases of TB in the camp, and the patients are isolated in a makeshift sanatorium behind the hospital. What if the doctors put Papa in there? How will he survive?

Papa coughs and sponges his moustache with his thread-bare handkerchief, leaving a tell-tail trail of pink sputum. 'It might not be TB.'

'Well, you'll have to see the doctors. I'll take you to the hospital tomorrow.'

'Getting back to that boy you've got involved with.' Papa clears his throat. 'I can't have you making a spectacle of yourself. It won't do your reputation any good, dear girl. You're growing up and you'll be seventeen soon.'

'Charles is just a friend. There's nothing going on between us.'

'Are you sure?'

I cross my fingers behind my back. 'Don't worry!'

\*\*\*

The doctors have put Papa in a side ward and keep him under observation. I'm free to spend as much time with Charles as our lack of privacy allows. Today, I'm sitting with him under the orchid tree, his arm around me. There's movement down on the beach. The Camp Commandant's Assistant is swinging a baseball bat, and shouting at a gang of European men unloading a consignment of supplies from a boat. I nudge Charles and point.

'He goes around slapping people's faces and laying into them with that paddle if they don't toe the line,' he says, taking my hand.

'Did you hear about his theories on eating grass?'

'He's been telling people they should live on it like Japanese soldiers hundreds of years ago.'

'Mr Chambers and Professor Morris have started making grass stews.'

'That can't be good for their stomachs. Human beings aren't able to digest the stuff. We're not cows,' Charles groans. 'The war has got to end one of these days, you know. And all this will just be a memory.'

'A bad one, I'm afraid.'

'All bad?' He smiles.

'Not you, of course. You make it bearable.'

I run my fingers through my tangled curls and push them back from my face. 'The Japanese are losing the war, though, aren't they?'

'Of course they are, bit by bit. We have to be patient.'

'But what if we all die of starvation before the Allies can get here?'

'We won't.' Charles puts his arms around me again.

I relax and snuggle against him. 'I love you.' The words spill out of my mouth before I've even thought about them. I hold my breath and wait for his response.

'I love you too. I want us to be together for always.'

His mouth comes down on mine and I melt into him.

A shout from lower down the hill. 'Kate,' Jessica calls out. 'Time to queue for supper . . .'

*I wish she would leave us alone.*

***

'Your father asked me to keep an eye on you,' Jessica says. 'He doesn't approve of your friendship with that young man.'

'Why? I don't understand.'

'Charles Pearce is neither one thing nor the other. He's not Chinese and he's not English.'

'Well, I think he's very lucky to have two cultures.'

'That's the problem, don't you see? The Chinese and the expatriates don't mix. We respect each other, of course, and we work together quite happily, but our backgrounds are too different. If the races inter-marry they become part of the Eurasian community, which isn't accepted by either side.'

'I don't see why we have to take sides. I really love my amah and her son is like a brother to me.'

'That's because they lived in your house and there were barriers, only you were just too young to notice them.'

'There aren't any barriers here in Stanley.'

'We won't be here much longer.'

'I hope not. Yet sometimes I think we will be, and we should live for now as we don't know what the future will bring.'

Jessica stands back and studies me with stern eyes. 'You have an old head on young shoulders, my dear. Just be careful!'

'What do you mean?'

'Have you started your periods yet?'

'Of course. But they stopped a few months after we got here. Mama said it was due to lack of food.'

'Don't let him take advantage of you, Kate. You're still

very innocent and your mother isn't here to warn you.'

'I don't understand.'

Jessica looks away. 'Take care not to lose your heart completely, that's all. We don't want you getting hurt.'

'I won't.' Charles would never hurt me. We talk about anything and everything, and, with him it's as if I've found the other part of myself, the part I didn't know existed. I can guess what Jessica was on about, but Charles is a gentleman and would never do anything I didn't want him to do. Trouble is, whenever he touches me I don't ever want him to stop . . .

# 13

Japanese voices jangle from just outside the door. I'm perched opposite Papa at the piled-up suitcases we use as a low table, sipping tepid water and nibbling from a bowl of cold rice. I'm wearing a cotton slip, but the summer air is so wet it drips down my skin and collects in the bends of my arms and behind my knees. I wipe my hands and get to my feet. *What's going on?*

Two officers are standing on the threshold, swords hanging from their waists. Three more men in white suits and Panama hats come up from behind them. My breath catches. *Kempeitai.*

Papa raises himself slowly from his mattress and bows. He's still weak; he was only discharged from the hospital yesterday. The blood he coughed up wasn't TB in the end. Just a severe case of bronchitis.

'You got radio?' a short, tubby man asks.

'No,' Papa says firmly.

'We do search.'

There isn't enough room for Papa and me, let alone for the contingent of Japanese. The officer gives a cursory glance around then mutters something incomprehensible. The rest of the Japanese laugh and back out of the door, still laughing.

Papa sits down heavily and I go to the window. The Japanese are heading off towards the Police Block. It's too late to warn Bob. I have to find Charles.

Within minutes I'm running up the stairs to his room. It's empty except for Ruth, who is sitting on a camp-bed, scooping congee from the bottom of her breakfast bowl. 'What's the matter?' she asks.

'The Japanese are prowling around looking for radios.'

'Well, they won't find any here.'

Legs shaking, I collapse on the bed. 'Are you sure?'

Ruth gives me a puzzled glance. 'Why?'

'No reason, kiddo.'

'I think my parents and Charles have gone to the canteen. Let's catch up with them.'

I link arms with Ruth and we walk up the main road. If only I could share my concern with her, but Charles told me Ruth doesn't know about the radio. Up ahead, I spot Derek Higgins approaching from the opposite direction.

'Guess what?' he says. 'They've arrested a top government chap, the number two in the police, and lots of other people.'

'Don't sound so pleased.' I push Ruth behind me.

Derek smirks. 'Isn't it about time we had some excitement in this boring place?'

'You're heartless and horrible.'

The echo of screams comes from the Commandant's house at the top of the hill, and I flinch.

Derek folds his arms. 'Do you know about Japanese water torture?'

I want to back away from him, but my legs have frozen.

'They tie the victims face-down on a board and pump liquid through their nose and mouth,' he says.

'H... h... how do they breathe?'

'They open their mouths even more, but the Japs fill them up with more water.'

'You're fibbing!'

Derek licks his lips. 'When the victims look like the swollen corpses of drowned people, the Japs jump on the poor buggers' stomachs.' He sniggers. 'Jets of water shoot out of their mouths, noses and even eyes.'

'You're such a sadist. I bet it's not true.'

''Tis so!'

Ruth comes out from behind me, and stamps her foot. 'I hate you. Leave us alone!'

I put my arm around her. 'Come on, kiddo! I'll take you home. We can wait for your parents and brother there.'

Back in the Married Quarters, we find Charles and his father sitting on their camp-beds.

'Ma's furious,' Charles whispers. 'She found us with the radio and has gone to bury it.'

'I was so worried about you.' I grab his hand, 'Thank God you're all right. And what about your mother? I hope she won't be caught.'

'She won't be. We smashed the radio into little pieces. Japs won't suspect a woman. She'll pretend to be planting something in our vegetable patch.'

I squeeze his fingers and kiss him right in front of his father and sister.

***

I hurry back to the Indian Quarters, but something's wrong. The village green is empty except for four men. My heart almost beats out of my chest. There's Bob, stumbling between two *Kempeitai* officers and a Chinese supervisor. They march him to the end of the blocks of flats. My whole body shakes. The officer makes him dig in the soft earth until he unearths a small grey box.

Tears gush down my face. Papa arrives and takes me by the arm. 'Come inside this instant! It's far too dangerous out here.'

I sniff and wipe my nose. 'What have you heard?'

'It's spreading around the camp like wildfire. Japs have discovered a fortune in banknotes hidden under the bandages of a chap sent to town for an x-ray. They've arrested the top man in the Hong Kong and Shanghai Bank and some of his underlings, the fellow in charge of Medical Services, and quite a few locals. Accused them of collaborating with the BAAG and forming a resistance.'

'Derek Higgins told me about the arrests.'

'They nabbed two of the Cable and Wireless staff, as well as our friend Bob, and said they were operating secret radios.'

'How did they find out they had radios?'

'Japs have discovered some spare parts smuggled in with our supplies.'

'Who told on them?'

'Some people would sell their own grandmothers for favours or for food.'

*\*\*\**

I lie awake all night; I can't stop thinking about Bob. In the morning I rush to the hot water queue to tell Charles. Where is he? I spin on my heel and dash to the Married Quarters.

Ruth and her mother are sitting next to each other, crying. Mr Pearce hovers over them, clutching at his hands. 'It's too terrible,' he says. 'They came for him last night. Said that, because he repaired their radio, he must have known about the others in the camp.'

My legs buckle and Charles' father gently helps me to a seat.

'We were kept up all night by the Japs,' Mrs Pearce sobs. 'They had a drunken party in the prison. We saw everything from our balcony.'

'One so-and-so, probably sozzled on *saké*, let loose into the yard and began firing his revolver into the air,' Mr Pearce says. 'All the Japs dived for cover, then an officer came out and shot him in the shoulder. They hauled the man away, and in the end everything quietened down.'

'What do you think will happen to Charles?' Numbness fills me, the frozen sensation only he can melt.

'I don't know,' Mr Pearce says. 'No one will tell us anything.'

'They'll let him out soon, though, won't they?' I wait for Mr Pearce to reassure me, but he remains silent.

*\*\**

The weeks pass and Charles is still being held in the gaol, along with the others who were arrested. Early one afternoon at the end of October, I'm lingering on the hillside above the cemetery with Ruth. I spend as much time as I can with Charles' sister. It started as a way of getting news of him; now I've become fond of her and enjoy our moments together.

I'm thinking about Charles. Hopefully, his arrest was a huge mistake and he'll soon be released. The Japanese said that, as Charles was over sixteen, he came under their authority and not that of the camp tribunal. He'll be tried and sentenced like everyone else. I hope it won't come to that. Mr Pearce said not to worry, as there was no proof that Charles had a radio or that he's been involved in anything untoward.

'I was with my friends by the main road this morning,' Ruth says, picking up a fallen pine cone. 'A van drove out of the prison and a hand waved through the window. Someone called out, "Goodbye".'

I look down at the shore. There's a stretch of sand near the jetty. It's usually deserted, but not today. Guards have appeared and someone has dug channels above the high-water mark.

Ruth points. 'What are those trenches for?'

'I don't know, kiddo. We'd better set off for school or we'll be late for our lessons.' I stare at the beach again.

Three trucks have driven up and the guards are opening the doors. 'Wait!'

The guards line up about thirty men and one woman, roped together in groups of three with their hands tied behind their backs. They wave their rifles and push the people down to sit on the sand, then they put blindfolds on them. There's Bob in the first trio! A guard leads him forward to kneel by a trench. Then a large man, his head close-shaven, unsheathes a sword and swings it in the air.

Down comes the blade, glinting in the sun. A streak of silver. Shining. Silent. Deadly. I yelp as Bob's body topples. Leaping to my feet I grab Ruth's hand, and we run. We run, our legs pounding the dry earth to get away from the scene of horror unfolding on the sand, our mouths open to let out our screams.

Ruth runs back to her family and I career full-tilt into Papa on the pathway leading down to the Indian Quarters.

'Steady, dear girl. What on earth's the matter?'

In gasping breaths I tell him.

He pulls me close and I sob against his chest. 'What a callous act! There's no excuse for it,' he says.

'They were laughing and j . . . j . . . joking. How can they be so cruel?'

Back in the Indian Quarters, Papa fetches a cloth and sponges vomit from my chin. I can't remember having been sick. He holds me as I weep. I spend the afternoon sitting listlessly on my mattress and go to bed early. Then I wake up screaming from a nightmares of Charles' instead of Bob's disconnected head rolling along the ground, blood spurting from his severed neck.

Papa sits down on the mattress next to me and pats my shoulder. 'There, there.'

I feel numb and empty of emotion; it's as if I've died too.

# 14

Sofia bends her fingers forward at a 90 degree angle to create a dragon claw. She must maintain the tension. It's a year since Leo's wedding, and she's practising her kung fu moves with him.

Her sister-in-law, Michiko, spends her time either in Leo's suite of rooms here at Father's, or at her family home. Michiko's mother is ill – some female problem no one will explain to Sofia – and needs Michiko to nurse her. She's there this afternoon, which is why Sofia has Leo's full attention.

After Japanese troops seized the British steamer *Sian* in the harbour, killing about twenty guards, the Japanese demanded the installation of their own advisors as an alternative to military occupation. Mr Kimura, it turns out, was what is known as a sleeper, and now advises the Portuguese administration on civilian defence. Not actually a spy, Uncle said, just waiting until the moment came to show his true colours . . .

Today, Sofia is the attacker and Leo is the defender. Sometimes they switch roles, but not often. Leo is still too strong for her and his attacks too rapid. One day she'll be good enough to resist him, hopefully.

They face each other and bow with their palms together. Sofia opens her arms wide and lets out a loud, '*Hai*!' She flies at Leo, hands flailing, flicking her wrist for extra force so that she can dig her fingers into his arm muscles. He blocks her move and she falls back. Up on her feet, she attacks. He throws out a kick and rolls away. She goes in for the assault again. Leo's superior technique pushes her across the terrace and she has to concede defeat.

'One more go,' she begs. This time she'll get him. She's determined. She goes at him like a whirling dervish, arms and legs flying out at the same time.

He aims a kick at her; she leaps up in the air and it misses its mark. Finally, she has the upper hand. She can feel victory within her grasp. She aims a zigzag motion kick at the top of Leo's foot, then grabs his leg and pushes him down. She's won.

'Well done, little sister. But you wouldn't have been able to do that if I'd used force on your pressure points.' He laughs.

'When will you teach me how to do that?'

'It's too dangerous. I could kill you and, judging by how much progress you've made recently, you could even end up killing me. Come on, let's go indoors and get ourselves something to drink. I'm parched.'

They sit in companionable silence at the large rosewood dining table, sipping iced jasmine tea. Sofia lets out a sigh of contentment. In spite of the Japanese practically controlling Macau, and the destitution of people on the streets, happiness bubbles up within her. She shouldn't feel happy. Not with all the wretchedness around her, but she can't help herself. A knock at the door, and she looks up. Father's houseman, Ah Chong, slinks into the room, his face pale. '*Aiyah!* Big fire. Master Leo you go quick. Missy Michiko hospital.'

Sofia lets out a gasp as Leo runs from the room. 'What happened?'

She perches next to Father in his study, waiting for news. She only saw Michiko this morning at breakfast. They talked about how they both missed going to the cinema, her brother's wife opening up to her at last.

'Michiko will be all right, won't she?'

'I hope so,' Father says.

Sofia takes his hand. 'Why didn't you object to Leo marrying a Japanese woman?' It's a question she's posed many times. Maybe today he'll finally tell her.

'I felt guilty for not giving him the love he craved from me. Michiko adores him, don't you know? I watched them together and couldn't refuse.'

'Oh,' Sofia says, frowning. She thinks back to the year between Leo's first meeting then marrying the girl. They must have seen each other in secret, because she can't remember him courting her openly. She squeezes her father's hand. 'Why couldn't you love Leo?'

'He reminds me too much of my own father, who only saw things in absolutes. There wasn't room for any compromises in his character. He could only see black or white, never the shades of grey. I'm sad to admit I disliked him, and, although I don't actually dislike Leo, I can't find it in myself to truly love him either. Not like I love you, my daughter.'

She's suspected this for years, but it's still a shock to have it confirmed. Another reason for Leo's jealousy. And an explanation for the change in him since he met Michiko; the Japanese girl seems to love him unreservedly.

*I hope she's all right.*

'What about Mr Kimura? Did you suspect he was a sleeper?'

'Absolutely not! He told me he wasn't in the military because he was colour-blind. I took it on good faith. I just wanted to get a cheap price for the pearls I'd promised Siu Yin. How was I to know Leo would start wooing the girl?'

Not long after the dinner party when Leo had first met Michiko, Siu Yin appeared with a long string of even bigger pearls than Mrs Kimura's. Why Father has to pander to her step-mother's every whim is something Sofia will never understand. Natalia has told her what she calls "the facts of life", of course. Could it be something to do with sex? Sofia can feel a blush creep up her neck just thinking about her father having sex with Siu Yin. 'I see,' she says, although she really doesn't.

The minutes stretch into an hour, then two hours. Ah Chong brings them a tray of supper. Cold bean curd. Sofia picks at it with her chop-sticks. She doesn't feel like eating. Something's wrong. Otherwise Leo would be back by now.

She can't wait any longer. She'll telephone Uncle. He'll know what's going on. 'I'll be back in a minute,' she says.

Natalia is in the front hall, standing straight-backed at the foot of the stairs. 'I've been waiting for you. Come up to your room, darlink. There's something I have to tell you.'

A sinking sensation in her chest, Sofia follows her governess up to the first-floor and into her bedroom. Natalia sits on the bed and pats the space next to her. 'I'm so sorry,' Natalia says softly. 'The whole Kimura family is dead.'

'No!' A chill creeps into Sofia's bones. 'How?' Her voice trembles.

'It wasn't supposed to be this way.'

'What do you mean?'

'Leo has been collaborating with the Japanese military. Your uncle found out he's been acting as an intermediary between Mr Kimura and a group of nationalists, who've been pretending to fight Japan when all they do is block the communist guerrillas.'

'How did Uncle find this out?'

'Because I've been following Mr Kimura. And the worst thing is, he saw me this morning when I tailed him to the harbour. I'd managed to creep up and hide behind an upturned sampan on the beach, where I listened to him conspiring with those traitors and heard them giving him details of guerrilla movements. Nationalists turning against their fellow-Chinese. Unspeakable!'

'How did he see you?'

'I was attacked by seagulls. Can you believe it? Even the seagulls are starving, and they must have thought my hat was edible. I sat there as they dive-bombed me, willing to brazen it out, but one of the men came to investigate and I ran off.' Natalia pauses. 'Leo will put two and two together. He'll think I had something to do with the arson attack on Michiko's family.'

'Why should he think that?'

'Firstly, because I was following Mr Kimura. Secondly, because only the guerrillas would have carried out the assault. They're the only people who dare to resist the Japanese around here.'

'You said it wasn't supposed to be this way.'

'Some young hotheads in the brigade took it on themselves to teach Mr Kimura a lesson. They didn't mean to kill anyone. Just to frighten him. Unfortunately, with the dry weather we've had recently, the house went up like a tinder-box. There were sacks of rice blocking the back door and the family was overcome by smoke inhalation.'

Sofia starts to sob. Her shoulders heave and snot runs from her nose. She grabs hold of her governess. 'What will you do now?'

'I can't stay here. I've just come to collect my things and say goodbye, my Sofichka. You're fifteen years old now, too grown-up to need a governess. When the war is over, your father should send you to school or employ the best tutors for you to finish your education. Make sure that he does!'

She goes with Natalia to her room and watches her pack. How to make Natalia change her mind? That would be foolish, though. Natalia's right; she has to leave. And soon. Sofia glances at her watch. Leo will be home any minute now. 'Hurry up!'

***

'Where is she? Where's that Russian bitch?' Leo shouts, coming through the door. He marches up to Sofia and her father. 'I know all about Natalia's shenanigans this morning. She's a spy. The police have found rags soaked in kerosene dropped on the road outside the house. The fire was started deliberately. If I discover you had anything to do with this, Sofia, I'll never forgive you.'

'Now, now, Leo,' Father gets up from his chair. 'Calm down! How can you accuse your sister of something so terrible? She's only a child, for heaven's sake. And what proof do you have that Natalia is a spy?' He turns to Sofia. 'Where is she, by the way?'

'She's gone.'

'Gone?' Father repeats, a frown crinkling his brow.

'She said to tell you both that she's very sorry. She didn't mean for this to happen.'

Father sits back down. He opens his mouth then shuts it again. He takes a handkerchief from his pocket and blows his nose. 'Did you know she'd been spying on us?'

Sofia has never lied to her father and she's not going to lie to him now. 'I knew she was a communist. I found out last year.'

'See!' Leo points at Sofia. 'My bastard step-sister is in cahoots with the Russian bitch.'

'I don't want to hear language like that in my house,' Father says, shaking his finger at Leo. 'Apologise to Sofia!'

'Never! She must have known about Natalia. They've always been thick as thieves. I'm sure there weren't any secrets between them.'

'I know I should have told you, Father, I realise that now. I thought she was harmless.' Should she tell him this is all Leo's fault for collaborating with the Japanese? She isn't a tell-tale-tit.

'Harmless?' Father's voice shakes with anger. 'How can deception ever be harmless? Go to your room, Sofia! I'll come up and talk to you when I've had a few words with

Leo.'

'All right,' she says, her mouth trembling. Tears prickle, but she won't cry. Not in front of Leo.

\*\*\*

The counterpane is cold beneath her fingers, like the icy feeling inside her. She runs her hands up and down the smooth silk. How will she cope without Natalia? She'll just have to and that's that. This war won't go on forever. When it's over, she'll start a new life. Maybe go to Hong Kong. She's always loved it there.

A knock at the door. 'I've been trying to talk some sense into the boy,' Father says, lowering himself onto the chair by the window. 'He won't listen. It's grief, I suppose. I can't help feeling responsible. I should never have allowed the marriage. It was bound to end in tears.'

'You weren't to know. I'm sorry for not telling you about Natalia. And I'm devastated for Leo about Michiko. Really, I am. And her family. It's so, so sad.'

'I don't understand why Leo thinks Natalia is responsible for this tragedy. He says Siu Yin's cousin caught her following him. He won't tell me anything else. Can you shed any light on this?'

What to do? She doesn't want to lie to Father. But if she says anything, Leo will find out and that'll make things even worse. Then, there's Uncle. No one must know he's been helping the guerrillas. She made a promise she can't break. That's it. A prior promise cancels out a future lie. She gets to her feet and makes eye contact with her father. 'I don't know anything.'

# 15

The Pearces' balcony directly overlooks the prison exercise yard. Every evening, from five to six, I'm there, watching Charles pace up and down with the rest of the prisoners, my heart going out to him with every step he takes. I've practically haunted the place in the eighteen months since his arrest.

Ruth tugs at my sleeve. 'Can you test me on my spellings?'

'Of course, kiddo.' How resilient Ruth is! Just like the rest of the children, she's full of joy at life, even in this terrible place. I've been trying hard to keep positive, telling myself the war is bound to end soon and that Charles will survive. It's hard, though . . .

Minutes later, after I've given Ruth full marks for her spellings, my heartbeat quickens. He's come into view. I can see him clearly. He turns his head in my direction and waves furtively. Like everyone else in the camp, he's deathly thin. At least he's still walking tall and doesn't look ill. Oh, how I long to take him in my arms . . .

Charles' family have been kind and welcoming. If they didn't know I loved their son before, they know it now. Papa wouldn't have been like them if it had been me who'd been imprisoned. He would have told Charles he didn't think him worthy. One day, I'll confront Papa about his prejudice, but only when liberation comes and I can love Charles openly.

I point to the flower from the orchid tree I've tucked behind my ear. If Charles can see it, he'll understand . . .

\*\*\*

On the fifteenth of January, air-raid sirens blare above Stanley. I rush to the window. American planes are flying overhead. They come often now to bomb the harbour, as well as targets on Hong Kong Island and Kowloon. Papa stands next to me. 'We haven't got any white crosses on the rooftops. How will they know we're an internment camp?'

Throughout the day I count the aircraft, over three hundred of them, the biggest raid yet. The next morning, the alarm sounds again. 'Look! They're back.' I go to the balcony. 'Thousands of them.'

'Not quite thousands,' Papa says. 'I've heard the Japs have put guns on top of the prison buildings. That's certain to attract attention.'

Japanese soldiers dash onto the village green, firing revolvers and rifles at planes miles high. 'They're running around like headless chickens,' I laugh, keeping my worry about Charles to myself. He'll be a sitting target in the prison . . .

A sudden roar. Four planes drop from the sky. They're heading straight for the Indian Quarters! Three American aircraft pass overhead, chasing a Japanese plane, their machine guns roaring.

'Quick! Get down!' Papa shouts.

A huge explosion rocks the building. Flinching, I peer over the parapet. The Americans have gunned down the Japanese plane, which has crashed into the hillside to our right - just above the bathing beach. A plume of smoke rises up. Tell-tale signs of more planes shot down: towers of smoke come from the outlying islands, from behind the hill on the other side of Stanley Bay, and from the cove itself.

The day wears on and the air-raids continue. I curl up on my mattress, holding my breath during the attacks, and letting it in and out while waiting for the next one. Papa sits next to me, grumbling and muttering about the lack of a proper shelter.

Late in the afternoon there's a massive bang. I stumble to the back of the flat, my legs shaking so much I can hardly move. A heavy cloud rises up from behind the cemetery and I grab Papa's arm. 'They must have hit one of the buildings at St Stephen's.'

*\*\*\**

Derek Higgins walks up to me the following morning in the water queue. 'Guess what?' he says with his habitual smirk. 'The Americans must have thought that rusty old wreck of a tanker in Stanley Bay had some strategic importance. A couple of aircraft turned to attack it, but their wings touched.'

'What happened to them?'

'The pilots had to jump out when the planes crashed into the hillside. One of them didn't make it and his parachute tangled up in the propellers. The other pilot got out and the Japanese shot him just as he landed.'

'Oh no! What about St Stephen's?'

'Bungalow C scored a direct hit. When the all-clear sounded, ten bodies were lying on the grass. Someone said they looked like they were asleep as they didn't have a scratch on them.'

'How do you know all this?'

'Because I went up there for a look.'

'Were they all right?'

'Of course not. They were dead. Six people were taken

to the infirmary. One woman died on the way there. Three more bodies were found in the wreckage. The funeral's later today and they'll be buried in a mass grave.'

'Another mass grave,' I murmur. Heavy-footed, I make my way back to the Indian Quarters, my chest aching. Of course they'll be buried in a mass grave. There's only one coffin in the camp. The base has been removed and it's used again and again for the many funerals, just like it was for Mama's. A picture comes into my mind of standing in the rain under a paper umbrella, and of strangers shovelling clods of earth onto my mother's shrouded body. I swallow the knot of sorrow in my throat and grip my bucket.

Papa is waiting for me. 'You haven't heard the worst.'

'What can be worse?'

'Some people didn't wait till the all-clear and looted the bungalow even before the bodies were removed.' He runs a hand through his hair. 'I often think we're interned with a bunch of animals.'

'Are you sure it was one of us? Isn't it something the Japanese would have done?'

Even as I ask the question, I remember Derek's description of the bodies and my stomach clenches.

'Japs mounted a guard as soon as they found out what happened then presented arms above the wreckage.'

'Such strange people . . .'

'They seem to think it's honourable to die in war, but equal to losing your soul if you're taken prisoner.'

'That explains a lot of things, but not their treatment of us.' I stretch out on my mattress and stare at the wall. Last October I turned eighteen. I've been in the camp for over three years and it's hard to imagine my life when peace eventually comes. What will it be like to no longer be hungry? To have proper clothes? To be able to go out and about? To be with Charles again?

And what will happen if peace doesn't come?

\*\*\*

A week after the air-raids, I'm on the Pearces' balcony, waiting to catch sight of Charles. Tailorbirds chirp in the bushes below and a kite soars above, gliding in circles among the thermals and giving an occasional long drawn-out squealing call. I look down at the exercise yard. It's getting late. Where is he?

A chill. The hairs on my arms stand up. A shift in the atmosphere. Anxiety radiates from Ruth, Mr and Mrs Pearce. A sudden terror. Everyone leaps to their feet. Charles isn't among the prisoners!

'I'll go and find out what's happened,' Mr Pearce says, making his way to the door.

Mrs Pearce seizes his arm. 'Be careful, dearest!'

The next hour drags. I bite what's left of my fingernails, which stopped growing ages ago for lack of nutrients. I pace up and down the balcony, then I sit on a camp-bed, then stand, then sit again, twirling my jade bangle round and round.

Mr Pearce returns and slumps down on a camp-bed, his face grey. 'Charles has been drafted to a labour camp in Japan along with some of the POWs from Shamshuipo camp.'

I let out a muffled cry. Charles has been weakened by years of semi-starvation. How will he survive? I can see in Mrs Pearce's eyes the same thoughts that I've been thinking. Ruth sobs, and I put my arm around her.

'Don't worry, kiddo! Charles will be fine. You'll see!'

\*\*\*

Time passes. Winter releases its hold, the orchid tree finishes its flowering season, and a muggy spring turns into a fierce summer. There has been no news of Charles.

I line up on the village green for a bowing lesson, heat and humidity enveloping me. The Camp Commandant is obsessed with military etiquette and seems convinced the prisoners aren't getting it right. I go through the movements, my mind elsewhere.

'How can the Japanese expect us to take this bowing seriously?' I whisper to Papa. In May, *The Hong Kong News* announced Germany's surrender. Soon afterwards, the Japanese said, "no more newspapers" and they became another item for black market traders. 'It's obvious they're losing the war.'

'They're doing it out of spite, I reckon.' Papa laughs, yet his eyes, staring blankly, give the lie to his apparent mirth. 'A guard said they've been tunnelling shelters and foxholes into the hills. Japs seem to think they can fight for Hong Kong. How desperate and pathetic . . .'

'Whenever I hear a guard coming, I run and hide or I give them my best bow.' I shrug. 'Everyone does. Don't they realise we're too weak for all this?'

To my left, Jessica Chambers is staring straight ahead. On the other side of the parade ground, a group of young men from the Hong Kong Police grin mockingly and make little effort to bow. I study the outline of Papa's ribs poking through his bare chest. Sweat pouring from his face, he stands to attention in the hot sunshine; I take his hand and it's like holding a bunch of twigs.

I glance at the Pearce family. Physically, they're surviving. Mentally, though, they've become listless and resigned to their circumstances, just like everyone else. They no longer mention Charles; they probably think talking about him will jeopardise his chances. So I try to do the same and carry on as if everything will turn out for the best. And I cling to that hope; it nestles next to the numbness that has seeped back into my soul.

The Commandant struts in front of us. 'Captain Ito show you.'

The Japanese officer stands on a table. He inclines at the waist, holding his body at a forty-five degree angle. We try to imitate him, struggling with the exertion, weak with exhaustion.

The new Formosan guards stand on the side-lines, their faces unreadable. The Commandant has put them through field training over the past couple of weeks, leading them around the camp, wielding a bamboo stick. He has no chance! The Formosans don't give a damn about fighting to keep Hong Kong in Japanese hands. The Japs treat them like dogs, unaware they participate in a thriving black market with the prisoners, keeping us informed about events in the outside world. Manila has already been liberated. Surely it won't be long before it's Hong Kong's turn? My hands shake. If freedom doesn't come soon, we'll all starve to death. The situation has become that serious.

And poor Charles stuck in Japan . . .

\*\*\*

The days go by in the same monotonous pattern – get up, queue for food, lie around too weak to do anything, queue again, sleep. Finally a copy of *The Hong Kong News* is smuggled into the camp with the information we've all been longing for. Japan has surrendered. I hear about it in the supper queue and join in as everyone hugs and kisses each other. Even though I've no energy, my step quickens. 'It's over,' I say to Papa back in our room. 'The war is over.'

He stares at me. 'I can't believe it. Far too sudden.' Then he breaks into a smile and hugs me as hard as his lack of strength allows.

The next day, a notice pinned to the canteen wall informs us officially that hostilities have ceased. The Representative of Internees, one-time Colonial Secretary, has accepted responsibility for the maintenance of discipline. I read the report slowly. Then I read it again so I can relay all the facts to Papa. I let out a sigh and close my eyes. I won't have to worry about survival any more.

From now on, I won't have to live behind barbed wire. Then I stare into the distance, as if by doing so I can see Charles.

Where is he? How is he?

I walk up the road and the camp is quiet. All the guards have disappeared and the Japanese are marching shamefaced to their headquarters. I make my way to the canteen. Passing the godowns, I spot a group of European policemen in uniform, patrolling the area. At least I don't have to bow anymore . . .

***

It seems liberation will never come. An American aeroplane flies over and drops pamphlets saying the internees should remain calm and not leave the camp until the Allied forces arrive. Time moves on slowly as we wait for the Royal Navy. The local Red Cross representative makes a speech, promising that the authorities will increase rations and provide buses to bring visitors from Victoria City and the Kowloon camps.

One afternoon, I'm reading to Ruth in her quarters. She looks up. Charles' Auntie Julie and Uncle Phillip come into the room. Phillip Noble, a tall man with silver hair, is a Portuguese-Chinese who married Mrs Pearce's sister ten years ago. They've spent the war in Macau.

'Conditions weren't much better than in Hong Kong,' Mrs Noble says. She looks so like Mrs Pearce they could be twins. 'We didn't have much food, but at least we didn't starve.' She hugs Mrs Pearce and stares at Ruth with a sympathetic expression. 'My poor dears! You're nothing but skin and bone. The sooner we get you out of here the better. And we'll do everything we can to find out about Charles.' She goes on to explain that the Pearces' old home was destroyed in the bombing. 'And the Japanese turned our place in Kowloon into an officers' club. Before they left, they did their business in the corners of every room.

Such barbarity! The whole place needs disinfecting and a fresh coat of paint.'

I shake hands with Charles' aunt. Should I beg her to get information about him quickly? That would be inappropriate, though. I'll just have to wait, and hope, and believe he'll soon be home.

\*\*\*

Food rations in the camp improve when the Red Cross send in beans and the Japanese manage to provide more vegetables and daily meat. For years I've dreamt of filling my stomach, and now I can't digest the unaccustomed protein.

The Colonial Secretary takes the oath as Officer Administrating the Government. Papa explains it's an important move, establishing British civilian authority over the colony.

A week later, I spot a familiar figure stepping off an open-topped lorry that has drawn up next to the canteen. A slight Chinese woman with thin black hair scraped into a bun turns and flashes a gold-toothed smile at me. 'Ah Ho!' I fling myself into her arms, then lead her to the Indian Quarters. Papa stares at her in evident amazement.

'You got any washing?' she asks.

Ah Ho tells us she set off for the colony as soon as she learned about the surrender, leaving Jimmy behind. She explains that he's joined up with the communists, but Ah Ho is glad to be back with Papa and me. She didn't like bunking down in the same room as the family's pigs and chickens in China.

Ah Ho sleeps on a mat in the passageway at the rear of the flat, and works alongside the other internees' amahs who've turned up in recent days, helping them prepare food in the communal kitchens. Her loyalty makes me feel humble.

A few days later, I go with Papa to visit our old home.

We catch a lift in one of the buses laid on to bring visitors to the camp. It's strange leaving Stanley after more than three and a half years. In town, I stare at the devastation, the bombed buildings, the craters in the roads, the piles of debris. On the Peak, the house has been stripped of its wooden flooring and black roof tiles. And the Japanese have sunk a well in the garden. Papa puts his hand to his forehead. 'It's right where Ah Woo and I buried our valuables.'

He finds an abandoned spade and digs. Before exhaustion claims him, he strikes something and bends down to reach for one of my silver riding cups. I study the object, won with such pride in my old life.

*What was all the fuss about?*

\*\*\*

At the end of August, the British fleet finally reach Hong Kong. The day before they arrive, planes fly over the camp and drop medicines and food that flutter down on green, red and white parachutes. I'm on the parade ground in front of the Married Quarters with Papa and we eagerly take a package each, nearly making ourselves sick gorging on chocolate. I grab one of the 'chutes; I've heard the rayon is perfect for making underwear.

I barely sleep I'm so excited and, when morning comes, the drone of planes sends me dashing onto the balcony; they sweep low in formations of two, three, four or eight. I wave, cheer and cry tears of happiness at being free at last. But how can I be happy when I don't know what's happened to Charles?

On the afternoon of the official flag raising ceremony, Papa opens a suitcase and presents me with one of Mama's dresses. It's light blue cotton with a fitted waist and puffed sleeves. I rummage in the case and find a pair of leather high-heeled shoes. After parting my hair at the centre, I pin it into a Victory roll. If only I had a mirror to see my reflection . . .

Papa puts on a shirt and tie then escorts me to the parade ground, where we take our places with the hundreds of internees.

A strange-looking vehicle pulls up. Papa says it's called a jeep. Out of it steps the commander of the fleet, Rear Admiral Cecil Harcourt. A bugle plays the attention and the Union Jack is unfurled, followed by the flags of all the different nationalities that have been interned in the camp. Banners at half-mast, the Last Post is sounded and planes fly overhead. Everyone sings, *Oh God, Our Help in Ages Past.*

A light wind blows in from the bay, cooling my father and me in the August heat, and lifting the notes of the bugle. The flags unfurl and fly over the colony once more.

*Our hope for years to come,* I sing, and the expectation I'll see Charles soon swells my heart.

\*\*\*

A fortnight later, I'm standing at the railings of a small aircraft carrier converted from a merchant ship that will take Papa and me to Sydney, Australia. The vessel picked us up at Stanley and now we're heading out of Hong Kong waters. Chinese white dolphins frolic in the ship's bow-waves, escorting us towards the open sea. I said goodbye to Ah Ho yesterday. My amah is returning to China with the promise of a job as soon as Papa gets back from his extended leave. He's given her some of the silver dug up from the garden to help with expenses.

A blast from the ship's funnel sends vibrations through the railings. I run my hands down the cold metal then put my fingers to my mouth, tasting the salt. It reminds me of the tears I shed only hours ago.

I went to say goodbye to the Pearces straight after breakfast. They were sitting on their beds, their faces puffed from crying.

'Oh Kate,' Mrs Pearce said, getting to her feet and putting her arms around me. 'My sister visited last night. We've had the most dreadful news.' She pointed to a cushion. 'You'd better sit down.' She took both hands and made eye contact with me. 'Be prepared for a shock, my dear. The ship . . .'

Mrs Pearce controlled her breathing, let a full breath stutter out, and took another.

'The ship taking Charles . . . Charles and the other prisoners, to Japan . . .' She had to stop again. The blood rushed from my head and my feet began to swim away from me.

'The ship was bombed and sunk by the Americans,' Mr Pearce said quietly, his teeth clenching shut immediately the words were out. 'Charles isn't listed . . . among the survivors.'

I sobbed and pleaded with his family that it couldn't be true, but they said Phillip Noble had telegraphed Shanghai, where the survivors had been taken, and Charles' name wasn't recorded among them.

I went completely silent then, shutting out the horror. I didn't look at anyone, because if I had done so it would have become real. I stared out the window and kept my body as still as I could. Ruth ran to fetch help, and there was a commotion when Papa came with Tony Chambers. They half-carried me back to the Indian Quarters. I hadn't even managed to get the Pearces' address in London.

\*\*\*

The ship heads towards the horizon now and I turn my gaze to the back of the Peak, swathed in fog. Up there, in the swirling mists, is my home. Hong Kong recedes in the distance, and the image of Charles' face comes into my mind: high cheekbones, warm eyes and dark brown hair that flops across his forehead. I step away from the railings and glance at the back of my left hand. It's bleeding. The blood has caked under my newly-grown fingernails.

# PART TWO
# 1948-1949

# 16

James Stevens stood next to Tony Chambers on the armour-plated bridge of the Customs Preventive ship. He glanced at the sky. Nearly daybreak. Shouldn't be long now. Catching smugglers would make a welcome change from surveying.

He steadied himself and rolled with the swell, breathing in the scents of China carried by the wind: the musk of wood smoke, the bitter stench of the communal latrines and the flowery fragrance of myriad joss sticks. So different to the smell of coal fires and the rotten-egg pong of the Thames in London.

Stubbing out his cigarette, he heard his father's words as if they were being spoken right next to him, 'Join the Navy and see the world, son.'

Hot tears welled up. James was a man now, twenty-five, and he'd taken his demob two years ago. He touched his inside pocket where that final letter from home nestled with his cigarettes. No need to read it, he knew it by heart.

*Last night one of those German doodlebugs flew over,* Mother had written. *We held our breaths as the terrible rasping, grating noise cut out and the rocket came crashing down on the newsagents up the road. I can't tell you how terrified we were.*

James' vision blurred. A week after the letter had arrived, he'd received a telegram informing him his parents had died in a raid from another deadly flying bomb. At first, he hadn't believed it. How could they both have been carted lifeless from under a pile of debris? Mother had always tried to make the best of herself by sleeping with her chestnut-coloured hair in rag curlers every night and putting on fresh lipstick every morning. Dad never left the house unshaven. Mother would have been taken from the wreckage with pale lips and her hair still in rags. Dad's chin would have been covered in stubble.

James had gone home on leave shortly afterwards, and then he'd finally accepted the truth. A heavy sensation in his stomach, he'd stumbled over the rubble until he'd reached the two-up-two-down house where he'd grown up. The wallpaper he'd helped hang flapped in the wind, the picture of a battleship was still pinned to his bedroom wall, but the side of the building had opened to the world. Broken glass crunched as he'd dragged his feet from room to room and, in the air, lingered the sour smell of plaster made wet by the rain.

James dried his eyes. There was no reason for him to return to London, or even England. His family was dead and the letter was the one thing he had left of them. If only he could tell Mother and Dad he'd got a job in the Far East. They would have been so proud of him; they'd never been farther than Brighton.

Timbers creaked in the distance and sails flapped. Bouncing on his toes, James gave the command, 'Full ahead!'

Sirens screamed as the ship surged forward. Phosphorescence from plankton glowed in the moonlight, lighting up the bow-wave. They were closing in on a large fishing junk.

He glanced at his Chief Officer. Tony wiped spray from his grey-flecked beard. 'Get ready to shoot!'

James switched on the searchlight and supervised the

loading of the Vickers three-pounder. He sighted the three masts and fish-fin sails of the vessel, ploughing through the waves about three hundred yards away. A shot across the bow should do the trick. He would board the junk, order the halyards sliced, and tow it back to Hong Kong. The smugglers would have to find their own way home. 'One round ahead!'

Third Officer Wang aimed to the side and with enough range to drop the shell in front of the junk. But it had changed tack and was going flat out to disappear around the back of a large island silhouetted against the stars.

'Bugger!' What were they playing at? It was a fair cop and they should give themselves up.

The Customs ship followed, propellers thumping, searchlight at full beam. The junk had entered a narrow inlet. James hadn't surveyed this area yet. He turned to Coxswain, a sinewy Chinese man. 'Can we get up there?'

'Sometime can. Sometime no can.'

'Cut the engines!' James took a sounding by lowering a lead line. 'No go.'

'We'll follow them in the motorboat,' Tony said, handing James a pistol.

They lowered the runner, winching it down from its position on deck. The boat hit the water with a splash. Barely keeping his footing, James followed Tony, Wang and three sailors armed with rifles down a rope ladder that flapped in the breeze.

The sky lightened and James steered the boat up the creek, carefully avoiding the dark rocks looming below the surface. They rounded a bend. The junk had run ashore and the crew were scuttling like ants around a dead cockroach, carrying what looked like cans of kerosene from the flat-bottomed vessel.

The motorboat beached. James jumped out behind Tony, his boots squelching in the sludge. Exhilaration coursed through him. The sun had risen fully now; night turned to day quickly in these parts. The gang had vanished into the mangroves, but a slim youth wearing a bobble hat pulled down to his eyes, in a tunic and baggy black trousers, was struggling on the mud flats.

Tony pointed. 'Grab him!'

James made a move in the direction of the youth, but Wang got there before him. With deft movements, the Third Officer yanked the boy's hands behind his back and tied them.

'How dare you do this to me?' the prisoner called out in a shrill voice.

'Lash him to that iron ring at the bottom of the junk,' Tony yelled to Wang. 'The tide has turned. With any luck it'll cover him before too long.'

James stared at his Chief Officer; he couldn't believe what he was hearing. 'Is this some kind of joke?'

'They won't let him drown. Someone will come before we have to set the lad free. And it'll save us the trouble of flushing the smugglers out of the undergrowth.'

'What makes you so sure?'

'Experience. You'll see.'

James shrugged. An ex-Royal Navy Lieutenant Commander, Tony had been in the Chinese Maritime Customs since before the war. He was in his early fifties now, twice James' age. He bowed to Tony's superior knowledge and turned away.

Wang marched the boy across the shingle, through the waist-high water, and up to the junk, where he tied him to the ring. James lowered himself down on a smooth rock, took out his cigarette case, and gave a Player's to Tony. He leaned forward. His Chief Officer pulled a lighter from his pocket and held it out.

James inhaled until his head buzzed. He turned and peered at the hostage. They were in a typical tidal creek that dried to a muddy channel at low tide, but would be flooded quickly when the tide came in. The sea had already risen as far as the boy's chest. He must be freezing; water temperatures in winter were a far cry from the tepid seas of summer. James tapped his index finger against his mouth, doubt twisting his gut. 'Are you sure this is going to work?'

'Trust me!'

James shook his head slowly. Tony must know what he was doing. Everything was under control. He gazed at the top of the beach. In the pale sunlight, the roots of the mangrove opened out like giant fingers; they would be flooded soon. The bottom of the junk would be submerged in no time and the boy with it. The smugglers were probably watching from behind the scrub and they might be armed. His hand hovered over his gun.

A scream reverberated across the waves. Water was lapping at the prisoner's chin. *Enough!* James leapt to his feet. 'If you don't untie him, I will,' he said to Tony.

'Calm down!' Tony grabbed his arm. 'Someone's coming.'

A portly Chinese man waddled towards them from the edge of the mangroves. 'Let go my niece!'

Niece? James stared at the man. The smuggler hawked phlegm from his throat, and spat it onto the sand.

'Before we untie anybody,' Tony said, 'hand over the goods!'

The man wagged a finger. 'You let go my niece first!'

'The goods first,' Tony repeated.

Another scream resounded from the junk. 'Uncle!'

The smuggler barked orders to his men, and they reappeared from the mangroves with the cans.

'Go to it,' Tony said, handing James a knife.

James gave his pistol to Wang, kicked off his shoes, shrugged off his shirt, and waded into the sea. He swam hard, making frantic strokes for the final couple of yards. Then he dived underwater. In the murk he searched around for the ropes, and sliced into them.

Hands freed, the prisoner slid from his grip and swam towards the beach. James followed, but a wave came from nowhere and knocked his head against the side of the junk.

He gulped salt water, his heartbeat echoing in his ears. His arms flailed and his eyes lost focus. He clutched at his throat, gasping for breath.

Someone grabbed his waistband and pulled him upwards. A hand cupped his chin; he was being hauled back to the shore.

James dragged himself to his feet, staring at the person who'd rescued him. Hat removed, wet hair fell dark and long over the slight shoulders of a young woman. *Bloody hell!*

'I thought you were supposed to be rescuing me,' she said, jutting out her chin. She shivered and rubbed her wrists where the rope had left red marks.

James coughed, and a searing pain slashed through his lungs. 'So did I,' he said, taking an agonising breath. He retched, and vomited brine. The girl studied him, her arms folded.

Wang and the smuggler came up. Teeth chattering, James took his shirt from the Third Officer. Where was Tony? James gazed around. His Chief Officer was busy seizing the goods and loading them into the motor boat. They would have to make several journeys to ferry them to the ship. James took one step forward, but his knees gave way and he grabbed hold of Wang.

Wang lifted him into the boat, James' legs scraping the rails. Tony's face came into view. 'What the hell happened to you?'

'Nearly drowned,' James coughed.

'We'd better get you to a hospital.'

He lay on the deck. Tony had gone off somewhere. Was that him in a huddle with the smugglers? James couldn't be sure. Bizarrely, the mangroves behind the beach had turned into a dragon, similar to the one the locals danced with at Chinese New Year. A niggle at the back of his mind. Why hadn't Tony given the order to seize the junk? James coughed again; he could hardly breathe.

# 17

Sofia marched up the plank to the prow of the junk. She stared at the departing Englishmen. Her so-called rescuer's cropped curls had reminded her of the burnished copper coins she'd collected as a child. Interesting, but he was a *gwailo* foreigner and a Customs' man; she doubted she'd see him again.

'Why didn't you send someone to free me sooner?' she asked her uncle. 'I was frightened.'

'You? Afraid? What about all that kung fu?' He laughed. 'In any case, you shouldn't have stowed away on my junk.'

Uncle was right; she shouldn't have. He often took her with him now the war was over. After he'd refused this time she'd wanted to find out why. Once he'd discovered her hiding among the kerosene cans, he'd told her about his plan. His ingenious plan. Uncle was so clever.

Movement at the edge of the swamp, and Uncle's assistant, Derek Higgins, approached, blond hair plastered to his damp forehead and a knapsack hanging from his shoulder. He negotiated the gangplank and opened his bag. With a satisfied grin, he let two gold bars drop onto the deck.

Sofia laughed. The Customs' men had fallen for the ruse. Half-drowning hadn't been part of the plan, but she was safe and so was the gold. She went down to her cabin and took off her peasant outfit. The padded tunic had been warm at first, and the binding with which she'd swathed her breasts had made it easier to run. Such a pity her shoes had got stuck . . .

Adrenaline had kept her going through the night, yet now her legs wobbled so much she could barely stand. She towel-dried her hair, pulled back the blanket, and climbed into her bunk. Closing her eyes, she hugged herself to stop the tremors. Uncle was wrong. For a few moments she'd been terrified nobody would cut those ropes in time.

***

The next evening, Sofia sat with Father drinking tea. 'It's time for my opium,' he said. 'Will you prepare my pipe?'

She followed his stooped frame to the large front room divided by a black lacquered antique Chinese screen. Despite seeing it practically every day of her life, she still loved the beauty of the Sung Dynasty city depicted in gold, the river spanned by a bridge crowded with ordinary people and aristocrats in their sedan chairs.

When she was little she used to imagine all sorts of stories about the screen, the workers on foot carrying their goods up the path to the tea-houses, the farmers tending their crops and livestock, the boats on the river lining up to dock. An idyllic scene. It was a shame real life wasn't like that . . .

Father grunted. She gazed at his ravaged face. Until a year ago, he'd been handsome, but now the strains of illness had robbed him of his looks. His mouth, once full, was a thin scar; his cheeks had hollowed and his eyes seemed sunken. Tears stung and Sofia opened a drawer.

The stem of the pipe was fashioned out of carved ivory that had yellowed with age. She smeared a pinch of thick, sticky black resin over a pinhole in the spherical bowl at the base, lit a lamp, and held the bowl over the flame. The opium vaporised. With trembling hands, she handed the pipe to him.

Tonight she prepared one for herself as well. It would help her cope. She sucked the rich, sweet-tasting vapour into her lungs and exhaled through her nostrils. Almost immediately, it was as if her mind had been freed. Her body relaxed. Although it wasn't customary to chat while smoking opium, there was something she needed to know. 'Father,' she said, stroking his fingers. 'Uncle told me you haven't much time left. Please say it isn't true.'

'I'm sorry, *querida.*' Father lifted his bony shoulders in a sigh. 'The cancer has spread. Don't worry, you'll be well looked after. Your brother will make sure of it. Promise me you'll be nice to him!'

Eyes half-closed, Sofia caught the sharp note in his voice. She wasn't a regular user and the rare times she smoked with him, she fell into dreams before he did.

'Promise me!'

His voice seemed to come from far away. She wanted to answer, but the opium had taken hold and she drifted off.

\*\*\*

Sofia packed away her books in Father's study. She'd just had her last lesson with Senhor Pereira. Officially, her education was over. Father had done what Natalia had wished for her; he'd employed the best tutors. Sofia's chest squeezed. She still missed her governess so much. News had come via Uncle when the war had ended that Natalia had gone back to Russia, where she'd become a teacher. *I hope she's happy.*

As for herself, Sofia still had a lot to learn, and she couldn't wait to go out into the world and learn it. Tomorrow she would start her job with Uncle, helping him set up a cotton-spinning factory in Hong Kong. She would continue taking her turn nursing Father, of course, but she couldn't wait to learn about business. That was the future for her. She'd begged Father to let her work for him in the Consortium; he'd said it was Leo's domain now and, given their animosity towards each other, he couldn't allow it.

How to be nice to Leo? Leo no longer taught her martial arts. Leo no longer smiled at her. Leo no longer even talked to her if he could help it. Nearly five years had gone by since Michiko and her family had died. A deed for which he blamed Natalia, and, by association, Sofia. At first, each time she saw him, she'd pleaded with him that she'd known nothing about Natalia's subterfuge. Father had been right about Leo's character – he only saw things in black and white. And his jealousy had returned. It wasn't the jealousy of a boy; it was the jealousy of a grown man, insidious and so much worse.

The study door swung open, and there he was. Wasn't there a saying that you shouldn't think of the devil or you'll conjure him up? *Ha!* Leo wasn't a devil; he was just flawed.

'I've come from your uncle's. He's let me down. I won't be using him for any of my shipments in future.'

'Oh?'

'You're welcome to him. I wouldn't trust him farther than I could throw him.' He spun on his heel and left the room.

A ridiculous urge to stick out her tongue, but she wouldn't do it. She was too old for such nonsense. Sofia picked up her last English grammar book and shoved it into the box by her feet. The servants would deal with it later. She needed to check on Father before her martial arts teacher arrived for her weekly lesson.

# 18

At the stern of his launch in Macau's Inner Harbour, James eyed the sampans and junks clustered along the foreshore. It was his first day back at work after two days in hospital and a week on leave. His lungs were back to normal, thank God, but he still hadn't tackled Tony about his failure to seize the junk. Scratching his head, James looked down at the muddy water. A sampan, deftly sculled by an old Chinese woman, had come alongside.

A lanky blond man, sat at the prow, shaded his eyes with a hand. 'Are you Lieutenant James Stevens?'

'I am.'

'Then Mr K C Leung would like you to have dinner in the Bela Vista Hotel at eight o'clock.'

'I'm sorry.' *Who the hell is K C Leung?* 'I don't accept invitations from people I don't know.'

'Mr Leung is the uncle of the girl you freed a couple of weeks ago. I'm Derek Higgins, by the way.'

James laughed. 'You already know who I am.'

'My employer makes it his business to know everything that goes on in Macau. And he knows you've been surveying the coastline.'

'It's a heck of a task. Hasn't been updated since before

the war.'

'Haven't you bitten off a bit more than you can chew?'

James straightened his back. 'Not at all.'

Higgins smirked. 'I'll see you at eight?'

'I apologise again. But I can't have dinner with a smuggler.'

'Mr Leung doesn't wish to compromise you. He merely wishes to discuss a proposal. Who knows? He might even be able to help you in your anti-smuggling operation.'

*Curiouser and curiouser. Maybe Leung will shed some light on Tony's recent activities?*

'The Bela Vista, you say? Why not? I've heard the food is excellent.'

Up on the bridge, James took out the charts he'd prepared from his last visit here. The shifting tides, sandbanks and mud from the Pearl River were making completion of his survey more difficult than he cared to admit. He rolled up his papers and gave his six-man crew the order to leave.

James spent the rest of the day crisscrossing the narrow straits separating Macau from China, taking soundings of the depths and recording information to be drawn up into charts. From the corner of his eye, he could see a distant junk keeping pace with his launch. He rubbed his chin. One junk looked much like another, but it was definitely the same junk, unmistakable for the rectangular patch in one of its sails.

\*\*\*

He climbed down to his dinghy, the setting sun pinking the sky. He'd put on the white full dress uniform with gold epaulettes, kept on board for meeting local dignitaries. Not that Leung could be considered a dignitary. James had a feeling he'd need to put on a show tonight, even if he had no jurisdiction in Portuguese Macau. Why had Leung invited him to dinner?

His boatswain rowed him towards the pier. At the top of the barnacle-covered steps James signalled for a rickshaw. A middle-aged man, with teeth that were just blackened stumps, stopped chewing a stick of sugarcane and grinned at James. Calf muscles bulging, the man loped between the shafts of the vehicle, pulling him at a steady pace down a narrow street.

The aroma of sizzling pork from the pavement kitchens mingled with the swampy stench of old drains. Zigzagging between bicycles, rickshaws and cars, a coolie in a straw hat carried a bamboo pole bent over his shoulder, bow-shaped from the weight of his load. A woman with a baby in a sling on her back stepped right into the path of the rickshaw.

A swerve, and the woman pushed her way between the stalls and into the open doorway of a jewellery shop. From the upstairs windows the clack of mah-jong tiles clashed with the hubbub of music and voices shouting in Macanese. One day soon he would spend longer in Macau, maybe even his next leave, James promised himself. He'd love to explore the cobbled streets of the old town and immerse himself in the exotic atmosphere.

After loping along an avenue lined with banyan trees and up a small hill, they arrived at the Bela Vista. Higgins was leaning against the door frame of the elegant nineteenth century mansion. 'At last,' he said, holding a cigarette between his thumb and forefinger and flicking ash.

James settled his fare. It was only five minutes past eight; he wasn't late. He lengthened his stride and followed Higgins through the foyer, up a staircase to a mezzanine floor, then past a reception desk and bar.

In the restaurant, the smuggler got up from his seat and pulled out the chair next to him. 'Let me introduce myself properly,' he said in heavily accented English. 'I am K C Leung.'

'How do you do?' James shook hands. He sat down

and glanced at the woman sitting opposite Leung. Not the dishevelled girl he'd "rescued", but one so striking he had to look away in order not to be thought rude for staring.

'This is Miss Sofia Rodrigues,' Higgins said from the other side of the table. 'I believe you swam together, but haven't met formally.'

James leaned forward and extended his hand, briefly glancing at her tight-fitting *cheongsam* dress, her small breasts outlined against the silk.

Sofia's warm fingers pressed his. He sat back and contemplated his surroundings. Potted palms stood like sentinels in the corners of the room. A Latin crooner, accompanied by a pianist, was singing *I've got you under my skin*. Wooden ceiling fans stirred the air, although the heat and humidity of summer had passed.

The Bela Vista was everything he'd imagined: starched linen, silverware and candlesticks on the tables, waiters jumping to light his cigarette.

*Shame you're almost certainly not here for the pleasure of your company.*

Leung confirmed his order of the most expensive choices on the menu: shark's fin soup, abalone and fried shrimp.

'I hope you're fully recovered,' Sofia said, smiling at James.

'No after-effects. What about you?'

'None whatsoever. Do you like Macau?'

'Very much.'

'My niece would prefer live in Hong Kong.' Leung gestured towards the girl. 'She think Macau dull. Anyway, she grew up here. Macau neutral and safer place during last war. But people starving. I got a friend who drank soup. Found human finger floating in it.'

'How disgusting.' James had heard the story before and doubted it was true.

'I was in Hong Kong during the war,' Higgins butted in. 'The Japs locked me up in the internment camp at

Stanley.'

'My Chief Officer was there too,' James said. 'Commander Tony Chambers. Perhaps you remember him?'

Higgins tugged at his collar. 'The name doesn't ring a bell.'

'Are you based in Macau?' James asked.

'Here and in Hong Kong. I look after Mr Leung's business interests there. But I have a fireworks factory here.'

'Fascinating.' James smiled at Leung. 'Might I ask what those interests are?'

'This and that. This and that.'

Sofia leaned across the table. 'Our food is arriving,' she said to her uncle. 'Remember it is impolite to chat too much while eating. Let's save our energy for digestion!'

They ate in relative silence, making small talk about the dishes and toasting them with *Mao-tai* wine.

After dinner, James shot a glance at Sofia. She was regarding him in a thoughtful way. 'Derek and I will leave you now.' She stood up. 'Uncle wishes to talk to you alone.'

'You have interesting job, Lieutenant Stevens,' Leung said, fishing an ivory toothpick from his pocket and slipping it into his mouth.

James took a sip of water, watching Leung move the toothpick with his tongue.

'You found out if ships can navigate the straits?'

James rubbed his chin. 'That will depend on the tides.'

Leung removed the toothpick and put it back in his pocket. 'I think even at high tide it will be impossible.'

'Why?'

'Because mud from river always clogging up the estuary.'

'Not true. There are channels deep enough.'

'I have fleet of junks that trade between Macau and China.' Leung gave him a cold, hard stare. 'We know these waters.'

'The charts will be published.' James put his glass down. 'And, at high tide, it'll be perfectly possible for ships to navigate.'

'Maybe you make error in one of your measurements? The sea will be too shallow for ocean-going vessels.'

'I haven't made any mistakes.'

Leung laughed and slapped his thighs, great guffaws escaping from his throat. 'I give you ten thousand dollars, help you make a mistake.'

James blinked. Ten thousand dollars was more cash than he could save in years. 'I'm sorry. I can't do it.'

Leung's eyes narrowed; his mouth became a straight line. His cheeks flushed red and anger blazed in his dark irises. Then his expression changed, as if a blackboard rubber had wiped the frown off his face, and he laughed again. 'I admire your integrity, Lieutenant Stevens. You think I smuggle for my own profit? You are wrong. I am helping my country be great again. China is sleeping dragon that will wake as soon as we get rid of Kuomintang.'

'The Customs is a Chinese government organisation. I work for your country.'

'Unfortunately, you work for wrong side. What will happen to your job when communists win?'

'I'll find something else if push comes to shove.'

'Not if, but when,' Leung said.

'Well, thank you for an interesting evening and a delicious dinner.' James got to his feet. 'It's late and I need to return to my launch. Please give my compliments to your niece.'

Leung lit a cigar and waved him off. He strode past the bar. Sofia and Higgins were deep in conversation. Envy stabbed James at the thought of Higgins with the girl. She was off-limits to him, however; he'd be drummed out of the Customs if he were seen with the niece of a smuggler. God she was beautiful. And exotic, with those dark-grey eyes. She spoke English with an intriguing accent, too. How did she come by that?

Back on his launch, the cool night air was a gentle caress. He lit a cigarette and stared at gas lights on the sea-wall reflecting in the harbour. A full moon had launched a glimmer of silver across the swell of the waves.

He gazed at the silent sea shining in the moonlight. The fishing fleet had already sailed out, the sampans like dozens of fireflies hovering on the horizon. He hoped Leung was wrong about the outcome of the civil war in China, but only a few months ago the Nationalist Government had instructed the Customs to transfer their gold reserves to Taiwan.

*Not a good sign.*

A rumble, similar to the sound of a London bus straining uphill, and James spun around. A motorised cargo junk was heading straight for his launch!

'Weigh anchor,' he yelled to his crew.

Heart pounding, he hauled himself up the steps to the bridge. The bows of the heavily-built junk curved towards him. His launch would become driftwood! Cold sweat dripped down the back of his neck.

He braced himself, ready for the collision. Then, at the last moment, the junk veered and shaved the launch's starboard quarter. Wash splashed the foredecks and the boat rocked from side to side.

Knuckles white, James gripped the railing as the junk disappeared into the darkness. An accident? Or deliberate? Could this have something to do with Leung? James wiped his forehead. He had to find out more about the smuggler and his connections . . .

\*\*\*

James stepped onto a sampan at North Point. A diminutive woman sculled him across the harbour towards small, rocky Kellett Island, the Royal Hong Kong Yacht

Club headquarters.

They passed through a cluster of fishing boats. The chatter of conversations floated across the water. James breathed in the aroma of salty spices and his mouth watered. A family was squatting at their low table on the deck of their junk, dipping chopsticks into the communal dishes. A chow dog barked as James' sampan passed the stern of a large trawler, and a bare-bottomed boy peed into the sea, sending an arc of urine into the air.

At the island's landing stage, James paid the boatwoman and clambered ashore. Steps led to a dining room overlooking the harbour. There were Tony and Jessica Chambers, sitting at a table by the window!

'James, darling,' Jessica said, pecking him on the cheek. She bore an uncanny resemblance to Rita Hayworth. 'How lovely to see you. We must introduce you to Hong Kong society.' She tilted her head. 'Can't have you eating on your own like this.' Jessica took a black Russian cigarette with a gold foil filter from her silver cigarette case, and offered him one.

James declined and held out his lighter.

Jessica inhaled deeply, her red hair catching the candlelight as she blew smoke towards him. 'There aren't many suitable ladies around.' She laughed. 'But a good-looking chap like you shouldn't have any trouble . . .'

'Just don't get involved with a Chinese or Eurasian woman,' Tony chipped in. 'It's not considered appropriate.'

James tensed; he'd see whomever he liked. To hell with the snobbery and prejudice that flourished in the colony. But he had to make his way in this place, where colonial attitudes governed society. From what he'd seen, and he hadn't needed to see much to form an opinion, the expatriate population was determined to keep up appearances and live as if they were in one of those glitzy nineteen thirties films. It was unlike anything he'd ever experienced, and he'd almost had to reinvent himself here, so far from his roots.

***

'Can I ask you something?' James said to Tony in the office the following morning. 'With all the time off I've had recently, I haven't had the chance until now. Why didn't we seize that junk?'

'What junk?'

'You know. When I nearly drowned.'

'Ah, yes. I'll tell you in a few weeks' time.'

'But . . .'

Tony put a finger to the side of his nose. 'Trust me and be patient.'

James picked up a stone seal with his Chinese name, *Shen Je-man*, on it. He dipped it into a flat bowl of red ink and stamped his chart of the Pearl River estuary.

*Bloody Tony. What was he up to? Could he be taking kickbacks from Leung? Surely not. There has to be another explanation . . .*

# 19

I sat next to Lieutenant James Stevens in the Customs motor boat, spots of blood seeping through my cotton gloves, the breeze blowing my hair away from my face. Even at this time of day, the port was busy: barges clustered around ships at anchor; beetle-shaped ferries plied their way towards the mainland; neon advertising signs lit up the tenements on the waterfront. It was just as I remembered and my nerves tingled in anticipation.

In spite of everything that had happened, I was glad to be back. When I'd arrived in Sydney I'd lived with Papa, who'd taken extended leave to recover from internment. Our rented house in Pymble was near the Ladies' College where I'd repeated my final year of school. The appalling conditions in Stanley towards the end had meant that I hadn't been able to concentrate on my studies.

After that first Christmas in Australia, I became a weekly boarder. Papa was soon his old self; he'd joined a golf club where he spent the days putting about on the greens or socialising in the bar, knocking back the whisky sodas, and smoking his pipe as much as before the war.

To begin with I found the unaccustomed freedom and abundance of food strange. At school the girls were pleasant enough, but they'd already formed their cliques. I made friends, but not close ones. Having lost touch with my pre-war chum, Mary, and pining for Charles, I'd found it difficult to form any attachments.

A year later, Papa returned to Hong Kong as *Taipan* of Wellspring Trading, the company he'd been in charge of before the war, and I started at Teacher Training College. It was a fast-track course, only two years, to meet a shortage. And now, here I was – back in Hong Kong.

Engines grumbling, the boat was approaching its destination. Ahead, bobbing sampans lined the shore. Elegant arcaded colonial buildings took up virtually every inch of space alongside the strip of flat land, and green slopes lifted sharply behind them to the Peak. I'd lived a pampered life there in those untroubled days before the Japanese invaded; everything would be different now.

We arrived at a pier with a roof pitched like a Chinese temple and there was Papa, standing in the shade next to his chauffeur-driven Daimler. I jumped off the boat and propelled myself into his arms. 'I thought we'd never get you home in time for Christmas,' he said, hugging me. 'Was that cargo ship all right?'

'Quite comfortable, actually.' I kissed him and his moustache brushed my cheek, the sensation as familiar as the aroma of tobacco radiating from him. 'You look well,' I said. He was much too thin, though - almost as thin as me.

'Thank you for meeting my daughter,' Papa said to Lieutenant Stevens. 'I really should get my own boat one day.' He let out a self-deprecating laugh. 'Why don't I organise a dinner one evening when Tony and Jessica are free, and you can join us?'

Lieutenant Stevens shook hands with Papa. 'I'd be delighted,' he said, smiling directly at me. I thanked him and followed Papa to the car, where porters had already stowed my suitcases.

In the back of the Daimler, I sank into the soft leather,

my gloved hand tucked under me. I looked out at the buildings I'd known my whole life: the hundred year-old St John's Cathedral with its gothic bell tower, the sloping roof of the Peak Tram station and its large clock face. I glanced at the back of the driver's head and my smile wavered. 'What happened to Ah Fong?'

'He died while we were in Stanley,' Papa whispered, patting my arm. 'Starvation, apparently. Dreadfully sad . . . This is George. Lots of locals are using European first names these days.'

Twirling my jade bangle, I thought about Jimmy. He'd changed his name as soon as he'd learnt to speak English. Did he still call himself Jimmy? Or had he gone back to his Chinese name? I frowned, trying to remember. Chun? Chun, Chun – Oh, Ming, like the vase. A tease from over a decade ago tickled my mouth. His name had been Chun Ming, or Ah Chun to his family and friends.

Gravel crunched under the Daimler's tyres. I rolled down the window. The house was nothing like the shell I'd last seen. The windows were intact again, the outside walls gleaming white, the black roof tiles all in position. Potted poinsettias lined the driveway like they'd done every December of my childhood.

The door opened, and Ah Ho stepped out. Gold teeth catching the sunlight, my old amah seemed just the same. I clambered from the car, flung my arms out wide, and ran forward. 'How are you?' I caught the scent of Chinese herbs and gripped Ah Ho's bony frame.

'Wah! You very beautiful now!'

I laughed. 'How's Jimmy?'

'He in China. He teacher like you.'

Papa gave a tolerant smile. 'Don't stand out here on the doorstep, dear girl! You can catch up with Ah Ho later.' He made his way into the hall. 'Time for a drink before lunch.'

Heels clicking on the parquet floor, I followed him into the sitting room. Papa sat in an armchair, and dear Ah

Woo, our old houseman, arrived with a whisky soda on a tray. I greeted him and was rewarded with a grin practically as wide as his face.

I let myself out through the veranda doors and took a seat on the patio. My gaze was immediately drawn to the spot where, before we'd left for internment, I'd watched Papa and Ah Woo bury the family silver. The heady scent of the Bauhinia flowers wafted towards me. *Such memories!* I peeled off my blood-soaked glove, and stared at the scabs on my hand. Sobs welled up.

A shout from Papa, 'Kate, where have you got to? Lunch is nearly ready!'

I dried my eyes and stared at the place where Papa and Ah Woo had dug that grave-like trench. I stuffed my gloves into my pocket. I should bury the past and everything that had happened - just like I'd buried the silver photograph all those years ago. I wouldn't harm myself anymore. Straightening my shoulders, I turned and headed back into the house.

\*\*\*

A month after my return to the colony I was standing on the veranda overlooking the harbour, waiting for Papa's guests. Light radiated from myriad buildings boasting neon signs below me. On the dark water, ships shimmered in the evening glow. Ferries festooned with fairy lights made their way to and from Kowloon, a giant pool of illuminations watched over by the shadowy shape of the encircling hills. All the years I'd been away, I'd dreamed of this view, and I'd looked at it every night since I'd returned, never tiring of it.

The grumble of a car engine from the driveway, and I went indoors.

Tony and Jessica Chambers, followed by Lieutenant James Stevens, came through from the entrance hall. 'Jessica, how glamorous you're looking tonight,' Papa said, getting up from his armchair. He held out his hand to James. 'Welcome. What would you like to drink?'

'A gin gimlet, please.'

Papa summoned Ah Woo by ringing the small brass bell from the sideboard. 'Where has Kate got to? Oh, there she is!'

I hesitated in the doorway and then walked forward, the gold silk of my gown swishing. 'Hello, everyone!'

'Kate, darling!' Jessica aimed a kiss at my cheek. 'My goodness. You're all grown up. And so pretty. Not that you weren't before, but that ghastly camp made us all look like ghouls by the end.'

Tony strode across the room and enveloped me in a hug. I pushed down the panic spreading through me. I should have realised seeing Tony and Jessica again would crack the thin veneer with which I'd sealed the past.

At dinner, talk soon turned to the civil war in China. 'Looks as if the communists are getting the upper hand,' Tony said.

'Humph. I heard Peking has fallen without a fight,' Papa muttered.

I swallowed a knot of apprehension. 'The communists aren't going to want Hong Kong, are they?'

'They have to respect the treaties,' Jessica said. 'Don't we have a lease on the New Territories until 1997?'

Tony helped himself to a slice of Beef Wellington from the dish held out by Ah Woo. 'I doubt the colony will be able to hold out against the People's Liberation Army any better than against the Japanese. Not unless we reinforce the garrison.'

'But I've only just come home,' I said, my mouth dry.

Papa reached across the table and patted my hand. 'Don't worry! China is in a complete mess. She's not going to risk the wrath of the world by attempting to invade us.'

'Good thing too,' James said. 'I've had enough war to last a lifetime.'

'What do you think of Hong Kong?' I asked him.

'Very friendly. It's a bit like a village. I mean, the European population is small so it's easy to get to know people.'

'You're right, I suppose. I just wish we had more Chinese friends. That's something I hope will change. It must be interesting for you to work for the Customs and spend so much time in China.'

'Actually, I'm planning to hand in my notice and find a shore job. The Chinese won't employ Europeans for much longer, not with the communists taking over. Tony's managed to get himself appointed General Manager of Holden's Wharf. He wants me to be his deputy as soon as he can wangle it.'

'Good luck!'

'Thanks. Are you working?'

'I met the Director of Education last week. He said there was a shortage of teachers and, as I've just qualified, he offered me a job at my old primary school. I start on Monday.'

James lifted his glass. 'Congratulations!'

The evening ended with coffee, liqueurs and dancing to a Bing Crosby gramophone record. *You must've been a beautiful baby,* Crosby crooned as James whispered the lyrics in my ear.

'Don't!' I stiffened. 'You're embarrassing me.'

'I apologise for that, but I've never spoken truer words, Miss Wolseley.'

'Please, call me Kate.'

'Only if you stop referring to me as Lieutenant Stevens. I'm James.'

'James. It's a nice name.'

'And I rather like Kate.'

'Well, at least we agree on something,' I said, my lips twitching. 'I wonder if we'll be in agreement on anything else . . .'

'Only one way to find out.'

'Oh?'

'We could have dinner together.'

'Let's see,' I said, regarding him sideways. *How to let him down?* 'I'm terribly booked up, you know. Perhaps you'll telephone me in a day or two?'

'Can't you tell me now?'

'I'm sorry. I really am. For some reason, I'm invited out almost every night to parties, dinner and dances. I think it's because there aren't many young women for people to invite.'

'Certainly none as lovely as you,' he said with a smile. 'Shall I ring you tomorrow when you've consulted your diary?'

'Now you're making me sound pretentious. Come onto the veranda and I'll show you the view!'

I linked my arm with his and led him outside.

'It's fabulous,' he said.

'Did you know that the Chinese believe the earth is a living entity and its breath *chi*, dragon vapour?' I pointed. 'Those hills are actually dragons that have rolled themselves south across China. Kowloon, *gau lung*, means "nine dragons". Except there're only eight of them as the emperor himself was considered a dragon, the ninth one.'

'Fascinating.'

'Hong Kong is a real dragon's lair. When I was little, I used to fantasise about the creatures coming to life while I slept. They'd be protecting the territory and keeping us safe in this haven. Pity they took a break from their duties and let the Japanese invade.'

I gripped my arms so hard I felt a sharp pain. *Stop!* I mustn't think about it; I'd resolved to leave the past buried, hadn't I? I hadn't harmed myself since I'd got back and I wouldn't start again now. That had been part of my previous life, the lonely time in Australia when all I had were my memories.

Back inside, I sat next to Jessica on the sofa, letting her prattle on about the best shops to buy silk. How to get out of having dinner with James Stevens? He was charming, admittedly. Easy to talk to and good-looking. But there was only one person who could melt the ice within me. One person who could light my inner flame. One person whom I could love.

## 20

*Heung Kong*, Fragrant Harbour. James let out a wry laugh. *Not very fragrant today.* Such a stench: bilge, sewage, seaweed, dead fish and a rotting pig's carcass, the flotsam of a busy port, borne on the muggy April air. James picked his way along the quayside and stepped aside. A bloody great crane was lifting a crate from the hold of a vessel. He stared at the Holden's Wharf godowns, lined up like army barracks, an office block in the centre. It was here that Tony was waiting for him to start his new job.

*A new challenge. I can't wait.*

James thought about his duties. He'd have to help oversee the unloading of European imports destined for the colony from the company's Red Funnel ships. They'd be loaded with Hong Kong re-exports, mainly of goods from China, on the return journey to England. All he needed, apparently, were good organisational skills and a degree of honesty. The last deputy had left under a black cloud, something to do with demanding too many kick-backs from the stevedores. James' administration skills were excellent. As for honesty, he'd proved his integrity by not accepting that bribe from Leung, hadn't he?

The lift boy slammed shut the doors and the old

machine clanked up to the second floor. James stepped into the office. Fans whirred on the ceiling, stirring the heat and humidity of early summer. *Urgh!* Spring was practically non-existent in Hong Kong; the season had changed from cool and damp to hot and wet overnight. For the next six months he'd be scraping mould from his shoes and books, and taking salt tablets to replenish the minerals he'd lose sweating. But not to worry, it was a small price to pay for getting out of war-torn Britain.

'There's your desk, old chap.' Tony pointed towards the centre of the room. 'The blackboard behind you is to keep track of all the ships unloading from the wharves and loading from junks in the harbour. There's a stack of paperwork from the godowns for you to tackle as well.'

'I'll get cracking then.' James didn't mind being Tony's workhorse; it wouldn't be forever. His salary was even better than it had been with the customs, but as soon as he found someone to back him, he wanted to start an import-export business. There was money to be made in Hong Kong, and he'd be one of those who made it.

Work kept him busy all morning and at lunchtime he was enjoying bacon and tomato sandwiches with Tony at the USRC, the United Services Recreation Club, in the heart of Kowloon. They sat sipping coffee in the members' lounge and leafing through the newspapers.

'Bloody hell! My old ship *the Amethyst* has been caught up in the communist advance.' James put down *The South China Morning Post*. 'Apparently she ran aground on the Yangtze, came under heavy fire, and there were a huge number of casualties.'

'That's a bit of a poor show.' Tony sat back in his armchair. 'We haven't taken sides in their civil war. What the hell was *Amethyst* doing up there anyway?'

'She was supposed to relieve *Consort* and evacuate British and Commonwealth citizens from Nanking.'

'Thank God we left the Customs when we did. I wouldn't like to be in China with all this malarkey going on.'

'You're damn right. I only hope they leave us in peace here.'

'We can't defend the colony. If it comes to that, we'll just have to hand it back. But I don't think it'll come to that, old boy.'

'I bloody hope not.' It would be just his luck if the Chinese came over the border and fucked everything up. 'Hong Kong seems to be full of nationalist Kuomintang supporters. Don't know which group is worse. The communists or the nationalists.'

'As far as I'm concerned,' Tony said, 'they're each as bad as the other. Our friend K C Leung, for instance.'

James shuffled forward in his seat. Finally, Tony had mentioned the smuggler. 'Can you tell me now why we didn't seize his junk?'

'Been meaning to fill you in, but have only just got the go-ahead from Special Branch.'

'Go-ahead? Special Branch?'

'I helped them out when I was in the Customs. Found out Leung has been smuggling goods into China. He's involved with the same guerrillas who helped some of our POWs escape during the war.'

'So that's why you let him go . . .'

'That and his links, or rather his niece's links, with the Macau Consortium.'

'Macau Consortium?'

'A gold trading monopoly backed by the corrupt Portuguese administration. They fly the gold into Macau from Hong Kong on seaplanes.'

'I thought gold trading was regulated by international agreements.'

'Portugal didn't sign up to them. They decided to play the open market. The China price for gold is higher than anywhere else. It isn't supposed to leave Macau, and officially it never does.'

'But unofficially . . . ?'

'Special Branch has heard that Sofia's half-brother is smuggling the gold back into Hong Kong. They suspect local banks are buying some of it. They want to find out which ones.'

James leaned in closer, intrigued. 'And . . . ?'

'Special Branch needs someone to keep an eye on Leo Rodrigues, and I'm no longer up to it. Also, they want someone to get the confidence of Leung's niece. She's the daughter of Paulo Rodrigues, who runs the Consortium.'

'What are you asking, exactly?'

'The Head of Special Branch, Gerry Watkins, knows Leung invited you to dinner the last time you were in Macau.'

'And?'

'Gerry wants you to go back there. Pretend to be a tourist. Contact Leung's niece. Perfectly legitimate thing to do. After all, she's quite a beauty.'

James sat back and thought for a moment. 'Do you need my answer straight away?'

Tony lit a cigarette. 'Mull it over for a couple of days then let me know. You'll be richly rewarded if you do decide to accept. Well, that's enough talk for now. We'd better get a taxi back to the office.'

At his desk James checked bills of lading. He was finding his new job just as easy as his previous one; it hardly required any intelligence at all, and he prided himself on his intelligence. In spite of his inadequate schooling, he'd pulled himself up by his own efforts to be the match of anyone he came across. He read voraciously and was addicted to a wide range of fact and fiction. Only last night, he'd had his nose buried in *The Naked and the Dead*, one of the best war stories ever written. It was thanks to his officer training in the Navy that he'd received an education of sorts, but he'd kept on learning ever since. One thing he did lack, though, was wealth. And a place in society. He'd get both before too long. He'd bloody better . . .

He glanced at his watch. Time to call it a day. He'd go for a bath and a massage before catching the ferry over to the Hong Kong Island side of the harbour. It would be the ideal place to think about Tony's proposition.

\*\*\*

In the bath house cubicle, he undressed and locked away his things in a drawer beside the bed. A uniformed attendant in soft-soled slippers wrapped him in a towel. He'd been here several times and no longer felt any shame at standing naked before another man. In fact, the whole experience had become quite impersonal. He sipped a San Miguel and relaxed.

The attendant returned and indicated that he should follow him to a room, which bore a surprising resemblance to his bathroom back at the small hotel where he'd been staying since he'd arrived in the colony: white enamel bath, wooden soap-and-sponge tray, brass taps. The attendant prepared the water, stirring it to make sure the temperature was right and adding pine scented salts.

James immersed himself. Should he get involved with Special Branch? The sum Tony had mentioned on the way back to the office meant he'd be able to afford that Dragon yacht he was hankering after, not to mention have a bit of cash to fall back on.

*I'm very tempted* . . .

A bath boy opened the door. The slim young man with a shaven head was stark naked. Having the bath boys work nude was probably a way of saving on drying their clothes.

'Can do?'

'Yes. Can do.' James closed his eyes and prepared to be ministered to like a baby. The boy lifted each of his limbs out of the warm soapy water. The sense of relaxation was so complete James began to drift off. But the youth stopped washing between his toes, prodded him, and made motions with his hands that he should stand up.

After placing two boards on top of the bath at right angles to form a T, the boy signalled that James should stretch out on the stem. The young man wrapped a hot, dry towel around his forearm and rubbed him with it, rubbing and rubbing until he sloughed off the top layer of James' skin. It came away in filthy black sheets. How could there be so much dirt? He was meticulous about cleanliness and showered morning and night.

Back in the cubicle he lay on the bed. The uniformed attendant returned and covered him with a towel, through which he massaged his arms and chest. James let his thoughts drift again. Sofia Rodrigues intrigued him. Could she be involved with the disreputable side of her family's business?

*I'll have to tread carefully* . . .

The attendant stopped pummelling and pinching and asked him to roll over. He climbed onto James' back and walked up and down his spine, kneading him with his feet. It was impossible to concentrate and James gave himself up to the massage. The attendant bent his legs up towards the back of his neck. 'Ouch!'

'*Finishy... Tippu?*' The masseur held out his trousers.

Out on the street, the heat hit James like a punch in the guts, and he was sweating again, moisture prickling his armpits and hairline.

He walked past shops selling embroidered linen, carved ivory statuettes, jade jewellery and other curios. Better go back to his hotel; he had to get ready. After repeated requests, at long last, he was taking Kate Wolseley out to dinner.

## 21

A fan on my dressing table stirred the warm evening air as I sat marking a set of exercise books. In spite of the memories, I was glad I'd come back to Hong Kong. I loved teaching at the Peak School; my job filled my days and the loneliness of Australia was fast becoming just a memory.

Sometimes, in Sydney, I used to go out to the pictures and dancing in the evenings with casual male acquaintances in order not to feel so alone. None of them could take Charles' place in my heart, though.

I shut my eyes and remembered the feel of his smooth skin against mine. One day, I'd go to the area where that ship had been sunk and lay a wreath of orchid tree flowers over his watery grave. Heart aching, I covered my face with my hands.

A knock, and Papa peered around the door. 'Aren't you having dinner with Lieutenant Stevens?'

I rubbed my eyes. 'Yes. With James.'

'He's a very nice young man. Entirely suitable.'

I put my pen down. 'What do you mean?'

'I think he could be right for you.'

'I'm only going out for dinner with him. Nothing

more.'

'You should consider your options. I'll be retiring next year and you need to find yourself a husband if you want to stay on. Someone who can keep you in the style to which you've become accustomed, as they say.'

Papa shut the door. I picked up my pen and scratched it across a spare sheet of paper. Papa treated me like a child, and no wonder, for I was still living at home. I'd looked for a flat, but accommodation was at a premium because of all the war-damage. I'd just have to put up with him babying me for now. As soon as the right place became available, or I found a flat-mate, I'd move.

I scrunched up the paper and threw it into the wastepaper basket. I had no intention of getting involved with James Stevens. I had no intention of getting involved with anyone. I'd only agreed to have dinner with him when he'd asked me so many times it was impolite to refuse.

I went to my wardrobe. What to wear? Something not too alluring. I flicked through my dresses and found a yellow taffeta frock with a V neckline and fitted waist.

After a bath, I dressed, left the house, and strolled to the Peak Tram station. The bell rang and the funicular started its descent. From my seat at the front of the car, I looked out at the thick sub-tropical jungle dropping steeply down to the city below. Once, I'd glimpsed a cobra curled in the shadows; I'd seen it raise its head and spread its hood as the tram rattled by. But today there were no reptiles lurking in the undergrowth, and soon we arrived at the terminus. Stepping onto the pavement, I found a rickshaw to take me to Jimmy's Kitchen, the oldest European restaurant in Hong Kong.

James was waiting at the bar, gin gimlet in one hand and a cigarette in the other.

I took the stool next to him. 'Am I late?'

'Not at all. You're looking beautiful. That colour really suits you. What would you like to drink?'

'A brandy soda, please.' Glancing up, I was startled by

the intensity of his gaze, and felt a flush up the side of my neck. 'How's the job at Holden's Wharf?' Best keep him talking about himself. That way he wouldn't be able to ask too many personal questions. Even if his deep blue eyes smiled attractively in that fine English face . . .

'The work is hardly exciting, but the best thing is, the company's building some flats in Kowloon.' James signalled the waiter. 'So I'll be able to move out of my hotel. Have you always lived on the Peak?'

'Yes. The servants love living at number eight.'

'Oh. Why?'

'The Chinese consider eight an excellent number.' A safe topic of conversation, not intimate at all. 'The word for eight sounds the same as prosperous and is also the *yinnest* of the *yin* numbers from one to nine.'

'*Yin* numbers?'

'Like everything else in nature, numbers have *yin* and *yang* qualities.' Our waiter placed my drink on the table, and I took a sip. 'Odd numbers are considered *yang* and even numbers are considered *yin*.'

'Shall we order?' James picked up the menu and handed it to me. 'Then you can tell me all about it.'

'The Mulligatawny soup is a speciality.' I pointed. 'As it says here: lightly spiced and delicious.'

'Sounds perfect. What about the Beef Stroganoff to follow?'

'You go ahead, James. My stomach can't digest much, so I'll just have a salad.'

'Are you sure?'

'Absolutely. It's nice to be back here, though. I used to come with my parents before the war. It was a bare-boned type of place then, with scrubbed table-tops and naked light bulbs, but the food was always excellent.'

James ordered then turned to me. 'What's the difference between *yin* and *yang*?'

'It's a very ancient concept. How do I explain without boring you?'

'I won't be bored. It's fascinating.'

I didn't care if I was boring him to death. It would stop him from inviting me out again, and I wouldn't need to put up with the intense way he looked at me. '*Yin* represents femininity, darkness and passivity. I don't agree females are necessarily passive, though.'

'I see your point. What about *yang* then?'

'It's the opposite: masculine, bright and active. Everything has an opposite, but never absolute.'

'What do you mean?'

'No one thing is completely *yin* or totally *yang*. For example "night", which is *yin,* can turn into "day", which is *yang.* If there's an imbalance, an excess or deficiency of one or the other, that's relative as well. A surplus of *yang* makes the *yin* become more intense.'

'Seems complex. How do you know so much about all this?'

The waiter led us to a table in the corner, and I told James about my childhood friendship with Jimmy.

'How unusual to have a Chinese lad for a companion. As far as I'm aware, the British and the Chinese seem to lead a sort of parallel existence in Hong Kong.'

'It's different with the servants. They're almost part of the family and we get to know them. Even so, we must be careful not to make them lose face.'

'Yes, I understand a bit about face. I used to feel as if I was treading on eggshells in the Customs.'

We finished eating, and James suggested we go on to a night club. I yawned, covering my mouth with my fingers. 'I'm sorry to be a wet blanket, but I've got to be up early for school tomorrow. Would you mind dreadfully if we didn't?'

'Not if you promise we can do this again.' He reached across the table and took my hand. 'I'm serious about my intentions towards you, Kate. Dare I hope you might feel the same way?'

This wasn't supposed to happen. I pulled away from

him, and made the excuse that I needed the loo. In the powder room, I stared at my reflection. Had I been sending the wrong signals? What the hell was I supposed to do now?

Back at our table, James was swirling a brandy. 'I'm sorry for rushing you, Kate. Please forgive me.'

I smiled at him. 'Of course.'

Outside the restaurant he hailed a taxi. 'Shall I come with you as far as the Peak? The driver can take me to my hotel afterwards.'

'I'll be fine, thanks.'

I waved through the back window of the cab. I couldn't help liking James. He was good-looking and charming. I'd enjoy seeing him again, but I didn't want him to get the wrong idea. I would never love anyone but Charles.

## 22

By the open grave in St Michael's cemetery, Sofia picked up a handful of earth, and threw it onto Father's coffin. The smell of the soil rose in the air: musty, sweet and clinging.

Father had died three days ago in his sleep; for the first and last time in his life Paulo Rodrigues had lost a fight and the cancer had finally defeated him. She stared at the wooden casket. He lay inside, dressed in his finest suit. Her chin wobbled and she breathed in gently; she mustn't lose control. Father had brought her up to be strong; he would have expected her to show that strength now.

How could she leave him here in this dismal depressing place, crammed with Victorian marble tombs and smelling of rot? Sorrow surged through her, but she couldn't let herself break down in front of all these people. She turned to go.

'Not so fast,' Leo said. 'We have to greet everyone first.'

Sofia stood next to him. A queue of dark-suited men had formed. They bowed and shook Leo's hand, then shuffled past and ignored her. Leo had probably orchestrated this charade to humiliate her. The last mourner presented himself. Uncle. 'I'm so sorry,' he said in Chiu Chow, taking a handkerchief from his pocket. 'I hope your father was in no pain at the end.' He dabbed eyes that were almost in danger of disappearing into his fat cheeks.

'The opium took care of that.' Her voice trembled with sadness. 'He spent his last days dreaming.'

'For the best, I expect.' Uncle walked with her to the waiting car. 'What are your plans now?'

'Father has left me half his shares in the Consortium. I want to sell them to Leo and move into your house.'

Uncle patted her hand. 'It is better you come and live with me. Your mother was my dearest sister, and she would have wanted it.' He sighed. 'Why don't you have dinner with me tonight?'

'Not tonight. I'm too miserable. Can we make it tomorrow at the usual place?' Despite being in mourning she had to eat. She also had to get out of Father's house. She kept expecting to bump into him around every corner and, when she didn't, the sense of loss was so, so overwhelming.

*** 

In her bedroom, she changed out of her black funeral dress and put on the baggy kung fu trousers and grey tunic she usually wore at home. She went into the bathroom and splashed cold water onto her cheeks. Her face was pinched with grief and dark circles spoiled the skin under her eyes. She left the room, marched down the corridor, and knocked at Leo's door. 'We need to talk.'

'I'll meet you in Father's study. Just give me ten minutes.'

She looked him up and down. The only thing different about him since Father's death was that the arrogance, once simmering beneath the surface, now rose from him like steam from fresh horse dung.

At Father's antique desk, she pulled out a chair and waited. She didn't wait long. Leo crossed the room and took the seat opposite; his newly-acquired Boxer dog, Balthazar, at his feet.

She pushed back her sleeves. 'I want to sell you my shares in the Consortium. And I'm planning to live at my uncle's.'

'That traitor!' Leo leaned down and fondled Balthazar's ears. 'He's not as clever as he thinks he is. When he was so careless with my shipment, I had him investigated. And it's not over yet.'

'What do you mean?'

'You'll find out soon enough. The terms of Father's will state that I am your legal guardian until you turn twenty-one.'

'My birthday's in October. You might as well let me go now, as you won't be able to stop me then.'

'You can go.' He slammed his hand down and sent a sheaf of papers cascading to the floor. Balthazar barked twice. 'But your shares in the Consortium will remain under my control until October.'

She clenched her fists so hard her arms shook. 'You bastard!'

'It's not me who's the bastard.' Leo's lips twisted into a smirk. 'You're an educated young woman. Think about your prospects and don't be too hasty! There are huge changes taking place in China, and the Consortium is rightly placed to take advantage.'

'I don't want to get involved with your cronies.'

'They're just members of an anti-communist action group, but Mao is gaining ground so they've fled here.'

'And now they're in Macau to make their living by pimping and extortion. I think it's revolting.'

'Your ideals will get you nowhere, Sofia. Life isn't as simple as you seem to believe.'

'There's no point in discussing it further.' She got to her feet. Of course, she knew it wasn't that simple. She wasn't an idiot. Leo's associates must have found it hard to leave everything behind in China. She wouldn't have liked to have been forced to give up her life. She'd give it up voluntarily when the time was right.

She strode out of the room and across the hall to the staircase. As she passed the front door, the bell rang and she opened it. Derek Higgins was standing on the doorstep.

'Derek! What are you doing here?'

'I've come to give my condolences to you and your brother. I couldn't make it to the funeral.'

'Thank you. I'll call the houseman and he'll take you through to Leo.'

Sofia stared at Derek's back as he followed the servant down the corridor. What was he up to?

*** 

Sofia put down her menu and glanced around the Solmar. She'd told Uncle all about her conversation with Leo. She'd tried to persuade him to intervene on her behalf, but he'd told her she'd be better off biding her time. Five months were nothing, he'd said; they would pass quickly.

Should she tell Uncle that she'd seen Derek at the house? No. She had nothing to go on. All she could do was keep an eye on him. And what about Leo's ambiguous remark? She looked up again and put a hand to her mouth. That Englishman, James Stevens, had just walked into the restaurant.

'Good evening,' he said, coming up to the table and beaming a smile.

'Why don't you join us?' She turned to her uncle. 'That would be all right by you, wouldn't it?'

Uncle grunted his agreement, and James pulled out a chair. 'This restaurant was recommended to me,' James said. 'I'm here for a bit of sight-seeing, and I was going to give my sympathy to you tomorrow. So sorry to hear about your father.'

'He's at peace now.' Best to change the topic of conversation. Talking about Father made her too sad. 'The Solmar is famous for Macau cuisine,' she said.

'Oh?'

'Portuguese traders brought spices from Africa, India and Malaya hundreds of years ago and blended them with native vegetables and seafood. You won't find food like this anywhere else in the world.'

James shuffled his chair closer. 'Fascinating.'

'The most popular dish is *bacalhau*.'

'What's that?'

'It's salted, dried codfish imported from Portugal. Before cooking, the fish slices are soaked in water for hours and hours to get rid of the salt.'

'I don't fancy eating a fish that has come half way across the world, even if it was in a dried state.' James laughed. 'My boss said I should try the sole.'

'You can order *Linguado Macau* if you want to play it safe. As it says on the menu,' she read, 'fresh and tender Macau soles fried and served with green salad together with cheese, shrimps and seafood.'

'Sounds superb, but I think I'll be daring and try the *bacalhau* after all.'

*Ha! He rises well to a challenge. Good to know.* 'Portuguese wines are excellent.' She glanced at her uncle. 'Why don't we order a bottle?'

'The best thing to drink with Macau food,' Uncle said, snapping his fingers. 'Waiter!'

They chatted about the history of the Portuguese territory. James didn't know much about it and seemed genuinely interested.

After dinner, Uncle said, 'I was expecting Derek Higgins to meet me here. I'd better find him. He has to go to Hong Kong for me tomorrow, and I need to give him my instructions.'

Uncle signed a chit then made his way out of the

restaurant. This was the first time in her life Sofia had been left alone with a man, and a *gwailo* foreigner at that. Her uncle *must* be worried about Derek.

She pulled a fan from her handbag and cooled the sudden glow to her cheeks. 'James, how do you fancy visiting a den of iniquity?'

His eyes widened. 'Depends on what sort of iniquity you mean.'

She giggled to cover her embarrassment. What had she said? 'Isn't Macau known as the Monte Carlo of the orient? Maybe we could try a spot of gambling?'

'You had me going there for a minute,' James laughed.

Outside, he placed his hand on the small of her back and ushered her into a taxi. At his touch, a shiver went through her and her breath quickened. She gave the address to the driver and stared out of the window, bringing her emotions under control. This wasn't right; she couldn't allow herself to be attracted to an Englishman.

In the doorway of the Municipal Gaming House, she pushed past a curtain, reeling at the stench of stale tobacco. People stood shoulder to shoulder around the gambling tables, shouting their bets. 'Let's go up these stairs here to get away from the crowds!'

She gazed across the gallery circling the mezzanine floor. Customers were sitting on uncomfortable-looking stools, lowering their stakes in rattan baskets on string to the pit below. 'They're playing *Fan-tan*.' She grabbed a seat. 'We have to gamble on how many buttons are left when the croupier has finished dividing the piles. Or you can bet on whether there will be an odd or even number.'

She threw herself into the game, exhilaration gripping her. First she was winning, then she was losing, then she was winning again. Her grief at losing Father still festered, but he wouldn't have wanted her to be miserable. She would think about him in her quiet moments, and live life to the full.

James squirmed on his seat. 'Let's quit while the going

is good!' 'I've got the impression this game is rigged. Why don't we go to the casino in the Central Hotel instead? I've heard they've got a cabaret and a good bar. This stool is killing me.'

Out on the Street of Eternal Felicity it was raining. A rickshaw pulled up in front of them. 'We can squeeze in together,' James said.

Sofia took out her fan again; she made a desperate attempt to cool the heat spreading to her face. She caught the scent of James' after shave and felt the hardness of his body against her own. This *gwailo* was doing strange things to her equilibrium.

The rickshaw stopped in front of the only skyscraper towering above the surrounding two-storey buildings. A neon sign flashed a single Chinese character, the name of the hotel and the symbol for China, China being the centre of the earth.

They found a table in the nightclub on the ground floor. An electronic noticeboard on the wall behind the small orchestra disclosed the results of play from the roulette tables next door. Hostesses in *cheongsam* dresses fluttered like brightly-coloured butterflies around the male clientele.

'What can I get you to drink?' James asked.

'A martini, please.' Cary Grant's favourite. James would think she was so sophisticated.

On the stage a group of young women in tail feathers were dancing to the beat of the band.

'Shall we place a bet?' James signalled one of the hostesses.

Sofia chose her numbers and their drinks arrived.

'Cheers!' The cool, dry, slightly spicy liquid slipped down her throat. She put down her glass and grabbed James' arm. There, at a table tucked behind a screen dislodged by a passing waitress, sat Derek Higgins and Leo, their heads bowed together.

# 23

James was nursing a glass of cold San Miguel opposite Gerry Watkins of Special Branch in the bar at the United Services Recreation Club. Watkins sported one of those handlebar moustaches that only certain types of men could get away with. James told him about his visit to Macau. 'When Sofia spotted her half-brother and Higgins in the casino, it was as if she'd seen a couple of ghosts. She ducked her head below the table then made me shield her from view as we sneaked out like a pair of thieves.'

Watkins took a drag from his cigarette. 'What happened then?'

'We found a rickshaw, and I left her at her uncle's mansion. She didn't invite me in, but I got the distinct impression she was about to have it out with Leung regarding Higgins' disloyalty.'

'Any idea what Higgins could have been up to?'

'I've no proof, but I'd hazard a guess he's sold out to Leo.'

'What about maintaining your contact with the girl?'

'She told me her uncle is opening a cotton-spinning factory in Kowloon next month, and said she'd send me an invitation.'

'That's good. Try and get closer to her, if you know what I mean. There must be something she needs. Find out what it is and offer to help her. As you know, the Consortium is sitting on a pile of gold and we know a lot of it is making its way into the colony. Could be the Fourteen K Triad are some of the likely recipients.'

'Fourteen K. Who are they?'

'Kuomintang supporters. Some say the name is because there're fourteen big shots. Others reckon the fourteen comes from their original address. We're in the process of identifying them and finding out what they're up to. They're called Triads because of the symbol used.'

'What sort of symbol?'

'The Chinese character, *Hung*, encased in a triangle. Represents the union of heaven, earth and man.'

'Are all Triads criminals?'

'Not necessarily. Sun Yat Sen was the founding father of the Republic of China. Well, apparently, he was a Triad, as are many of the nationalists. There are various factions, but the Fourteen K is a much bigger organisation and much more violent than any of the others.'

'I'll do my best to get closer to Sofia,' James said, intrigued. 'I'll invite her out to dinner and take it from there.'

'Perfect. By the way, a chum of mine, Duncan Smith, District Officer in Tai Po, used to row at Cambridge. He's keen to raise a crew to compete in the dragon boat races.'

'Sounds like fun. When?'

'On the first of June. Tony's game for a laugh as well. We'll have to practise a bit first to get the hang of paddling.'

James nodded. He'd been a good oarsman in the Navy. Joining in with this lark would be a way to show he was "one of the boys".

\*\*\*

Dressed in a pair of shorts and nothing else, James sat in a fishing sampan stripped of its gear, a carved dragon's head attached to the bow, and a tail fixed to the stern. For the past month he'd trained with Gerry, Tony, and Duncan Smith, a well-muscled ginger fellow. He'd gone like the clappers up and down Tolo Harbour in the New Territories, day after day, sweating buckets and trying to get the hang of driving the blade of his paddle through the water. Now he was as ready as he'd ever be.

James and Tony were perched at the front, with Gerry Watkins and Duncan Smith behind. A Chinese man beat a drum in the prow of the boat, synchronising the paddling. Another local acted as coxswain at the stern, and steered the vessel with a long oar.

Last week a religious ritual had taken place to wake the dragon from its slumber, when the head and tail had been fixed onto the boat. The village elder of the Tai Po clan, who managed the affairs of the district under the eye of the colonial administration, had dotted the dragon's fierce eyes with black ink. To all intents and purposes, the dragon had come alive. James smiled at the superstition of it all. Apparently, he was a dragon himself in the Chinese zodiac. He rather liked the fact that Julius Caesar and Abraham Lincoln had been dragons, but not that Hermann Göring and Francisco Franco had also belonged to the same club.

A large crowd had gathered on the waterfront to watch the races, attracted by the spectacle of seeing a *gwailo* team of foreigners competing against seasoned locals. Hot sunshine beat through clouds of humidity and the air was heavy with the stench of drying fish on the quayside, and rotting seaweed on the rocks by the shore. James prodded Tony. 'Why are they staring?'

'It's our hairy chests, old chap. We're like apes as far as they're concerned.'

Gongs signalled the start. James plunged his paddle into the water on the beat of the drum. It took him and his team-mates a minute or two to get going. Striking the sea fast and furiously, they started to make good headway and were catching up with the fishermen. James gasped. They were heading for a direct collision!

'Hard over,' he shouted to Coxwain. The Chinese man changed the direction of his oar. The boat heeled brusquely and tipped. James and Duncan, on the outside of the turn, fell into the harbour. Tony and Gerry sat in their seats and the boat slowly filled with water. The crowd on the waterfront giggled loudly, clearly embarrassed for the Englishmen at their acute loss of face.

James stood on the seabed. He clutched his sides and laughed. Tony, Gerry and Duncan chortled with him as they waded ashore. 'Well, here's another nice mess you've got me into,' James said, removing seaweed from his hair. He fell against Tony, shoulder to shoulder, and held onto him for support, letting out more belly laughs.

'Duncan's invited us for a beer and a spot of dinner back at his house,' Tony said, chuckling.

'Sorry!' James gulped in air and collected himself. 'But I've got to get a move on. Sofia and her uncle are expecting me at the opening of their factory.'

Tony winked. 'Off you go, then. I'll make your excuses.'

James took a taxi home to his new flat in Kowloon Tong. He stood at his bedroom window and lifted his gaze over the rooftops towards Lion Rock, the tallest crag in the centre of the hills that formed a back-drop to Kowloon, its shape like one of the lions in Trafalgar Square.

His flat was on the ground floor and had a garden, which made it almost like living in a house. Kowloon Tong was developing into quite a posh residential area. Not the Peak, of course, but it would do for now. One day, he would move up the social ladder and get a place that would be worthy of Kate Wolseley.

Only last night he'd taken her to dinner at the Parisian

Grill and told her about his new apartment.

'I wish I didn't have to stay with my father,' she'd said, wistfully. 'It's a bit stifling. There's a teacher at school I've become friendly with and we're thinking of getting a place together. She's in a hostel at the moment, the Helena May. But we can't find anything.'

'I'll keep my ear to the ground. Something's bound to come up,' he said, making an effort to sound more optimistic than he felt. The colony was reaching saturation point with all the refugees pouring in from across the border.

'I wonder what will happen when the dust settles. I mean, when the civil war in China is over.'

'We live our lives in complete isolation, don't we?'

'My father says, whenever there's trouble in China, people come to Hong Kong. In the past they would go back again, but I don't know if that'll happen now.'

'You're probably right. What's going on there will change the place out of all recognition.'

'When I was growing up here, I was pampered and spoilt. It's the way we lived then, but things are different now. I want to contribute. To really be a part of this place.'

'How?'

'There's an orphanage in the New Territories that's run by an Englishwoman. She's looking for volunteers and I'm going to offer my services on Sundays.'

'What a good idea! I'm impressed.'

They'd spent the rest of the meal talking about their respective jobs, but whenever James had tried to steer the conversation towards more personal matters such as Kate's tastes in music and reading matter, she'd turned the questions round. He'd found he was talking more about himself than he was listening to her.

After dinner he'd taken her dancing and she'd let him kiss her for the first time. Somehow, though, it seemed her heart wasn't in it. Something to do with the way she'd avoided a second kiss. *The proverbial ice-maiden.*

\*\*\*

James showered, letting the tepid water wash away the smell of seaweed. Then he changed into a pair of beige slacks and an open-necked white shirt. The weather was too hot for a jacket and tie. He sent his houseboy to flag down a taxi, and knocked back a glass of beer.

Half an hour later he stood in front of the two-storey factory watching the fireworks that trailed in a long line from the top; they erupted in a cacophony, supposedly to chase away the evil spirits. The sign above the premises, *Leung's Textiles*, showed he was in the right place. James pushed open the door.

The factory floor was crowded with looms, and a receptionist ushered him up the stairs to a large suite of offices. Sofia came forward, her uncle by her side. 'We're honoured you could be our guest.' She indicated a passing waiter. 'Do help yourself to a glass of champagne.'

James glanced at Sofia; she'd moved away and was talking animatedly to another invitee. She was dressed in a simple, elegant, red *cheongsam* with a split up the sides revealing her impossibly long, slender legs. God, she was beautiful. He walked over to her, reeled in by an invisible thread. 'Thanks for inviting me. And please give your uncle my congratulations. I was wondering, though, if you're free to have dinner with me?'

'I was going to invite you to come with us. Uncle has arranged for his launch to take the three of us to Aberdeen fishing village. To a floating restaurant.'

'Sounds wonderful.'

## 24

They boarded the launch at Kowloon pier. The evening air had turned cooler, and Sofia wrapped her silk stole around her. The vessel crossed the harbour and headed out past Green Island. Would James fall in with Uncle's plan? At Aberdeen, the boat nudged into a space at the waterfront and they stepped ashore.

Immediately, a crowd of boat women clad in black trousers, aprons, and round woven straw hats, surrounded them like a flock of vultures. Sofia had thought James might have found it more amusing to cross the short stretch of water to the restaurant by sampan. A big mistake. The women pulled at James' shirt and jabbered at him in Cantonese. Sofia looked around for Uncle's boat. Too late. It was already half-way across the bay.

She negotiated a price with the most forceful of the vultures. The woman then led them down the stone landing steps to her sampan. Sofia settled herself carefully with James on low rattan chairs. She eyed him contemplating the woman; he appeared mesmerised by her as she revolved a single oar in her hand, rocking back and forth on the heel and sole of her foot. The sea was flat and black as ink, and ahead shone the gaudy neon signs of the restaurant boat: Chinese characters a foot long and wide in red, blue and green. The night air was balmy now and redolent with the odour of brine, mixed with the aromas of spices and rice cooking in the village. The voices of the fishing people, sitting at the prows of their junks, carried across the water.

On board the restaurant, the manager greeted them and showed them the floating pantry. Moored to the seaward side, four large wooden pens had been fastened at water level, their walls bored with holes for fresh sea-water. A man rode the brine in a small shell boat.

Sofia pointed to a sleek, grey grouper. The boatman tossed the fish onto a platform floating at right angles to the restaurant. A boy caught it in another net and flung it to the first in a line of cooks. With the flat of his chopper the cook stunned the fish on a large round board, then passed it on to a second man, who gutted the fish with one stroke of a sharp knife, and handed it to a third cook squatting on a stool in front of a brazier.

The fish eventually emerged on a flowered porcelain dish, steeped in soy sauce, bamboo shoots and seasoning. 'Fascinating,' James said. 'This is marvellous.'

A shout, and the boy with the net held up an enormous lobster for Sofia's inspection. It waved its claws in protest as the boy took it to the cook, who chopped it up and pan-fried it with green onion and ginger.

Another man showed Sofia blue and gold speckled crab and pearl-grey translucent shrimp. She nodded her approval, then led James to a round table overlooking the harbour. Uncle was already there.

Sofia watched the men feasting, until they obviously couldn't eat another morsel, and drinking rice wine until their heads must have been spinning. She took care to eat and drink little; she had to keep her wits about her. James was affecting her equilibrium again; his mere presence was making her pulse dance.

\*\*\*

'I'll leave you and take the boat back to Kowloon,' Uncle said after dinner. 'I have business to attend to on the island.'

Uncle's so-called business was a woman he'd set up in a flat in Wanchai. The plan had always been to leave Sofia alone with James. Uncle had said the Englishman would sniff around for some information and he'd told her precisely what to divulge. How did Uncle know this? She shrugged to herself and looked out the window. The launch had tied up to the side of the restaurant. 'Time to go, James,' she said.

There was plush seating at the stern of the boat and a table for their drinks. Sofia sat next to James, poured him a brandy, then leaned back. 'One day I'll move to Hong Kong,' she said. 'When the time is right.'

'And when will that be?'

'When I've sorted out some family matters.'

'I've been meaning to ask about your family. You never mention your mother.'

'She died giving birth to me.'

'I'm sorry.'

'She was Uncle's favourite sister and Father's concubine. Uncle considered it an honour. Twenty years ago he wasn't as well off as he is now, but I sometimes wonder if it was more than that. Father passed a lot of business his way over the years.'

'Your English is very good. You have a Russian accent, if I'm not mistaken. How did that come about?'

'I had a Russian governess. What about you? Where did you go to school?'

He seemed to hesitate a moment. 'What if I were to tell you that I'm not exactly top drawer?'

'What do you mean?'

'I didn't go to the right school.'

'I've never understood why the British call that top drawer.'

James swilled the alcohol in his glass then sipped it.

'Oh, these things matter. Cost me the job of my dreams, at least.'

'Oh?'

'I went for an interview to be a Navy Pilot, along with a friend of mine. Nick. He'd been to a grammar school . . .' Another sip went down with a swallow. ' . . . I'd been an apprenticed plumber. He got in, I didn't.'

Sofia shook her head slowly. Should she touch his hand? No. Too forward.

'Mind you, I took it on the chin. I got my commission eventually, and became a First Lieutenant. Then the end of the war came, of course. I've done well . . .'

'*Joss.*'

'*Joss?*'

'Luck, or fate. We're the same, you and I. We have to fight harder than anyone else. I'm a Eurasian woman and I'm not from what is considered to be a good family. I'm a survivor and so are you. That's what's important.'

'Tell me about the family matters you need to resolve.'

'You know the Consortium imports gold freely, because Portugal didn't sign up to the gold regulation agreement?'

'Yes.'

'My father was too ill in recent years to realise Leo was getting his employees to melt down the international gold bars. Those bars weighed around twenty-seven pounds each. His men converted them into portable nine ounce ingots or thin gold sheets. The smugglers preferred the lower weights as they were easier to transport.'

'What smugglers? We didn't catch anyone smuggling gold when I was in the Customs.'

'They weren't smuggling the gold into China, but to Hong Kong.'

'And your uncle was involved?'

'Uncle's junks used to run some of that gold. Do you remember the first time we met?'

'How could I forget?'

'It was part of a bluff. Uncle told Leo that Customs had seized the gold at the same time they confiscated the cans of kerosene. Leo was suspicious, but he accepted the story.'

'I gather he's found out the truth.'

'Yes. From Derek Higgins. And now Leo wants compensation.'

'Can't say I'm surprised about Higgins.'

'He no longer works for Uncle but has become Leo's henchman.'

'Any reason for that?'

'Derek can't resist money. He'll sell out to the highest bidder every time. Apparently, he helps his parents in England, but he's also addicted to gambling, I've heard.'

'So Higgins has a human side to him after all. Who'd have thought it?' A pause. 'Why did your uncle take the gold?'

'To give to the guerrillas in China.'

'And what sort of compensation is your brother asking for?'

'He's not my brother. Leo is my half-brother and he wants to get his hands on our factory. The amount owed is twenty-eight thousand US dollars and Uncle doesn't have the ready cash.'

'I'm sorry.'

'Leo doesn't need the factory. He's doing this out of spite. He's got his shares in the Consortium and his finger in practically every pie in Macau. Uncle has transferred almost all his interests to Hong Kong, and Leo can't abide that. I think it's also because a number of Shanghai industrialists are setting up factories near ours. They're nationalists, just like Leo's mother's family.'

'Can Leo legitimately force your uncle to give him the factory?'

'Not legitimately, of course, as he can't admit to the smuggling. But he also has contacts through his mother with the Triads. They're gangsters.'

'I know about the Triads.' James took another sip of brandy. 'And I know someone who would be interested in more information about Leo's associates. I can't promise anything, but they might be able to help. Leave it with me for a week or so!'

'Thank you, James.' She slipped her hand into his and squeezed it gently. She couldn't help herself. He lifted her fingers and kissed the inside of her wrist. A tingle crept up her arm and heat rose up from between her legs to her neck. She glanced away from him.

'Sofia. Look at me!'

She turned back to him, and placed his hand over her heart.

James' eyes were so bright they appeared to burn. He lifted her chin and kissed her on the lips. She resisted for a second but he pulled her to him, his hand on the small of her back, and she melded against him. The hardness of his chest pressed against her breasts. The sounds of the harbour receded; all she could hear was the blood rushing through her veins. It felt so, so wonderful.

James' hands entwined in her hair and she kissed him back. He reached under her dress, his touch sending currents of pleasure rushing through her. Their kisses grew deeper. This was her first time kissing a man, but she knew what to do instinctively, abandoning herself to the deliciousness of it. She broke off and looked at him, hands on his face. His eyes were heavy with longing.

'Let's go down to the cabin,' she said, not caring about the consequences.

The darkness was soft and enveloping; the aroma of polished wood mixed with the scent of the sea. Wrapped around each other, they stumbled onto the bunk. She couldn't see him but felt him stretched out next to her, his mouth on hers, his hands in her hair.

'Tell me to stop,' he whispered.

She shook her head.

'Oh, God . . .'

They were desperate. His breath came in deep gasps. The split in the side of her dress allowed her to lift one leg and drape it over his. Their kisses became more urgent.

A sharp knock on the cabin door. 'We arrive Kowloon pier,' the boatswain said.

Sofia sat up and put a hand to her mouth. It felt bruised but ripe, like a soft peach ready to be devoured. She reached for the light switch.

James blinked in the fluorescence. 'I'd say we got the timing absolutely spot-on there.'

'We were a bit hasty, don't you think?' She giggled. 'There's plenty of time for us to get to know each other. Especially if you're going to help me save the factory.'

The launch dropped James off and Sofia returned to the cabin. She lay on the bunk, stretching like a lazy cat. She'd been about to give her virginity to a man she barely knew. Only she felt as if she didn't need to get to know him; she knew him already. A shiver of worry stroked her spine, but she ignored it. No need to fret about James feeling the same way; she would trust in *Joss*.

# 25

*You are entering The New Territories. Please drive carefully!* I smiled at the notice. Weren't you always supposed to drive carefully? But we'd left the city behind and the people who lived here weren't used to traffic. It was good to get away on my own for once; the constant attention of James, circling around me like a moth, had started to get on my nerves.

The taxi driver slammed on his brakes. A water buffalo had got out of its field and was wandering on the narrow road. We set off again past paddy fields, walled villages, deep valleys, vegetable-plots and fruit orchards. Old women sat winnowing rice in rattan baskets, their wide-brimmed straw hats bobbing up and down. Graves and jars of human bones dotted the steep hillsides, sited with care so *yin* and *yang* were in perfect harmony. Bare-bottomed toddlers at the side of the road waved and called out, 'Hallo, bye-bye.'

I thought about the children in Stanley. Once, I'd lined them up for their Carol Service; it was our last one in the camp even though we didn't know it then. I'd gazed fondly at the Japanese man conducting. The Reverend Kiyoshi Watanabe had been our latest interpreter and a more sympathetic man than any we'd had previously.

A Lutheran minister, he'd studied at the Gettysburg Seminary in the United States, where he'd been given the name John. The children in the camp called him Uncle John. The infants had sung, *away in a manger, no crib for a bed*, and I'd joined in. Uncle John then launched into a rendition of *Holy Night* in Japanese, his tone strong and true. Yet, in the audience, a number of people had talked loudly and spoilt his performance. Papa told me only the other day he'd heard that Uncle John's wife and daughter had been vaporized by the Hiroshima atomic bomb. So much suffering . . .

The gates of the Children's Home, as it was called, rose up. A formidable-looking European woman was striding down the drive, mud-coloured hair a mass of frizz, and steel-grey eyes framed by tortoiseshell glasses.

I held out my hand to the woman I'd heard so much about: Miss Denning. A missionary sent to Hong Kong in the early 1930s, I recalled, Miss Denning had been struck by the plight of hundreds of babies abandoned as a result of poverty and superstition. With support from local missionaries, she'd started the orphanage and had managed to keep going through charitable donations. During the war, she and her helpers had suffered violence, starvation, dysentery and recurrent malaria, but they'd refused to abandon their charges. I felt a rush of admiration.

'You'll find we're like a family,' Miss Denning said. 'The children call me Mum and our main aim is to love them as if they're truly ours. You're a teacher, I believe?' Without waiting for a reply, Miss Denning continued. 'Excellent. You can help the children with their reading. We all speak English with them and we teach them in English. If you can promise to come every Sunday, that will be perfect. We have a team of volunteers during the week, but no one on Sundays.'

The building had been converted from an old police station. Miss Denning showed me around the ground floor dining room, children's dormitories, and staff sitting room. Upstairs was another sitting room, a kitchen, bathroom, dispensary, sick room and a superintendent's bedroom.

Miss Denning pointed through the window to a smaller building at the back. 'That's for me and Mary Williams, my right-hand-lady. Oh, and the amahs.'

Downstairs, we traipsed into the schoolroom built by the side of the block. Rows of faces looked up at us, straight black hair and cheeky grins. The vast majority of them were girls. Girl babies were of less value in Chinese culture and therefore more likely to be abandoned. My heart swelled with sympathy for them. If only I could adopt them all . . .

Another European woman, with mousey brown hair cut in a severe bob, came forward. I shook hands with Miss Williams. Miss Denning's "right-hand-lady" promptly put me to work. I sat on a stool, surrounded by the infants, and flipped open *The Three Little Pigs*. I felt a tug at my sleeve. A girl nestled by my side: wide eyes, small mouth and pointed chin. 'Hello,' I said. 'What's your name?'

'Mei Ling,' the child whispered, shyly. She clambered onto my lap and told me she was five years old. I stroked her soft round cheek and hugged her. Then I stared over Mei Ling's shoulder at the far wall and thought about Papa. He visited Mama's grave every Sunday, but I hadn't been able to face going with him. I'd managed to keep my memories of Stanley sealed away; working at the orphanage would be the perfect pretext not to return.

\*\*\*

At home that evening, the telephone rang and I picked up the receiver. It would be James. He usually called me at this time on a Sunday, to suggest meeting up for dinner mid-week.

'It's Chun Ming here,' a familiar voice said.

'Jimmy!' He'd given his Chinese name. 'What a

surprise! Where are you?'

'I've just arrived and I have a job teaching English at the Chinese school in Waterloo Road.' It was one of the many communist schools the Government allowed to operate, just like they turned a blind eye to the news agency, communist newspapers, and other such organisations that were springing up all over the colony.

'It's wonderful you're back. What a coincidence we've both become teachers!'

'May I please speak with my mother?' Jimmy's voice was stiff and unfriendly, not like my Chinese brother at all.

I rang the hand bell on the table in front of me and sent the houseman to fetch Ah Ho. She talked at length with her son. Pretending not to listen, I picked up a magazine and flicked through the pages, my heart crumpling with every word.

'*Aiyah!*' Ah Ho put down the receiver. 'Ah Chun got married. He want me go live in his flat in Mong Kok. He say no good his mama work as amah. Say very bad face for him.'

I embraced Ah Ho. 'How are we going to manage without you?' I stepped back. 'I'm sorry. Of course you must go and be with Jimmy. I'm just being selfish.'

\*\*\*

Jimmy came to collect his mother a week later. He arrived with his wife, Li, and they sat on the sofa, their backs straight. I poured them tea. Ah Ho, even though invited, had refused to take her place next to them.

I held out a plate of cucumber sandwiches. 'Tell me what you've been doing since I last saw you,' I said to Jimmy.

'I struggled with myself for many months when I went back to China after the British surrendered.' He paused, bit into his sandwich, chewed, then swallowed. 'I joined the guerrillas and we had to fight in secret. I'd seen the corruption of the Kuomintang. They made me sick.' He sipped his tea. 'Now the revolution has triumphed and, because of my knowledge of Hong Kong, I've been sent here to live among the running dogs of imperialism. It is a great sacrifice, but I'm willing to make it for my country.'

*How zealous he sounds!*

'Please allow your mother to visit often.'

Jimmy smiled his crooked-teeth smile and, for a couple of seconds, I caught a glimpse of my childhood friend. 'That will be acceptable,' he said.

'We want to give her a monthly pension. It's the least we can do.'

'I think she will appreciate your consideration.'

Later, her paltry luggage loaded into the car Papa had organised to take her to Jimmy's flat, Ah Ho stood sobbing in front of the house. Earlier, she'd told me she didn't want to leave but had to do her duty to her son.

I kissed my amah's wrinkled cheek. 'I'm going to miss you and I want you to know that, if ever you need anything, you only have to call me.'

Ah Ho waved from the back seat as the car drove out the gates. I wiped my tears. Li had hardly spoken a word to me; she seemed such a quiet person. If only I could have broken through the barrier that seemed to have risen between me and Jimmy, but he'd seemed not to have even noticed I still wore the jade bangle he and Ah Ho had given me. I doubted he'd kept my book.

I remembered the games of hopscotch on the path to the tennis courts, the walks around the Peak, my parties when he'd always been included at my insistence. At the time of the Mid-Autumn Festival, Mama and Papa used to let me stay up late with Ah Ho and Jimmy to watch the moon and eat moon cakes. Ah Ho's English was even more limited then and she called the festival "the Moon's Birthday". We had lanterns and mine was always shaped like a horse and Jimmy's like a goldfish and I would play hide and seek with him in the dark. Those days would live on in my memory, but Jimmy almost certainly never thought back to his time on the Peak. He was so wrapped up in revolutionary zeal he'd probably blocked it from his mind.

I went up to my bedroom and sat at my dressing table. I'd finally lost that gaunt look I'd had since Stanley. My cheeks had rounded out and my breasts were more distinct. Charles would hardly recognise me if he saw me again. Only Charles would never see me again. Charles was dead.

I thought about Jimmy, fired with enthusiasm for his cause. I needed a cause myself. Something I could believe in. Something to lift me out of this dreadful despondency and give me a reason to get on with my life.

# 26

Charles was pacing the forward deck of the *SS Canton* in the warmth of a late summer dawn. He'd been up here for the past hour and the ship had just passed the lights of a sampan or, possibly, a junk. He was back. At last.

Feeling in his pocket, he crumpled the well-worn draft of the letter he'd sent to Kate nearly four years ago.

*27, Groombridge Road*
*Hackney, London E9*
*1st December 1945*

*Dearest Kate*

*I miss you so much, and the past eighteen months have been such hell, looking up and seeing you on that balcony, your beautiful face, and not being able to hold you in my arms and tell you how much I love you, then not being able to see you. Oh, how I've wanted to feel your sweet lips on mine and stroke your soft, warm cheek. There hasn't been a minute of every day when I haven't thought about you, my darling.*

*You must be wondering what happened to me. As you know, I was due to be drafted to Japan. After an overnight stay at a camp* near the airport, the guards loaded us onto lorries that took us to Holden's Wharf, but there was an air-raid and pandemonium broke out. Bombs were flying everywhere and the Japs ran for cover. Everyone else was frozen with fear, but I took the opportunity to make a dash for it. And thank God I did as so many died on that ship. Such a terrible tragedy!

Did you know the communist guerrillas rescued Allied soldiers who escaped from camps? They also picked up almost all of the shot-down American pilots. One of the guerrillas was shadowing our lorry, and took me straight to a safe house in Sai Kung. I was scared out of my mind. They kept me there for a fortnight until I'd recovered my strength enough to carry on. I'll never forget those fisher people: they shared their meagre food with me and I can't tell you what a difference it made. When I got there, I could hardly walk, I was so weak, and all I could think of was holding you again.

One night, I was told to get ready to leave. Someone found me a Chinese peasant outfit, you know the sort of thing - baggy black cotton trousers and a black padded tunic. I expect I looked more local than ever and my Cantonese was good enough to fake it if we met any Japs. We set off by sampan under cover of darkness as if we were going fishing.

I had been entrusted to a sixteen-year-old. Can you imagine? Except he was the fiercest sixteen-year-old I've ever met. His name was Fei, and he'd left school at thirteen because there were Japs to fight. He'd been with the guerrillas for nearly a year and boasted six kills. He said they took few prisoners on either side. "When the Japanese catch one of our men, do you know what they do?" he asked me. "They press lighted cigarettes all over his face and kill him slowly. When we take one of them we cut off his head immediately." I just hope the same thing happens to those sadists who murdered Bob and the others. Ruth told me all about what you both saw. It must have been terrifying for you, my love. Makes me feel ill to think that you witnessed such horror.

We landed on the other side of Mirs Bay and I thought we'd arrived at a ghost village. Completely silent. No dogs barking, no chickens clucking. We could see vegetable plots stretching up towards the darkness of the mountains behind. Bit by bit, figures came out *from behind the bushes and soon we were surrounded by villagers and insurgents. They gave us condensed milk and biscuits before we started marching up the valley towards unoccupied China. We spent the night at a stronghold of the anti-Japanese resistance, in a village house together with the family's livestock.*

*After a breakfast of sweet cakes we marched along the raised paths through the paddy fields. We stopped to catch our breath at several villages, and were given tea and steamed buns by the women, whose men were all off fighting the Japanese. As in most of China, the only communication lines were the ribbon-like footways we were walking on, made up of low walls of mud running from one rice field to the next.*

*We were in smugglers' territory and climbed up wide steps, hidden under a canopy of overhanging trees and shrubs. The great flat stones had been worn smooth by the passage of thousands of padding feet, carrying merchandise unloaded from junks on the coast. At the top of the steps we had our last view of Hong Kong – a distant peak on the west coast of the bay. I thought about you, Kate, stuck in Stanley, and I prayed it would not be long before we could be together again.*

*On the fourth day we reached Waichow. Fei took me to the Seventh Day Adventist Mission, which overlooked the East River and the mountains beyond. It was a haven of tranquillity, with lawns shaded by old trees, flower gardens and a lake. I stayed with the pastor and enjoyed the luxury of a bath and a shave, wishing with all my heart that you could have been there with me, you would have adored the place, Kate.*

*Having done his duty, Fei said goodbye. I was sad to see him go as I'd grown used to his cheerful company and had felt safe with someone who had six Japs under his belt. From then onwards, I was in the hands of the BAAG, the British Army Aid Group, which was the resistance movement we were in touch with in the camp. Shortly after Chinese New Year we were evacuated upriver and, a few months later, sent farther north again, as the enemy was on the move.*

*When the Japs surrendered, I was able to make my way back to Hong Kong and found out I'd missed your departure by one day. One day! Can you believe that? Desperate, I went to your house on the*

*Peak, but it was almost in ruins and there was no one around. I couldn't find anyone who knew how to get in touch with you. But I expect the house will be renovated and I just hope someone will forward this letter.*

*Darling Kate, if you get this, please write to the above address. I long for your news and to know you still love me as I love you.*

*Yours,*

*Charles xxx*

Why hadn't Kate answered his letters? He'd written to her every month for nearly a year. Perhaps she'd had second thoughts and had decided not to answer. No, that couldn't be. They'd been so close, so in love. He knew Kate and he knew she'd never forget him. The only explanation could be that his letters hadn't got through to her. Simple as that. She was probably still in Australia and, as soon as she returned to Hong Kong and found out he was here, she'd get in touch with him. He couldn't wait to see her dear, darling face again and to feel her in his arms.

He'd enjoyed the month-long voyage from Southampton, once he'd got over the initial sea sickness and the wrench of saying goodbye to his family. His cabin was air-conditioned and his fellow-passengers friendly. Especially the young, single women making their way out to the colony to stay with friends and relations and, possibly, meet someone to marry. They wouldn't consider him a suitable catch as he was half-Chinese, he knew, but that hadn't prevented them from flirting with him. He'd got used to flirting with girls and keeping them at arm's length. Kate was the only one for him.

At Port Said an Egyptian, or *gully-gully man* as everyone called him, came on board and delighted people with his antics. Dressed in a long white robe and brown sandals, the man had waved his magician's wand and conjured up live baby chicks from behind the children's ears.

A first class passenger, Charles had to dress formally

for dinner - except the first night and nights in port. He'd enjoyed the deck quoits, dancing, and a peculiar ceremony when they crossed the Equator, with first-timers having to give a present to King Neptune. Luckily, he didn't qualify; he'd already gone through that on his voyage out to England.

The farther east they'd sailed, the closer he'd felt to his roots. There'd been some spectacular sunsets over the Indian Ocean. In Colombo he went ashore and bought tiny wooden carved elephants; they'd make useful presents. Singapore reminded him of a quieter, cleaner Hong Kong and he'd relished hearing Cantonese in the shops.

Now, the dull drone of the turbines and the song of the wind were in his ears. The sky was lightening and the shadowy shape of islands came into sight. Ships, and freighters, and barges, and Hong Kong Island rose out of the gloom. Other people emerged on deck and Charles greeted them with a smile. Tugboats guided the *SS Canton* towards Holden's Wharf through the melee of water craft thronging the harbour.

He stood at the railings and eyed the crowd gathered on the quay. There were Uncle Phillip and Auntie Julie! He waved frantically until they returned his greeting.

Disembarkation formalities completed, he ran down the gangway and they threw their arms around him. Auntie kissed his cheek. 'Welcome home.'

Soon afterwards Charles was sitting in their spacious sitting room. Peking carpets covered the waxed parquet flooring, and the antique lacquer chests and jade screens he remembered were in their usual places. The last time he'd been here, they were still in storage. 'It hardly seems any different.'

'We've redecorated it to be the same as before the war.' Uncle Phillip rubbed his brow. 'As you know, we managed to hide our choice pieces in an out-of-the-way warehouse.'

Uncle, whose real estate business was flourishing after he'd made some wise investments, had arranged a job for

Charles at Beacons law firm.

'It's very kind of you to help me,' he said, touching Uncle's shoulder.

Auntie poured tea. 'How is your mother?'

Charles smiled at his aunt. Her resemblance to Ma was uncanny. It would be years before he'd see his family again, but he didn't regret his decision to return to Hong Kong. He'd been a stranger in England. It had been a struggle to adapt at first, but thanks to his paternal uncle's generosity they hadn't wanted for anything. Initially they'd lived in the East End, but they'd moved to Chelsea after the war and Pa had started his own business dealing in Chinese antiques.

'Ma is well and so are Pa and Ruth,' he said to Aunt Julie. She was still childless after many years of marriage, and he knew she considered Ruth and him almost like her own children.

'You'll find Hong Kong is changing.' Uncle offered him a cigarette.

'Thanks, but I don't smoke. Please tell me about the changes.'

'Masses of people are pouring over the border because of the troubles in China. I'm a member of a *Kaifong* Association and we're doing our best to provide free education and health care.'

'Where do all the refugees live?'

'Most of them are in squatter huts on the hillsides. The rest are on rooftops, in alleyways, anywhere they can find.'

Auntie wagged a finger. 'I think the Government needs to wake up to its responsibilities and send them back to China.'

'These poor people must have good reason to abandon their homes, sever their family ties, and renounce their traditional allegiances to come here.' Uncle smiled indulgently. 'We have to accept them in the name of humanity.'

After lunch, Charles went to his room to unpack. But

the amahs had got there before him and all his clothes had been tidied away, his books placed in neat piles on the chest of drawers. He'd have to get used to a house full of servants again and there would be many other changes he'd have to deal with. Returning to his roots had been the second goal that kept him focused while he'd been away. The first goal, of course, was that he'd see Kate again and rekindle their love.

\*\*\*

Charles crossed the harbour on the Ferry the next morning, and walked the short distance to Alexandra House. The Star Ferry was still just the "Ferry" - some things didn't change.

The union flag flew from the domed cupola on top of an elegant four-storey building perched on portico arcades up ahead. It was as familiar to Charles as a pair of old shoes. But the roads were even more crowded than he remembered: tramcars, buses, taxis, bicycles and rickshaws all vying for space with private cars in the rubbish-strewn streets. People scurried between the vehicles and the noise was thunderous: horns hooting, trams jangling, bells ringing, people shouting. Charles inhaled the petrol fumes, the smell of wok oil and the stink of humanity living cheek by jowl and let out a happy sigh. He'd truly come home.

His office was on the fifth floor and he rode up in an antiquated bird cage lift, to be met by his secretary, Mabel, a Portuguese Eurasian, plump and middle-aged. The Cantonese office boy, a relation to one of Uncle Phillip's messengers, busied himself reading the paper and providing endless cups of tea. Charles and his secretary got on with the correspondence, the ordering of business cards and the like. His workmates seemed friendly, a mix of British, Eurasians and Chinese solicitors. The barriers had never been there when it came to business.

At lunchtime Charles strolled down Queen's Road. On

his right loomed the granite-faced fortress of The Hong Kong and Shanghai Bank. A pair of polished bronze lions guarded the door, symbolising the financial stability of the colony. He patted the lions like everyone else, for luck. He had it on good authority the building possessed excellent *feng shui*; the life-force of the dragon of the mountain flowed down from the Peak to the harbour via its premises, bringing wealth and prosperity to all who banked there.

He glanced across the road and caught sight of the back of a tall lady with long, wavy dark-brown hair getting onto a tram. Could it be Kate? His heart quickened, but he was too late to catch up with her. If it had been her. The tram was already clanking its way towards Wanchai.

The Supreme Court rose up on his left and Charles walked to the entrance. A statue of a blindfolded woman, witness to the impartiality of the law, stood with scales in her right hand. She held a sword in her left one to remind the population of the law's power of punishment. It wouldn't be long before he walked through that hallowed door, ready to work with a barrister and try a case to the bench.

Charles bowed his head and said a silent prayer in front of the Cenotaph, remembering Bob and all the others who had died at Stanley.

*The Glorious Dead 1914-1918*
*1939-1945*

He stared at The Hong Kong Club building. That was one place where he wouldn't be setting foot. Its constitution excluded the membership of shopkeepers, Chinese, Indians, women and other undesirables. Not that he fell into any of those categories, but Pa hadn't been considered when he'd applied to join before the war. It didn't take much intelligence to work out why.

Charles felt proud of his background, however, and

ready to take on the establishment. He didn't need to be a member of any of their clubs. There were enough clubs he could join that would accept him. He thought about Henry Wolseley. Should he telephone him and ask about Kate? No, he'd find her himself. It had been too problematic from London, the distance too great, communication too erratic. Now he was back in Hong Kong, the difficulties would be different . . .

# 27

On board his Dragon yacht, *Jade Princess*, moored at the Yacht Club, James was checking the lines and making sure they were separated, ready for departure. The boat had been built in the 1930s, and he'd bought it from a fellow about to retire in England.

Sofia was due to arrive from one of her uncle's trading junks, anchored nearby. Should he feel guilty about her? He shook his head. It wasn't as if he and Kate were engaged to be married. They were simply seeing each other socially. Perhaps he really had reinvented himself in Hong Kong; he certainly wasn't the same man he'd been brought up to be. He'd never imagined himself as the type to take a mistress.

*And such a mistress!*

So beautiful and exotic. What he felt for Sofia was pure intoxication. She hadn't hinted she wanted anything more from him other than the occasional assignation. Was he pleased or annoyed at her casual approach? Just grateful their relationship had been kept secret; he didn't care for the disapproval of Hong Kong society. He was certain he would be ostracised if anyone found out. If only he didn't have to consider the social taboos of this bigoted place . . .

Sofia had taken to sailing as if it were in her blood. She appeared to have an instinctive feel for it, and could have managed *Jade* quite well on her own if he'd let her. This was the third time they'd slipped away at first light. They'd cruise out of the harbour on *Jade's* inboard engine and unfurl her powerful sails to find a deserted cove, where they would skinny-dip and make love in the shallows. He smiled to himself, remembering the first time. She'd laughed at the speed of his love making and had made him lie back afterwards while she'd tantalised him, instructing him not to move as she ran her hands down his body.

She'd taught him the ancient Chinese art of love that she'd learnt from reading the books in her uncle's library. James was relieved Sofia hadn't learnt it from another man. She'd been a virgin and he could hardly believe his luck that she'd chosen him. Heat crept up his neck as he thought about their lovemaking. He'd learnt to prolong the pleasure and not to come too quickly.

The creak of the single oar being sculled on a sampan, and he reached out his hand to help her aboard. They set off and soon they anchored in Rocky Bay.

The sun had risen and the early morning sea was still as glass. At this time of day and mid-week, the beach was deserted. Sofia dived off the side of the boat. Her body was spare but shapely, and she swam with the assurance of someone who'd practically grown up in the sea, unlike him; he'd only learnt to swim in the Navy. He slipped on his bathing shorts and dived into the cool depths. Surfacing next to her, he shook the droplets from his hair.

He kissed Sofia deeply and she laced her legs around him. Treading water, he manoeuvred her backwards until they reached the side of the yacht, then placed her between himself and the ladder, holding onto the rungs with both hands. She pulled off her swimming costume and tossed it into the boat. He did the same, then lifted her onto his erection. They moved in unison, the tepid seawater caressing them, every nerve in his body tingling. 'Now,'

Sofia said, at last. He came, then, losing himself in her, hot pleasure shooting through him. Intoxicating pleasure. No words spoken, just a physical need assuaged.

They climbed aboard the yacht and sipped the piping hot coffee Sofia brewed in *Jade's* tiny galley. Overlooking the bay perched the exclusive bungalows of the wealthy expatriates, whose residents' committee kept out locals and undesirables. Last week he'd been invited to a party with Kate there, given by the *Taipan* of one of the Hongs, as the larger trading companies were known. The *Taipan* and his wife were friends of Kate's father, and they had a weekend retreat on a ridge overlooking the Shek-o golf course.

James had been envious of the fabulous location, although at the time he'd called it a bit remote. It had been an excellent opportunity to make the right contacts, but he'd longed to be with Sofia and his passion had fought against the sensible voice inside his head that told him no good would come of his affair with her.

He glanced at her towel-drying her hair. *God, she's beautiful! What does she see in me?*

'Have you any news yet about helping us save the factory?' she asked, putting on fresh lipstick.

'My contacts are keen for me to meet with your uncle. To discuss possible cooperation.'

Maybe Sofia was seeing him to keep him soft for K C Leung? The sudden thought soured the coffee in James' mouth.

\*\*\*

He met Leung at a restaurant in Kowloon, where K C had booked a private room. Sofia hadn't been included in the meeting. Why? Her uncle greeted him jovially and showed him to the table.

'I'll lay my cards on the table,' James said, sipping brandy and picking at the crispy seaweed with his chopsticks. 'I've been asked to find out about Leo

200

Rodrigues' Triad contacts and the banks in receipt of smuggled gold. Sofia tells me you're in debt to him.'

'That's right. But I don't want to repay.' Leung thrust out his chest. 'I want trick him into thinking I repay.'

'How do you propose to do that?'

'He flies the gold into Macau regularly on Catalina seaplane. I'll arrange for a robbery to take place after aircraft leaves Hong Kong. I need you be on my launch, pick up my men and the loot.' K C laughed and settled back in his chair with exaggerated casualness. 'I'll repay Leo with his own gold.'

'Who will steal the gold?' James blinked. The plan was foolhardy. No other word to describe it. 'And what will happen to the plane?'

'One of my associates trained to fly Catalina seaplane in Philippines. He and other man will board flight from Hong Kong to Macau, and hold gun to pilot's head when seaplane reaches cruising height.'

James laughed. 'And you expect them to just hand over the plane?'

Leung's smiled. 'If they don't want get killed.'

'Then what?'

'My man will take over controls and land aircraft near Soko Islands, in most south-western waters of Hong Kong Territory.'

'Why do you need me?'

'I will give you name of Hong Kong banks that buy gold from Macau illegally. Also will find out where new Triads have set up. I know you work for Special Branch. You tell them keep out of my business in return for this.'

'What will happen to the gold?'

'My men will conceal plane and tie up captives. I want you to pick up my men and gold.'

'I still don't understand why you need me. Can't you get one of your men to do it?'

'If you involved, I know Hong Kong police not trick me.'

'Fair enough. I'll let you know as soon as I've been given the green light.' James crossed his arms. Special Branch was unlikely to want Leung's information enough to countenance an in-flight robbery. '*If* I'm given the green light, that is.'

'You will be. Or we won't be able to stop any violence between the nationalists and the communists. Big trouble coming from China. And new Triads very big trouble-makers.' Leung lifted his glass and smiled. '*Yum sing!* Or "bottoms up" as you British say.' And he drained his brandy in one gulp.

They ate quickly, talking about the food (delicious) and weather (too hot and wet). They had little in common, apart from Sofia. Did her uncle know about their affair? If so, he must have sanctioned it.

James couldn't fathom the man. Because he was Chinese, he supposed, but also for his political convictions. China was an enigma to him and the people so different to any he'd encountered before. Fascinating, though. He'd like to learn more about them. James was starting to feel more intrigued by the locals than by the stuffy expatriates.

Take Henry Wolseley, a typical Colonel Blimp character, almost a stereotype, but then most of the expatriates in Hong Kong were like that. How had he produced such a sweet daughter as Kate? *Ah, Kate!* He was fond of her and glad he wasn't exactly two-timing her. She deserved better.

Heat spread up from James' groin. God, Sofia was enticing. What if he risked everything and allowed himself to fall in love with her? Perhaps she didn't want that. After all, she'd given him no indication . . .

## 28

'I don't understand why you want to leave the Consortium, Sofia.' Leo lit a cigarette. 'Why give up all the power and influence we have here in Macau for the life of an ordinary person in Hong Kong?'

'I don't intend to be *ordinary*,' she said, straightening her back. She sat opposite him in Father's study. Balthazar, as usual, lay on the rug at his feet. The dog went everywhere with him; he spoilt it with titbits from the table and employed a servant solely to take the it for walks.

'Hong Kong will flourish. And I intend to flourish with it.'

'How's that? With a piddling factory spinning cotton?' He laughed, blowing smoke towards her. 'That's hardly going to make you a millionaire.'

'The factory is just a start. I'll invest my capital in the company. Uncle and I will develop it into a proper textiles business, manufacturing clothing.'

'And set yourselves up to rival businesses in England?' He sneered. 'I don't think so.'

'Our labour costs will be much lower. We'll be more competitive.'

'What about quality control?'

'I'll go to Britain and learn from the experts.'

'All these plans of yours will come to nothing when I take over the factory,' he said, balancing his cigarette on the edge of the ashtray. 'I'll sell it to the highest bidder to get back my money. Many industrialists are leaving Shanghai to set up in Hong Kong.'

'Uncle will pay you back. Give him time!'

'Time is at a premium, haven't you heard? Run along now, little bastard sister.' He waved her off. 'I've got a meeting to go to.'

Sofia concealed herself behind the rhododendron bushes in the front garden and waited until Leo emerged from the house. Derek Higgins was with him. How she hated that man! He'd served Uncle like a slave and here he was kow-towing to Leo as if he were some sort of god.

She remembered that Derek needed money for his family. And he had to feed his gambling habit. Uncle had paid him a fair wage, only it wouldn't have made Derek rich. Neither would his fireworks factory, a small concern he ran on a shoestring. But it wasn't an excuse to betray Uncle.

Sofia followed Leo and Derek, keeping out of sight as they walked to the old Inner Harbour. The deep-sea junks clustered five abreast, washing hanging from a forest of bare masts. The temperature must have been in the nineties and the humidity was so high the air practically dripped moisture. She hardly noticed she was so used to it.

She strode past the shipwrights, constructing their junks on cradles over a canal. Spicy aromas of food mingled with the stench of rotting rubbish. She ducked down a dark alley-way and hid behind a stall. Leo and Derek disappeared into a tea-house. Sofia crept up to the shuttered window and, peered through the cracks. She stiffened. They were talking to three Chinese men. One of the men leaned back in his chair; his jacket fell open. There was a gun in a holster strapped to his chest!

She stared at the men for a long time and memorised

their features. Then she rushed home and marched into the sitting room. Uncle was sitting under the ceiling fan.

'If the men are returning to Hong Kong on the afternoon ferry I need to be on it too,' she said after she'd told him what she'd been doing. 'Now I know what they look like, it'll be easy enough to keep an eye on them.'

'You did well.' Uncle handed her a wad of Hong Kong dollars. 'Make sure you treat yourself to something nice at Lane Crawford.'

'Thank you. I just hope I'll be able to follow those men without problems.'

'I'll telephone one of my associates to meet you as you disembark.'

Four hours later, a slight young man with a round face and crooked teeth greeted her at the pier on Hong Kong Island. 'My name is Chun Ming,' he said.

The three Triads took rickshaws to the Ferry. Sofia and Chun Ming followed in a taxi. They managed to get onto the same boat across the harbour, and stood behind the men in the queue for another taxi.

Past the airport, they stopped in front of what looked like a shanty town. There were shacks everywhere but for some crumbling old buildings in the centre. 'I feared as much,' Chun Ming said. 'Kowloon Walled City.'

'Oh?'

'It's the only part of Hong Kong that has stayed under the control of China. About six and a half acres of land, it wasn't and never has been a city.'

'Now I remember. Wasn't it a Chinese military fort when Hong Kong was ceded to Britain over a hundred years ago?'

'You mean when Britain grabbed Hong Kong in an unequal treaty. There's no point following them in there. It's full of Kuomintang supporters. No wonder the Triads have moved in . . .'

'Thank you for bringing me here, Chun Ming. This information will be invaluable.'

Sofia dropped him at his flat. In Tsuen Wan, she paid the taxi driver and went up to her office. She dialled James's number and asked if they could meet.

'I'm sorry, sweetheart. If I'd known you were going to be in town, I wouldn't have made prior arrangements. I'm having dinner with my boss and his wife at the Parisian Grill. When do you go back to Macau?'

Should she tell him not until tomorrow? *No.* 'On the evening ferry,' she lied.

\*\*\*

At eight o'clock Sofia was hiding behind a stall on the pavement outside the Parisian Grill. Why hadn't James invited her to meet his friends? Perhaps he wasn't ready. She wanted to see what they looked like. One day, she'd meet them properly. When James realised how much he loved her and didn't care what others thought.

A taxi pulled up. James was in the back seat. *Oh, no!* He wasn't alone. He was with a European woman, just the two of them, and no sign of anyone who could be his boss. The girl seemed much too young to be Tony Chambers' wife, and she was beautiful, willowy, with a heart-shaped face, and a fragile look that would make any man want to protect her.

Sofia chewed her thumbnail. Should she march up to them and demand an explanation? But she had no rights over James, no rights at all. Hadn't she'd played it cool with him up until now? The next time she saw him she'd find out about the Englishwoman and she'd let him know how she felt. It was time to tell him she loved him. The physical attraction she'd felt for him initially had grown into a deep love. If anyone were to ask her why that was, she'd find it difficult to explain other than the fact she wouldn't be happy if she had to live without him. He made her feel complete.

She wrapped her arms around herself. Uncle would be

pleased with her spying this afternoon. Now he had something to give James in exchange for helping to save the factory. Uncle hadn't told her what his plans were, but she had her own thoughts on what was needed, and those thoughts included James, Englishwoman or no Englishwoman.

## 29

In the Wellspring box at the Happy Valley racecourse, I was tapping my foot and listening to Papa chat with Arnaud de Montreuil, the French Consul-General. I'd much rather have spent the afternoon at home, but my father had insisted on bringing me with him, saying he had important guests and needed me to help entertain them. Also, I suspected he'd wanted me here because he'd invited James.

'Love,' Papa had said when I'd told him I hadn't forgotten Charles. 'Love comes when you make a life together.'

'Is that what happened between you and Mama?' I'd asked. 'I know the story. After you met her in Southampton at the end of the first war, you came out to Hong Kong to better your prospects. Six months later, Mama embarked on a P & O liner, leaving behind everything familiar to her. You must have loved each other right from the start.'

'Your mother and I came from the same background.'

I stopped tapping my foot and went to stand next to James, who was watching the race, a betting slip in his hand. An electric machine on the other side of the track showed the enormous sums of money being gambled. People were leaning over the balcony in the next box, the majority of them Chinese. Unlike Papa's other clubs, the Hong Kong Jockey Club approved of local members.

A tall man turned around. Seconds passed; he was staring right at me. My heart thudded, and my knees began to give way. I stepped back, found a seat and undid the top button of my blouse. The walls of the box were closing in on me. Taking a few deep breaths, I got up and excused myself. 'I need some fresh air,' I murmured to no one in particular.

'You do seem rather peaky.' James glanced at me. 'Shall I come with you?'

'Don't worry! I'll be fine.'

Outside, I fought my way through the crowds towards the entrance of the Jockey Club. Across the road, there was a cemetery. *Another damn cemetery!* I walked through the pillared entrance, climbed the steep hillside, and sat on a patch of grass. I had a clear view of the clock tower in the centre of the two members' stands. On the other side of the valley was Blue Pool Road, where Papa and I used to ride every Sunday.

A lone figure came through the gates of the race-track. He walked just like Charles used to, swinging his right arm with each step. The man crossed the road and climbed up the hill. Sudden fine drizzle fell and soaked my hat.

My heart sang. *It's Charles! He's alive!* He stood in front of me and unfurled his umbrella. His adult face had become even more finely chiselled, his shoulders had broadened and his body, under a well-tailored suit, had filled out. But his hair still flopped across his forehead in that same maddening way.

'I saw you leave and wondered where you were going with such a determined look on your face,' he said, taking off his jacket and spreading it on the grass. 'The ground is damp, let's sit on this.'

Feeling hot, I removed my cotton gloves and stuffed

them into my handbag. Charles was looking away, probably to avoid meeting my eyes. As well he might, not having contacted me. Should I ask him why? *No.* He was sitting so stiffly; the years had turned him into a stranger. It wasn't the sort of question you could put to a stranger.

I pulled down my skirt. 'Did you know the Japanese kept the Jockey Club open during the war?' *Might as well fill the silence with small-talk.* 'They called it the Hong Kong Race Club and changed the names of the ponies from English to Chinese.'

'Apparently, they used the ponies to pull passenger carts when the buses stopped running after the petrol ran out.'

'They even ate some of them.' I shuddered. 'How's your family?' I was aware of his gaze on my face now.

'Ruth is doing well at school. She wants to become a doctor.'

'Gosh, how clever of her!'

'I expect she'll come back to Hong Kong when she's qualified. She keeps going on and on about how much she misses this place.'

I glanced at my watch. 'I'd better be getting back before they start worrying about me.'

Charles got to his feet and held out his hand. His touch was so familiar a mad impulse took hold of me to reach out and stroke his face. Before I could stop myself my fingers were laced in his and I was kissing him. 'Oh God, Charles, I thought you were dead,' I said between kisses. 'Why didn't you contact me?'

'B . . . b . . . but I did. I wrote to you.'

'Well, I didn't receive your letters.'

'I wrote every month for a year.'

'How can they have all gone missing?'

'I wrote to your address on the Peak in the hopes someone would forward them.'

'I never received them,' I repeated, looking into his eyes.

'I was worried you'd had second thoughts, but then I told myself you'd never do that. I'm right, aren't I, Kate?'

I kissed him again, full on the lips, and it was like coming home after a long, long journey. I was where I should be, in Charles' arms. How could anything ever part us again?

As if he'd read my thoughts, Charles said, 'What about your father? Do you think he could have intercepted my letters?'

'No, I'm sure he wouldn't have. I expect the letters got lost in the post. Or they weren't forwarded. That's much more probable.'

Charles took my hand and kissed it. 'Your father didn't approve of us in Stanley. He's hardly likely to have changed his mind now. Perhaps we should keep our love a secret until we know where we stand with him? I don't want to cause a rift between you.'

A bubble of disappointment formed in my chest and I turned away from him. 'I don't care about that, my darling. I don't care about anything but us, and I want to tell everyone.'

'We will when the time is right,' he said, turning me towards him. He stroked my cheek. 'Oh, Kate, how I've longed to do that. I want everything to be perfect for you. No arguments with your father. And I need to prepare my family as well.'

His family? Surely there wouldn't be any problems with them? 'Why's that?'

'My uncle and aunt have become very Chinese since the war. I'm sure they'll grow to love you, but I need to give them time to get used to the idea.'

'It's all so complicated. I wish people were more open-minded.'

'Hong Kong has become a melting pot of China. A place of refugees and my uncle and aunt fit in better with the Chinese community than the English. There's an old saying: all rivers running into the China Sea turn salty.'

'What's that mean?'

'All ethnic groups living in China get assimilated eventually.'

'I think they're privileged to have a dual background.'

'How can they fit in with both cultures?' Charles shrugged. 'Before the war, they could be part of the Eurasian community. Where's it now? Disappeared.'

'I suppose you're talking about yourself as well.' I reached for his hand. 'What about me? Am I too English for you?'

Charles gave one of his heartbreakingly beautiful smiles. 'Oh, my sweet love. I don't think of you like that. You're Kate, the other part of me. Together we can overcome all this prejudice. I'm sure of it. We just need to take things slowly so we get what's best for us.'

'Fair enough. Only an hour ago I believed you were dead. Now I know different my life has meaning again. I'll be satisfied with seeing you in secret for a while.' I sighed. 'How will we know when the time is right to tell everyone, though?'

'We'll know. Will you trust me?'

'I suppose so. At least come back with me to the Wellspring box and say hello. That can be the first step.'

'Of course,' he said, and we kissed again.

In the race-stand, Jessica and Tony welcomed Charles as if he were a long-lost friend. And Papa's guests seemed fascinated to meet him, the nephew of millionaire Phillip Noble no less! The French Consul-General even promised a dinner invitation. But Papa stared at Charles as if he'd seen some sort of apparition.

Charles exchanged business cards with James and Arnaud. 'My uncle is expecting me. Nice to see you again, Kate.'

'Nice to see you too.' *How long will I be able to keep up this silly pretence?*

From the other side of me, James pointed. 'You've dropped one of your gloves, Kate.'

Before I could do anything, Charles retrieved it. The message in his eyes was clear: love mixed with the fundamental decency that was essentially Charles. My Charles.

\*\*\*

In the car on the way home, Papa lit his pipe. 'Did you know how Charles Pearce's uncle came to be so filthy rich?'

'Filthy rich. What a horrible expression. Please enlighten me!'

Seemingly unfazed, Papa sucked on his pipe. 'His father was an ordinary Portuguese Eurasian bank clerk. I believe Phillip Noble was educated at one of those elite schools that offered scholarships to local boys.'

'Oh?' *What was he on about?*

'Before the war, he'd already started building his real estate empire. From the safety of Macau, he gave instructions to his contacts to buy up duress notes.'

'Duress notes?'

'Hong Kong dollars issued by local bankers under Japanese orders. Noble got them at a fraction of their face value. Of course, on liberation, the Hong Kong and Shanghai Bank honoured the notes at their full worth and he made millions.'

'That's not exactly dishonest. He gambled and won.'

'We're getting too many of these rich Chinese in the colony. Place isn't the same at all.'

I clenched my jaw. It was useless to argue with Papa and far too distressing. Didn't he realise Hong Kong was changing? I saw it all around me. More and more people were flooding in from China. Because of all the wealth the rich immigrants were bringing with them, the shops were booming. The Chinese *taitais* went on shopping sprees all morning and played mah-jong all afternoon, just like the bored British missies did before the war. In the old days, they only went to Lane Crawford's and Whiteaway's department stores. Now there was much more choice and you could buy anything - if you had the money.

It was such a contrast to the abject poverty of those who'd crossed the border with nothing. Beggars thronged the streets and shanty towns were springing up everywhere. Papa seemed oblivious to their misery, but I couldn't ignore it. I was determined to find a way to help; I just hadn't found it yet.

I thought about Charles, and happiness fizzed through me. *Hopefully, it won't be long before we can announce our love to the world.*

## 30

Charles was one of the first guests to arrive at the Consul-General's villa. He was standing in the garden with a glass of chilled white wine and gazing at the view. Balanced on a rocky promontory between Repulse Bay and Deep Water Bay, the property overlooked Middle Island and the South China Sea beyond.

'Just like the Côte d'Azur,' Arnaud had said a minute ago before he went off to greet other people.

Charles hadn't been able to stop thinking about Kate since last Saturday. Mid-week he'd called her, but her father had answered the phone and he'd made up the excuse of a wrong number. Although he had no evidence, he was certain Henry Wolseley had intercepted his letters. A gut feeling. How to win the man over? Charles wanted everything to be perfect for Kate, for her to have the wedding of her dreams with her father in doting attendance. He chewed his lip and looked around.

Arnaud, a flashy character, was circulating among his guests. 'I only invite beautiful women to my parties,' Charles remembered him saying when they were introduced at the races. The Frenchman had stared pointedly at Kate. As if on cue, her laughter tinkled from the other side of the lawn.

She was standing next to that Englishman, James. Kate looked across the garden and met Charles' eyes.

*I'd give anything to sweep her off to a quiet place and make love to her.*

He stood in the shadows and watched her. In the camp, she'd almost been a beauty, but semi-starvation had kept her from blooming into the lovely woman she'd now become. Her bow-shaped lips parted in a half-smile and his heart-rate quickened. She was still slim, even thin, but her figure was curvy.

*Don't do this to yourself! Be patient!*

At dinner, he sat next to Jessica Chambers. She must have been in her early thirties, and the years as well as his new position in society had shrunk the gap that used to exist between them. Jessica leaned towards him. 'How do you find life in Hong Kong these days?'

'Different in some ways, yet fundamentally it's the same old place.'

'Where are you living?' She lifted her soup spoon and swallowed a mouthful of *vichyssoise.*

'Still at my uncle's but I'm moving into a flat in Pokfulam next week.'

'And how is work?' Jessica's bright red lipstick had smeared the wine glass she held to her lips.

Most of his cases involved petty family disputes. Bigger cases would come his way once he became better known. 'So far so good. It helps to have the right contacts, of course.'

'Of course.' Jessica stared around. 'Isn't this an interesting mix of people? Quite different from the stuffy parties we used to go to before the war.'

Charles studied the other tables. Kate was at Arnaud's table and James had been placed to the left of Arnaud's wife, Adèle, at the head of her own table. Two standard poodles sprawled at her feet, and she was feeding them scraps from her plate. The other guests were a varied bunch, and the ladies beautiful.

Charles listened to the woman on his left. Statuesque, blonde, probably Danish judging by her accent, with a voluptuous bosom in danger of escaping from her low-cut dress. She was discussing a development at exclusive Shek-o with the Englishman on her right. 'I don't understand why they don't let the Chinese buy houses next to the golf club.'

Hong Kong was changing, but some changes were taking longer than others. Charles was the only Oriental at his table. He gazed around the room again; each table had its own token local representative. How open-minded of Arnaud . . .

The blonde now smiled at Charles. 'I'm delighted to meet you. I hardly meet any Chinese. Everyone here keeps to a small social circle of like-minded people, inviting each other and being invited by each other to an endless round of parties. I do think Arnaud is clever to give these mixed dos.'

After coffee, the ladies disappeared to the powder-rooms, and the men smoked cigars and drank port. Charles lowered himself down next to Tony Chambers on a plush, white sofa. Through the open doors, servants were clearing the tables from the terrace. 'What happens next?'

Tony blew cigar smoke. 'Usually dancing to gramophone records.'

Charles took his leave and wandered into the garden, separated from the main road by a high boundary wall with Chinese roof tiles on top. He walked to the place where he'd stood earlier. A full moon reflected in the inky blackness of the sea below. On the horizon, the lights of the fishing sampans flickered in the September night. He wasn't surprised when Kate came up; their minds had always been in tune.

'It's glorious, isn't it?' she said.

'Absolutely.'

'Can you smell those roses?'

Bushes lined the bank below and steps led down to the beach, where white sand glittered in the moonlight. Kate's floral perfume mixed with the heady scent of the flowers. If only he could take her in his arms and crush her against him! He gripped the iron rail so hard his knuckles turned white.

The Englishman appeared at his elbow. 'Ah, here you are, Kate. I've come to claim you for a dance. Good to see you again, Charles.'

Kate walked to the veranda with James and they performed a slow waltz. Was something going on between them? Charles shoved his fists into his pockets. No, Kate wouldn't . . .

He strode across the lawn and bumped into Jessica. She grabbed his arm. 'I hope you're a good dancer.'

The music switched to a tango, and he led Jessica in an open embrace. Out of the corner of his eye, he saw Kate standing on the side, watching him. Jessica performed a leg hook and, after what seemed like hours, the record finished.

'I'm exhausted,' Jessica said. 'Let me hand you over.'

What could he say? He was holding Kate before he could think of anything, and doing the slow-slow-quick-quick of a foxtrot. 'You're good,' she whispered. 'I knew you would be.'

Charles held her gently, not too close, but she pressed her lovely body against his and he started to respond.

'I was expecting you to ring me,' she said.

'I did, but your father answered. I think it'll be better if you rang me.'

Kate leant back and regarded him in a thoughtful way. 'All right.'

Charles felt her melding into him again. *Oh God! Oh God!* He wanted her so desperately it was like a knife twisting his gut. 'Do you mind if we take a break?' He dropped his hold. 'I'll get us some refreshments. What would you like?'

'A brandy soda, please.'

Ten minutes later, he returned with their drinks. *Damn!* She was sitting on the side talking with James. Charles handed Kate her brandy and pulled up a chair, but she was giggling at something James had said and hardly seemed to notice him. *Damn again!* The Englishman had taken her hand and was patting it while laughing at himself. Charles could feel his cheeks burning. Perhaps there *was* something going on between them? No. Kate was a beautiful young woman and was bound to have admirers. Especially as she'd thought he was dead until a few days ago. He could trust her, he knew he could. Whether he could trust James Stevens, however, was another matter . . .

# 31

I was on my way back from the orphanage. My taxi halted at traffic lights, and I stared out of the window. A man was striding up a rough track leading to a steep hillside on the far side of the crossing, swinging his arms like Charles did. I told the driver to stop, and paid the fare. I had to see him again. If it was him. I'd spoken to him on the phone a couple of times, but it wasn't the same as being with him face to face. He'd asked me about James Stevens, and I'd told him James was just a friend. I couldn't help feeling pleased Charles loved me enough to be jealous.

I set off at a brisk pace, walking past coolies carrying heavy bundles on their shoulder-poles, and rickshaws laden with packages. Then I came to a flattened area, almost a plateau at the top of the path. Built in close proximity stood thousands of huts made of thin wood, corrugated iron, and old packing cases. A whole city had risen from bare ground. People turned and stared at me.

A bare-bottomed toddler, his lower lip quivering, nose running with phlegm and tears streaming, hid behind his mother's legs. The woman, a baby slung from her back, picked up her child and ran off down a narrow alleyway. Everywhere washing hung out to dry. Where did these poor women get the water to wash their clothes? There was a standpipe down by the main road; they must have to carry buckets all the way up here. Obviously there were no sewerage facilities and a stench in the air reminded me of Stanley.

I looked around for Charles. He'd disappeared and I doubted it had been really him that I'd seen. I was out of place here; it was so different from my usual haunts. And I was frightened. Not of the people, who seemed more scared of me than I of them, but of the poverty. I started to trace my steps back down to Waterloo Road. Someone tapped on me on the shoulder, and I turned around.

'What are you doing here?' Charles asked.

'I could ask the same thing of you,' I said, smiling.

'My uncle has built cheap blocks of flats on some land he bought. I was getting the names of people to re-house. It's a drop in the ocean, though. There are far too many refugees.'

Charles offered me a lift home, and I walked with him to where he'd parked his car in Kadoorie Avenue, breathing in the faint citrus smell of him, intensely aware of his physical presence, his broad shoulders tapering to a slim waist. 'It's turned out to be a gorgeous afternoon,' I said, falling into the safe refuge of small-talk.

Bright sunshine had cleared away the humidity that had clung to me like a blanket while I'd been at the orphanage. I pointed at two magpies, perched in an orchid tree. 'One for sorrow, two for joy.'

Charles took his keys from his pocket and led me to an MGA Coupé parked in front of his uncle's house. 'Shall we take the car hood off?'

'What fun.' I glanced back at the tree, remembering the one in Stanley. Had Charles made the same connection?

'How about a spin?' he said.

We crossed the harbour in the vehicular ferry, headed through the mid-levels, skirted Happy Valley, went over the gap and down towards the south. Charles turned right onto Island Road, the MG's engine making a purring sound, and we motored towards Aberdeen fishing village.

'This was the fragrant harbour that gave Hong Kong its name,' he said. 'In the last century the British would stop off and get fresh water from a waterfall. The fragrance came from the scent of the joss sticks traded here.'

'I always thought the name referred to Victoria Harbour, which isn't fragrant at all.'

Charles seemed to relax behind the wheel of his car, sure of himself as he drove me around the back of the island. I was so aware of him it hurt - his thigh long and lean on the other side of the gear stick, his strong, capable hands on the steering wheel.

'I've just rented a flat in Bisney Road,' he said. 'Moved in yesterday. Would you like to see it?'

The apartment was on the second floor of a new three-storey block. There were staff quarters and three bedrooms, but so far he'd only furnished one of them. I stood at the door to his room and stared at his bed, a flush spreading through me. Turning abruptly, I collided with him.

He took me in his arms and kissed me. My body fused to his and I kissed him back, real kisses, the years of longing unravelling like a dropped stitch. He lifted his head and his eyes sought mine. 'Kate?' His voice cracked with emotion.

I nodded.

Charles steered me backwards and we toppled onto the quilt. My hand slipped under his shirt and I caressed his smooth chest. He undid the buttons of my blouse, reached behind, and unclasped my bra.

His mouth explored my breasts. 'Oh Charles . . .' I was losing myself to the pleasure. I couldn't think of anything but him. My one and only love. He pulled down my panties, and I unbuckled his trouser belt.

It was my first time and I'd expected discomfort. But all I wanted was to keep him inside me forever. Exquisite sensation filled my body.

*Oh Charles, oh Charles, at last.*

The pleasure built and built and I was melting with it. Then something happened, something I'd read about yet never imagined could be so extraordinary, and I let out a low shuddering moan. Charles quickly withdrew. 'I love you so much,' I said, turning to smile at him.

'And I love you too, my darling.' He stroked my cheek. 'I want you here with me, you know I do, but we have to be patient. So I think it's time I got you home to your father.'

I wanted to shake him and tell him Papa didn't matter. But something stopped me. Of course my father mattered. Hands trembling, I put on my panties, buttoned up my blouse, and picked up my handbag. 'Let's go, then.'

All the way back up to the Peak, I maintained silence. I'd made love with Charles, I should have been bubbling with happiness. Instead, though, my insides were tied up in knots.

# 32

Charles dropped Kate off at her front gate. He watched her marching away from him, and an invisible hand squeezed his heart. She'd been so quiet in the car. Too quiet. Should he run after her? Charles grabbed the door handle. He pushed down, then stopped himself. He had to be cautious, otherwise he'd make mistakes and he wouldn't achieve his goal. Kate meant the world to him; her happiness was paramount.

He drove back to his flat. Thankfully, his amah had been out at the market when he'd brought Kate here earlier. Tittle-tattle spread around the colony through the servants' grapevine and God forbid Kate should be the subject of the latest gossip.

Stepping into the hallway, he called for Ah Tong and requested an early supper. Emotions drained, he collapsed on the sofa and sipped a beer, listening to his amah's clattering in the kitchen. Shame he had little appetite, but he had to give Ah Tong face and do honour to the meal.

The sweet and sour fish eaten, every bite an effort, he drew a bath. Lying back in the tub, he remembered the first time he'd met Kate. She was sitting in the cemetery, unaware he was watching her twirl her plaits like a little girl. Later he'd fallen in love with her sweet face, her amber eyes and irrepressible giggle. She'd been young for her age and he'd loved her innocence, probably the result of her sheltered upbringing. Kate was the apple of Henry Wolseley's eye, anyone could see that. And she reciprocated her father's adoration. If Charles were to cause a breach between them, it would affect Kate for the rest of her life. He couldn't do that to her.

***

The following evening, he drove towards the car ferry terminal through streets lined with four-storey buildings, their flimsy wooden balconies festooned with washing strung on bamboo poles. The poor of the city lived here in sub-standard housing. Most of the flats had no bathrooms, no toilets, no courtyards and only one kitchen for about twenty families. Far worse than Stanley. The apartments were divided into eight foot square cubicles shared by five or more people. Charles had experienced overcrowding, but this was on a much greater scale than in the internment camp.

Filthy pavements were lined with stalls selling everything from congee to cans of cola, and in between stretched the mats of the street sleepers - whole families who hadn't been able to find anywhere to live. He opened the window and reeled at the stink of human ordure, rotten fruit, decaying vegetables and cooking oil. Strident Cantonese voices filled the air - shouted conversations interspersed with the cries of the hawkers. Rain pummelled the roof of his car and ran down the windscreen. Charles wound up the window.

On the ferry he stayed in his MG. He thought about Kate, as Kowloon emerged from the mist with its hills and teeming tenements. Perhaps they shouldn't have made love, they weren't married yet, but it had been just how he'd dreamt it would be. When they'd melted into each other, he'd pulsed with such love for her he could have died at that moment and felt fulfilled.

Except he hadn't died, of course, and, hopefully, he and Kate would have a future together. He stared around him. Living here was like living in a human ant colony: people building, toiling, making, striving and always hoping for better days to come. Everyone wanted to accumulate wealth; it was the goal of every person, from the lowly street sleeper to those who were already rich but who had every intention of getting richer. Part of the Chinese character, and he didn't disapprove. Hong Kong was an amalgamation of east and west, just like he was. Charles sighed. How to break through Henry Wolseley's prejudice and be accepted as a suitable match for his daughter? The ferry was docking, and Charles started the car. There had to be a way, there just had to be . . .

'You've got too thin,' Auntie exclaimed, greeting him at the door of the house. Charles kissed her cheek as she dragged him over the threshold. She led him to a tray of *dim sum*. 'You eat,' she ordered. 'I'll go check on dinner.'

Uncle came into the room, dressed casually in an open-necked shirt. 'Good to see you, Charles. How're things?'

He talked about his current case, a family dispute about a Last Will and Testament (taking care not to reveal any names). Uncle listened and cracked sunflower seeds between his teeth. 'Seems you're already doing well. Isn't it time you married? In fact, your aunt and I have been looking out for you and we think we've found you the perfect wife.'

Surely his uncle wasn't being serious? 'Thank you,' Charles mumbled, his English side taking over. 'But I'll find my own wife, if you don't mind.'

Auntie returned with a tray of drinks and placed it on the coffee table. 'When do you have the time to meet the right girl? We'll invite a young lady we know, and her parents, to dinner.'

'Don't forget the Chinese are matchmakers and we're half-Chinese,' Uncle said. 'People with the same social status are expected to marry each other. If their families don't intervene, then how else can they meet?'

'Seems to me more like a business arrangement than finding a person you love,' Charles laughed.

'Love? Very romantic of you.' Uncle lit a cigarette. 'Believe me! It's much better to marry someone from the right background.'

'Actually, I've already met my future wife. Kate Wolseley.'

Uncle sat up straight and blew out a puff of smoke. He coughed. 'Who?'

'The girl we met at Stanley?' Auntie turned to Charles. 'She's not for the likes of you.'

'How can you say that? Excuse me for being blunt, but you're in a mixed marriage and so is Ma.'

'We're women. It's easier for a Chinese woman to marry a foreigner. But when I say easier, it wasn't that easy. Our family was against it.'

'The other way round is very rare,' Uncle said. 'Miss Wolseley will be shunned by her circle. You'll make her very unhappy.'

It was as he'd feared. They didn't understand. Hong Kong was changing and he and Kate would be at the forefront of that change. 'Don't worry! I know what I'm doing.'

Uncle shrugged. 'I certainly hope so.'

'Please can I introduce her to you properly?'

'We'll invite her to dinner,' Auntie said.

Charles grinned. Kate would knock them off their feet, he knew she would.

*** 

Two days later Charles waited with his relatives in the private room of a Kowloon restaurant. He hadn't seen

Kate since they'd made love, and he longed for her so much it was as if he'd been living in a vacuum. Their waiter placed a dish of appetizers on the table. Charles breathed in the aromas of ginger, garlic and sesame oil. The food would be good here; at the entrance he'd spied tanks full of fish swimming about in happy ignorance of their destiny. He couldn't wait to see Kate again. How would she get on with his uncle and aunt? And, more importantly, how would they get on with her?

The door swung open and in she walked. Her eyes sought his and she gave a tentative smile. Dressed in a pale blue cotton dress, nipped in at the waist with a full skirt, she looked stunning. Charles got to his feet and squeezed her fingers. 'Uncle, Aunt, this is Kate, my soul-mate.' He knew he was being corny, but couldn't help himself.

Formalities over, Kate sat down next to him. She beamed at Aunt Julie. 'I do like your *cheongsam*, Mrs Noble. I wish I could wear one myself, only I'm not sure I have the figure for it.'

'You're very slim, so should be no problem. I'll take you to my tailor.'

Charles clasped Kate's hand under the table. So far so good. Then Uncle butted in, 'What opinion does your father have about my nephew, Miss Wolseley?'

Kate blushed. 'What do you mean?'

'Uncle,' Charles said. 'Do you have to be so outspoken?'

'I'm sorry. I didn't mean to be rude. Just concerned for you both.'

'We're taking things slowly, Mr Noble,' Kate said. 'My father will come round to the idea of Charles and I being together eventually.'

'Do you really believe that? I know of no other Englishwoman involved with someone from our background.'

'Now, now, Phillip,' Aunt Julie said. 'Can't you see how in love these two are?'

Auntie was practically cooing, but Uncle's face had taken on a stern expression.

Kate smiled at him. 'Mr Noble, we're not rushing into anything.'

'I don't want Charles to get hurt.'

'Neither do I,' she said, firmly.

'Good.' Uncle rang the bell for their waiter. 'We'll discuss this no further. Let's enjoy our meal.'

'Thank God,' Charles said, keeping his voice neutral. 'I was beginning to think we'd never get anything to eat.' He'd been on the point of making his excuses and leaving the restaurant with Kate. This was supposed to be a social event, not an interrogation.

\*\*\*

The rest of the meal passed with no major hiccoughs, although it seemed that Uncle ordered specific dishes to test Kate's resilience: from braised chicken feet to noodles served with one thousand year-old eggs. However, she did Charles proud and tried everything, all the while speaking only when she was spoken to and smiling her sweet smile. He could see she was working her magic on his uncle, charming him into compliance. She already had Aunt Julie eating out of her hand. They'd arranged a shopping expedition to buy the right silk for a *cheongsam*. What would Henry Wolseley say when he saw his daughter dressed like a local? He'd probably have a fit. Charles chortled to himself, then sipped from his cup of Jasmine tea.

Dinner over, he stepped outside with his arm around Kate. A forest of neon signs lit up the night and crowds of people thronged the street, pushing past each other into the open doorways of shops selling Chinese medicines, jade, cameras, and linen. The clack-clack of abacuses totalling up sales echoed down the pavement. Most of the women shoppers were dressed in black: from their baggy cotton trousers to their high-necked jackets buttoned diagonally across their bodies. Charles knew from experience that they only dressed in bright colours on special occasions. He couldn't wait to see Kate in a *cheongsam*. Turning to her, he said, 'That didn't go too badly, did it?'

'Your aunt was lovely to me. But your uncle still needs convincing, I think.'

'Just his character, darling. He's always been cautious. Never does anything without giving it a lot of thought. He'll come round eventually. How could anyone not love you?'

She laughed and squeezed his arm. 'And you. We need to tell my father soon. I can't bear not seeing you every day. And I hate lying to him. He thinks I'm having dinner with James tonight.'

He kissed her. 'We'll tell him soon, I promise.' A bubble of jealousy. 'We can't have him thinking you're serious about James, can we?'

'You know I'm nothing of the sort,' she said, kissing him back.

Charles spotted a taxi and lifted his hand. 'Time to get you back to Hong Kong side, I suppose. I don't like the thought we'll have to part for the night. I'd give anything to wake up with you tomorrow morning.'

They settled into the back seat of the cab, and he put his arms around her. She snuggled against him then lifted her chin. His mouth came down on hers, love for her throbbing through him. Kate's lips parted and he kissed her deeply, his hands cupping her breasts. *God, how I want her.* She gave a soft moan, and he made himself pull away. 'We're behaving like a couple of adolescents not wanting their parents to find out what they're up to.' He stroked her cheek. 'One thing is certain, though. I can't go on like this much longer . . .'

# 33

Dressed in a halterneck top and shorts, Sofia stepped out of the sampan and paid the boatwoman. She'd accepted James' invitation to spend the day on his yacht. A whole day! *My first time seen in public with him.* She pushed away her worries about the Englishwoman.

Laden down with her picnic basket and swimming things, she clambered aboard *Jade* to be enfolded in James' warm embrace. The yacht putt-putted out of the harbour, its inboard engine just about coping with the swell. In Junk Bay, James unfurled the sails and the yacht bucked at a list. Sofia tossed back her hair, tasting the salt of the sea on her lips, and feeling the exhilaration of running with the wind.

They rounded the headland and tied up to a jetty in Joss House Bay. Here, it was calm and the air redolent with the odour of brine. She changed into her swimsuit in the miniscule cabin, then looked over the side of the boat. 'It's so clear you can see right down to the sand on the seabed,' she said.

She swam with James in the deserted cove, then climbed back onto the yacht, put on her shorts, and unpacked sandwiches while James opened two bottles of Tiger beer. 'Shall we go for a walk after lunch?' She would ask him about the Englishwoman later.

They ate in comfortable silence, rinsed their plates with seawater, and then stepped ashore. Cicadas screeched in the undergrowth as they strolled towards the temple at the base of the hill. The air was pungent with the stench of fish drying on rattan mats under the portals of the grey-walled, green-roof-tiled buildings. Mongrels sat in the shade scratching their fleas. Children gawked at them and called out, 'Hallo, bye-bye.'

In the cool of the darkened temple an old hag, with a few strands of grey hair scraped back in a bun, kow-towed before the altar with a statue of the goddess of the sea.

'That's Tin Hau. She protects fishermen and sailors.' Sofia pointed at the blackened face of the effigy and pulled at James' sleeve. 'We should pay our respects to her. Light joss-sticks, bow three times and she'll bring us good luck.'

James turned his head towards the Buddha-like image. 'I'd rather get out of here,' he whispered, his cheeks pale. 'This place is giving me the heebie-jeebies.'

He grabbed her hand and pulled her out into the sunshine. His fingers were ice-cold, even in this heat. 'I've got the distinct impression someone just walked over my grave.'

Back on the yacht she stretched out next to him. 'I'm curious,' he said after kissing her. 'What do you see in me?'

'I don't understand.'

'You're incredibly beautiful, Sofia, and I'm just an ordinary bloke.'

'I just seem exotic to you, that's all. I feel as though I've known you all my life. Maybe even in another life.'

'Do you believe in reincarnation?'

'I'm not sure . . . I definitely believe in the supernatural. You can't help but feel it in Hong Kong. The Chinese belief in ghosts is so strong.'

'Then you aren't a Buddhist?'

'No. My uncle is one, you could say, but he's a typical Chinese in that he is also a Taoist and follows Confucius.

And he venerates his ancestors and believes in all the different deities, just to be on the safe side and in spite of being a communist. I was brought up a Roman Catholic, because of my father.'

'That temple gave me the creeps.' James shuddered. 'The smell of the incense made me think of nothing but death.'

'Let me rub your back. You know how it soothes you.' Not a good moment to ask him about the Englishwoman.

***

It was two days later, and Sofia was working on the solo martial art forms she practised most afternoons in order to build up her flexibility. Her teacher had told her to train her form as if she were sparring and to spar as if it were a form. Sofia placed her hands on the carpet in her office and pushed herself to her feet. She blocked and punched the air, flowing with the movements and, as she did so, she imagined she was fighting Leo.

Uncle had finally let her in on his plan; it was a daring scheme, but it was also ingenious. Chun Ming and one of Uncle's associates would commit air piracy. Sofia couldn't wait to see Leo's face when he found out he'd been robbed. He wouldn't be able to find any proof to connect the deed with Uncle, even if he suspected it. Chun Ming would fade into obscurity, knowing he'd helped derail a nationalist, and Uncle's associate would leave for America to rally support for Mao.

It was time the Americans were told they'd backed the wrong horse. Chang Kai Shek was a war lord and his Kuomintang party so corrupt they would bleed sleaze if you pricked them. She remembered Uncle's attempt to bribe James last December. Uncle was an old rogue and many of his business practices suspect, but he loved China and knew the only way for it to prosper was through radical change.

Sofia went down to the shop floor. The heads of her workers bowed over the looms, the clamour of the machinery deafening. She walked alongside the rows of young women. They were here to earn a wage that might have been considered subsistence-level by some, but for these people it was a means of subsistence they wouldn't otherwise have. They deserved her respect and she should become more involved in their interests. She would put a stop to using the girls to work the looms at night. It might halve profits, but the practice had to end. If she set up sleeping facilities and ensured her workers were adequately fed, productivity would almost certainly improve.

Back in her office she dialled James' number. She needed to check he'd been given the go-ahead by Special Branch. And it was time she asked him about the Englishwoman.

They arranged to meet at their usual place - a quiet hotel on the road from Kowloon to the New Territories. She phoned for a taxi to pick her up, then took a shower.

James was waiting for her on the veranda skirting the back of the hotel. A clear view stretched towards Hong Kong Island - rivers and rivers of lights. A plane was coming in from the west, banking low before lining up for the runway at Kai Tak Airport. The warm evening air, rich with the perfume of frangipani, caressed her bare arms.

'I'd love to have dinner with you at the Parisian Grill one evening,' she said to James. 'I've heard the food is excellent.'

'I went there the other week, as a matter of fact.' He paused. 'Of course I'll take you.'

'Did you go alone?'

James glanced away, appearing to consider the question. He lifted his shoulders in a brief shrug. 'I met this girl, Kate Wolseley, who has all the right connections for me to make my way in Hong Kong.' His eyes searched hers and he gave a sheepish smile. 'I'd been hoping one of her father's friends would back me in an import-export business and I suppose I was using her. I'm ashamed of that now.'

'There is another way, you know. Import-export is too old-fashioned. The future is in manufacturing.' She thought for a moment. *Is it too soon to ask him? No.* 'I'd like to offer you a partnership in the factory.'

'Sofia, you don't have to do that.' He put his arms around her and nuzzled her ear, sending a wave of pleasure through her. 'I'm totally smitten with you and should have told you before now.'

'Totally smitten?'

'I mean I'm in love with you. Dare I believe you feel the same way about me?'

Her mouth too dry to speak, she wrapped her arms around his waist and hugged him. *James loves me, not the Englishwoman.*

He led her to their room. They undressed and she stretched out next to him on the cool sheets, the ceiling fans stirring the air around them. She touched him, bending over him so that her hair caressed his face. She kissed his eyelids and moved her mouth down his body, burying her fingers in his chest hair. Then she pressed her lips to his flat stomach.

She took him in her hand, feeling him grow until the size of him made her smile. She wanted the whole of him, every inch. She straddled him, and, once he was fully inside her, she moved slowly up and down.

'Ah, Sofia, what are you doing to me?'

'Shush, relax,' she said, her voice throaty. She kept her movements unhurried, and concentrated hard to contain her rising desire.

'Oh, yes,' he said, moving in time with her. 'Oh, yes!'

'My love,' she said, pushing down on him, rotating her pelvis, finally allowing her pleasure to build as James thrust back at her. Hot throbbing ripples of sensation, again and again and again. She collapsed next to him, spent.

'Darling, shall we call for room service? I'm hungry.'

'You little minx,' James said, laughing. 'You've had your wicked way with me and now all you can think about is food.'

'Didn't I please you?' she asked with a kiss to his chest.

'You more than pleased me,' he said, his hand cupping her chin. He traced his fingers over her mouth then down to her breasts.

With a giggle, she slapped his hand away. 'If I don't have supper soon I'll faint.' Much as she longed to repeat the love-making, she had to talk to him first.

They washed, dressed, and ate at a table in the corner of the room: steaming hot wonton soup, chicken with cashew nuts, and crispy noodles followed by pomelo and star fruit. Sofia sat back in her chair and watched James wipe his mouth with a linen napkin. 'Have you held your meeting with Special Branch yet?'

'They won't commit themselves to approving an actual robbery. I didn't think they would,' he said. 'However, provided everything goes according to plan and we get the gold off the plane before the police arrive, they won't pursue the matter.'

'And in return?'

'The names of the banks receiving the smuggled gold, as well as the details of your half-brother's contacts.'

'Uncle knows the banks and he already has the details of Leo's associates. He bribed Derek Higgins. As you know, Derek needs money.'

'Strange fellow. Bit of an enigma, don't you think?'

'Most definitely.' She stroked his hand. 'What shall we do now?'

'What would you like to do?' James leaned forward and kissed her lips.

'I'm serious about you becoming a partner in the factory,' she said, ignoring the heat rising between her thighs. Business first, pleasure later. 'We would make a great team.'

'But I don't know anything about cotton-spinning.'

'I'll teach you. We import raw cotton from Pakistan at the moment. You could help us secure suppliers in America and Mexico. It would mean travelling to those countries and making contacts. You'd be the right person for the job.'

'I might enjoy that. Who do you ship the yarn to?'

'Mainly Indonesia and Malaya. Uncle has family there. But markets in Asia are wide open, as much of Japan's textile industry has been bombed to smithereens. In fact, Uncle bought his looms from the Japanese. He told me it gave him a sense of satisfaction buying them from the defeated enemy.'

'How do you see the future of the factory?'

'Currently, we can only produce coarse yarn, because of Hong Kong's summer heat and humidity. I want to install air conditioning as soon as we can afford it and then conditions will be suitable to spin finer yarn. I'd like to move into weaving, dyeing and eventually garment manufacturing.'

'Sounds like you've got it all mapped out, sweetheart.'

Could she hope that she and James would have a future together? She sighed to herself. Only if everything went according to Uncle's plan and she could get away from Leo. *Leo*, she shuddered. *I won't think about him now.*

James carried her back to the bed. 'This time, let me do the work,' he said, sitting her down. 'Open your legs.'

Her first thought was, thank God she'd had a wash. Then, she couldn't think anymore, just feel, as his tongue explored her folds. And it was wonderful, so, so, wonderful. She couldn't stop coming, wave after wave, her pleasure as great as the ocean. He lifted his head and rolled her back. She parted her thighs for him, swallowing him into her until they were one. James and Sofia. The perfect partnership. She looked deep into his eyes while they rocked together. 'I love you, James.'

# 34

I had stepped onto the veranda to enjoy the evening view. Glancing at my watch; I realised it was time to get on with some marking and preparing tomorrow's lessons. I'd been distracting myself from my frustration at not seeing Charles by concentrating on my job. I'd even taken my pupils on a day-trip to the Children's Home, where they'd each given the orphans new toys donated by their parents. Every day, for the past week, I'd spoken at length with Charles on the phone, but only when Papa was out. Was Charles being too cautious? He was like his uncle in that respect. Maybe I should come right out and tell Papa myself . . .

I lowered my gaze towards Kowloon, then stepped back in surprise. Billows of black smoke were rising from a hillside and an orange glow lit up the sky. I ran indoors. 'It looks like one of the squatter camps is on fire,' I said to Papa, my hands flailing. 'We've got to help. Come on! Those poor, poor people.'

In the kitchen, I asked Ah Woo to find some food and fill as many vacuum flasks as he could with hot tea. Murmuring under his breath and clearly thinking his young missy had gone mad, he opened a cupboard and removed a large Dundee cake which he sliced into small pieces. Then he put some old teacups into a cardboard box.

I went back to the veranda. Papa was holding a pair of binoculars to his eyes. 'You aren't seriously thinking of going over there?'

'I've got to do something.'

'What can you do? Leave it to the authorities, dear girl!'

'It's George's day off. Can you give me a lift?'

'All right. All right. Hold on!'

Papa fetched his keys. I raided the linen cupboard for blankets, bundling them up and taking them to the car. Ah Woo carried baskets of flasks and food. Papa loaded everything into the boot. All three of us got into the Daimler and set off down the Peak. 'Can't you go a bit faster?'

'These hairpin bends are too dangerous for speed. Be patient!'

We took the car ferry across the harbour, then drove until we arrived at a road block. 'I'm a doctor,' I lied to the Chinese policeman at the barricade. 'Please let me through!'

There was nowhere to park, so Ah Woo and I left Papa with the car. Thousands of people, evacuated from the inferno, were sitting on the streets. The air was bitter with the acrid stench of burning rubber and textiles. Flakes of ash floated down; some of them still glowed red from the flames. A fire engine, its hose attached to a street hydrant, sprayed water in a high arc that hardly seemed to make any difference.

I ran backwards and forwards to the car with Ah Woo, distributing blankets, slices of cake, and tea to the shocked refugees. A young woman sat on the kerb, clutching a small child to her breast. Silent tears squeezed from her eyes. Her husband cradled their other child, a baby, and made soothing sounds. I went up to them with a thermos flask and a china cup. They took the tea from me, and nodded their thanks.

I went back to Papa, Ah Woo at my heels. 'It seems as if everyone got out, thank God.'

'Good. Can we go home now? I'm missing a concert on the wireless.'

'Is that all you can think about? Haven't you got any conscience?'

'Of course I have, but I'm realistic as well. This mess isn't of our making. I've said it before and I'll say it again. Let the authorities handle it, dear girl!'

'I can't stand by and watch. I've got to help these people. Surely, there must be something I can do?'

'You could start a charity, I suppose,' Papa said, shaking his head. 'Involve Jessica! She's good at organising things. Remember the amateur dramatics in the camp?'

A vision of Mama tripping the boards flashed into my mind, and I swallowed my guilt. One day I'd visit Mama's grave. But only when I was ready. The memories were still too painful. I stared at the thin white scars on the backs of my hands . . .

\*\*\*

The Ladies' Recreation Club sprawled down the side of the Peak at the mid-levels: a clubhouse, tennis courts and a couple of swimming pools. A waiter showed me to a table in the corner.

Jessica came through the door and took the chair opposite. She delved into her handbag for her cigarette case. 'I'm not late, am I?'

'No. I'm early. Shall we order straight away?'

'Definitely. I could eat a horse.'

'I hope not.' I let out a laugh. 'I'd never eat horse meat.'

'Ever since Stanley my stomach always seems to be crying out for food.' Jessica flicked open her lighter and lit a cigarette. 'Thankfully, I've managed to keep my figure in spite of becoming a complete glutton.'

The waiter took our orders - steak for Jessica and fillet

of sole for me. Jessica moved to sit on the edge of her chair. 'So, you want to set up a charity to help the refugees?'

'I thought we could begin by organising a ball at the Peninsula Hotel. We could sell the tickets above the odds and get people to donate prizes for a raffle. It's not much, but it would be a start.'

'And it'll be fun.'

We chatted about setting up the charity until our food arrived, then went on to discuss my teaching job and work at the orphanage.

'And here I am, living a life of leisure,' Jessica said. 'Tony and I have been trying to start a family, but no go I'm afraid. Seems semi-starvation has buggered up my baby works.'

'I'm so sorry,' I said, shocked.

'There's a specialist in London I plan to visit next year. Now, tell me! I'm dying to know. Why aren't you seeing James anymore?'

I stiffened. 'What a question!'

'Tony heard it from James himself. He was a bit concerned, as he bumped into him with the daughter of Paulo Rodrigues on the Ferry the other day. Then James told Tony he wanted to resign from Holden's Wharf and help the girl expand her cotton spinning business.'

I gripped the table cloth. 'I wondered why he hasn't phoned recently. I thought it was because I was giving him the cold-shoulder.'

'And why did you do that? As if I can't guess ...'

'Charles Pearce, of course.'

'I hope you know what you're doing, Kate. Crossing over the cultural gap is a huge step.'

'That's why we're keeping it secret from Papa until the time is right. Promise me you won't tell him!'

'Of course not. I'm on your side, as a matter of fact. Charles is a charming young man. I sat next to him at dinner the other week, remember? And he can certainly

241

dance. Actually, he doesn't even look terribly Chinese. If I didn't know, I'd say he was Mexican . . .'

*Just the sort of thing Jessica would say but kindly meant, I suppose.*

In the taxi on the way back to the Peak, I wound down the window and let the night air blow through my hair. I slumped back in my seat. It wasn't that I wanted to be with James, but I envied him and Sofia managing to be together in spite of their different backgrounds. I straightened my back and set my jaw. How to resolve the problem of Papa? Jessica had said during lunch that he would be a tough nut to crack. It was true; he was set in his old-fashioned ways. What I needed was a catalyst. Something to jolt him into the twentieth century. *Perhaps I should pack my bags and leave. But where would I go?* The Helena May had a waiting list as long as a train and I'd searched for a flat, but hadn't been able to find anything. I slumped back in my seat again.

# 35

Sofia lay in the cabin of her uncle's launch. The nausea had subsided, but she'd spent the two hours since they'd left Kowloon going to and from the heads and vomiting. She ran a jerky hand through her hair. It had to be some kind of tummy bug. She swung her feet slowly to the floor and went up to the bridge.

'I don't know what came over me,' she said to James. 'I'm feeling a lot better now.'

'That's good.' He put his arm around her and kissed the top of her head. 'I was worried about you. You still look a bit pale, though.'

'I'll be all right once I've eaten something.' She kissed the pulse beneath his ear. 'Come down to the lower deck for some lunch. The plane won't be here for a while yet.'

At the stern of the launch she sipped a soda water and munched on a cream cracker. They were motoring past Siu A Chau, the northernmost of the dozen or so islands making up the Soko group south of Lan Tau - Hong Kong's largest island. She eyed crystal-white sands and lush green vegetation rising up to a small hill. Supposedly there was a hamlet hidden there somewhere, but otherwise the place was uninhabited. A small shrine nestled by the shore, painted bright red, and rocks at the far end stood up like ninepins.

The Catalina seaplane would touch down between Siu A Chau and Tai A Chau, the largest of the Sokos, just within the colony's territorial waters. She glanced upwards and caught sight of Lantau Peak - a broad cone to the north.

Once they'd put masks on to conceal their identities, she and James would secure the Catalina and its prisoners with the help of Chun Ming and Uncle's pilot, Wing Yan. Then they'd pick up the gold and head back to Kowloon by way of the dumbbell-shaped island of Cheung Chau, where it had been arranged for them to leave Uncle's men in a safe house. The Marine Police would be tipped off by Special Branch as soon as the plane took off. By the time their boats arrived, Sofia and the others would be long gone.

Staring at the island across the short stretch of sea before them, she said to James, 'Have you heard the story of Cheung Po-tsai, the famous pirate?'

'Can't say that I have.'

'According to legend, he had a fleet of over one thousand war-junks equipped with cannon and over ten thousand men at his command.'

'How long ago was that?'

'The last decades of the eighteenth and beginning of the nineteenth century. Apparently, he had an English concubine and he lived with her in a sumptuously furnished cavern on Cheung Chau.'

'Strange he should meet an Englishwoman in those days.'

'She fell in love with him after he'd captured a British clipper and held her for ransom.'

'Just like I've fallen in love with you.'

'I'm not a pirate,' she said, laughing.

'Ah, but your uncle is. This whole malarkey smacks of piracy, in my opinion.'

Ignoring his remark, she pointed ahead. 'They say the Englishwoman's grave is on that island.'

\*\*\*

After they'd eaten, she went back to the bridge with James. The rumble of an engine, and she shaded her eyes. The seaplane had levelled out over Lantau, but instead of starting its descent, it was tossing from one side to the other. Sofia clapped her hands to her cheeks. It had overshot its intended landing spot. *Holy Mother of God!* The plane had gone into a nosedive.

James swung around. 'What the hell?'

In the distance, the Catalina plunged into the sea.

'Oh no!' Sofia felt sick again.

'Bugger!' James grabbed the charts, hung onto the table, and ran a finger down the map. 'She's ditched about ten miles away, I reckon,' he said, his voice a pitch higher than usual. 'We must go there straight away.'

They approached the crash site at high speed. Within minutes, it seemed, although it probably took longer, they spotted jetsam bobbing on top of the waves. Sofia looked around for the plane. Nothing. Suitcases floated on the surface and coldness spread through her.

James caught hold of her arm. 'Look!'

She followed his gaze and there was someone, a man, clutching a piece of wreckage.

James grabbed a lifebuoy and threw it to the man. Sofia went to fetch a blanket while James and the boat-boy lifted the survivor onto the deck.

Chun Ming lay stretched out, his face white and heavily bruised; he was shaking and his leg dangled limply - obviously badly broken. 'What happened?' Sofia wrapped the blanket around him, but he stared at her as if he had no idea who she was.

James made radio contact with Gerry Watkins. Sofia listened to the brief conversation, trembling. 'Fair enough,'

James said to Watkins. 'We'll take him to Queen Mary Hospital.'

'He's washed his hands of the matter,' James said, pacing the deck. 'We're off the hook because of the deal with your uncle. But the plane has crashed, and the police are in the know, so Chun Ming will be investigated. There's no chance of recovering the gold, I'm afraid.'

Sofia cradled Chun Ming's head in her lap. She didn't care about the gold. All she could think about was the plane's final moments as it went down, taking everyone on board but Chun Ming with it.

*\*\**

Two days later, Sofia stood by the foot of Chun Ming's hospital bed. He was sleeping, his face serene against the white of the sheets. His pyjamas had been buttoned up wrongly and she longed to re-button them, but she didn't want to disturb him. His leg was in a pulley and covered in bandages. She sat down on the chair by his bedside.

He opened his eyes and smiled weakly.

A Chinese nurse, a wisp of black hair poking out from her cap, busied around arranging the red gladioli Sofia had brought. After plumping up Chun Ming's pillows and helping him take a sip of water, the nurse left the room.

Sofia took hold of Chun Ming's hand. 'How do you feel?'

His face wore a pained expression. 'I'll be all right.'

'What happened?'

'I can't remember much.'

'Do you think you can piece things together if I prompt you?'

'I'll try.' Chun Ming grimaced. 'Well, a few minutes after take-off, I think it was, Wing Yan put a gun to the pilot's head. He demanded the controls, but the pilot refused.'

'What happened next?'

'Let me think . . .' Chun Ming stared at the opposite wall for what seemed like an age, his forehead wrinkling. 'I know. I ordered the co-pilot and Derek Higgins, who was carrying the gold for your half-brother, and the other passengers to move to the side of the cabin so I could cover them with my gun.'

'And then what?'

'The plane hit a patch of turbulence and Higgins drew his own gun.'

'Did he fire it?'

'No. Higgins lunged at Wing Yan, who lost his balance. Both guns went off and a bullet hit the pilot in the back of the neck.'

'How terrible!'

'The pilot's body fell forward onto the flight controls. The plane veered left, then right, and then nose-dived. Everyone was screaming and I managed to jump out the door just before we hit the sea.'

'There's no easy way to tell you this, Chun Ming, but you've got to know.' Sofia leaned forward. 'There's a policeman outside this room. Now that you've regained consciousness, he will want to interview you.'

'Why?'

'They knew about the robbery and they've recovered the pilot's body.'

'I didn't shoot him.'

'I know. But you're the only survivor.'

'I'm sorry about those who died. I never expected this outcome.'

'I'm sorry too about them all, even Derek Higgins.' She glanced down at the bed sheet.

'I agree. He was very unpleasant, but I didn't want him to die.'

'Uncle will send some money to his parents,' Sofia said, patting Chung Ming's hand. 'He has great respect for family.' *As if that will make it all right!*

'What about the factory?'

'You're not to worry about that. The main thing is you will get better. We'll find you a good lawyer. In fact, I don't think that policeman can interrogate you until you have one.'

A trolley rattled past the door and she stood up. 'I must go, but I'll be back tomorrow.'

She picked up her handbag. Two Chinese women were coming into the room. The Englishwoman, the one she'd seen with James, followed them.

'Li! Ma!' Chun Ming called out.

'Hello. I'm Kate Wolseley.' The Englishwoman smiled at Sofia. 'Chun Ming and I grew up together.'

Sofia took a step back and touched her throat. Dizziness spread through her. She grabbed hold of the side of the chair. Her legs folded beneath her and she slipped to the floor.

# 36

I took a taxi to the Ferry. The cymbals and high-pitched song of Cantonese opera were playing on the radio and the cab stank of stale cigarette smoke. Outside, though, Hong Kong shimmered in shades of green and blue. The humid clouds of summer had given way to the lucidity that only happened at this time of the year, when it truly became a place of mountains, sea and sky. But the sound of pile drivers echoed in the air. Such a shame that so many hills were being bulldozed down to fill in parts of the harbour and make room for unrelenting construction work.

Poor Sofia. I'd rushed forward to catch hold of her and help her to sit on a chair when she'd nearly fainted. Her face was greyish and perspiration shone on her forehead. Ah Ho grabbed a glass and filled it from the water jug on Chun Ming's bedside table. Sofia resolutely refused to see a doctor. What an incredibly beautiful woman she was, with her thick dark-brown hair and large grey oriental eyes, not to mention an almost perfect figure (perhaps her chest was a bit flat). No wonder James had fallen for her . . .

I was furious with him. Between them, Chun Ming and Sofia had told me the whole story. James should have persuaded K C Leung to find another way to repay Leo

Rodrigues. People had died as a result of Leung's so-called ruse.

Leaning back, I shut my eyes. Charles had responded to my call from the hospital's reception desk with a swift agreement to meet me at the Peninsula Hotel. If anyone could help Jimmy, Charles would be that person. He said he had a client to see in Kowloon beforehand. That suited me fine; I'd combine meeting Charles with confirming the final details of the ball, which was due to take place the day before my twenty-third birthday.

I found a seat on the top deck of the ferry in the covered central section. The sides were open to the view and a sampan floated past with an old man holding a fishing line, his long grey goatee flapping in the breeze. All around us vessels weaved and crossed, passed and turned, like a pool of carp in a feeding frenzy.

On Kowloon side, as everyone always called it, I walked for five minutes until I arrived at the Peninsula. It was here that the Governor had surrendered to the Japanese on Christmas Day, 1941. Japanese officers had occupied the hotel, which became their headquarters. Now it was "the finest hotel east of Suez" again. A sudden sensation of loss spread through me; Mama used to bring me here and treat me to a milkshake sometimes after school.

A fountain played in the forecourt and I climbed the steps, glancing upwards at the horseshoe-shaped structure. Two bellboys in white uniforms opened the double doors. I crossed the marble floor to the manager's office, where I confirmed the menu for the ball and made sure all the arrangements were in place.

Thanking the manager, I stepped into the lobby. A string quartet on the corner balcony was playing *Greensleeves*. There was Charles in an armchair at a table across the room. I drank in the sight of him: his broad shoulders, lean body and long legs. He looked up and smiled his wonderful smile, making my pulse race.

Last week we'd gone to the pictures together and had seen the film *Easter Parade,* starring Judy Garland and Fred Astaire, but that had been the only time we'd managed a date since dinner with Charles' relatives. I'd loved the Irving Berlin soundtrack and had been humming *Stepping out with My Baby* so much I'd been driving my school colleagues mad. In the cinema, Charles and I had kissed in the darkness. He'd held me in his arms and I'd felt the hardness of his chest against my breasts. How I longed to make love with him again ...

The clink of cutlery mixed with the murmur of conversation as Charles pulled out a chair and gave me a peck on the cheek. 'How wonderful to see you, darling,' he said. He signalled the bow-tied waiter. 'Indian, Earl Grey or Jasmine tea?'

'Indian, please.'

Charles gave our order. Then he placed the tips of his fingers together. 'Tell me, my love, why did you want to see me so urgently? Purely business, you said. What business?'

'The Catalina sea plane.'

A frown creased his forehead. 'What's that got to do with you?'

'Not me. My old amah's son.'

I explained about my hospital visit and we both expressed surprise that Derek Higgins had also been involved in the catastrophe. 'It would mean so much if you could help,' I said. 'Not just to me. Ah Ho must be worried sick about Chun Ming.'

A bicycle bell rang, as one of the pageboys walked past us, holding a small blackboard aloft to page someone. Charles leant forward. 'Where did you say the plane went down?'

'Beyond the Soko Islands.'

'Have the police interviewed Chun Ming yet?'

'No. They'll wait until you can be there.'

'Good. I'll get my secretary to make the arrangements.'

Our waiter arrived and placed a silver tray on the table, laden with a typical English afternoon tea: wafer-thin sandwiches, sponge cake and scones. I lifted the silver teapot and poured.

Charles offered me a cucumber sandwich then took one for himself. 'Tell me more about James' involvement.'

'Sofia said he was working secretly for Special Branch. Apparently, James brokered a deal with Leung for information about local banks smuggling the Consortium's gold into Hong Kong.' I sipped my tea. 'Leung also provided details of a new group of Triads from China who are setting up here. In return, Special Branch agreed to let him get away with the robbery.'

'Right. That will make it easier. Special Branch won't want this to get out.'

I crumpled my linen napkin, stiff with starch. Charles was looking at me intensely, bathing me in the warmth of his regard. 'Jessica and I are organising a charity ball here to coincide with the Mid-Autumn Festival next week,' I said. 'Would you like to buy a ticket? It's Fancy Dress and the theme is China.'

'Why not? What are you wearing?'

'The *cheongsam* I'm having made. I'm going as Madam Chiang Kai Shek. I bought the material with your aunt yesterday.'

'So glad you two are getting on. Auntie will convince Uncle, you'll see. He always comes round to her way of seeing things in the end.'

We lapsed into silence while Charles ate his way through all the cake and sandwiches. Putting my napkin down, I pushed back my chair. 'Well, I'd better be off. I took an afternoon's leave of absence from school to visit Chun Ming, and my headmistress will be cross if she gets reports that I've been seen having tea at the Pen. Are you going back to Hong Kong side now?'

'Yes, my love, I'll take the Ferry with you.'

I held his hand and we walked past the bus station to

the concourse. I didn't care if any of Papa's chums saw us, and Charles didn't seem to mind either. A stiff breeze was blowing and I held onto my hat with my other hand. We went through the turnstile then up the ramp to the ferry.

'Did you know a tropical cyclone is headed our way?' Charles said. 'The Royal Observatory has launched typhoon signal number one. I've heard the storm won't be here for a couple of days, but do take care, my darling.'

'I wondered why it has turned so windy. Don't worry, I'll be safe on the Peak. Papa has perfected the art of organising typhoon shutters.' A sudden thought occurred to me. 'I've just had a brilliant idea. We can tell Papa you're helping Jimmy, I mean Chun Ming. That will be a perfectly legitimate excuse for us to see each other. Then, once he gets used to you being around, we'll inform him we're in love.'

A doubtful expression crossed Charles' face. 'Something tells me it isn't going to be that simple.'

'Well, have you got a better plan?'

'No,' he said, taking my face in his hands and kissing me.

'Good. I'll tell Papa about you helping us.'

# 37

Charles dialled Kate's number. He wanted to fill her in on developments in Chun Ming's case, but her houseboy answered the phone and said she'd gone to the Children's Home in the New Territories. Apparently, she went every Sunday.

Charles put down the phone. Why hadn't Kate told him that's what she did on her day off? It was a marvellous thing for her to do. Except, it was so like her not to tell him; she wouldn't want him to think she was boasting. They'd spoken only yesterday and she'd said her father hadn't batted an eyelid when she'd explained he was helping Chun Ming. Charles was under no illusions, however. Expatriates and locals always worked well together as far as business was concerned. It was only in their personal lives that they didn't mix.

The wireless blared from the kitchen. Yesterday, typhoon signal number three had gone up and winds had strengthened throughout the day, but by early this morning it seemed the storm had turned away. Charles glanced out of the window; the trees were bending in an alarming fashion. A news flash came on and he jumped to his feet. The typhoon had turned around and was heading straight for Hong Kong!

Wendy, as the storm was known, was expected to pass near the colony late that afternoon at the same time as the predicted high tide. There were fears of a tidal wave in Tolo Harbour.

*Good God! That's close to the Children's Home . . .*

Charles grabbed his car keys, ran downstairs and jumped into his MG. The wind whipped the trees by the side of the road and sent rubbish flying up into the air, buffeting his small car. He had to use all his strength to keep it on the road.

At the Ferry a policeman stopped him. The boats had all gone to the typhoon shelters. He wouldn't be able to get across.

Charles drove frantically round to the back of the Hong Kong Club, found a space, reversed into it, and ran to the pier.

There was a man in a walla walla motorboat, his craft cresting the waves like a roller-coaster. 'You wan' go Kowloon side?'

'How much?'

'Fifty dollar!'

'Too much!'

'Fifty dollar!'

Charles looked around; there weren't any other boats. He climbed down the ladder and jumped into the vessel. Warm rain drenching him, he sat next to the boatman and held on for dear life as the walla walla jerked, plunged, and pitched its way across the harbour.

On Kowloon side Charles clambered ashore, found a phone booth, and dialled the Wolseleys' number. Henry answered.

'I'm on my way to the New Territories,' Charles said. 'Have you heard from Kate?'

'I can't get through to the orphanage. The phone lines must be down. Very grateful to you if you'd check on my daughter.'

'I'll try my best.'

'Just make sure she's all right!'

Charles got into the back of the only cab prepared to take him to Sha Tin. Rain sheeted horizontally across the road, broken glass flew in the air and shop signs swayed. The streets, normally crowded with people, were eerily empty.

Half an hour later, the taxi skirted the edge of the rising waters and pulled up outside the gates of the orphanage. Charles paid the driver. The man told him he lived locally and was heading home anyway, but that didn't stop him from charging thirty dollars.

Charles ran up the steep driveway to the front door. It was swinging on its hinges. A corridor spanned the front of the building and he went into the first room, a dining room with long tables down the centre and a smell of burnt rice. No one. Next he strode into a sitting room boasting chintz-covered sofas and rattan armchairs. Empty. Three children's dormitories with unmade beds made up the rest of the rooms. Where was Kate? There was a door at the end of the corridor, and he pushed it open.

There she was, in a large schoolroom, mopping up rainwater that had come in through the shuttered windows. She stared at him. 'What are you doing here?'

'God, Kate! Why didn't you tell me this is what you do with your time?'

'Well, now you're here, you can help,' she said with a wry smile. 'Sorry I'm not more welcoming, but I'm exhausted.' She handed him the mop, and waved towards a frizzy-haired European woman sitting with a group of children in the dry patch at the far end of the room. 'Miss Denning, this is Charles. Looks like he's come to give us a hand.'

'Good. You stay here with the little ones, Kate, and I'll go and find Mary. I think she's with the amahs and the older children.'

Charles gazed out through a crack in the shutters. The fields below, a short time ago sodden with water, were now completely submerged. People had moved up to the green-tiled roofs of the nearby walled village, clutching their possessions; some had even carried up pigs, chickens and dogs. The orphanage was on a hill, but it was a small one. Would the waters reach them here?

He mopped up as much as he could, then went over to Kate; she was sitting with a small girl on her lap.

'Who's this?'

'Mei Ling.' Kate kissed the girl on the cheek.

He lowered himself to sit cross-legged next to her. The child regarded him suspiciously. 'I don't suppose she sees many men,' he said, unable to keep the emotion from his voice. He really admired Kate for what she was doing, but couldn't find the words to say so in front of the children.

'Why don't you read Mei Ling a story? She likes *The Three Little Pigs*.'

Gradually, the child's eyes lost their mistrustful look. Charles enjoyed reading to her; it reminded him of the times he'd read to Ruth when she was Mei Ling's age. The girl's eyelids closed and she drifted off to sleep.

Outside, the wind bellowed and rattled the windows. What was happening to those poor people in the village below? He couldn't bear to think. And what would happen to them if the sea rose further?

'You didn't explain why you came here,' Kate whispered.

'I wanted to tell you that Chun Ming will be sent back to China when his leg is out of plaster. He won't stand trial in Hong Kong.'

'Good!'

'Yesterday I spoke to the senior partner in my firm and he confirmed my belief that, because the plane came down in Chinese waters, the colony won't have jurisdiction. I contacted James Stevens, and he got in touch with Special Branch. I found out he'd done the deal this morning.'

'I wonder what will happen to Chun Ming when he's in China . . .'

'He'll probably receive a hero's welcome from the communists. They're poised to take Canton and he's an ardent party member. Also, he fought with them during the occupation, didn't he?'

'Of course. That should make it easier for him.'

'When I interviewed him yesterday morning, he told me he knew Fei, the fierce young man I met at the end of the war who got me through Japanese lines. I was glad to have been of help to Chun Ming, my love. I don't condone what he did, though. It was misguided to say the least.'

'What did James have to say for himself?'

'Nothing much. I got the impression he didn't want to talk about it.'

*\*\**

In the late afternoon, the wind died down and the rain abated. There was nothing more he and Kate could do here, as Miss Denning had returned and taken charge. They said goodbye to the children and walked down the slope towards the village. Kate cried out in dismay at the devastation: debris everywhere, people wailing and frantically digging in the wreckage as they searched for their loved ones, torn-up vegetation strewn across the road, a large fishing junk tossed up on the land. Dead animals floated on the receding waters, and the shanty town he'd seen by the main road had been reduced to splintered planks of wood. It was incredible that so much damage could have happened in such a short time. Charles put his arm around Kate and she burrowed into his shoulder, sobbing.

Sirens shrilled and three fire engines arrived, followed by five ambulances and a police car. There was little he and Kate could do to help, other than comfort the grieving. In the early evening, Charles found a taxi and took Kate to the Ferry. She was silent throughout the journey, her face pale with apparent shock and tiredness. They arrived on Hong Kong side, and he walked with her to his car.

'Thank you for getting Chun Ming off, my darling,' Kate said. 'I don't mean to sound ungrateful, but you could have waited to tell me tomorrow, couldn't you?'

'I was worried about you. Also, when I phoned your father to find out if he'd heard from you, he asked me to make sure you were all right.'

'Then please come in for a drink when we get to my place.'

\*\*\*

A gardener was sweeping up leaves, and repositioning flowerpots at the edge of the driveway. Charles parked to the side, steering clear of a couple of amahs taking down the typhoon shutters.

'This is quite a house,' he said.

Kate led him through the front door. 'I suppose it *is* a bit big for the two of us. I'm longing to get away, but you know how difficult it is to find somewhere. You were lucky to have your uncle's contacts to get your flat, weren't you?'

She was right; he would have found it impossible if Uncle Phillip hadn't been a friend of his landlord. Waiting lists for accommodation were notoriously long.

In the sitting room, Henry Wolseley got up from his armchair and held out his hand to Charles. 'Dashed grateful to you.' Henry went up to Kate and hugged her. 'Bally typhoon. Wasn't supposed to change course like that. Are you all right?'

'We're fine,' Kate said. 'But lots of other people aren't, I'm afraid. We could do with a drink.'

'Of course.' Henry rang a hand bell. 'Where's Ah Woo? Ah! There he is.'

Charles asked for a San Miguel and Kate a brandy soda.

Their drinks arrived, and Kate led him to the veranda to admire the view. The typhoon had cleared the air and, from this height, it was possible to see the mountains of China on the distant horizon behind the Kowloon hills.

'You'll stay for supper, won't you?'

'As long as your father doesn't mind.'

'Of course he won't mind. He thinks we're just friends. Friends have supper together, don't they?'

'We should be able to tell him we're more than friends soon, my darling. Your plan might just work . . .'

# 38

Sofia unlocked the front door of Father's villa (she'd never think of it as Leo's) and strode across the tiled hall to the sideboard. She rang for the houseboy. 'Is my brother home?'

'Yes, missy.'

'Please tell him I'm here.'

Within seconds, Balthazar at his heels, Leo stood in front of her and folded his arms. 'What can I do for you?'

'I'm very well thank you, how are you?'

'Sarcasm will get you nowhere,' Leo said, his mouth turning up at one corner. 'Why are you here?'

'I have your money.' She handed him an envelope containing a banker's draft.

'How did you manage that?' Leo slid out the cheque. 'You haven't received your inheritance yet.'

'I went to the biggest bank in Hong Kong and they were quite happy to lend me the money, secured on the factory and its machinery.' James had helped organise the loan once his partnership in the business had been confirmed.

'Fair enough. You win, little sister. For now.'

'Here are my house keys. I'm leaving Macau for good

so I won't need them anymore.'

Leo frowned. 'Tell your uncle I know he was involved with the seaplane catastrophe. Someone has talked. Leung had better watch his back.'

'What are you on about?'

'I think you know perfectly well.'

'I know nothing of the sort. And there is no way you can connect my uncle with that tragedy.'

'He was seen with a man known to have trained as a pilot in the Philippines.'

'You're just making this up, Leo.'

'The Consortium has lost nearly thirty thousand American dollars. That's a lot of money by any reckoning, over one hundred and forty thousand Hong Kong dollars in fact. Strangely enough, roughly similar in value to your bank draft.'

'Only a coincidence. I'll go upstairs now and pack the last of my things.'

*Dratted Leo. He's too clever by far. Too, too clever.*

\*\*\*

Sofia took the afternoon steamer. Whenever she left Macau for the bright lights of the British colony, it was as if she were being jolted from the nineteenth into the twentieth century. In Macau, time seemed to have stood still and nothing had changed in decades. Many of the buildings in the beautiful old terraces were crumbling into decay, and the whole place had a feeling of decadence. She was glad to be on this ship, with her trunk of clothes in the hold and her jewellery in a bag by her side. Finally, she was getting away from Leo and everything to do with him.

Apparently, Derek Higgins had been able to manufacture fire-crackers in Macau, whereas in Hong Kong factory regulations would have made his methods impossible. Derek's workers had caught terrible illnesses by inhaling poisonous vapours. Some had even blown themselves up. No questions had ever been asked by the authorities. People had done the work because they'd been desperate for employment. They would find other, healthier jobs now, hopefully. She wasn't sorry Derek's body hadn't been found. He'd been a shark and he'd ended up a shark's dinner, for sure.

As for Leo, no doubt he'd continue his trajectory to become the most powerful man in Macau. Almost certainly, he would be running the place in a few years' time. She was well out of it. If she'd stayed he would have involved her in no end of shady dealings; it was the way he operated.

Her future lay with the factory. She and James would develop it into a profitable, legitimate business together. She had to build security. Not just for herself, but for her child. She was pregnant; she'd found out from her doctor yesterday, although she'd suspected it since nearly fainting at the hospital. After each lovemaking session with James, she'd douched with Chinese herbs, the advice she'd read in one of Uncle's books. Not the right advice, as it had turned out . . .

Sofia looked out of the porthole. The colour of the sea had changed from muddy to turquoise blue, so they must have left the Pearl River Estuary. Soon, they passed Lantau Island and entered Hong Kong's Victoria Harbour. Here was her future. Here was James, the man she loved. Here she would bring up their child.

***

She passed through immigration. James was waiting for her. She went up to him, her heartbeat quickening. How would he react when she told him about the baby? When would she tell him? He came up and took her hand luggage. 'Where's this trunk you warned me about?'

'Over there.' She pointed.

'Good thing I organised a lorry, then,' he said, laughing.

'It's enormous.'

They clambered into the front cab, and the vehicle made its way to the car ferry. Crossing the harbour, they got out and stood on the foredeck.

James hooked his arm around her waist. 'How did things go when you paid off Leo?'

'He's not stupid, you know.' She leaned against him. 'He suspects Uncle set up the robbery. He can't prove it, but we need to be aware we have a dangerous enemy.'

'How far does his influence extend? Surely not to Hong Kong?'

'He's only a big fish in the small pond of Macau. But, don't forget he has connections with the Triads here.'

'I haven't forgotten. I'll make sure Special Branch keep me informed if they hear anything. What news of Chun Ming?'

'The only people who know of his involvement are us, his family, Kate Wolseley and Charles Pearce. Let's hope it stays that way. If Leo gets wind of his participation in the robbery, it'll be difficult to keep him safe. I wonder if we can get him back to China before his leg is out of plaster . . '

'I'll have a word with Gerry Watkins.'

They returned to the lorry and disembarked. After twenty minutes they arrived at their hotel, the one they always used. Only this time they'd booked a suite to tide them over until they found a flat. James had given up his lodgings in Kowloon Tong when he'd resigned from Holden's Wharf.

James took off his shoes and stretched out on the bed cover. She sat next to him and took his hand. 'There's something I need to tell you.'

'Oh,' he said with a frown. 'Something good or something bad?'

'Something good. At least, I think it is.'

'Well, then, tell me.'

'I'm pregnant,' she said, meeting his gaze.

A smile spread across his face. 'Are you sure?'

'I saw my doctor yesterday. You'll be a father next April.'

'Sweetheart, that's wonderful. I was going to do this in a more romantic setting, but there's no time like the present, as they say.'

'What were you going to do?'

'Ask you to marry me. Will you, Sofia? You'll make me the happiest man alive.'

'Yes. Oh, yes,' she said, her heart singing.

'We can get a special license. Do it as soon as possible to avoid any scandal. You know what this place is like.'

She lay next to him. 'It will be scandalous enough you marrying me without the extra gossip about when our baby was conceived.'

He held out his arms. 'I love you, Sofia Rodrigues, and I'll love you as long as I live.'

'I love you too, James. In this life and the next.'

# 39

I was looking for some scissors. Spread out on my desk were the pictures painted by my class of eight-year-olds; I wanted to cut them out and paste them onto a frieze. I'd searched everywhere in my bedroom; I must have left the wretched things at school. *How annoying!* I ran downstairs to Papa's study and leafed through the papers on the top of the desk. Nothing.

I checked the top drawer. No luck.

Then I tried the bottom one. Locked.

*Is it worth all this bother for a pair of scissors? One last try . . .*

I opened the top drawer again. A key was sticking out from under Papa's writing folder. I picked it up and inserted it in the bottom drawer.

*Success!*

I slid open the drawer and rummaged through it. *Why aren't there any damn scissors here, for heaven's sake?* I'd have to try the kitchen. As I began to shut the drawer, I caught sight of envelopes tied up in string.

Sucking in a quick breath, I picked them up and peered at the post-marks. London. I flicked through ten letters sent between October 1945 and October 1946. Someone had scribbled out our address on the Peak and had forwarded them to Sydney.

*Charles' handwriting. I'd know it anywhere.*

I struggled with the knot, fingers shaking. Eventually it loosened and the letters spilled out onto the desk. I picked them up and stared at them, one by one. Hands trembling, I opened the first envelope and started to read.

*Dearest Kate*

*I miss you so much, and the past eighteen months have been such hell . . .*

\*\*\*

How could Papa have kept them from me all these years? Didn't he realise how unhappy I'd been? With heavy arms, I dragged myself up the stairs and flung myself onto the bed, clutching the envelopes to my chest. The front door slammed and I rushed downstairs. Papa had already sat in his armchair, lit his pipe, and unfurled his newspaper. 'My goodness, you look as if your feathers have been well and truly ruffled, dear girl.'

'I've found Charles' letters.' I lifted my chin. 'That was a bit remiss of you, don't you think? It would have been safer to have destroyed them.'

Papa was silent for a moment. 'Would have been against the law,' he said, sucking on his pipe and putting down *The South China Morning Post.*

'And not giving them to me wasn't?'

'I would have given them to you eventually. When you'd settled down with a proper chap.'

'And Charles Pearce isn't a "proper chap"? Is that it? How could you?' I curled my lip. 'You let me think he was dead.'

'I believed there could be no future for the two of you in Hong Kong. I didn't want my daughter excluded by society and made unhappy. Time is a huge healer. I thought you'd forget all about him.'

'What a horrible cliché! In any case, time hasn't healed

anything,' I spat. 'You broke my heart and I'd be grateful if you no longer interfered in my life.'

I turned on my heel and bounded back up to my room. Determinedly ignoring Papa knocking on the door, I read through the other nine letters. Charles wrote about how he'd started a law degree at King's College. He described his course and his fellow students, his life in London and how Ruth and his parents were getting on. Each letter pleaded for a response until the final one stated he would no longer be writing; it was clearly a useless exercise.

The knocking continued. 'I'm sorry,' Papa said. 'It was wrong of me. Can you forgive me?'

'It's not just me who needs to forgive you. Charles and I are in love. If you won't accept that then I'm afraid you'll lose me. The truth is, I can't live without him.'

\*\*\*

'Can you do up my buttons, please?' I asked Ah Ho. She'd come back to work for us after Chun Ming and his wife had left for China yesterday. My amah and I were in the room I'd taken for the night at the Peninsula Hotel, and I was putting on my dress – the *cheongsam* I'd had made at Aunt Julie's tailor's.

'*Aiyah!* Missy, you very beautiful,' Ah Ho said, smiling her gold-toothed smile.

I glanced down at my figure: the green silk clung to my breasts, my stomach and my hips. 'Ah Ho, what are you calling me missy for? I'm Katie.'

'Now you grown up, you missy,' Ah Ho huffed, folding her arms.

'I'm sorry,' I said, giving myself a mental kick for making her lose face.

I stole a glance at Ah Ho: her hair was thinning more than ever and there were new wrinkles in her cheeks. The worry about Chun Ming had aged her. Of course Ah Ho would visit her son in China, but she was probably missing him already. It must have been a huge wrench seeing him off at the train station. Everything had happened so quickly. One minute he was in the hospital and the next he was leaving, still on crutches, Li by his side. I'd got there just in time to say goodbye.

Ah Ho fastened my last button. I looked down at myself again and blushed; I should have asked the tailor not to make the slits up the side of my legs so high.

A knock at the door. I slipped on my mask and stared at the apparition in the doorway. Jessica's face was heavily made up with white powder, thick black eyebrows and ruby red lips; a black wig covered her hair. 'What a marvellous Empress of China you make, Jessica!'

'How did you know it was me?'

'The masks only cover our eyes. It will be easy to recognise people, won't it?'

'Just a bit of fun. And we'll be taking them off before supper, won't we? Come on! Time to get the show on the road, as they say.'

I hugged my amah. 'Thank you for helping me, Ah Ho. George will take you home now.'

I picked up my evening-bag and made sure my dance card, lipstick and powder were inside. Then I followed Jessica down the corridor to the lift where Tony, dressed as the Emperor of China, was waiting.

All the way down to the mezzanine floor, I worried. What if we didn't sell enough raffle tickets? And what about Charles? Tonight I would tell him my father had hidden his letters. He'd been right all along . . .

\*\*\*

The ballroom, capable of seating eight hundred guests, overlooked the harbour. Pillars with Corinthian capitals lined the doors onto what was called the roof terrace. (Not the top of the multi-storey building, but the roof over the hotel's entrance.) I walked across the parquet floor, glistening after its daily polish, and glanced up at the slightly domed ceiling, painted rain-washed blue. On a podium at the far end, members of the Filipino swing band I'd arranged were tuning their instruments. I checked the table numbers and verified the names of the guests at each table, making sure Charles and I were placed together with Sofia and James. I'd put Papa at the grandees' table, with Jessica and Tony, the Governor, the *Taipans* of the trading companies and their wives. Everything was ready and, within minutes, people began filing in through the double doors.

'Isn't that Charles?' Jessica pointed towards a tall man next to the bar, he was dressed as an ancient Chinese warrior, knee high boots and leather armour. My heart skipped a beat; I quickly glanced around at the other guests. There were James and Sofia, in People's Liberation Army uniforms (how on earth?), standing slightly apart from everyone else.

I went up to them. 'I'm so glad you could come,' I said, squeezing Sofia's hand. 'Let's get ourselves something to drink then we should fill in our dance cards.'

'Already done,' James said. 'I'm not having my fiancée dance with anyone else.'

I made an effort to stop my mouth from falling open; I didn't succeed. 'Congratulations!' I embraced them both. 'When's the happy day?'

'Pretty soon, actually,' James grinned. 'Needs must, as they say.'

I stood back and stared at him. What did he mean? Realisation dawned and I smiled. 'Then let me congratulate you again.'

'We were wondering if you and Charles would be witnesses at the civil service,' James said. 'We've managed to get a special license.'

'I'd be delighted. But you'll have to ask Charles yourself.'

'Ask me what?' Charles said, coming up and shaking

hands with James.

'We're tying the knot. Kate has said she'll be a witness. We'd be honoured if you'd agree to be one as well.'

'With great pleasure. The City Hall, I presume?'

'Ten in the morning next Saturday.' James signalled a passing waiter carrying a tray of champagne cocktails.

I took a glass and lifted it to my lips, my eyes meeting Charles'. 'Have you got any space on your dance card?' he asked.

'I've only pencilled in Tony and my father.'

'Please may I have the honour of dancing with you for all the others? That dress is far too enticing.'

'Well, my darling, I can't dance every dance, you know. I have to make sure our volunteers go round and sell all the tickets for the raffles. And I have to sell some myself.'

'Then let me help you.'

*\*\*\**

During supper Tony performed his role as Master of Ceremonies with aplomb, making the draws for the donated prizes between each course. The meal seemed to go on forever, but money had poured in and there would be enough to begin funding a children's clinic in one of the squatter areas. It was a small start, but a good one.

Papa, dressed as a Mandarin, joined Tony on the podium. 'Ladies and Gentlemen,' he said. 'I would like to propose a toast to my dear daughter, Kate, whose birthday it is tomorrow, and who has organised this marvellous ball with the help of Jessica Chambers. And thank-you to all who've donated prizes. You've been hugely generous and I'm sure you'll agree a splendid time has been had by everyone. Raise your glasses! To Kate and to Jessica!'

There was a resounding cheer and my cheeks burned. Charles came up. 'This is my dance, I think. The last waltz.'

He twirled me closer and closer to the double doors

until we were standing on the roof terrace - alone the two of us. Then he kissed me. I felt as if I was swimming underwater as the kiss went on and on and on: delicious, sweet, tender and utterly perfect.

'It's midnight. Happy Birthday, darling Kate.'

'Thank you.' I took a deep breath. 'There's something I have to tell you.' The sound of a ship's horn reverberated in the distance, and I stared at the neon lights reflecting in the harbour. I steeled myself. 'I found your letters. My father seems to have "forgotten" to give them to me.'

'What!' Charles frowned. 'He was almost civil when I had supper with you the other night, and I'd started to think the letters had simply got lost.'

'He'll apologise to you in person. It was very wrong of him. I told him that I loved you and wanted to be with you, come what may. He blathered on about how difficult my life would be and I said I didn't care.'

'I hope I haven't caused a rift between you,' Charles said, putting his arms around me again.

'Papa always spoiled me when I was a child.' I rubbed my cheek against the leather armour of Charles' costume. 'It was as if he had to make up for Mama being the way she was, unable to show affection.' I breathed in Charles' citrus scent. 'Papa seemed genuinely sorry about the letters. He loves me and wants me to be happy. Only now does he understand how much my happiness is tied to you.'

'And mine to you,' Charles said, kissing me again. 'And mine to you.'

I kissed him back, drowning in him, melting with love and desire for him. He cupped my breasts and a zing went through me as my nipples hardened. Then footsteps sounded; another couple had come onto the terrace. I shook myself and took Charles' hand. 'Let's see how James and Sofia are getting on,' I said, leading him back into the ballroom. 'Everyone seems to be giving them the cold shoulder.'

# 40

James woke early on his first Monday as a married man. He glanced at Sofia, sleeping peacefully next to him, her luxurious hair spread over the pillow. He wrapped a tendril around his finger and lifted it to his lips, inhaling the vanilla scent of the *Shalimar* perfume she used. God, he was lucky. To think he'd once been ashamed to be seen with her. All because he'd wanted to fit in. He didn't need to fit in with the expatriates. He didn't give a flying fuck about the majority of them. He didn't need anyone or anything but his darling wife.

Sofia stretched and yawned. 'What time is it?'

'Time to get up and go to work. It's the tenth of October, the Double Tenth, don't forget. The nationalists will be celebrating the anniversary of the end of imperial rule. We need to establish our presence at the factory.'

'Are you expecting any trouble?'

'We did have a spot of bother after Mao declared his Republic ten days ago, and our workers flew their flags with communist slogans. They upset the right-wingers next door.'

'Why didn't you tell me this before?'

'I've got the situation fully under control.'

'Are you sure?'

'On Friday, one of the girls told me she'd seen a flag with the slogan *Long Live the Chinese Republic* flying across the road. Don't worry! I promptly told the right-wingers there to take it down. The wording was too political, I said, and it would stir up trouble with those who'd been celebrating the foundation of the People's Republic. I said it was inappropriate for a British colony.'

'I hope you haven't made things worse,' Sofia said, pouring him a coffee from the tray by their bed.

'Most of the locals have no interest whatsoever in politics. Their allegiances are more a way of affirming they belong to a specific community. There's absolutely nothing to worry about, sweetheart.'

'If you say so, James,' she said. But from her expression and lack of a smile, she appeared unconvinced. Unease spread through him.

\*\*\*

They arrived at the factory, and James made a tour of the floor. The young single women, the bulk of their labour force, were sitting in rows bent over their looms. They were paid at piece rather than time-rate, so it was in their interests to get on with their work.

He went to the office and helped Sofia with the correspondence - letters to cotton suppliers in the United States and Mexico.

The phone rang and Sofia picked up the receiver. She was speaking Chinese, her tone agitated. She put down the receiver. 'That was my uncle. There's a rumour you've told the nationalists not to celebrate.'

'Not true at all. I just didn't want them to provoke the communists.'

Another shrill from the telephone, and Sofia picked up again. She passed the receiver to James.

It was Special Branch. 'Gerry. What can I do for you?'

274

'Word is the Triads are agitating the nationalists next door to your factory. The police are sending backup for you.'

Shouts, and James went to the window. Below, a crowd of men and women were milling around yelling slogans. His breath caught. 'Come downstairs,' he said to Sofia. 'We'd better make sure all the doors are locked.'

They rushed to the factory entrance. Too late. The mob was forcing its way inside. The women who worked on the looms cowered on the floor, their arms over their heads.

James' ears pounded. If only he'd learnt to speak Cantonese, he would tell the rabble a thing or two. 'This is outrageous,' he shouted. 'Go away! You've got no business to be here.'

Pure hatred shone on their faces. A young woman, black hair in a pigtail, bared her teeth. A burly bald man screamed his rage, spittle flying, the whites of his eyes blazing. The group pushed and shoved their way towards James. He raised his fists to fight them off. More people came up from behind.

Someone grabbed him and tied his hands behind his back. The mob pushed him down on the floor, and he struggled against the bindings. A skinny young man slapped him on the face, unleashing a stream of foul language; that much he understood. He fought against the cords. The youth slapped him again, harder. Blood trickled from the corner of his mouth.

More rioters burst through the doors and hurled Molotov cocktails into the air. Explosions went off all over the factory. The looms caught fire. The first group appeared distracted by what was going on. Keeping his eye on them, James inched his way over to where Sofia had curled into a ball by the wall. He had to protect her and their child.

He threw himself over her, covering her body with his. Something struck him below his mouth. A sharp pain pierced his neck. Then he was falling, falling, falling into the darkness . . .

# 41

Sofia opened her eyes; there was blood everywhere. Blood covered her face, her arms and her chest.

*Holy Mary, Mother of God!*

James lay slumped to the side, a gurgling sound coming from him.

*Sweet Jesus!*

A glass shard stuck out of his neck. Blood spurted from the wound.

*Please God, let him be all right!*

Hands shaking, she pulled off her blouse and clasped it around the glass. Must stem the flow. Her fingers were cold... so, so cold. James' eyes were closed and his face had gone white. She looked around for help. The rioters had already run off.

*Cowards!*

Smoke billowed from the looms. The factory girls were still cowering with their arms over their heads. The sound of sirens, and her teeth chattered uncontrollably.

Four policemen burst through the door - a European and three Chinese. The *gwailo* came up and lifted James' wrist, then shook his head slowly. Sofia sat back and let out a keening wail.

'No no no!'

The policeman barked orders to his men to help the girls leave the factory. He handed Sofia his jacket, then lifted James. She glanced down; she was only wearing her bra. She quickly covered herself.

'We have to leave the building,' the policeman said. 'The fire's taking hold, but we've radioed for assistance. Where's the cotton stored? That stuff is extremely flammable.'

The policeman's words seemed to be coming from the end of a long tunnel. What was he asking her? She couldn't think . . .

Outside, a crowd had gathered and the policemen were setting up a safety cordon. Sofia staggered to the pavement.

*Where was James?*

More sirens. An ambulance and two fire engines pulled up. Sofia stared around. She couldn't see James. 'Where's my husband?' she cried out, clutching at her blood-stained skirt.

A nurse draped a blanket around her shoulders, led her to the ambulance, and sat her down. Then she went to a water boiler and came back to Sofia with a cup of hot sweet tea. Sofia swallowed the warm liquid and her tears, frozen until then, gushed freely. She cried for the brave man who'd died saving her and their child. She cried for a life cut short in its prime. She cried for her baby who wouldn't know its father. And she cried for herself.

The nurse spoke to her in Cantonese and patted her back. Sofia sobbed until she had no tears left. Lifting her chin, she could see the stretcher at the side of the ambulance holding a body wrapped in a sheet. James.

'We'll take you to Kowloon Hospital,' the nurse said. 'When the doctor has examined you, you'll need somewhere to rest and someone to look after you. Do you have anyone who can take care of you while you get over the shock?'

Sofia thought for a moment. Uncle? She would phone him from the hospital, but she wouldn't go to his flat. He'd installed his mistress there and she wouldn't be welcome. And some of this was Uncle's fault. If James hadn't got involved with him, he'd still be alive. Guilt flooded through her; James had died because he loved her, not because of Uncle.

There was only one person Sofia could call on. A most unlikely person, but something told her that person would comfort her and make her feel safe.

\*\*\*

It was early evening by the time she rang the bell at Kate's home. She'd gone back to the hotel to change and had cried again when she'd caught sight of James' comb by the side of the basin, with a few of his hairs still in it. She'd lain on his side of the bed and had hugged his pillow, which still had the scent of *Old Spice*. If she'd stayed there she'd have gone mad.

A servant opened the gate and ushered her into the Wolseleys' sitting room. Within minutes, Kate was by her side. 'I'm so relieved to see you,' Kate said, leading her to the sofa and sitting her down. 'I heard the news on the radio and I've been trying to find out how to locate you. Please stay here. My father and I rattle around in this big old place. I'm so sorry, Sofia. I can't begin to imagine what you must be going through.'

'What about your father? Won't he mind?'

'Leave him to me. He's out tonight at a dinner party, so it's just the two of us. You don't have to talk if you don't want to. Oh dear, I didn't mean to make you cry. Here, have my handkerchief . . .'

Sofia described the assault on the factory, and Kate listened quietly. Then she told Kate about the hospital. Kate asked about the baby, and she said her child wasn't in any danger. She was grateful Kate didn't question her about her future plans. She needed time to think. In the meantime, she was secure in this sumptuous mansion. Leo wouldn't be able to get at her here.

\*\*\*

Two days later Sofia stood in the visitation room of the funeral parlour. James was laid out in front of her. Had he known, at that last moment of consciousness, he was going to die? One life given for two saved. James wouldn't have thought twice.

Tears streaming, she shivered in the air-conditioned atmosphere. It was freezing, of course; it needed to be. No stinking corpses in this sanitary place. She took her gloves from her handbag, but they made little difference.

James was covered in a white silk sheet that had been pulled up to his ears, to hide his mortal wound and the signs of an autopsy carried out under police orders. His fine-looking face was almost unscathed, just a small cut above the left eye. The glass shard from the Molotov cocktail had shattered on his chin and had severed the jugular vein in his neck. She reached down and touched his icy cheek, kissed him on the forehead, and whispered, 'Goodbye, my one and only love.'

It was hard to shake off the feeling of unreality. How could this be James lying there? James had been so full of life, so wonderful and so, so gallant. How could fate have dealt him such a blow? It wasn't fair. He was in his mid-twenties - far too young to die.

The Wolseleys' driver took her to the Victoria business district. The Daimler meandered through the usual motley collection of trams, cars and rickshaws and pulled up outside Alexandra House. She got out and rode up to the fifth floor in the lift, then strode down the hallway. The receptionist showed her to a meeting room where Charles Pearce, James' recently appointed solicitor, was waiting for her.

'It's really quite simple,' Charles said. 'James has left you his stake in Leung's Textiles and all his chattels. He has also willed you his yacht, *Jade Princess*.'

Everything was exactly as he'd said it would be when Uncle had handed over his shares in the business. Could it only have been last month? All had been done according to the book; she would have security for herself and the child.

'I've started the insurance claim,' Charles said. 'Thankfully, the fire brigade managed to save the building. It's just the looms that need replacing.'

'Thank you.'

'Did you see the newspapers this morning? The Government is launching a full investigation.' He picked up the paper and read, '*It is clear that the tragedy isn't attributable primarily to the crowd excitement which might have been engendered by the Double Tenth celebrations. The attack was clearly fomented by criminals.*'

'My half-brother is linked to the Triads, you know. I strongly suspect him of being behind James' death, but I won't be able to prove it.'

'The police will find out something that can be proved, surely?'

'I wouldn't count on it. Leo is very clever. He'll have covered his tracks.'

'You know him better than anyone, of course.'

'And I hope I'll be able to live in peace from him.'

\*\*\*

James' funeral was held the next day at St John's Cathedral; the church was almost full. Dressed in black with a veil over her face, she sat next to Uncle and Kate. James' catafalque appeared, covered in white orchids, with Tony Chambers, Arnaud de Montreuil, Charles Pearce and Henry Wolseley walking alongside. Everyone got to their feet and the men placed James' coffin before the altar.

Sofia stood as straight as a reed, her head upright, keeping a tight rein on her emotions. She wouldn't let her grief show; if she did, she wouldn't be able to control herself. She could feel James' spirit watching her; he would know how she felt as he lingered between this world and the next. She wanted him to be proud of her.

It was cool in the church, the air stirred by fans attached to long poles hanging from the ceiling. Their whirring almost drowned out the sound of the traffic, changing gear to climb the steep road outside. She looked up at the stained glass windows that had replaced those removed by the Japanese during the war. The window in the east showed Christ on the cross with his mother and Mary gazing up at him, placed there as a memorial to those who had suffered during the occupation and to those who had given their lives.

Everyone got to their feet and she picked up her hymn book. *The Lord's my shepherd, I'll not want*; she joined in, clasping the back of the pew in front of her. The singing finished. Sofia kneeled and prayed. She was out of practice and could only think of the Lord's Prayer. The service continued, and she went through the mechanical responses she'd practised in her childhood; they came back to her like an often-repeated rhyme, the Anglican Service remarkably like the Roman Catholic, although the latter had usually been in Latin.

The dean said a prayer of farewell, entrusting James to God. 'We will now proceed in cortege to Happy Valley.'

An hour later, Sofia stood in front of the group of people gathered around the open grave. She'd deliberately distanced herself from Kate and Charles. This was her cross to bear and she'd do so with dignity. James' spirit was fading into the next world now; she could sense it.

The dean's cassock swayed gently in the breeze. 'We therefore commit James' body to the ground, earth to earth, ashes to ashes, dust to dust, in the sure and certain hope of the Resurrection to eternal life.'

Sofia stuffed the corner of her handkerchief into her mouth to stop herself from wailing.

\*\*\*

The next day, she visited the factory and surveyed the destruction. Her workforce was sweeping up the mess made by the damaged looms. The girls came up and commiserated with her.

In the office she sat in front of her desk and determination surged through her. She would build the business up again as a memorial to James. Leo would have to hand over her inheritance next week, and she would use some of it to buy a flat. She couldn't presume on the Wolseleys any longer, nor did she want to; she valued her independence.

Kate had battled her father to let her stay with them, reminding him she was James' wife and he couldn't turn his back on her. Mr Wolseley had been stiff and resistant at first, but he'd mellowed as the days had gone by and now it seemed he couldn't do enough for her. As for Kate, Sofia had come to realise the Englishwoman had an inner strength that would help her overcome the obstacles to her happiness. It was obvious Kate and Charles belonged together, and the sooner Henry Wolseley got used to the idea the better.

# 42

I hugged Sofia. 'I'll miss you terribly,' I said. And I would. I'd grown really fond of her. 'Make sure you keep in touch.'

'I will.' Sofia got into her taxi. 'You must come and visit soon.' Through her uncle's connections, Sofia had managed to find a flat in the mid-levels. She'd told me that she would apply for a British passport as soon as possible. Her marriage to James meant that she could claim nationality. She wanted to sever all ties with her family in Macau.

As I stepped into the hall, the telephone shrilled. I picked up the receiver.

'How do you fancy a spin out to Stanley?' Charles said. 'It's a beautiful day.'

I still hadn't visited the cemetery; I'd told Charles at James' funeral that I hadn't been able to face it, and he'd squeezed my hand in sympathy. 'I don't know if I'm ready to go back there yet.'

'I think it's time. Come on, darling. It will do you good.'

I changed into a pair of navy slacks and a white linen blouse, then went to tell Papa where I was going. He looked up at me as I stepped into his study. 'Charles is driving me to Stanley,' I said. 'I'll take some flowers for Mama's grave.'

'Would you, my dear? The ones I put there last week will need replacing, and it will save me having to do it tomorrow. Your young man is turning out to be a pleasant surprise, I must say. A very pleasant surprise.'

'So he's a proper chap after all, is he?'

Papa had the grace to look flustered. 'His handling of Jimmy's debacle and the way he brought you home after the typhoon certainly impressed me. And I apologised to him about the letters, didn't I?'

Papa had invited Charles for dinner last week, just the two of them. I wished I could have been a fly on the wall. Neither of them had told me much about what they'd said, other than the fact that Papa had agreed that I could see Charles openly.

'Thank you for that, and for making Sofia so welcome in the end. I don't know what she would have done otherwise.'

Papa cleared his throat. 'Nonsense! I like Sofia. She'll go far, mark my words!'

\*\*\*

The nearer we drove to Stanley, the more my nerves jangled. Charles was right, though, I had to do this; I'd bottled it up too long.

'I know what you're thinking, my love,' Charles said. 'You're strong enough. Believe me.'

He parked in front of a small temple on the other side of the village.

'What are we doing here?' I asked, surprised.

Charles led me up a small flight of steps to the portal. Inside, it was cool and dark. Incense perfumed the air and, in the dull light of myriad joss sticks, a glass pane shimmered on the far wall. 'Come closer!'

'How bizarre!' Behind the glass was a tiger skin. I read the notice fixed to the left, *This tiger weighed two hundred and forty pounds and was seventy-three inches long and three feet high. It was shot by an Indian policeman in front of Stanley police station in the year of nineteen forty-two.*

'I wonder why it's here . . .'

Charles held me close. 'Well, I think this is a fitting resting place, don't you?'

'Yes, I do.' I glanced at the blackened face of the statue of Tin Hau, in an alcove behind offerings of fruit. There were fresh flowers on an altar in the centre of the temple. It had been good to come here. The tiger had brought me closer to Charles in Stanley. And the beast was working its enchantment on me even now. 'I'm ready. Let's go to the cemetery!'

Charles drove through the village, past the police station and the school, and parked below the path leading up to the graveyard.

I reached for the bouquet of purple orchids and my rucksack on the back seat. We went up a flight of newly-built steps with grassy slopes on either side. Mama's grave was at the top. The roughly-hewn headstone had been replaced by a proper marble plinth.

Kneeling, I removed the dried-out chrysanthemums from the vase at the base, then filled it with water from the bottle I'd stashed in my bag. I put my hand on the cool stone and whispered, 'I'm here. I haven't forgotten you. I'm so sorry I haven't come before now.' I looked up and caught Charles watching me, love in his eyes. Getting to my feet, I dusted down my slacks. 'Let's pay our respects to Bob.'

A line of headstones with the names of those whose final resting place was unknown had been placed here after the war. Beyond, we found Bob's grave and bowed our heads. I remembered the last time I'd seen him. There was a question I'd been meaning to ask Charles.

'Did the Japanese torture you when you were in the

prison?'

'No,' he said quietly. 'But I heard screams. Those poor policemen . . .'

I took his hand. 'Thank you for bringing me here, my darling. It hasn't been as bad as I thought.'

'They say we should always confront our fears, don't they? Look! There's our orchid tree. It's still here. Shall we sit for a bit?'

We sat side by side. Charles put his arms around me, and I lifted my face to receive his kiss. The rich, heady fragrance of the Bauhinia flowers filled my nostrils. I plucked a heart-shaped leaf and crushed it between my fingers.

'I love you so much, Kate,' he said, looking into my eyes. 'What happened to James has made me realise we have to take every chance of happiness we're given. Who knows how much time we have left?'

I studied the headstones and nodded. Then I gazed at his face. His hair was in his eyes. I reached up and brushed it back. 'When we're married. And only if you agree, of course, I'd like us to adopt Mei Ling. Oh, and I want Ah Ho to come and work for us.'

'Is that a proposal, Kate?'

'Yes.'

'Then, I accept.' He stroked my cheek, his fingers warm against my skin.

He kissed me again, more possessively this time, and I met his passion with my own. It had always been Charles. Ever him. Since the first moment I saw him. I thought about James and Sofia. Charles was right, we had to take every chance of happiness we were given, but also pay it back tenfold. 'And Mei Ling?'

'She can be the first of our children.'

'How many shall we have?'

'That's entirely up to you. As many as you like, and of course Ah Ho can be their amah.'

The leaves of the orchid tree sighed in the breeze. I

rested my head on his shoulder, twirled my jade bangle, and contemplated the sampans at anchor in the bay below.

# AUTHOR'S NOTE

I was privileged to have grown up in Hong Kong during the post-war era, and I hope that my personal experience of a time and place which no longer exist has lent an authenticity to my writing. *The Orchid* Tree is, however, a work of fiction. All the characters are products of my imagination. My mother had an amah, Ah Ho, who looked after me when I was a child; I loved her dearly, but the Ah Ho of my novel is simply inspired by her.

My grandparents, Doris and Vernon Walker, were interned in Stanley. I remember my grandmother telling me Ah Ho's first words to her on liberation, which I have used in *The Orchid Tree*. Gran and Grandpa didn't like to talk about their harrowing time in the camp. Like Flora with Henry, Doris was caught nursing Vernon during a bout of TB when the Japanese attacked. My mother, Veronica, had been evacuated to Australia. From the age of 14 to 18 she learnt to cope without her parents, an experience which affected her for the rest of her life.

When my grandparents were finally liberated, they were so thin they resembled walking skeletons, and both died relatively young due to post-starvation-related illnesses. Their lives were similar to Henry and Flora's, in that they lived on the Peak in a house with nine servants and shared some of the colonial attitudes of my expatriate characters, however that's as far as the similarities go.

Family stories did inspire parts of *The Orchid Tree*. My father, Douglas Bland, was an officer in The Chinese Maritime Customs from 1946 to 1948, making charts and chasing smugglers up and down the South China Coast. He told me of an incident when a young man had been tied to a junk, and also about a bribery attempt. James and Sofia's story is not that of my parents, however. Dad was a businessman and a prominent Hong Kong artist; I have used one of his paintings on this book cover.

Mum was a teacher like Kate, and shared some of her physical characteristics, but that's all. I wanted to take a girl from my mother's background, and have her fall in love with a man whom my grandparents would have considered unsuitable. Hong Kong today is a different place to the old colony, and mixed-marriages have become commonplace. I like to think Kate and Charles would have been at the forefront of that change.

As I said, this is not a family history; it's a romance. All the locations in my story are real, however, as are the events which took place in Stanley. I have used George Wright Nooth's involvement with smuggling chocolate fortified with vitamins into the prison as a reason for Charles to fall under the suspicion of the Japanese.

A ship, *Lisbon Maru*, taking POWs to Japan was sunk by the Americans, but that happened in 1942 not 1945. I have also taken the liberty of bringing forward in time the violence in Tsuen Wan, caused by escalating tensions between pro-Nationalist and pro-Communist factions. There wasn't a Typhoon Wendy in Hong Kong in 1949; I have based my typhoon on the notorious Typhoon Wanda.

The Children's Home is inspired by Miss Dibden's Shatin Babies' Home. James' hapless dragon boat race is taken from the first competition between expatriates and locals, recounted by Denis Bray. James and Sofia's dinner on the floating restaurant was inspired by the one in *A Many Splendoured Thing*. And K C Leung's attempt to steal Leo's gold was based on the world's first air piracy, an attempted skyjack that went disastrously wrong in Hong Kong on 16th July 1948.

With respect to the spelling of Chinese names, I've used the orthography that was current in the 1940s. My title, *The Orchid Tree*, not only is a feature of the novel, but also another name for the *Bauhinia blakeana*, which originated in Hong Kong. Since the handover of the ex-colony to China in 1997, the flower has appeared on the territory's flag and coins. The place of my birth, Hong Kong will forever be my home.

The following books have provided me with inspiration and information:

Alan Birch &Martin Cole, *Captive Christmas*
Martin Booth, *Golden Boy*
Denis Bray, *Hong Kong Metamorphosis*
Christopher Briggs, *The Sea Gate*
Jean Gittins, *Stanley: Behind Barbed Wire*
Vicky Lee, *Being Eurasian*
Tim Luard, *Escape from Hong Kong*
F.D. Ommanney, *Fragrant Harbour*
Gwen Priestwood, *Through Japanese Barbed Wire*
Han Suyin, *A Many Splendoured Thing*
George WrightNooth, *Prisoner of the Turnip Heads*

I hope you have enjoyed reading *The Orchid Tree* as much as I enjoyed writing it. Your feedback is important to me and I would love to know what you thought of Kate, Charles, Sofia and James. You can connect with me on Twitter @siobhandaiko or by email info@fragrantpublishing.com.

Lightning Source UK Ltd.
Milton Keynes UK
UKHW01f0623121018
330430UK00001B/279/P

# THOMAS COOK
## *Travellers*

# GREECE

BY
ROBIN GAULDIE

**AA**

Produced by AA Publishing

**Written by** Robin Gauldie

**Original photography by** Terry Harris

Edited, designed and produced by AA Publishing.
© The Automobile Association 1995.
Maps © The Automobile Association 1995.

Distributed in the United Kingdom by AA Publishing, Norfolk
House, Priestley Road, Basingstoke, Hampshire RG24 9NY.

A CIP catalogue record for this book is available from the
British Library.

ISBN 0 7495 0951 1

Published by AA Publishing (a trading name of Automobile Association
Developments Limited, whose registered office is Norfolk House,
Priestley Road, Basingstoke, Hampshire RG24 9NY. Registered number
1878835) and the Thomas Cook Group Ltd.

Colour separation: BTB Colour Reproduction, Whitchurch, Hampshire.

Printed by: Edicoes ASA, Oporto, Portugal.

Cover picture: Temple of Poseidon, Akra Soúnion (Cape Soúnion)
Title page: Greek Orthodox priest
Above: Metéora

# Contents

# About this Book

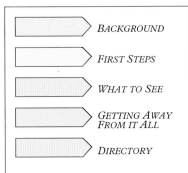

> BACKGROUND

> FIRST STEPS

> WHAT TO SEE

> GETTING AWAY
> FROM IT ALL

> DIRECTORY

This book is divided into five sections,
identified by the above colour coding.

The **Background** gives an introduction
to Greece – its history, geography,
politics and culture.
**First Steps** offers practical advice on
getting to grips with the language and
customs of the country and getting
around.

**What to See** is an alphabetical listing of
places to visit, interspersed with walks
and tours.
**Getting Away From it All** highlights
places off the beaten track where it is
possible to relax and enjoy peace and
quiet.
Finally, the **Directory** provides practical
information – from shopping and
entertainment to children and sport,
including a section on business matters.
Special highly illustrated *features* on
specific aspects of Greece appear
throughout the book.

### Mapping
The maps in this book use internationally
recognised country abbreviations:
AL Albania  BG Bulgaria  TR Turkey

Donkeys and mules still play an important part
in the life of many rural communities

# BACKGROUND

*Other countries may offer you discoveries
in manners or lore or landscape; Greece offers you
something harder – the discovery of yourself.*

LAWRENCE DURRELL
*Prospero's Cell* (1937)

# Introduction

$G$reece is where the distant past and the vital present meet; a land of big cities and empty hillsides, snow-capped peaks and sandy beaches, ancient temples and busy summer holiday resorts. No other European country has such deep cultural roots, tapping into more than 4,000 years of Hellenic history – and few other European countries offer such a variety of things to do and places to see.

Apart from its ancient archaeological sites, mainland Greece offers some of the last wilderness areas and uncrowded beaches in Europe, many of them unknown to the millions who visit the Greek islands each year.

Though most Greeks have abandoned their colourful traditional costumes, the country's folklore still comes to life during the many summer festivals and saints' days, when Greeks celebrate with feasting, music and dancing.

Life is lived outdoors most of the year, and there is nothing to beat sitting

## LOCATOR

Fishing boats at Astakos

# MAINLAND GREECE

at a shady harbour-side table eating fish or octopus caught only that morning, with a glass of ice-cold beer or a carafe of strong-tasting *retsina*. Food in Greece is simple, hearty – and cheap.

In addition to the fine beaches, Greece offers ancient cities, lost temples, crusader castles and mighty sea fortresses amid striking scenery. For accommodation you can choose from bright, modern apartments and small hotels, big, bustling resorts, or comfortably restored traditional mansions, castles or former monasteries.

Lovers of nature will find isolated mountain wildernesses and giant freshwater lakes which attract Europe's rarest birds, and fields and forests full of wild flowers and dazzling butterflies.

For those in search of sport, Greece offers the best yachting and windsurfing in Europe, plus waterskiing from dozens of sunny beaches, parascending, diving and snorkelling. Few other countries pack such an array of delights into such a small space.

# History

**BC**
**1700–1600**
Mycenaean culture emerges on mainland.
**1200**
Collapse of Mycenaean culture.
**1100**
Arrival of the Dorian Greeks.
**776**
First Olympic Games.
**800–600**
City-state system takes shape.
**490**
First Persian invasion. Athenian victory at the battle of Marathon.
**480**
Second Persian invasion. Greek army annihilated at Thermopylae, and Athens captured. Persian navy defeated at Salamis.
**479**
Persians defeated at Plataiai and Mycale. End of the Persian Wars.
**478**
Athens at the height of its power as leader of the Delian League.
**431–404**
Peloponnesian War between Sparta and Athens ending in Athenian defeat.
**371**
Thebes defeats Sparta at the Battle of Lévktra.
**359–336**
Rise of Macedonia.
**338**
Macedonia defeats southern cities at Battle of Khairónia.
**336–323**
Reign of Alexander the Great.

The 'Mask of Agamemnon'

**323–196**
Macedonian kings.
**200–146**
Wars with Rome, culminating in the end of Greek and Macedonian independence.

**AD**
**242–251**
Goths appear on the Greek frontier for the first time.
**260–268**
Gothic raids into Greece begin.
**324**
The Roman Emperor Constantine moves his capital to Byzantium (Istanbul), renaming it Constantinople and founding the Christian (Byzantine) empire in Greece and the east.
**393**
Olympic Games banned by the Roman Emperor Theodosius.
**529**
Last schools of philosophy suppressed in Athens.
**600–700**
Pagan Slavs and Goths invade Greece as far as the Peloponnese.
**800–900**
Byzantine recovery.
**1204**
Frankish/Venetian Fourth Crusade sacks Constantinople. Franks and Venetians divide Greece.
**1261–62**
Byzantine Empire recovers Constantinople and most of mainland Greece.
**1354**
Ottoman Turks capture Gallipoli.

**1429**
Turks take Thessaloníki.
**1453**
Fall of Constantinople and the end of the Byzantine Empire.
**1460**
Fall of Mistra.
**1499**
Turks take Návpaktos, Koróni and Methóni from Venice.
**1537–40**
Turks take Monemvasía and Návplion.
**1571**
Turks checked at Battle of Lepanto by Holy League led by Don John of Austria.
**1685–99**
Venice recovers the Peloponnese.
**1821–30**
War of Independence. The Peloponnese, Athens and Attica, Sterea Ellas, the Cyclades and the Argo-Saronic islands become the new Republic of Greece.
**1831**
President Capodistrias assassinated.
**1833**
Bavarian Prince Otto becomes King Otho I of the Hellenes.
**1881**
Turkey cedes Thessaly to Greece.
**1912**
First Balkan War. Greece gains Thessaloniki, Ionina and Epirus from Turkey.
**1913**
Second Balkan War. Greece allied with Serbia against Bulgaria.
**1917**
Greece joins World War I on the side of Britain and France.
**1919**
Encouraged by Britain and France, Greece lands troops at Smyrna (Izmir) in Turkey.
**1920–23**
War between Greece and Turkey ends in defeat for Greece. Around one million Greeks driven from Turkey; 400,000 Muslims driven out of Greece.
**1924–36**
Political chaos, leading to suspension of constitution. General Metaxas becomes dictator.
**1939**
Italy invades Albania.
**1940**
Italy demands access to Greek ports. Metaxas refuses. Italian invasion defeated in Epirus.
**1941–1944**
German occupation. Varied resistance groups active in many areas, including growing Communist faction.
**1946–49**
Civil war, with the USA and Britain supporting the Royalist right-wing government forces against the Communists.
**1967–74**
Military junta rules Greece, led by Colonel Papadopoulos. King Constantine expelled. Referendum ends the monarchy.
**1974**
Collapse of the junta after the Turkish invasion of Cyprus. Restoration of democracy.
**1981**
Greece joins the European Community. Left-wing PASOK party led by Andreas Papandreou elected.
**1984**
PASOK re-elected.
**1989**
PASOK defeated. Series of short-lived caretaker governments.
**1990**
Nea Dimokratia party elected under Konstantinos Mitsotakis.
**1993**
PASOK re-elected.

# Empires, Hegemonies and Invasions

## The Mycenaeans and Dorians

These Bronze Age warriors built citadels ringed by massive boulder walls in the Peloponnese, Athens, Thebes and elsewhere, and traded with Egypt and the empires of the Middle East. Their civilisation toppled around 1200BC. About 150 years later, the first Greek-speaking, iron-using Dorians arrived from the north, settled among the ruins of the Mycenaean civilisation, and over the next 300 years developed their own culture.

Silver head of a bull (*rhyton*) found at Mycenae, dating from the 16th century BC

## The city-states

By the 8th century BC Greece was divided among dozens of small, fiercely independent city-states. Not all were Athenian-style democracies. Sparta was an authoritarian, militarised state ruled by two kings. Other cities were democracies, oligarchies controlled by a group of powerful men, or tyrannies under an absolute ruler. The rival cities banded together against Persia in the early 5th century BC, but after the invasion Athens and Sparta fought each other for almost 30 years. Sparta, the victor in 404BC, was in turn defeated by Thebes, which dominated Greece until the rise of Macedonia (see page 132).

## The Macedonians and Hellenistic Greece

Macedonia and a number of smaller kingdoms created by Alexander's generals dominated the Greek world from the end of the 4th century BC until the Roman conquest. Other Hellenistic kingdoms were created in the Middle East, giving the Greeks broader horizons. Despite political chaos and frequent conflict among Alexander's successors, trade, philosophy and the arts flourished in the wider Greek world, but the mainland cities stagnated.

## The Romans in Greece

Roman legions first landed in Greece in 201BC. Over the next century Rome became increasingly powerful and was frequently at war with Macedonia. Greek cities which resisted Roman hegemony were destroyed, as Corinth was in 146BC. The Roman conquest was completed in 86BC when Athens fell, bringing almost three centuries of stability, during which Athens flourished with the building of a new Roman city beside the ancient Greek one. Corinth, too, was rebuilt and in the later Roman period Thessaloníki became a great trade centre.

## The Byzantine Empire
In AD330 the Roman Emperor Constantine dedicated his new capital of Byzantium (now Istanbul) and renamed it Constantinople. The city became the heart of a Christian empire which was more Greek than Roman, with territory which included all of Greece and Asia Minor and much of the Middle East. It lasted for more than 1,000 years, withstanding invasions by Slavs, Bulgars, Persians, Saracens and Turks until its final defeat in 1453.

## The Venetians
Venice, with its eyes on the Greek islands, encouraged its Frankish allies of the Fourth Crusade to sack Constantinople in 1204. The Venetians then seized Évvoia (Evia), the Ionian islands, and strategic harbours throughout Greece. When Constantinople fell to the Turks, the Venetians held on to mainland and island strongholds including Monemvasía, Methóni and Koróni,

Top: bronze helmet of Miltiades, hero of the battle of Marathón, found at Olympia (490BC)
Left: bronze head of a 5th-century BC Athenian warrior

Návplion, Návpaktos, Rion and Andírrion, and as late as the end of the 17th century reconquered most of the Peloponnese from Turkey before being finally driven out of the mainland for good in 1715.

## The Turks in Greece
The Turkish conquest cut Greece off from the Christian West but made it part of a vast Muslim Ottoman empire. The seafaring Greeks carried on much of the trade of this empire, and Greek traders and shipbuilders flourished. The Turks tolerated other religions but punished rebellion with extreme ferocity. Despite this, risings against the Turks were frequent. In 1821 a final struggle for independence began, leading to the creation of the first independent Greek state in 1830.

# Politics

*P*olitics is a favourite topic of Greek conversation. Memories of the 1946–9 Civil War and of the 1967–74 military junta have begun to fade, but political discussion is guaranteed to raise voices and tempers and the fiercest debate is often between those who are on the same side. In 1993 passionate protest followed the unofficial visit of ex-king Constantine, who had been rejected in the referendum of 1973.

Since 1974, Greece has been a parliamentary democracy with an elected president whose role is mainly ceremonial. Real power is in the hands of an elected prime minister.

### Political parties

Two major parties dominate Greek politics. PASOK, a left-wing alliance, ruled through much of the 1980s, was voted out in 1989 and returned to power in 1993. The aggressively right-wing Nea Dimokratia (New Democracy) party, in power between 1990 and 1993, made itself unpopular by a wide-ranging programme of privatisation of state enterprises and a drive to collect tax from a workforce which is nearly 50 per cent self-employed.

Nea Dimokratia was toppled by the defection of one of its ministers, Antonios Samaras, whose Politiki Anoikti (Political Spring) party campaigned on a fiercely nationalist platform to win a handful of seats.

Two other minority parties, the old-style KKE (Greek Communist Party) and a reformed socialist party, are also represented in the national parliament.

Left: Vouli (parliament building) in Athens
Bottom: PASOK's leader, Andreas Papandreou

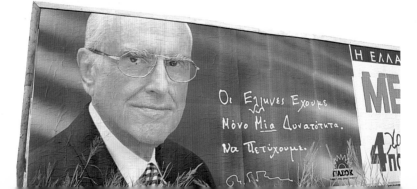

Campaign posters flash all the colours of the Greek political spectrum

## Greece and Europe

Anything touching on Greece's hard-won sovereignty quickly becomes a hot political issue, often overshadowing rational discussion of the shaky state of the Greek economy – partly kept afloat by the European Union – which has urged Greece to privatise its unwieldy nationalised enterprises and reduce a huge economic deficit. Modernisation measures (including higher taxes) are widely disliked and universally blamed on Brussels, but many Greeks seem able to ignore the visible benefits of EU membership.

The PASOK government, which was stridently anti-American during its first two terms, began its third spell in office with peace overtures towards the USA, partly to balance grass-roots anti-European feeling.

Neighbouring Turkey, though a NATO ally, is still seen as a threat, and Greece spends proportionately more on defence than any other European country. The hottest issue in recent years has been Macedonia – a name to which Greece claims sole rights but which is also claimed by the former Yugoslav republic across the border. Greek

ministers refuse to recognise the newly independent state under that name, referring to it instead as the Republic of Skopje (after its capital) or as FYROM, an acronym for Former Yugoslav Republic of Macedonia. Recognition of the former Yugoslav republic by European nations brought howls of protest from Greece.

### THE COLONELS' JUNTA

On 21 April 1967 a group of army officers staged a *coup d'état* to prevent the election of a left-wing government. The junta, led by Colonel Yioryios Papadopoulos, censored the press, banned trade unions, imprisoned thousands of opponents and banned free speech, popular music, short skirts, long hair and beards. Despite this mixture of terror and petty stupidity, the colonels were strongly supported by the USA, and many Greeks believe their *coup* was a CIA plot. The junta fell in 1974 after its backing for a right-wing Greek coup in Cyprus led to Turkish invasion of the island.

# POLITICS AND PHILOSOPHY

*...Plato points upward to heaven, Aristotle downward to the earth.*
Clement C J Webb, *A History of Philosophy*, Oxford University Press (1915)

**A**thens was the most democratic of the Greek city-states, but it was a strictly limited democracy. Only free men born in the city might vote, and even at the best of times the man in the street might be more easily inspired by charismatic orators than by level-headed statesmen.

Philosophical debate was as intense as political argument, and the philosophers who entered political discussion are those best known today.

The philosophers who took an active part in the political life of the city are nevertheless outnumbered by those who stood aloof from it, preferring the discussion of ideals to realities. In fact, the schools of Hellenic philosophy flowered in the 4th and 3rd centuries BC, when Athens was no longer the greatest power in the Greek world, and many of the most influential teachers argued for individual self-sufficiency rather than engagement with the fickle world. To the Ancient Greeks, 'philosopher' meant no more than 'lover of knowledge', and philosophy embraced the entire realm of thought from pure mathematics to morality and ethics.

and arguably the most influential on later Western thinkers. Much of his rigorously logical thinking aimed to explain organic and physical phenomena; today, he might be a physicist rather than a philosopher.

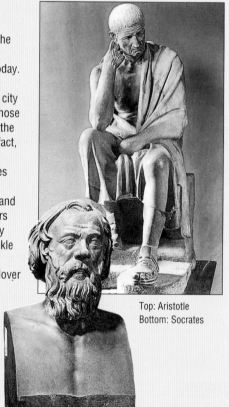

Top: Aristotle
Bottom: Socrates

## ARISTOTLE (843–322BC)

The tutor of Alexander the Great and pupil of Plato (his name means 'the best student'), he is the least mystical of the Greeks

# IN ANCIENT ATHENS

## DEMOCRITUS (c.460–c.370BC)

A contemporary of Plato, Democritus argued that the world could not be perceived through the senses alone but must be understood intellectually. He conceived the universe as consisting of tiny, indestructible units, for which he coined the term 'atoms'.

## DIOGENES OF SINOPE (c. 410–c.320BC)

Founder of the school of philosophers called the Cynics, Diogenes might be called the first drop-out. He argued for the simple life and rejected the everyday demands of convention, owned as little as possible and lived in a barrel.

*The death of Socrates*, by Jacques-Louis David (19th century)

## EPICURUS (341–270BC)

Epicurus and his followers argued that there is no after-life and that therefore happiness in this one is the chief good, and therefore the only reasonable aim.

## PLATO (427–347BC)

Plato is among the best-known of all the Greek philosophers, not only because he was the most prolific writer but because so many of his writings have survived. His central argument was that deeper nature and the meaning of things could be determined only by thought, not through the senses.

## SOCRATES (469–399BC)

Socrates lived and taught when Athens was at its zenith, paving the way for all those who came after him. He left no writings of his own, but is known to us through the work of his followers Plato and Xenophon, and his opponent the playwright Aristophanes, who caricatured him in his play *The Clouds*. His championing of reason over superstition and his delight in argument for its own sake made him many enemies among Athenian conservatives, who ultimately succeeded in having him tried and convicted on a charge of corrupting Athenian youth. The penalty was death by poison. Socrates might have escaped execution by pleading guilty, but refused to do so.

## ZENO OF CITIUM (334–262BC)

Zeno and his followers, the Stoics (who take their name from the *stoa* or porch of the market-place where they gathered), held that the world was ordered by a divine reason, and Stoic influences are apparent in Christianity. Both Stoics and Cynics were more concerned with finding a philosophy suited to everyday life than with ultimate truths, and the debate which they started continues, one way or another, today.

# Culture

### New ways for old

Visitors to Greece only a quarter of a
century ago might have seen grain being
threshed on a stone threshing-floor,
taken to the mill by mules, ground by
wind-power and baked in a wood-fired
village oven.

Pack-mules still carry heavy loads in villages all
over Greece

Greece has come a long way since
then. Mules are still useful load-carriers
all over the country, but they are no
longer the lifeline of many villages. New
roads and shiny pick-up trucks are the
signs of a new prosperity.

### Windows on the world

Television, no longer an unattainable
luxury, is a fixture in most Greek homes.
Video and satellite TV have turned out-
of-the-way hamlets into suburbs of the
global information village. Taverna-
owners who used to add up the bill on
the paper tablecloth or the back of a
cigarette packet are now just as likely to
use a brand-new personal computer, and
although it can take up to two years to
have a telephone installed, many
shepherds and villagers find cheap

walkie-talkies a convenient substitute.
Fishermen, too, benefit from new
technology, and most of the larger vessels
have ship-to-shore radio and radar.

### The tourism boom

Transport within Greece has become
faster and more efficient. Perhaps even
more importantly, for a country cut off by
sea and international politics from its
Western European trading partners,
international transport links have
improved. Holiday jets bring millions of
tourists into Athens and other mainland
airports at Kalamata, Préveza and
Thessaloníki, but they also take Greeks
abroad.

### Change for the better?

Not all the changes have been positive –
at least from the visitor's point of view.
Those seeking tranquillity will be
disappointed by the national fondness for
massively amplified music and unsilenced
motorcycles, and the microwave oven has
done more to undermine the reputation
of Greek cooking than oil or garlic ever

New prosperity buys bigger bikes

could. Traffic in Athens has grown worse with more widespread car ownership. Having said that, however, Greece is still a wonderful place in which to get away from it all, and much of the country away from the main tourist resorts remains completely unspoilt.

**The Greeks abroad**

During the 19th century millions of Greeks emigrated. There are large Greek communities in the USA, Canada, Australia and South Africa, all of them aiming to strike it rich and return home. Visitors who have seen hard-working expatriate Greeks in action may be surprised by how laid-back they seem to be in Greece.

A brighter future for Greece has also encouraged many younger overseas Greeks to return, often bringing fresh ideas and initiatives to the conservative villages their grandparents left. Many young men are put off by the prospect of a spell in uniform. All Greek men must spend two years in the armed forces on turning 21, and these reluctant soldiers are paid only a pittance.

Other Greeks have returned to the land of their ancestors after an even longer absence. As early as the 4th century BC, Greeks had settled on the shores of the Black Sea. With the fall of the Byzantine Empire, they preferred the rule of a Russian Orthodox tsar to that of an Ottoman Muslim sultan. Until the collapse of the USSR, 400,000 Greeks lived in the Soviet republics, many of whom have now chosen to live in Greece.

**Greek personality**

You may well meet an Aristotle (Aristotelis) in the corner store or find that your waiter's name is Socrates, but modern Greeks seem to have surprisingly

THOMAS COOK'S
## *Greece*

*Thomas Cook first visited Greece as part of a tour to the Nile, Palestine, Turkey and Italy in 1869; the party visited Epirus to see the ruins. By 1870 Athens was included in many of Cook's tours to Italy and Switzerland and an office was opened in Athens in Place Royale (now Platia Syntagma) in 1883. The building of Greek railways and interest aroused by archaeological excavations ensured a constant stream of customers for Cook's Greek tours. The restarting of the original Olympic Games in Athens in 1896 also attracted many visitors. The first conducted tour to Greece took place in 1904.*

The company of contemporaries

little in common with their heroic ancestors. There is still a real pride in their achievements, and today's Greeks have inherited the philosopher's delight in ideas and debate, but 2,500 years of change separate them from the builders of the Parthenon. On first acquaintance, Greeks may seem indifferent one moment and pushy the next, but they become firm friends more quickly than any people in Europe.

# Geography

*M*ainland Greece covers some 130,000 sq km. To the west, the Adriatic separates it from Italy. To the south lies the Mediterranean and to the east are the Aegean and its islands. Greece has some of the most spectacular landscapes and wide open spaces in Europe, from the peaks of Ólimbos (Olympus) to the rolling farmlands of Thrace.

Much of the country is mountainous, and throughout history the mountains have provided a defence against invasion and a refuge for those resisting occupying powers. Wherever you are in Greece there are mountains on the horizon, and you are never more than a few hours' drive from the sea.

### Economy and population

Greece has a population of 10.5 million, more than 4 million of whom live in and around Athens. More than one in three Greeks work on the land, many of them on small, family-owned farms, and almost half are self-employed. It is still a poor country, and many people hold down several jobs in order to make ends meet. Money sent home by Greeks living overseas helps many families manage.

### Farming

Oranges and lemons, cotton, tobacco, grapes and, above all, olives grow in abundance in the fertile valleys and plains and are among the country's major exports. Sheep and goats graze on higher, barren ground.

### Flora and fauna

Intense farming has taken its toll of Greek wildlife over thousands of years, as it has throughout Europe, but low population density has left niches for many rare and endangered species (see pages 138–9).

### Geology and climate

Beneath the thin topsoil, most of Greece is porous limestone. Water drains through it quickly, giving mountains and hillsides a parched, near-desert look for much of the year. Underground rivers have cut through the rock in many places, creating echoing caverns lined with coloured spires and stalactites. Topsoil washed from the mountainsides has accumulated over millennia in fertile valleys watered by rivers which swell with winter rains and melting snow but

A prickly pear cactus clings to the barren rocks of the *kastro* at Monemvasía

The northern Pindhos mountain range is one of the last areas of wilderness in southern Europe

dwindle to a trickle in the hot summers. Winters are short, mild and wet on the plains and around the coasts, but can be bitterly cold in the mountains.

**The sea**

If the mountains defend and divide Greece, the sea unites it with the outside world and provides a living for thousands of sailors and fishermen. The Greek merchant navy is one of the world's biggest and rivals tourism as the country's biggest foreign currency earner and one of its biggest employers. All over Greece you will meet retired seamen whose encyclopaedic knowledge of the world's ports comes from a spell on one of the thousands of tankers and freighters which fly the blue and white colours of Greece. Ready access to the sea also made it easy for Greeks to leave their country when times were hard, and more

than 4 million Greeks live overseas, most of them in the USA, Australia, Canada and South Africa – though it is said that you can find a Greek in any seaport in the world.

In ancient times the sea linked the enterprising Greeks with the great empires of the Middle East, and adventurous mariners from the Greek city-states founded colonies as far afield as Marseilles and Sicily in the west and the shores of the Black Sea in the east. Well into this century it was easier to travel by sea than by road and little mainland ports like Yíthion, Neapoli or Yerolimín were thriving centres of import and export to Athens and abroad. Much of their trade now goes by road, and these sleepy, forgotten harbours with their rows of merchants' mansions are some of the pleasantest places in which to spend a Greek holiday.

# ENVIRONMENT

Greece's record on the environment could be better. There are no votes in cleaning up rivers, seas and countryside at the expense of farmers, fishermen or industrialists, so Greek governments tend to ignore environmental issues. Interference (or even comment) from abroad is widely resented, and Greeks often argue that the tourists who complain about litter-strewn beaches are the very people who create the litter. They have a point, but the heaps of festering garbage which accumulate wherever there is space to pull off the road are not the work of visitors. Unfortunately, local authorities have neither the money nor the powers to clean up the mess, and national government in Athens has yet to show any real interest in doing so.

Less obvious to the holiday visitor is the environmental damage being inadvertently caused by misdirected European Union investment. Greece, the poorest country in the EU, is a major beneficiary of its regional funds, and Greek farmers have been quick to see the benefits of the EU's agricultural subsidy system. On the mainland, tobacco and cotton cultivation is booming as never before and European glut of both crops means farmers are paid to plough them back into the soil. The farmers can hardly be blamed for trying to make easy money, but the consequences are worrying. Many of Greece's rivers have been reduced to a mere trickle by dams built to meet the country's fast-growing need for hydroelectric power. At their mouths, delta wetlands which shelter thousands of rare birds are being drained by tobacco and cotton farmers. Greece's longest and mightiest river, the Akhelóös (see pages 94–5), is threatened by a new set of dams which will cut off water from the wetlands at its mouth, drown a remote and historic monastery and village in the Píndhos mountains, and cut off water from existing dams down river. Ironically, the EU, which is backing the multi-million ECU project, has already prosecuted Greece in the European Court for failing to protect the same wetlands that the dam threatens.

Huge man-made lakes, like this one near Marathón, have changed Greece's landscape

# *FIRST STEPS*

> *You know what the Greeks are like; we can't talk without using our hands.*
>
> BUS DRIVER
> quoted by Patrick Leigh Fermor in
> *Roumeli: Travels in Northern Greece* (1966)

## THE ALPHABET AND VOCABULARY

Romanised spellings of Greek names can vary. In placename headings and in the index, this book uses the transliterations which correspond to AA maps. More familiar Anglicised spellings (given in brackets in the headings) are sometimes used in the text. This leads to inconsistencies when compared with other books and maps: *Nafplion, Navplion, Nauplion, Nafplio, Navplio* and *Nauplio* are all the same town. The differences are rarely so great as to make a name unrecognisable. The names of museums and other places of interest may also be translated differently, so that what one source interprets as 'Historical and Ethnological Museum' may be translated elsewhere as 'National Historical Museum'. To avoid confusion, placename headings give the name in romanised Greek, followed by the most usual English translation in brackets.

It is helpful to know the Greek alphabet so that you can recognise placenames, while the few words and phrases following the alphabet will also come in handy.

### Alphabet

| | | | | | |
|---------|---------------------------|--------|-----------------------|---------|-------------------|
| Alpha | short *a*, as in hat | Iota | short *i* sound, as in hit | Sigma | *s* sound |
| Beta | *v* sound | | | Taf | *t* sound |
| Gamma | *y* sound, as in you | Kappa | *k* sound | Ipsilon | long *e*, as in feet |
| Delta | *th* sound, as in father | Lambda | *l* sound | | |
| | | Mu | *m* sound | Phi | *f* sound |
| Epsilon | short *e* | Nu | *n* sound | Chi | guttural *ch* sound, as in lock |
| Zita | *z* sound | Omicron | *o* | | |
| Eta | long *e*, as in feet | Pi | *p* sound | | |
| Theta | hard *th* sound, as in think | Rho | *r* sound | Psi | *ps*, as in lamps |
| | | | | Omega | *o* |

### Basic vocabulary

| | |
|---|---|
| good morning | *kalimera* |
| good evening | *kalispera* |
| goodnight | *kalinikhta* |
| hello | *yasou* |
| thank you | *efkharisto* |
| please/you're welcome | *parakalo* |
| yes | *ne* |
| no | *ochi* |
| where is...? | *pou ine?* |
| how much is...? | *poso kani?* |
| do you speak English? | *milate anglika?* |
| I don't speak Greek | *dhen milo ellinika* |

### Travelling

| | |
|---|---|
| car | *avtokiniton* |
| bus | *leoforion* |
| ferry | *plion* |
| train | *trenon* |
| airport | *aerolimenon* |
| ticket | *isitirion* |

## Places

| | |
|---|---|
| street | *odhos* |
| square | *platia* |
| avenue | *leoforos* |
| restaurant | *estiatorion* |
| hotel | *xenodochio* |
| room | *dhomatio* |
| post office | *tachidhromio* |
| police | *astinomia* |
| pharmacy | *farmakio* |
| doctor | *iatros* |
| bank | *trapeza* |
| café | *kafeneion* |

## Food and drink

| | |
|---|---|
| food | *fagito* |
| bread | *psomi* |
| water | *nero* |
| wine | *krasi* |
| beer | *bira* |
| coffee | *kafes* |
| lobster | *astakos* |
| squid | *kalamares/kalama rakia* |
| otopus | *oktapodhi* |
| red mullet | *barbounia* |
| whitebait | *maridhes* |
| lamb | *arni* |
| chicken | *kotopoulo* |
| meat balls | *keftedhes* |
| skewered meat | *souvlakia* |
| pork | *chirini* |
| spinach | *spanaki* |
| courgette | *kolokithia* |
| beans | *fasoles* |
| chips | *patates tiganites* |
| cucumber | *angouri* |
| tomato | *tomata* |
| olives | *elies* |
| salad with feta | *horiatiki* |
| tomato salad | *salata* |
| yoghurt and cucumber dip | *tsatsiki* |

## PLACENAMES

Where a widely used English version of a placename exists, this is used throughout the text except in the initial placename heading. Such placenames include:

Athens (*Athínai*)
Corinth (*Kórinthos*)
Delphi (*Delfi*)
Epirus (*Ípiros*)
Kalamata (*Kalámai*)
Macedonia (*Makedhonia*)
Patras (*Pátrai*)
Sparta (*Spárti*)
Thebes (*Thivai*)
Thessaly (*Thessalia*)
Thrace (*Thráki*)

## Postal addresses and street names

*Odhos* (street), *platia* (place or square) and *leoforos* (avenue) are usually dropped from Greek postal addresses. In this book, *odhos* and *leoforos* have accordingly been ommitted but, in the interests of clarity, *platia* (as in Platia Sindagma) has been retained.

## Numbers

| | | | |
|---|---|---|---|
| 1 | *ena* | 14 | *dhekatessera* |
| 2 | *dhio* | 15 | *dhekapende* |
| 3 | *tria* | 16 | *dhekaexi* |
| 4 | *tessera* | 17 | *dhekaevta* |
| 5 | *pende* | 18 | *dhekaokto* |
| 6 | *exi* | 19 | *dhekenea* |
| 7 | *evta* | 20 | *ikosi* |
| 8 | *okhto* | 30 | *trianda* |
| 9 | *enea* | 40 | *seranda* |
| 10 | *dheka* | 50 | *peninda* |
| 11 | *endheka* | 100 | *ekaton* |
| 12 | *dhodheka* | 1000 | *khilies* |
| 13 | *dhekatria* | | |

## LANGUAGE, MANNERS AND CUSTOMS

### Hospitality

Greek hospitality is legendary. Traditionally, any stranger is a guest. That attitude of *philoxenia* ('love of guests') is dying hard with the growth of tourism, but it quickly starts to show itself as you travel away from the busy resorts – or even in them at less busy times of the year. A gift of a flower from someone's garden, nuts or fruit from an orchard you pass, or a carafe of wine sent to your table by a complete stranger comes as a surprise to visitors from less warm-hearted lands. It should come as no surprise, though, in a land where the trading tradition goes back 3,000 years, that Greeks can also drive a hard bargain.

### Queuing

Queuing for public transport is virtually unheard of, and you must expect a certain amount of pushing and shoving on boarding boats, trains and urban buses. In banks and post offices, however, there is usually a fairly orderly queue – though if you do not step forward promptly when it is your turn, somebody else will.

### Dress code

Topless sunbathing is now accepted on even the most public beaches, but total nudity will offend and may get you arrested. Shorts and T-shirts are acceptable summer wear everywhere except on visits to monasteries and churches, where men must wear long trousers, women skirts which cover the knees, and both sexes should wear long sleeves.

### Women travellers

Greece is still a male-dominated society (though it is changing) but many women feel less risk of harassment than in many other Mediterranean countries. Greek men certainly feel that a woman can only be flattered by their attention, but are unlikely to persist in the face of an unambiguous 'no'. You are more likely to meet with unwanted attention in summer resorts – from summer visitors – than from local people elsewhere.

### Language

The Greek language can be intimidating, if only because its alphabet is so different from the familiar Roman script, but a little Greek goes a very long way in making friends and influencing people.

Older Greeks like this retired shepherd jealously guard the tradition of *philoxenia*

A local farmer and his mule enjoy the contentment that a slower pace of life generates

Greeks firmly believe that their language is almost impossible for foreigners to learn, and even knowledge of a few simple phrases will be admired and extravagantly praised.

Greeks use a lot of body language (they say that to silence a Greek you need only tie his hands behind his back) which can be helpful and confusing by turns. One helpful hint: a backward jerk of the head which you might interpret as a nod is exactly the opposite. Often accompanied by a click of the tongue, it means 'no'. On the other hand, a rapid side-to-side shake of the head is not a negative – it means anything from 'I don't understand' to 'What can I do for you?'

The Greek alphabet is impossible to translate directly into other languages, and vice versa: it takes a while to puzzle out that *xampòurgker* means 'hamburger' or *kroyasan* means 'croissant'. Some Roman letters are missing from the Greek alphabet, and are represented by combining two Greek letters to make the appropriate sound. *Mu* and *pi* are combined to make a hard B as in bar; *nu* and *taf* to make a hard D as in dog; and *nu* and *kappa* are often used to approximate a hard G as in golf.

The white pebble beach at Ayios Ioannis, on the east coast of the Pílion (Pelion) peninsula

## WHERE TO GO

Mainland Greece has more than enough sights and landscapes to fill any holiday and offers endless scope for exploration off the beaten track.

### Ancient Greece

The ruins of ancient cities and temples clutter any map of Greece, but surprisingly few of the ancient sites which are so carefully marked and signposted are of interest to anyone except the keen archaeologist. They are, after all, up to 4,000 years old, and time has taken its toll. Even the best-preserved or most lovingly restored buildings lack roofs and many of the columns which supported them, while the statues and friezes which decorated them are either in museums or have been carted off by looters. The less well-preserved sites may be marked only by a single column, a scattering of masonry blocks, and a few holes in the ground. Of the scores of ancient sites carefully marked by the Greek Ministry of Culture, those of central Athens (see pages 36–9) and a dozen or so others are guaranteed not to disappoint. These include the Temple of

Poseidon at Soúnion (see pages 48 and 54–5); Mikínai (Mycenae); Árgos and Tiryns in the Argolid; the nearby Theatre of Epídhavros (see pages 62–3), and Corinth (see page 68); Olympia in the western Peloponnese (see page 78); and Delphi in the Sterea Ellas region (see pages 88–9). Equally impressive are the remains of the temple complex at Dhodhóni in Epirus (see page 104), and the sites of the lost cities of Dhion, below Mount Olympus (see page 128), and Philippi (see page 120). In the southern Peloponnese, the mighty walls of ancient Ithomi are worth a detour.

### Battlefields

Those interested in military history may like to visit the well-signposted battlefields where the decisive conflicts of classical Greece were fought out. A crescent of battlefields lies north of Athens, with Marathón (see page 50) to the northeast, while Thermopylae (see page 53), Lévktra (see page 53), Plataiaí (see page 53) and Chaironeia (see page 86) lie to the northwest. All five are within easy reach of Athens.

### Beaches

Mainland Greece offers excellent beaches, many of them surprisingly uncrowded. The longest and least developed sandy beaches run for many kilometres down the west coast of the Peloponnese, and in the southern Peloponnese there are also excellent sand beaches at Koróni, Methóni and Stoupa (see pages 64–5 and 76–7). The more sheltered east coast of the Peloponnese boasts many delightful little beaches of white pebbles and coarse shingle.

In the north, there are excellent sand beaches on the Khalkidhikí (Chalkidiki) peninsulas (see pages 122–3), at Párga (see page 107) on the west coast, and near Préveza (see page 107).

## Castles

Lovers of medieval romance should head for the Peloponnese, where it seems as though every hilltop and mountain pass is crowned by a Byzantine, Frankish or Turkish castle and every harbour has its Venetian fortress. Among the most striking are those at Mistra and Yeráki (see pages 74–5), Monemvasía (see pages 72–3), Koróni, Methóni and Pílos (see pages 64–5) and Chlemoútsi (see pages 78–9).

## Historic towns

Towns with historic quarters which have survived the ravages of war, fire, earthquake and modernisation are easiest to find in the northern mainland. They include Ioánnina (see page 104), Kastoría (see page 128), Kaválla, Komotiní and Xánthi (see pages 120–1). In the south, Návplion (see page 61) has a pretty town centre dating from its 18th-century Venetian heyday.

## Mountains

The finest mountain scenery in Greece is to be found in the Pindhos range, which forms the backbone of the northern mainland. The Parnassós massif is an awesomely beautiful backdrop to Delphi, and the lonely peaks of Olympus dominate the plains of Thessaly and Macedonia. In the Peloponnese, the saw-edged ridge of the Taíyetos runs from the north to meet the sea at Ákra Taínaron (Cape Matapan), the southernmost tip of mainland Greece.

## Picturesque villages

Mainland villages display a rich variety of traditional architectural styles, from the ruined towers of the Mani (see pages 70–1 and 80–1) to the half-timbered mansions of the Pílion (Pelion) peninsula (see pages 112–13), the stone-slab homes of the Zagória (see pages 114–15) or the mud-brick ghost villages around the Préspa lakes (see page 129).

The slopes of the Parnassós massif, backdrop for the beauties of ancient Delphi

## DRIVING

Driving in Greece requires a combination of caution, confidence and strong nerves. Roads have been improved greatly in recent years and most are now well-surfaced but Greece is a mountainous country and there are many steep hairpin bends. Greek bus drivers, who like to take these hairpins at speed, usually sound their horns almost continuously to tell you that they are coming. Among other typically Greek hazards are flocks of goats or sheep being herded across the main road, usually when you least expect them.

In places, wide, newly tarred roads degenerate abruptly and without warning into pot-holed tracks, a spine-jarring experience for driver and passengers. Greek drivers will take an ordinary saloon car over the roughest roads, but off the beaten track some roads are suitable only for four-wheel-drive vehicles.

Outside the three major cities and the main highways which connect them traffic is light. In the cities, it is another story: driving, navigating and finding somewhere to park can be demanding, and it is easier to leave your car and explore on foot or by public transport. There are one-way systems in even the smallest villages. These are widely ignored by locals.

Greeks are aggressive drivers, and a combination of winding roads and cavalier driving habits results in the worst road accident level in Europe, with almost 2,000 fatalities a year. Speed limits are treated with contempt (Greek drivers flash their lights at oncoming traffic to warn of police checkpoints) and though seat belts are compulsory for drivers and front-seat passengers it is unlikely that you will ever see a Greek wearing one.

If all this sounds intimidating, do not let it deter you from driving in Greece. Driving can be by far the best way to see the country, and a car will take you to places impossible to reach by public transport. The golden rule for drivers in Greece is: expect the unexpected.

Toll booths on the major highways help return the cost of road construction

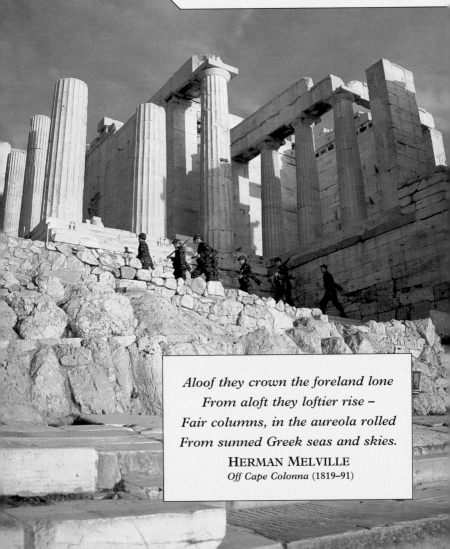

# WHAT TO SEE

*Aloof they crown the foreland lone*
*From aloft they loftier rise –*
*Fair columns, in the aureola rolled*
*From sunned Greek seas and skies.*

**HERMAN MELVILLE**
*Off Cape Colonna (1819–91)*

# Athínai

## (Athens)

## CENTRAL ATHENS

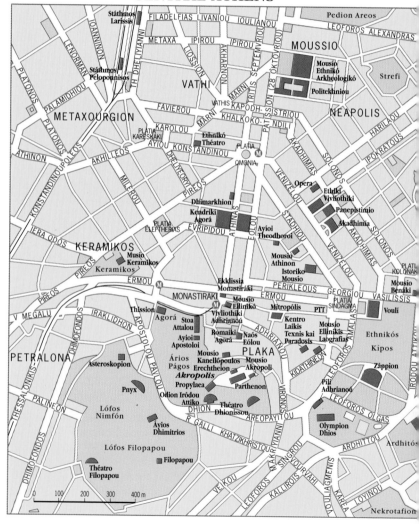

*A*thens is home to almost half the country's total population, and the glowing columns of the Parthenon, the city's best-loved landmark, rise above the crag of the Acropolis like an island of grace in a modern urban sea.

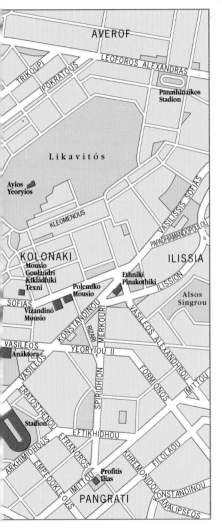

Much of Athens is surprisingly new, built since World War II to house an influx of people from the countryside. In 1940 only 850,000 people lived in the city. By 1970, there were 2.5 million. Today there are 4 million.

The city's apartment and office blocks nevertheless conceal happy surprises. Turn any corner and you may find yourself looking at a 1,000-year-old church, a tiny park cluttered with toppled ancient columns, a quaint old taverna or the high garden wall of a 19th-century mansion surrounded by exotic palm trees.

Athens has only one major city-centre park, Ethnikós Kípos (National Gardens), but makes up for its shortage of public green space with explosions of greenery and colour from gardens, balconies and window-boxes. Planes and orange trees line streets and squares, jasmine and honeysuckle cling to tumbledown walls and in spring even wasteland and roadside blaze briefly with wild poppies and daisies.

City life echoes the laid-back style of a rural village, and few corners are without a vendor peddling barbecued corn-cobs, nuts, sunflower seeds, or sesame-seed rings.

Most offices close for an afternoon siesta, and Athenians spend much leisure time playing backgammon or (as befits folk who live in the city where democracy was born) arguing politics at café tables.

Most of the city's ancient sites and museums are in a compact area within a 2-km radius of Platia Sindagma (Constitution Square), the hub of modern Athens.

# Akropolis
## (Acropolis)

*T*ime and weather have stripped the buildings of the Acropolis to bare white marble, making the perfect simplicity of their proportions all the more striking. Their impact reaches across more than two millennia.

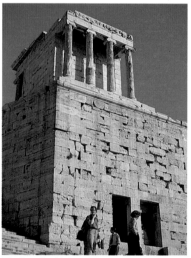

The Temple of Athena Nike was restored in the 19th century

The 100m limestone crag was first occupied more than 5,000 years ago, and there are traces of Mycenaean buildings dating from 1500BC. In the 5th century BC Pericles – the city's leading statesman and its guiding hand from 461 to 430BC – commissioned Kallikrates and Iktinos (both after 450BC) to rebuild the temples sacked by the Persians in 480BC, and the brilliant Phidias (500–432BC) to design their friezes and statues.

Later occupiers demolished some buildings. Others (including the Parthenon) were damaged or destroyed during the many sieges of the Acropolis between medieval and modern times. As late as the War of Independence, Greek rebels used it as a fortress.

The main buildings of the site are linked by the Sacred Way, running from the middle gate of the Propylaia to the Parthenon. The site is entered by the eastern Beulé Gate, to the left of which stands the plinth of a statue to the Roman general Agrippa.

*Acropolis (tel: 3210 219). Open: weekdays, 8am–4.45pm; weekends and holidays, 8.30am–2.45pm. Admission charge includes entry to museum and Acropolis site.*

### Erechtheion

Restored in the 1980s, the Erechtheion was the Acropolis's holiest shrine, dedicated to Athena as patroness of Athens. Standing opposite the Parthenon, its three Ionic porticos were built on different levels. The original *caryatids* (female figures) of the south portico have been replaced by copies.

### Mousío Akropoli (Acropolis Museum)

Collection includes figures of Athena, 6th-century BC *korae* (figures of draped maidens), friezes from the Erechtheion and the Temple of Athena Nike, and *caryatids* from the Erechtheion.

*Tel: 3236 665. Open: Monday, 11am–4.30pm; Tuesday to Friday, 8am–4.30pm; weekends, 8.30am–2.30pm.*

## Naos Athena Nike (Temple of Athena Nike)

The temple honours Athena as goddess of victory. Designed by Kallikrates in the mid-5th century BC to celebrate the Athenian defeat of Persia, it was completed in 424BC. Demolished by the Turks, it was restored in the 19th century.

## Parthenon

Phidias and his patron Pericles intended the Parthenon to be an act of worship in stone, celebrating Athens at the zenith of its power.

Dedicated to Athena in 438BC, the Parthenon was brightly painted and cluttered with elaborately decorated statues. The greatest, the gold and ivory statue of Athena, 12m high, was taken to Constantinople in AD426 and melted down. A copy is in the National Archaeological Museum (see page 42). The marble friezes which adorned the Parthenon and Temple of Athena Nike were removed by Lord Elgin, British ambassador to the Ottoman Sultan, in 1801, and are in the British Museum. Greeks strongly resent this and demand their return.

In the Middle Ages the Parthenon was used as a Christian church, and in 1466 it became a Turkish mosque. The Turks later used it as a powder magazine.

## Propylaea (Propylaia)

The Propylaia, the dramatic gateway to the Acropolis temple complex, combined Ionic and Doric features. Built between 437 and 432BC by the architect Mnesikles, its 46m-wide portico was pierced by five elaborate gates. The north wing of the Propylaia housed the Pinakotheke, which was built in the 5th century BC as a portrait gallery. The Pinakotheke was in use as a powder magazine when it was struck by lightning in 1645. It has been partly restored.

## The Sacred Way

After entering the temple site by the Propylaia, worshippers passed along the flag-stoned Sacred Way, lined with statues of deities and heroes, to the Parthenon, pausing to worship at one or all of the shrines on the way. There are fine views of Athens from here.

The south portico of the Erechtheion, the holiest shrine of the Acropolis temple complex

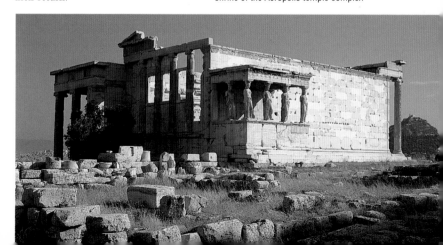

# CLASSICAL ARCHITECTURE

The temples of ancient Greece still have the power to move the visitor after two and a half millennia – an amazing tribute to their builders. The architects of classical Greece picked the setting for each temple as carefully as they planned its proportions. Besotted with the possibilities of geometry, they strove for simplicity, harmony and balance through a complex series of interrelated ratios. Few designers in the intervening centuries have matched their talents.

The temples of the 6th and 5th centuries BC, the golden age of Greek architecture, were built to a strict pattern. Steps surrounded a rectangular stone platform which supported fluted columns topped by a gabled roof and decorated with elaborate friezes depicting gods, heroes and monsters.

Again and again, the builders managed the brilliant trick of making the massive marble columns seem light and delicate, balancing height against width and horizontal against vertical by the use of the simplest of harmonic ratios.

Doric temple architecture, originating in mainland Greece, was the earliest and plainest of the three 'orders' of classical architecture.

Above: Corinthian capital
Left: Corinthian columns of the Olympion Dhios

Columns had no base, a simple capital at the top, and no more than 20 flutes or decorative grooves. Doric temples, like the superbly preserved Temple of Apollo at Vassai, can appear more massive than those built in the Ionian style. The Parthenon, finest of all the Doric buildings, avoids this by sleight

Left: caryatids of the Erechtheion
Below: the Parthenon

of hand: its columns slope slightly inward for strength, and the corner columns, which should appear larger than the others, are in fact slightly smaller, tricking the eye into seeing a larger space.

The Ionic style originated among the Greek cities of the Asia Minor coast. Ionic columns have a subdivided base, a shaft with 20 flutes, a decorated capital, and are often slimmer than the Doric column. The later Corinthian style, developed after the Roman conquest of Greece, is a fusion of Greek and Roman design. Base and shaft are similar to Ionic columns, while the cup-shaped capital is more floridly carved with leaves and garlands.

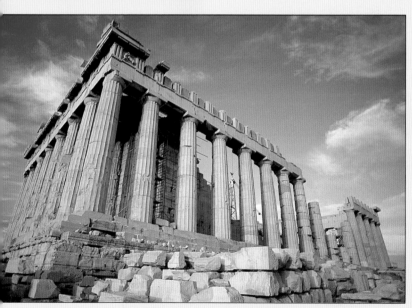

# AROUND THE ACROPOLIS

## ACROPOLIS INTERPRETATION CENTRE

Copies of the friezes from the Parthenon, including those in the British Museum and the Acropolis Museum, are the main attractions of this new centre for conservation and restoration. Copies of sculptures from the Erechtheion and Temple of Athena Nike will also be displayed, and it is planned to relocate the Acropolis Museum to a new building next to the Centre.

*2–4 Makriyianni (Makrigiani) (tel: 9239 381). Open: Monday to Friday, 9am–2pm; Monday, Wednesday and Friday, also 6pm–8pm; weekends, 10am–2pm. Admission free.*

## LOFOS FILOPAPOU
### (Hill of the Muses)

Named after the Roman consul Philopappos, the hill is topped by his 12m-high monumental tomb, built in AD116. Around it are the remnants of 3rd-century BC fortifications.

## ODION IRÓDOU ATTIKO
### (Odeon of Herod Atticus)

Built into the rock of the Acropolis in AD161, this huge theatre is the main venue for the annual Athens Festival of music, theatre and dance. It seats 6,000, and its superb acoustics carry voices to the highest of its many tiers of seats.

The theatre's well-preserved Roman façade with its tiers of arches can be viewed from the stepped path to the Acropolis, which runs past it.

*Dhionissou Areopayitou. Open: for performances only (see **Entertainment**, page 149).*

## OLYMPION DHIOS AND PÍLI ADHRIANOÚ (Olympion Zeus and Arch Of Hadrian)

The temple of Olympian Zeus was one of the ancient world's greatest, completed by the Roman Emperor Hadrian in AD132. It measured 107.45m by 41m. Only 15 of its 84 columns still stand, the rest having been taken by successive occupiers of Athens, including Genoese, Venetians and Turks, for building stone.

Next to the Temple of Olympian Zeus, the monumental arch divided Hadrian's new Roman city from older Hellenic Athens.

*Junction of Leoforos Singrou and Leoforos Amalias (tel: 9226 330). Open: daily, except Monday, 8.30am–3pm. Admission charge.*

Arch of Hadrian

Only 15 of the original columns of the Temple of Olympian Zeus still stand

## PNYX

On this low hill west of the Acropolis the Athenian popular assembly met until the late 4th century BC, when it relocated to the Théatro Dhionissou (Theatre of Dionysos) below the Acropolis. There is little to see during the day, but during the summer the Pnyx is the venue for the nightly Sound and Light show telling the story of the Acropolis (see **Entertainment**, page 153).

## THEATRO DHIONISSOU
### (Theatre of Dionysos)

The oldest of the buildings on the southern slope of the Acropolis, the 17,000-seat theatre with its 67 tiers of seats is separated from the Odeon of Herod Atticus by the sites of the Sanctuaries of Asklepios and of Dionysos Eleutheros, of which only two Corinthian columns remain. Built in the 4th century BC, the theatre was embellished and enlarged in the 1st century AD under the Roman emperor Nero, with the addition of elaborately carved front-row seats for the priests of Dionysos and other dignitaries.

Next to the theatre are the remains of two sanctuaries to Asklepios, god of healing, dating from the 4th and 5th centuries BC, and the rows of column bases which mark the site of the 2nd-century BC Stoa of Eumenes. *Dhionissou Areopayitou (tel: 3224 625). Open: daily, 8.30am–2.30pm.*

Tiers of seats ring the auditorium of the Theatre of Dionysos

# NORTH OF THE ACROPOLIS

## AGORÁ (Ancient Market-place)

This was the heart of everyday life in ancient Athens and after the Acropolis is the most important and evocative of the city's ancient sites. Highlights include the 5th-century BC Thission, the most intact of all Greece's temples. So called because its friezes (now badly damaged) showed the exploits of Theseus, the building with its 34 Doric columns was a temple to Ifestos (Hephaestos), the armourer of the gods and the deity of smiths and artisans.

Rebuilt after the Persian invasion of 480BC, the Agorá was ringed by long, colonnaded buildings called *stoas*. One of these, the 2nd-century BC Stoa Attalou (Stoa of Attalos II), was rebuilt by American archaeologists. A striking two-storey building with a Doric colonnade on the ground floor and an Ionic one above, it is now the Mousío

A tombstone at the Keramikos cemetery shows an Athenian noble family

Agorá (Agorá Museum), with a collection of vases and fragmented statues.

Just below the upper entrance to the site stands the Byzantine church of Ayioi Apostoloi, built in the 11th century AD on a site on which St Paul is said to have preached.

*Main entrance is on Adhrianoú (tel: 3210 185), 5 minutes walk from Monastiráki metro station. Open: daily, except Monday, 8.30am–2.45pm. Admission charge.*

## ÁRIOS PÁGOS (Areopagus)

According to legend it was on this rocky hilltop above the site of the ancient Agorá that Ares the war god was tried by the other Olympians for the murder of one of the sons of Poseidon. A cave in the hillside was the Sanctuary of the Eumenides (the Harpies), who were goddesses of revenge. The summit offers views of the Ancient Agorá and the Acropolis.

## KERAMIKOS CEMETERY AND MUSEÍO

The cemetery of ancient Athens was excavated in the 19th century, revealing rows of *stelae* (tombstones) of the Athenian élite. Others are on show in the small museum and in the National Archaeological Museum (see page 42). *Ermou 148 (tel: 3463 552). Open: daily, except Monday, 8.30am–3pm.*

## NÁOS EÓLOU
### (Tower of the Winds)

Overlooking the Roman Forum, this 13m-high octagonal marble building was built in the 1st century AD. The tower takes its name from the winged figures carved on each face to represent the winds, and housed a water-clock for those using the nearby Forum.

The Tower of the Winds and columns of the Roman market-place

*Near junction of Eólou and Adhrianoú, opposite Romaiki Agorá. Not open to the public.*

## ROMAIKI AGORÁ (Roman Forum)

The site of the Roman market-place, which complemented the nearby Ancient Agorá, is marked by the massive four-columned gateway built in the 2nd century AD. There is little else to see within the site.

*Pelopida and Eólou (tel: 3245 220). Open: daily, except Monday, 8.30am–2.45pm. Admission charge.*

The ancient Agorá in Athens, once the social and commercial hub of the city

### LIFE IN THE MARKET-PLACE

The Ancient Agorá and the later Forum were more than just places to buy and sell goods and services. The long porches of the *stoas* surrounding them provided shelter for philosophers and politicians as well as for traders. Below the Thission stood the government buildings of Ancient Athens. The city's 500 magistrates met in the Bouleuterion, and 50 of them lived in rotation for one month of the year in the circular Tholos next to it. The Metroon, built in the 2nd century BC, was both a ' temple and a state library.

# MODERN ATHENS

The main thoroughfares, squares and public buildings of modern Athens date from the 19th century, when Otho I, first king of independent Greece, decreed a new capital among the ancient ruins. Sadly, much of Otho's gracious little capital was destroyed during World War II, and post-war development has swamped the rest.

### ETHNIKÓS KÍPOS (National Gardens)

Laid out for Otho I's queen, Amalia, by a Bavarian landscape architect, the former garden of the Anáktora (Royal Palace, now the Voulí, the Parliament Building) is the only large green space in central Athens. A band plays at its open-air café on summer evenings.

*The entrance gates are on Amalias, Iródou and Vasilissis Sofías. Open: sunrise to sunset. Admission free.*

### KOLONAKI

The smartest shops, nightspots and restaurants in Athens are in this fashionable suburb on the slopes of Likavitós, 10 minutes' walk from Sindagma. The centre of Kolonaki is Platia Kolonaki, a central square ringed

The whitewashed chapel of Ayios Yioryios on Likavitós

by chic cafés and piano bars. Behind it, steep streets and steps climb the hill.

### LIKAVITÓS

This wooded 227m-high peak topped by the chapel of Ayios Yioryios (St George) is a prominent landmark, from which there are fine views of the Acropolis, the city and its surroundings. A path leads to the chapel from the Hotel St George-Lykabettos, Kleomenous 2. The lazy way is to take the funicular, also from Kleomenous.

### MITROPÓLIS (Cathedral)

The massive and ugly new cathedral, built in the 19th century, dwarfs the much prettier late 12th-century building next to it, uniquely built of fragments from ancient temples and medieval buildings. Many of the ancient fragments have had crosses carved on them later. *Platia Mitropólis.*

### OMONIA

Platia Omonia, at the opposite end of Stadhiou from Sindagma, is the city's other main square. Once elegant, it has become a busy traffic and public transport hub with little of its former charm.

### PIRAIÉVS (Piraeus)

The port of Athens, west of the city, is connected to it by a single metro line. You will have to pass through the harbour district to visit the islands of the Argolikós-Saronikós Kólpos (Argo-Saronic Gulf) (see Getting Away From it All, pages 134–5), though many of the excursion boats now leave from Faliron Bay to the west of Piraeus.

### MIKROLIMANO (Little Harbour)

Sometimes called Turkolimano (Turkish

Harbour), Mikrolimano is between Piraeus itself and Faliron. This lagoon-like one-time fishing harbour is now filled with yachts but is still surrounded by the best fish restaurants in Athens, almost two dozen of them.

## PLAKA

Below the Acropolis, on its north and east sides, the old-fashioned streets of the Plaka with their tall, stucco-fronted houses and occasional gardens full of palms or lemon trees are the prettiest part of Athens. There are few cars and plenty of shops, cafés, restaurants and leafy squares. Tourism plays a big role, but has not yet taken over the Plaka completely. The main shopping street is Adhrianoú, running around the northwest edge of the Plaka.

Brightly painted houses like this 19th-century mansion are typical of the old Plaka

## SINDAGMA

Platia Sindagma is the heart of modern Athens, surrounded by expensive hotels, banks and airline offices, and open-air cafés. The meeting-point of the city's main avenues – Ermou, Amalias, Stadhiou and Venizelou (also called Panepisthimiou) – Sindagma is an island in a sea of traffic. The drills and diggers at work on the new Athens underground system (scheduled for completion by the end of the century) somewhat detract from its undoubted appeal.

## STADION (Stadium)

This copy in marble of the ancient Stadium, built in stone in 330BC and rebuilt in marble in AD140, dates from the late 19th century. It was donated to the Greek people by the millionaire George Averof in time for the first modern Olympic Games in 1896.
*Junction of Vasileos Konstandinou and Iródou Attikou. Open for events only.*

## VOULÍ (Parliament)

Borrowing the name of the ancient Athenian citizens' council, the Voulí is the most imposing of the city's 19th-century buildings. Built in 1843 as the palace of Otho I, the building and the Tomb of the Unknown Soldier outside it are guarded by white-kilted élite soldiers of the Evzones regiment.
*Leoforos Amalias, east side of Syntagma. Not open to the public. Changing of the guard, 11am on Sundays.*

## ZÁPPION

This elegant cream-and-yellow building standing in formal gardens is the epitome of the neo-classical style popular in the reign of Otho I. Its most noteworthy feature is its mock-Corinthian portico. Completed in 1883, it was the gift to the city of millionaire Constantine Zappas, and is now a conference centre.
*Located within the National Gardens. Open: sunrise to sunset.*

# MUSEUMS OF ATHENS

## ETHNIKÍ PINAKOTHÍKI
### (National Art Gallery)
Three paintings by El Greco (born in Venetian-ruled Crete though he worked in Spain) are the jewels of the gallery's collection. Most of its other paintings are by 19th-century Romantics.
*Vasileos Konstandinou 50 (tel: 8217 717). Open: Monday to Saturday, 9am–3pm; Sunday, 10am–2pm. Admission charge.*

## ISTORIKO MOUSÍO
### (National Historical Museum)
This contains an exhibition of paintings, engravings, weapons and relics devoted to the Greek struggle for independence from the Middle Ages to the 20th century.
*Stadhiou 13 (tel: 3237 617). Open: Tuesday to Friday, 9am–1.30pm; Saturday and Sunday, 9am–12.30pm. Closed Monday. Admission charge.*

## MOUSÍO ATHINON
### (Athens Museum)
For a glimpse of Athens during its 19th-century revival, visit the former royal palace where a collection of paintings and exhibits is housed in one of the prettiest of the city's surviving neo-classical buildings.
*Paparigopoulou 7 (tel: 3246 164). Open: Monday, Wednesday, Friday and Saturday, 9am–1.30pm. Admission charge.*

## MOUSÍO BENÁKI
### (Benaki Museum)
This cramped but fascinating collection of Byzantine and Asian jewellery, icons and textiles and colourful displays of Greek national costume was closed in 1993 for refurbishment; its re-opening date is uncertain.

*Koumbari and Vasilissis Sofias (tel: 3611 617).*

## MOUSIO ELLINIKIS LAOGRAFIAS
### (Museum of Greek Folk Art)
Here you will find an eye-catching collection of delicate embroideries and magnificent clerical robes, and traditional pottery from the islands.
*Kidhathíneon 17 (tel: 3229 031). Open: daily, except Monday, 10am–2pm. Admission charge.*

## MOUSÍO ETHNIKÓ ARKHEOLOGIKÓ
### (National Archaeological Museum)
Whatever you do in Athens, do not miss the finest museum in Greece, where treasures from the royal tombs of Mycenae compete for your attention with the magnificent statue of Poseidon and other bronzes, classical sculpture, ceramics and statuettes. It is well worth devoting most of a day to the huge collection. If you try to rush round, you will miss some of the most striking highlights.

Top billing goes to the Mycenaean collection (Room 4), where pride of place is given to the dazzling golden 'Mask of Agamemnon'. Now known to belong to an earlier era than Homer's hero, its age and sheer beauty make a double impact. Around it are crammed cases of glittering Mycenaean jewellery and flowing frescos from the palace at Tiryns.

Bronze head in the National Archaeological Museum

The best way to view the breathtaking sculpture which is exhibited in the other halls of the ground floor is to begin at Room 7, left of the main entrance, and work your way round room by room. This way you get a tour in time from the earliest archaic *kouroi* (statues of graceful youths) through to the perfectly poised, mid-5th-century BC statue of Posiedon, found on the seabed off Évvoia about 70 years ago.

The first floor houses the Helen Stathatos collection of gold funerary decorations. The richly decorated black-and-red figure vases from the 6th and 5th century BC on the second floor afford fascinating glimpses of everyday life among the ancient temples and palaces.

*Patission 44 (tel: 8217 717). Open: Monday, 10.30am–5pm; Tuesday to Sunday, 8am–5pm. Admission charge.*

## MOUSÍO GOULANDRI KIKLÁDHIKI TEXNI
### (Goulandris Museum of Cycladic and Ancient Greek Art)

More than 200 startlingly modern-looking statuettes, tools, weapons and ceramics from the Cycladic civilisation which dominated Greece between 3000 and 2000BC are displayed here.

*Neofytou Douka 4 (tel: 7234 931). Open: Monday to Wednesday and Friday, 10am–4pm; Saturday, 10am–1pm. Admission charge.*

## MOUSÍO KANELLÓPOULOS
### (Kanelloupoulos Museum)

Feast your eyes here on glowing Byzantine icons, jewellery, and traditional weavings, furniture and embroidery in a 19th-century Plaka mansion.

*Corner of Theorias and Panos (tel: 3212*

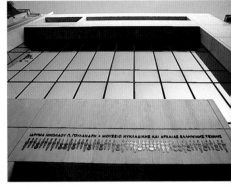

The Goulandris Museum

*313). Open: daily, except Monday, 8.30am–3pm. Admission charge.*

## POLEMIKO MOUSÍO
### (War Museum)

Housed in an ugly 1960s block, this museum was created by the Colonels' junta to glorify the army. It offers an insight into Greece's deep vein of patriotism, fostered by struggles against so many invaders, but the antique aircraft which sit outside and the collections of obsolete weapons and battle tableaux within are not very exciting.

*Vasilissis Sofias and Rizari (tel: 7290 543). Open: daily, except Monday, 9am–2pm. Admission free.*

## VIZANDINÓ MOUSÍO
### (Byzantine Museum)

Icons are the chief glory of this collection, though the best-known exhibit is the Epitaphios of Thessaloníki, a 14th-century embroidery depicting the Lamentation.

*Vasilissis Sofias 22 (tel: 7231 570). Open: daily, except Monday, 8.30am–3pm. Admission charge.*

# The Plaka and the Acropolis

The Plaka is the most picturesque part of Athens and alone of the older districts has survived fairly intact. Its narrow streets offer an escape from the manic Athens traffic. *Allow up to 4 hours.*

*Start at Monastiráki metro station and head down Ifaistou (Ifestou) into the Flea Market, a mix of jewellers, souvenir shops, shoemakers, boutiques, and army surplus stores.*

## 1 PLATIA AVISSINIAS

About 5 minutes' walk from Monastiráki, turn away from the boutiques and souvenir shops of Ifaistou for a look at an old-fashioned clutter of furniture-makers, antique stalls and street vendors selling junk of all kinds.

*At the end of Ifaistou turn left then left again on to Adhrianou.*

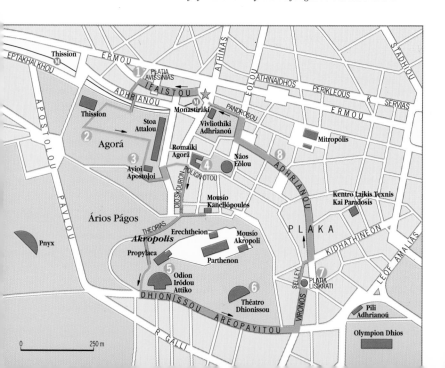

## 2 ANCIENT AGORÁ

Entering the Agorá by its lower gate, follow the signs to the Thission for one of the best views in Athens. Most of the modern city is hidden. Mount Imittós dominates the eastern skyline with the wooded slopes of Ários Págos to the south, and above them the crag of the Acropolis and the pillars of the Parthenon. As a bonus, the whole of the Agorá, the heart of the ancient city, is laid out in front of you (see page 38).

## 3 AYIOI APOSTOLOI

Before leaving the Agorá by the upper gate, pause to look at the domed Ayioi Apostoloi (Holy Apostles), a Byzantine church dating from the 11th century and built on a site where St Paul is said to have preached.

*Leaving the Agorá, turn left and left again, and then right on to Polignotou.*

## 4 ROMAIKI AGORÁ (THE ROMAN AGORÁ)

A four-columned portico marks the entrance to the site of the Roman Agorá. To the north stands the site of the Vivliothiki Adhrianoú (currently closed for excavation). On the east side of the site stands Náos Eólou (Tower of the Winds). Built in the 1st century BC, it was a combined sundial and water-clock.

*Turn right on Dioskouron, a steep street of old-fashioned, yellow-painted stucco houses which becomes a flight of steps before it joins Theorias.*

*Turn right to go direct to the Acropolis or detour left for 50m to visit the Mousío Kanellópoulos (Kanelloupoulos Museum, signposted, see pages 42–3).*

*Theorias runs above the Ancient Agorá, passes between the Acropolis and the Ários Págos and curves left to the entrance to the Acropolis (see pages 32–3).*

*The uphill part of the walk ends here. From the Acropolis take the stepped path downhill through pine trees for about 100m and turn left.*

## 5 ODION IRÓDOU ATTIKO (ODEON OF HEROD ATTICUS)

This fine Roman theatre was built in AD161. Athens Festival events are staged here in summer. It is open only for performances (see page 36).

*Descend a short flight of steps to emerge on to busy Dhionissou Areopayitou. Turn left and walk downhill for 200m past the Theatre of Dionysus.*

## 6 THÉATRO DHIONISSOU (THEATRE OF DIONYSUS)

The works of the great Athenian playwrights were first performed in this theatre, which dates from about 534BC (see page 37).

*At the foot of Dhionissou Areopayitou, turn left on to Vironos and follow it to Platia Lisikrati.*

## 7 PLATIA LISIKRATI

Marked by the 4th-century BC Lysikrates Monument whose six Corinthian half-columns commemorate a prizewinning *choregos* (choirmaster), this is a good place to stop for a drink or a meal.

*Vironos leads on to Selley. At its end, turn right then immediately left, back on to Adhrianoú.*

## 8 SHOPPING ON ADHRIANOÚ AND PANDROSOU

Adhrianoú is lined with shops selling pottery, clothes, and brightly coloured rugs and carpets.

*Turn right on to Eólou, then left on to Pandrosou. This 'new' flea-market street with its dozens of souvenir shops leads back to Monastiráki.*

# Attikí

## (Attica)

*A*ttica is the mythic heartland of ancient Greece and it takes only a little while to escape from Athens to the little-changed landscape of the Messogia, in the midst of the southern peninsula. Covered with vineyards and olive groves as it has been since antiquity, the region produces much of the *retsina* drunk in Athenian tavernas.

On the southern tip of the peninsula, the columns of the Temple of Poseidon, dramatically silhouetted against the sunset, are one of the great sights. Other delightful temples are to be seen at Vravróna and Thorikón (Thorikos), on the peninsula's east coast.

A string of fashionably casual seaside suburbs, beaches and marinas on the west coast of the Attica peninsula attracts droves of Athenians in summer. The best sandy beaches, though, are on the bay of Marathón, 42km from Athens, where a mound and a modern monument mark the grave of the Athenians who fell in battle against the Persians in 490BC. Northwest of Athens, grim fortresses and other ghostly battlefields mark the one-time frontier of Athens with Thebes, its rival, while the fortresses of Aigósthena, Elevtherai, and Plataiaí, mark where the Spartans, Athenians and their allies again defeated the Persians in 479.

West of Athens, the coastal highway to Corinth passes through industrial suburbs which generate much of the capital's notorious smog.

The ruins of Eleusis, once one of the most important religious shrines in Greece

The Temple of Themis (goddess of Justice) at Rhamnoós, destroyed by the Persians

# ATTICA

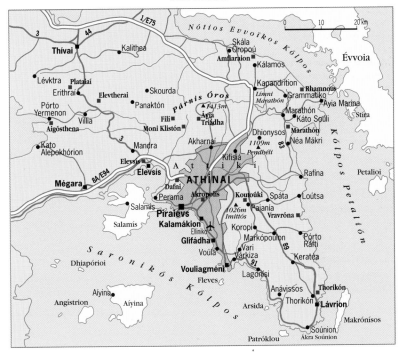

The Temple of Poseidon at Cape Soúnion, the southern tip of Attica

## THE PLAYGROUND OF ATHENS: AKTÍ APOLLONA (APOLLO COAST)

South of Athens lie the city's seaside suburbs and marinas, offering Athenians a summer getaway. Pollution is a problem on beaches closer to the busy harbour of Piraiévs (Piraeus), and swimming between Piraeus and Glifádha is not recommended. Beyond this, a string of clean beaches extends along the west-facing Aktí Apollona (Apollo Coast) to the tip of the peninsula.

### AKRA SOÚNION (CAPE SOÚNION)

After the Acropolis, the **Temple of Poseidon** in silhouette against the sunset is the best-known and most striking image of Attica. Perched 60m above the sea on the peninsula's southern tip, the temple was built between 444 and 440BC and dedicated to Poseidon. It was restored after independence in the 19th century, 16 Doric columns of the original 34 surviving. Just 6.10m high, the columns seem taller because of their

slimness, measuring only 1m in diameter at the base and 0.79m at the top. On one of the two columns of the entrance portico is carved the name of Lord Byron, who visited the temple in 1810.

The temple is at its most spectacular at sunset, when it is also at its most crowded as dozens of sightseeing coaches arrive from Athens.

*Temple of Poseidon, 70km south of Athens (tel: 0292 39363). Open: Monday to Saturday, 9am–sunset; Sunday, 10am–sunset. Admission charge.*

### GLIFÁDHA (GLYFADHA)

The best swimming near Athens is at Glyfadha , the smart suburb 18km from the city centre, favoured by wealthy Athenians and expatriates. There is a clean beach operated by the National Tourist Organisation, a marina, and the capital's only 18-hole golf course (see Sports, page 162).

### KOUTOÚKI CAVE

The Koutoúki Cave, discovered in 1926,

plunges into the side of Imittós. Within, water trickles down floodlit rose-coloured walls and needle-sharp stalactites.

*4km from the village of Paianía (Peania) and 18km from Athens (tel: 6642 910). Open: Tuesday to Sunday, 8.30am–3pm. Admission charge.*

## VARI

Vari comes to bubbling life after dark, when it is a favourite dinner destination for Athenians. Waiters dressed in the baggy pants and embroidered waistcoats of traditional costume drum up business for dozens of rival restaurants. Not for vegetarians or the faint-hearted, Vari's taverns cater to serious carnivores with dishes like whole lamb on the spit, skewered meat, *kokoretsi* (spit-roasted lamb entrails) and sheep's brains.
*27km from Athens.*

## VÁRKIZA

A lively resort and fishing harbour, Várkiza has a 750m stretch of sand with facilities operated by the National Tourist Organisation. Cafés and expensive restaurants surround its small port and many Athenians drive out for the evening, especially at weekends, to sample freshly caught seafood.
*31km south of Athens.*

## VOULIAGMÉNI

The smartest of all the resort suburbs, Vouliagméni is the haunt of Athenian shipping millionaires and other tycoons, as can be seen from the luxury yachts and cruisers at anchor in its marina. Villas and hotels are dotted among the pine trees of two wooded headlands

### ANCIENT ATTICA

Theseus, the mythical king who slew the Minotaur and thus freed Athens from paying tribute to the Minoan rulers of Knossos, united the petty kingdoms of Attica with Athens. Throughout ancient times the region remained part of the Athenian city-state, providing Athens with wine, bread, olives, marble for its great temples and silver from the Lavrion mines. During the Peloponnesian War of the 5th century BC, Sparta struck at Athens by invading Attica each year, systematically felling its olive groves and cutting off the city's food supply.

With the decline of Athens, Attica declined too and as Christianity took over its temples fell into disuse, to be rediscovered only in the 19th century.

framing Vouliagméni's natural harbour. Vouliagméni's beaches and luxury hotels are popular and crowded in summer.
*24km south of Athens.*

The richly stocked yacht marina in the fashionable Athenian suburb of Glyfadha

# MARATHÓN AND THE EAST COAST

## AMFIARAION

Located in a peaceful, pine-covered gully, rows of stone coffins and statue pedestals give a clear picture of the layout of the ancient site, a sanctuary dedicated to the legendary Amphiaraos, king of Argos, and dating from the 4th century BC. The lion-footed seats of the priests in the front row of its 3,000-seat theatre are well preserved.

*On the Kálamos road, 38km north of Athens. Open: Monday to Friday, 8am–6pm; weekends, 8.30am–3pm. Admission charge.*

## MARATHÓN

The name is legendary but there is little to see at Marathón. The only relic of the battle is the 12m-high mound marking the tomb of the 192 Athenians who fell. It stands among citrus groves behind a 2km crescent of sandy beach. The mound of the Plataians, allies of Athens, is 5km away on the opposite (inland) side of the main road near the small village of Vranas. Next to it, the Marathón Archaeological Museum houses finds from the tomb, gravestones and carvings from the mid-4th century

The burial mound at Marathón, beneath which archaeologists found bones of the Athenian dead

BC, pottery and stone tools from the Cycladic and Mycenaean eras, and an Egyptian-style *kouros* from the 2nd century BC. In the adjacent Bronze Age tomb, 10 skeletons dating from the 2nd millennium BC are open to view.

*Tomb and museum (tel: 0294 55155), 42km from Athens and 5km from the resort of Marathón. Open: daily, except Monday, 8.30am–3pm. Admission charge.*

## RAFÍNA

Ferries and hydrofoils to the Aegean islands lend an air of bustle to this small port. Its half-moon harbour front is packed with excellent fish tavernas, a lovely place for a night out. In the

### THE BATTLE OF MARATHÓN

With its long sweep of gently shelving beach the bay of Marathónas is the perfect place for a seaborne invasion, and it was here in 490BC that the Persian general Mardonios landed with a fleet and an army of perhaps 30,000. They were met by 10,000 Athenians and their Plataian allies. Though heavily outnumbered, the Athenians charged the Persians and routed them. The Athenian historians claimed only 192 of their citizen soldiers were killed (among them the Athenian commander Kallimakhos) for 6,400 Persian dead. Miltiades, the surviving commander, sent a runner to tell the city of the victory. He ran non-stop, gasping out his news before dying of exhaustion and inspiring the modern marathon event, run over a course which corresponds to the distance from the battlefield to the city of Athens.

Temple of Artemis at Vravróna, possibly founded by Iphigenia, daughter of Agamemnon. Beyond the temple foundations are the dining rooms and dormitories of the young priestesses that served here

daytime, Evia and the slopes of Oxi Oros tantalise on the horizon.
*40km east of Athens*

## RHAMNOÓS (RAMNOUS)

Ramnous is now off the beaten track, but in ancient times it controlled all the shipping passing through the Gulf of Evia. The most impressive part of the site, the 4th-century BC fortified harbour, is closed for further archaeological work. The site is famous for its Temple of Nemesis, the goddess of justice, retribution and atonement (build about 435BC), the only such temple known outside Asia Minor, and the Temple of Themis, the goddess of world order (built about 500BC).
*Káto Soúli (tel: 0294 63477), 55km northeast of Athens; follow signs from main Marathón road. Open: Monday to Saturday, 7am–6pm; Sunday, 8am–6pm. Admission charge.*

## THORIKÓN (THORIKOS)

A short distance from the ugly mining town of Lávrion, close to Attica's southern tip, ancient Thorikos is still being excavated. Quite densely populated from 2900BC onwards, the town became a Mycenaean stronghold, and three 16th-century BC beehive graves have been discovered. Its most interesting feature is an unusual 4th-century BC oval-shaped theatre with tiers of seats for 5,000 spectators. Little remains of the site's acropolis or other buildings.
*Signposted 'Theatre Antique' from Lávrion. Free access.*

## VRAVRÓNA (BRAURON)

Here you will find a cluster of graceful temple columns among vineyards and reedbeds. The earliest finds from the site are from as early as 1700BC, but the main ruins are those of the 5th-century BC Temple of Artemis, the goddess of female chastity, a cult which goes back to the 9th century BC. A small museum exhibits jewellery and sacred vessels from the temple. More interesting are the lively statues of the *arktoi* or 'bear-maidens' who were the priestesses of Artemis. The 15th-century AD chapel of Ayios Yioryios, within the temple precinct, has some interesting remains of frescos.
*Vravróna Archaeological Site (tel: 0299 27020), on the road to Pórto Ráfti, 7km from Markópoulon, signposted. Open: daily, except Monday, 8.30am–3pm. Admission charge.*

The east coast harbour of Rafina is Attica's gateway to the islands

The courtyard at the Dafni Monastery. The church interior is a treasure house of mid-Byzantine mosaics – even after Turkish troops attempted to melt the gold out of the fragments

# NORTHERN ATTIKA

## DAFNÍ MONASTERY

The monastery and church of the Virgin at Dafní date from the 11th century AD, though there has been a monastery on the site since the 6th century. Much of the splendid gold mosaic of the interior survives; its most striking feature is the mosaic of a characteristically stern-looking, Byzantine-style Christ, though the other portraits are very human, lively and almost classical in their rendering. The exterior, with its graceful arcade and portico using columns and fragments lifted from an earlier temple of Apollo, is less stolid than many modern Orthodox churches and is a typical Byzantine mix of brickwork and masonry.

*Signposted off the main Athens-Eleusís-Corinth highway, 11km from the centre of Athens (tel: 5811 558). Open: daily, 8.30am–3pm. Admission charge.*

## ELEVSÍS (ELEUSIS)

Set on a low hill overlooking the sea and surrounded by refineries and factories,

<br>

**DEMETER AND AND PERSEPHONE**

Persephone, daughter of Zeus and Demeter, goddess of the earth's fruits, was carried off by Hades (to whom Zeus had promised Persephone in marriage) to the underworld. During her search for her daughter, Demeter came to Eleusis where she gave the king permission to build a temple in her honour. To this she retired, vowing that until Persephone was returned she would neither reside in Olympus nor allow crops to grow on earth.

Zeus relented, commanding Hades to return Persephone. To this Hades consented but he gave Persephone part of a pomegranate to eat. Having eaten in the underworld she was bound to return there, and was allowed to live on the earth with her mother only between sowing time in the autumn and harvest in early summer. The hot, arid summer months she spent underground as 'goddess of the dead'. Demeter and Persephone were worshipped together as goddesses of growth, especially of cultivated grain.

<br>

Eleusis is now an unprepossessing place but it was one of the great sanctuaries of ancient times. Dedicated to the fertility goddesses Persephone and Demeter, the site was rediscovered and excavated in the 19th century. Roman ruins overlay the earlier Greek temple. Its main features are the great forecourt and entrance to the sanctuary built by the Romans in the 2nd century AD, the Telesterion, which was the centre of the sanctuary, and the classical-era defensive walls around the site.

*Eleusis Archaeological Site (tel: 5546 019), signposted from the main Athens-Eleusis-Corinth highway, 26km northwest of Athens. Open: daily, except Monday, 8.30am–3pm. Admission charge.*

## ELEVTHERAI

This 4th-century BC Athenian fortress guards the pass between the Pateras and Kitheron ranges through which the former National Road between Athens and Thebes still runs. One massive wall of grey limestone blocks still stands, and goats shelter in the ruins of its towers.

*Signposted to the north of the Athens–Thebes road, 1km north of the Pórto Germeno turning. Unenclosed.*

## PÓRTO YERMENO (PORTO GERMENO)

This delightful, quiet little resort at the head of an arm of the Korinthiakós Kólpos (Gulf of Corinth) seems more remote than it is. Ringed by steep, pine-covered slopes, it has a crescent of pebbly beach, busy only on summer weekends, and a handful of guesthouses and fish restaurants.

*Signposted from Athens-Thebes highway, 71km northwest of Athens.*

**Nearby** is the once-mighty Athenian fortress of Aigósthena, built in the 4th century BC as part of the defences on the Theban border. Its massive walls ring a low hilltop, and five of its 15 square towers are still standing.

*500m from Pórto Germeno village. Unenclosed.*

## THÍVAI (THEBES)

A ruined 13th-century Frankish tower stands atop the hill which was the acropolis of ancient Thebes, one of the most powerful of the city-states. Allied with the Persians against Athens in 480BC, Thebes remained a rival until Sparta defeated Athens in the Peloponnesian War. Thebes' finest hour came in 371BC when it defeated Sparta to become chief of the Hellenic states. It was destroyed by Alexander in 336BC. The main point of interest today is the Mousio Thivai Arkheologiko (Thebes Archaeological Museum); the collection includes a 6th-century BC *kouros*, some unique black tombstones, and Mycenaean sarcophagi.

*Thebes is 81km northwest of Athens. The Thebes Archaeological Museum (tel: 0262 27913) is next door to the castle. Open: daily, except Monday, 8.30am–3pm. Admission charge.*

---

### BATTLEFIELDS OF NORTHERN ATTICA

Three great battles for ancient Greece were fought in northern Attica. At Thermopylae (480BC), the pass connecting Attica and Thessaly, 300 Spartans under King Leonidas fought to the death against a much larger Persian force. They were avenged at Plataiaí (479BC) by a Greek alliance. At Lévktra (371BC) Thebes defeated mighty Sparta. There is little to see at the battlefields, but a statue of Leonidas stands near the site of Thermopylae, beside the OE1 highway.

**Lévktra**: 12km south of Thebes, signposted.

**Plataiaí** 17km south of Thebes, signposted.

**Thermopylae**: near Kamena Vourla on OE1 (National Road 1), signposted.

# Attika and Ákra Soúnion

The best way to see the countryside and the superb archaeological sites of Attica is by car. The high point of the tour is the magnificent Temple of Poseidon at Ákra Soúnion (Cape Soúnion), on the very southern tip of the Attica peninsula. *Starting from central Athens, the tour distance is 180km. Allow 4 to 6 hours driving.*

*Leave Athens by the main coast highway, passing through the seaside suburbs of Glifádha, Voúla and Vouliagméni. On a clear day the island of Aíyina can be seen to the west, and the waters of the Saronikós Kólpos (Saronic Gulf) are dotted with yachts and ferries.*

*At Várkiza, set on a scenic bay with a pay beach managed by the Greek National Tourist Organisation, turn inland, following the*

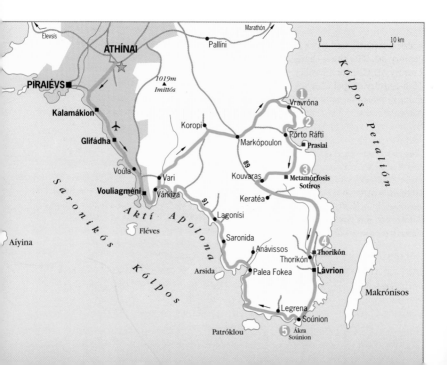

signs to *Vari (2km)*, then turn right in the direction of Koropi.

*Leaving the urban sprawl of Athens, the countryside is much scarred by marble quarrying. At the Koropi crossroads, take the second right, signposted to Markópoulon, and drive through prettier surroundings of rolling hills dotted with olive trees and vineyards.*

*At Markópoulon, follow signs first to Vravróna to visit the ancient temple site and museum, then to Pórto Ráfti. The road crosses a fertile plain covered with vineyards which sell their produce to the Kourtaki retsina winery in Markópoulo. The green vines are all the more striking in contrast to the barren hillsides around them.*

*After 7km turn right, following signs to Vravróna and Pórto Ráfti. 250m from the turning you will see the columns of ancient Vravróna (see page 51) on the left.*

## 1 VRAVRÓNA

The sanctuary was dedicated to the goddess Artemis and dates from the 5th century BC. The site is shared by a 6th-century AD Christian basilica and the 15th-century chapel of Ayios Yioryios.
*From Vravróna the road climbs through pine woods, descending after 3km to the sea.*

## 2 PÓRTO RÁFTI

The spectacularly located port and beach resort of Pórto Ráfti, on a broad, almost-enclosed blue bay, is a lovely place to stop for a snack and a swim.
*Leaving Pórto Ráfti turn right (signposted to Kouvaras), and keep right. The road climbs through a pine-wooded valley.*

## 3 MONASTERY OF METAMÓRFOSIS SOTIROS (METAMORPHOSIS SOTIROS)

The stately terracotta domes and bell towers of the monastery of

Mount Parnitha dominates the Athens skyline and offers escape from the summer heat

Metamorphosis Sotiros (Transformation of the Saviour) stand guard over its olives and vines, surrounded by cypresses and palms.
*The road zigzags through hills before joining the main road to Lávrion, which is soon bypassed as you press on to Cape Soúnion. Detour to the ancient site at Thorikón (signposted 'Theatre Antique' to the right of the road just before you enter Lávrion).*

## 4 THORIKÓN (THORIKOS)

An unusual oval-shaped theatre seating 5,000 is currently being excavated at this hillside site, which dates from the 5th century BC.

## 5 CAPE SOÚNION

Homer's 'sacred headland' is crowned by the Temple of Poseidon, set atop 60m-high sea-cliffs, and one of the most spectacular of Greece's ancient sites. The islands of Makrónisos and Kea float on the eastern horizon. The temple was built between 444 and 440BC and restored in the 19th century, the clifftop position making it an invaluable vantage point in war and it was at one time fortified. It was built as a tribute to the sea god Poseidon at a time of growing Athenian naval power.
*Head back to Várkiza and Athens by the winding corniche road which follows the bays and headlands of the Apollo Coast. The drive back takes around 1 hour.*

# Pelopónnisos

## (The Peloponnese)

*S*eparated from the northern mainland by the Korinthiakós Kólpos (Gulf of Corinth), the Peloponnese is rich in history and in natural beauty. Its coasts have some of Greece's longest sandy beaches and prettiest remote coves, its mountains offer unrivalled views, and it is dotted with ancient palaces, castles and fortresses spanning 5,000 years.

The Isthmus of Corinth connects the Peloponnese with the northern mainland, and is cut across by the Dióriga Korínthou (Corinth Canal). Much of the region is mountainous, with one mighty chain of peaks, culminating in the Taiyetos summit, running down the centre.

Nowhere else is Greece's many-layered history so clearly on show. The northeast corner of the region was the cradle of the Mycenaean civilisation celebrated by Homer. The classical and Hellenistic eras which followed are represented by Sparta, Corinth, Epídhavros and other sites.

The Byzantines built the fairy-tale castle of Mistra, above the Evrótas valley. Frankish princes left castles on a dozen hilltops. The Venetians fortified Návplion and Monemvasía and built grim strongholds at Methóni and Koróni. The Turks added yet another layer of history.

The Peloponnese is the birthplace of modern Greece. Here the War of Independence began in 1821, and here its fiercest battles were fought for

The Arcadian Gate at Ancient Messini stands as a testament to the monumental engineering skills of Sparta's great rival

possession of castles built hundreds of years earlier. Together with Athens and the Sterea Ellas, the Peloponnese was the nucleus of the new Greek state established in 1830.

The north coast between Corinth and Patras is backed by steeply rising mountain slopes. West of Patras, the coast is dominated by long, sandy beaches. Inland, every pass through the mountains is guarded by a medieval castle or classical temple, but one of the

magnets for visitors is the magical site of ancient Olympia.

Each of the three peninsulas has its own aura: Akritas, with its Venetian fortresses, Taínaron with its deserted towers and Maléa with its empty hillsides.

On the east coast, some charmingly remote towns, villages and untouched beaches are cut off from the hinterland of the Peloponnese by the bulk of Párnon Óros (Mount Parnon).

# THE PELOPONNESE

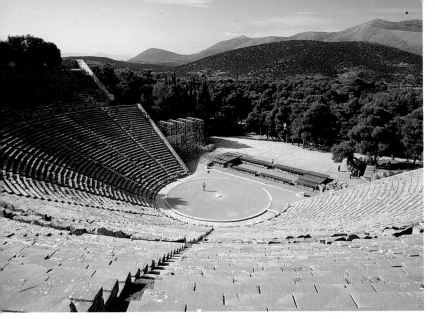

The theatre at Epídhavros

## THE ARGOLID

The Argolid is a blunt peninsula pointing southeast into the Aegean. The peninsula and the fertile plain at its landward end are rich in ancient and medieval sites.

There are beach resorts at Tolón, 4km from Návplion, and Portokhéli, on the peninsula's southern tip.

## ÁRGOS

The oldest continuously inhabited town in Europe – it was founded in 2000BC – stands amid olive and citrus groves, a grid of modern buildings surmounted by Larissa Castle 300m above.

### Kastro Larissis (Larissa Castle)

The 13th-century Frankish Kastro Larissis (Larissa Castle) is impressive from below and ghostly within, as only the outer walls and the shell of the inner keep survive, but there are fine views south down the east coast.

*Access is from the west side of the crag, 5km from the town centre. Signposted. Unenclosed.*

### Mousio Arkheologikou (Archaeological Museum)

The museum contains minor finds from ancient Argos, including pottery, weapons and mosaics and a suit of 8th-century BC bronze armour.

*Town centre (tel: 0751 28819). Open: daily, except Monday, 8.30am–3pm. Admission charge.*

Impressive remains of the 2nd-century AD Roman baths are to be found, along with the ruins of the largest theatre in Greece (capacity 20,000), on Gounaris, the road to Tripoli.

## EPÍDHAVROS

Set in a landscaped site among pines, the restored 4th-century BC theatre is the finest in Greece, seating 14,000 in 55 tiers, and is the main remnant of a sanctuary dedicated to Asklepios, the god of healing. Attending the theatre was thought to be beneficial to the spirit and the structure is still in use for the Epídhavros Festival from June to August each year, when the ancient plays are brought to life by its magnificent acoustics – you can clearly hear someone speaking in a normal voice, or even tearing a sheet of paper, from the top row of seats almost 23m above the stage. Only foundations remain of other buildings, though some of the tiered seats of the stadium still survive.

*Archaeological Site and Museum (tel: 0753 22009). 28km east of Návplion and 3km from the village of Ligoúrion (Lygourion). Open: Monday, 11am–5pm; Tuesday to Saturday, 8am–5pm; Sunday and holidays, 8.30am–3pm. Admission charge.*

### IRÉON (IREO)

Cyclopean blocks and column sections litter the site of the Sanctuary of Hera, the earth goddess of Argos. Tiers of walls and foundations give a clear view of the

The legendary wooden horse of Troy, visualised by a 19th-century artist

ground plan, but there are no signs to help make sense of the site, which is best appreciated from its highest point, the flagstoned floor of the 7th-century BC Doric Temple of Hera.

*Ireo Archaeological Site, 2km north of Inaxon, signposted erratically. Open: daily, 8.30am–3pm. Admission charge.*

### HOMER'S HEROES

In one of the greatest stories ever told, the blind poet Homer wrote, probably in the 8th century BC, about events which were already far in the past. Homer drew on earlier folk tales for the basic plot and characters of his epics, the *Iliad* and the *Odyssey*, which deal with the 10-year siege of Troy, in Asia Minor, by a league of Mycenaean kings and princes from the Greek mainland and islands.

The war began when Paris, younger son of King Priam of Troy, ran off with the beautiful Helen, wife of King Menelaus of Sparta. Menelaus summoned his allies – the mighty warrior and commander Agamemnon, king of Mycenae; Nestor, wise old king of Pilos and a skilled charioteer; cunning Odysseus, ruler of Ithaca; and the invincible Achilles, dipped by his mother in a sacred spring to protect him against all weapons. Homer's *Iliad* deals with the last year of the siege during which Achilles was killed by an arrow which pierced his ankle, his only vulnerable spot.

In the *Aeneid*, the Roman poet Virgil (70–19BC) tells how Troy fell not to the valour of Achilles but to a ruse. The Greeks built a giant wooden horse, which they left as an offering to Poseidon when the fleet sailed away. The Trojans dragged it into the city, not knowing that Greek warriors lurked within. That night, the fleet returned, the hidden commandos emerged to open the gates, and the city fell.

Top: the Lion Gate at Mycenae
Inset: Heinrich Schliemann

## MIKÍNAI (MYCENAE)

The most impressive of the Argolid's dramatic ancient sites, excavated by the German Heinrich Schliemann (1822–90) in 1876s.

He first found the ramparts, then a circle of royal tombs. The corpses found in them were decked in golden masks (including the famous so-called 'Mask of Agamemnon') and bracelets, now in the National Archaeological Museum in Athens.

Pass through the ramparts by the Lion Gate with its carved lionesses. Immediately within, to the right, are the first tombs discovered, dating from the 16th century BC. Below these and outside the walls is a second tomb circle,

### THE REAL MYCENAEANS

*I have gazed upon the face of Agamemnon.*
Heinrich Schliemann (1876)

In 1871 the German archaeologist Heinrich Schliemann staggered the world by finding proof that Homer's epics were more than myth. Inspired by the *Iliad*, he discovered the site of Troy near Canakkale in western Turkey. Three years later he made his first tentative excavations at Hycenae, and two years after that he uncovered the palace and tombs. In the tombs were gold-bedecked skeletons, one of them wearing the breathtaking golden mask now in the National Archaeological Museum in Athens. His discovery began an archaeologists' gold rush to excavate the rich sites surrounding Mycenae and ushered in a golden age of archaeological discovery.

The Mycenaeans were a Bronze-Age people who came to Greece from Asia around 2100BC, and over the next five centuries they created a world of tiny kingdoms ruled from hilltop palaces built of crude but imposing massive stone blocks. They settled throughout southern Greece and established colonies in the islands and overseas, trading with the great empires of Egypt and the Middle East and with the Minoans of Crete. This first Greek civilisation fell quite suddenly around 1200BC, leaving a treasury of finely detailed figurines of people, gods and animals in bronze, gold and ceramics, elaborate seals and frescos depicting scenes from everyday life, and gorgeous golden grave-goods. The later, Dorian Greeks, who settled among the mighty ruins of the Mycenaean civilisation, wove a tapestry of legend around the dimly-remembered Mycenaeans and their palaces, kings and heroes.

excavated in 1951 and dating from the 17th century BC. Next to this is the so-called Tomb of Clytemnestra, a 14th-century BC domed royal grave. Above the tombs, the tiers of the Royal Palace are connected by zigzagging marble stairs rising to a fortified acropolis.

Opposite the main site is the splendid Treasury of Atreus, a 13th-century BC beehive tomb over 13m high quarried out of the hillside.

*The site is 2km from modern Mikínai, 7km southeast of the main Corinth-Argos road. Signposted. Archaeological Site and Treasury of Atreus (tel: 0751 66585). Open: weekdays, 8.30am–5pm; weekends and holidays, 8.30am–3pm. Admission charge.*

## NÁVPLION

A delightfully pretty harbour town whose shuttered stucco façades date from Návplion's brief 19th-century moment of glory as free Greece's first capital.

### Akronavplion (Its Kale)

A rugged ring of impressive Turkish–Venetian ramparts on the site of an earlier Frankish stronghold occupies a headland above the harbour. The Byzantine gatehouse has fine frescos dated to AD1291. The main area of the old citadel has now been converted into a hotel.

### Bourtzi

A quaint miniature fortress built by the Venetians in 1471, with a six-sided tower, adorns the island in the middle of Návplion's harbour. It also served in the past as a prison and the local hangman's home, but is now deserted.

### Palamidhi

Built on the heights between 1711 and 1714, when the town was Venice's regional capital, the imposing stronghold is entered through gateways bearing the Lion of St Mark. The view from the top is magnificent.

*Palamidhi Fortress (tel: 0752 28036). Open: weekdays, 8am–5pm; weekends and holidays, 8.30am–3pm. Admission charge.*

## TIRYNS

'Cyclopean' limestone boulder walls, up to 7m high and 700m in circumference, led later Greeks to believe that this 13th-century BC stronghold was built not by men but by giants like the one-eyed Cyclops of the myths. It is, in fact, the finest surviving example of Mycenaean military architecture. Historians estimate that the original height of the walls may have been as much as 20m – they are 10m thick in places. Little is known of the builders or of the ruling family, but it is clear that the fortress suffered a violent end, the palace within being gutted by fire well before the classical period.

*The fort is 4km north of Návplion (tel: 0752 22657). Open: weekdays, 8am–5pm; weekends and holidays, 8.30am–3pm. Admission charge.*

The island fortress of Bourtzi guards the harbour at Návplion

# DRAMA IN ANCIENT

The plays performed in theatres like Epídhavros were far more than mere entertainment. They began as religious experiences, and their purpose was to explain the ways of gods to men. They also, however, often commented on society and politics in the city. Later, the works of the great Greek dramatists influenced Roman theatre, and later still they inspired generation after generation of Western playwrights, including Shakespeare and his 16th- and 17th-century contemporaries. Modern theatre is still in their debt.

To the playwrights of ancient Athens, a comedy was more than merely a play to make people laugh, and a tragedy more than just a tear-jerker. Essentially, tragedy dealt with deeper religious or moral themes, and comedy with everyday affairs, but both forms were highly stylised and conventional. Actors were disguised in masks which portrayed their character's attributes and an on-stage chorus provided a running commentary.

Tragedies were presented in Athens at great annual festivals and were surrounded by splendid rituals. Every citizen (that is, every free-born Athenian man) was entitled and expected to attend.

Writers had a solemn social and religious responsibility and the most successful were richly rewarded.

Cutout: actor's mask

The plot was less important than the exposition of the dramatist's theme, since the audience was already familiar with the story-line. Athenian audiences, in particular, instead, wanted to see how a new play interpreted an old story, and one purpose of the drama was to keep alive tales which were a central part of Greek culture.

Though described as 'hard to analyse, impossible to translate', the ancient plays of writers like the tragedians Sophocles (496–406BC), Aeschylus (*c.*525–456BC) and Euripides (484–406BC), and the comedian

Cutout: actor's mask

Works of the great Greek dramatists were performed at the great Theatre of Epídhavros

# GREECE

Aristophanes (448–380BC), are re-enacted each year at festivals in Athens and Epídhavros (see Entertainment, pages 148–49). These can be moving events, especially if you have an English translation of the script, and their themes and even their humour are as relevant and fresh today as when they were written.

Cutout: actor's mask

Actors preparing for a performance

# ÁKRA AKRITAS (CAPE AKRITAS)

### ANÁKTORA NESTOROS
(Palace of Nestor)

It is hard to picture the 13th-century BC palace of the great elder statesman of the Trojan War from its mud and stone foundations, but the site has a fine view across Navarino Bay. There is a cavernous 13th-century BC beehive tomb about 100m from the palace site.

*17km north of Pílos. Open: daily, except Monday, 8.30am–3pm. Admission charge.*

Only the stone foundations of the Palace of Nestor survived a fire in the 12th century BC

### KASTRO TON PARAMYTHION
(Castle of the Fairy-tales)

Winged horses, 5m-high stucco statues and tableaux from Greek history surround the extraordinary three-storey folly with its red and yellow spires and white plaster battlements built in the 1950s by the late Dr Haralambos Fournarakis.

*On the shore, between Kiparissía and Filiatrá. From Kiparissia, follow signs to Agrili. The building is not open to the public.*

The Castle of the Fairy-tales, a unique and colourful Greek folly

### KIPARISSÍA

A pocket-sized Byzantine castle sits crumbling on a pine-covered hilltop above this farming and fishing town which spreads between the coastal hills and a long strip of pebbly beach.

*1km from town centre.*

### KORÓNI

The lovely castle at Koróni looks east to the summits of Taïyetos (Taiyetos) and the cliffs of Outer Mani, and down on to the red roofs, esplanade and palm trees of the town itself. Koróni and Methóni, known in the Middle Ages as 'the Eyes of Venice', guarded the sea routes to Venice's eastern colonies. To the south, you can see Koróni's 1km sweep of sandy beach.

The ramparts surround houses, gardens, and a cemetery and monastery among pines and olives.

*500m from the esplanade. Unenclosed.*

### METHÓNI

A fortified city from a historical romance, Methóni occupies a headland jutting into a vast bay sheltered by the island of

Sapiéntza, protected to landward by impregnable walls and a deep moat. Within, a 750m cobbled road leads from the inner keep past ruined mosques and churches, cracked spires and toppling arches to the octagonal Bourtzi tower on an island connected by a causeway. The Lion of St Mark, symbol of Venice, is emblazoned on the stonework to the left of the main gate, close to the sea. Sunset over the Bourtzi is best viewed from the long sandy beach east of the castle.

Modern Methóni, outside the walls, is a lively tourist resort in summer, reverting to a somnolent farming and fishing town out of season.

*63km southwest of Kalamata. Castle, overlooking Methóni harbour (tel: 0731 25363). Open: daily, except Monday, 8.30am–3pm. Admission charge.*

Rusting Venetian cannon adorn the battlements overlooking the tranquil harbour at Methóni

## PÍLOS

The peaceful town of white- and cream-painted 19th-century houses overlooking the lagoon-like bay of Navarino is built around a small harbour (slated for development as a marina), guarded by the huge Neo Kastro.

*51km west of Kalamata.*

### Neo Kastro (New Castle)

The castle was built by the Turks in the late 16th century to control the bay of Navarino and counter the Venetian forts at Methóni and Koróni. Recently restored, it contains a small museum with a fine, colourful collection of prints and lithographs of fantastically-costumed heroes of the War of Independence. The etching *Lendemain de Navarin* (*The Day After Navarino*) shows a disconsolate Turk clinging to a spar among the wreckage of his fleet.

*Above Pílos, 500m from the harbour. Open: daily, 8.30am–3pm. Admission charge.*

### NAVARINO

The calm bay sheltered by the islands of Navarino and Sfaktiria attracted seafarers to Pílos from King Nestor, the elder statesman of the *Iliad* and the *Odyssey*, Homer's epics of the Trojan War, to Venetian and Turkish fleets in medieval and modern times.

On 20 October 1827, a Turkish fleet anchored in the bay was sunk by a flotilla of British, French and Russian ships commanded by the British Admiral Lord Codrington. Codrington's instructions were to observe, but when the Turks fired on one of the allied ships they responded in kind. The sinking of the Turkish fleet helped to decide the War of Independence in favour of the Greeks.

Precarious wooden balconies overhang
Andhritsaina's streets

# THE CENTRAL
# PELOPONNESE

The heartland of the Peloponnese is a
blend of rugged mountains, rolling hills
and farming valleys filled with olive trees.

### ANDRÍTSAINA (ANDHRITSAINA)

A charming, old-fashioned hill town
surrounded by barren peaks,
Andhritsaina rises from a main square
dominated by an enormous plane tree,
and in summer is full of café tables.
Many of its older houses have tiled roofs
and overhanging second storeys.
*65km from Tripolis.*

### KARÍTAINA

Commanding the Alfiós valley, the 13th-
century baronial castle of the Frankish de

Bruyères family balances precariously
above the half-deserted medieval village.
Halfway up the steep path to the citadel
stands a marble bust, erected in 1939, of
Theodoros Kolokotronis, the great
general whose forces garrisoned the
castle in the 1821–30 War of
Independence.
*55km from Tripolis. Unenclosed.*

### MANTINEIA

Founded in about 500BC, Mantineia was
destroyed by the Spartans in 385BC and
rebuilt in 371BC when Thebes was
victorious over Sparta. The ruins date
from the 371 rebuilding, and of
particular interest are the massive town
walls, over 4m thick and almost 4km in
length, with 10 gates and 120 towers.
*Unenclosed. 11km north of Tripolis on the
main road to Olympia.*

### MEGALÓPOLIS (MAGALOPOLI)

Relics of the ancient city, built between
371 and 368BC by Epaminondas of
Thebes to curb the power of Sparta,
include the foundations of the 66m by
53m assembly hall and the lower rows of
a 59-tier theatre which seated nearly
20,000.
*1km north of the modern town of
Magalopoli on the Karitaina road.
Signposted. Open: daily, except Monday,
8.30am–3pm. Admission free.*

### TRIPOLIS

The quiet market town of Tripolis is the
hub of the Peloponnese road and rail
networks, and the gateway to the more
exciting southern Peloponnese. Tripolis
stands amid farmland on a 600m plateau
ringed by mountains. Destroyed by the
Turkish general Ibrahim Pasha during
the War of Independence, it is a far cry
from the holiday hotspots and a good

place to come if you want to see everyday Greek life unaffected by the tourism business.

*180km southwest of Athens.*

## VASSAI

The dramatically sited Temple of Apollo Epikourios (Apollo the Succourer) at Vassai stands 1,128m above sea level, looking out over the blue slopes of the Arkadian mountain ranges. The temple's tottering pillars are braced by a web of scaffolding and it is protected from the elements by a vast high-tech marquee. Built in 450–420BC, it is one of the best preserved of the ancient temples and is attributed to Iktinos, one of the builders of the Parthenon. It was rediscovered, almost intact, by the French architect and archaeologist Joachim Bocher in 1765. Like those of the Parthenon, its friezes were acquired by the British Museum in the early 19th century and are still exhibited in London.

With 15 Doric columns on its long sides and six on each end, the temple is much narrower than is common and, unusually, is oriented north to south instead of east to west.

*65km southeast from Olympia. Signposted. Unenclosed.*

---

**THE FRANKS OF THE MOREA**

In 1204 the Frankish soldiers of the Fourth Crusade turned on the Byzantine Empire, sacked Constantinople, and carved the empire (of which Greece was then part) into a federation of Latin kingdoms. One of these knights, Geoffrey de Villehardouin, took the Peloponnese, then called Achaia or the Morea, dividing it into 12 baronies which he gave to his followers. The Frankish barons occupied and added to Byzantine castles such as Acrocorinth and Monemvasía, or built new ones like Karitaina and Mistra. The Latin mini-states in Greece lasted just half a century before being driven out by a newly assertive Byzantium. In 1259 William de Villehardouin was among the Frankish knights defeated and captured at Pelagonia in northern Greece by the exiled Byzantine Emperor, Michael VIII Paleologos. He was forced to surrender his three strongest castles, Monemvasia, Mystra and Great Maina. Two years later, the Byzantines reconquered Constantinople and gradually drove the Franks from their remaining strongholds.

---

The main square in Andhritsaina where a large plane tree provides shelter from the sun

The seven Doric columns of the Temple of Apollo are all that remain standing of Ancient Corinth

# CORINTH AND AROUND

### ARKHEA KÓRINTHOS
### (Ancient Corinth)

Corinth's varying fortunes through the ages are reflected in the ruins of the ancient city, which span 800 years, from the 5th century BC to the 3rd century AD. A great power in the 8th century BC, Corinth was later overshadowed by Athens until again ascendant as chief of the League of Corinth under the Macedonian kings. In Roman times the city was one of the great imperial cities, but the fall of Rome, barbarian invasions and Turkish conquest eventually obliterated it. Ancient Corinth is actually situated at the foot of the hill of Akrokórinthos (Acrocorinth), 7km southwest of the modern city.

Highlights of the site are the Temple of Apollo, with seven of its 38 Doric columns intact, dating from the 6th century BC, and the Peirene Fountain with its stone arches and colonnade. Other relics include the 150m by 90m site of the Agorá and the foundations of the enormous *stoa* which occupied its south side. The seats of a small Roman *odeon*, carved from the rock in the 1st century AD, are clearly visible next to the much larger 18,000-seat theatre built in the 5th century BC and enlarged in the 3rd century BC by the Romans, who used it for gladiatorial contests.

The museum features Roman mosaics and statues, pottery and several small bronzes.

*Ancient Corinth is 7km southwest of modern Corinth, signposted. Mousio Arkheologikou (Archaeological Museum) (tel: 0741 31207). Open: Monday, 11am–6pm; Tuesday to Sunday, 8am–6pm. Archaeological site (tel: 0741 31207). Open: daily, except Monday, 8am–6pm. Admission charge includes both.*

## AKROKÓRINTHOS
### (Acrocorinth)
Towering on its 500m crag above the site of ancient Corinth, the immense ramparts of this medieval stronghold embrace Ancient Greek, Roman, Frankish and Turkish remnants. A Byzantine fortress, it was taken by the Franks in 1211 and added to by Frankish princes over the next 180 years. It passed back to Byzantium in 1394 and was later held by the Knights of St John, the Venetians and the Turks. The 15th-century ramparts, 3km long, are pierced by three gates, and inside there are two more walls built by the Byzantines. Within the walls are a dilapidated mosque and minaret, and a small church among the tumbled walls of the Turkish town. Beside the minaret is an ancient well, still providing water.

From the highest point, marked by a Corinthian capital atop a concrete pillar, there are awe-inspiring 360-degree views. *Acrocorinth Archaeological Site (tel: 0741 31207). Two kilometres above the archaeological site of ancient Corinth. Open: daily, except Monday, 8.30am–6pm. Admission charge.*

## DIÓRIGA KORÍNTHOU
### (Corinth Canal)
The Corinth Canal, begun by a French company in 1882 and completed by the Greeks 11 years later, is today more a landmark than a shipping route. The canal helped make Piraeus Greece's major port, but it is too narrow for modern vessels and is used only by smaller cruise ships. It is 6.34km long, 23m wide and 80m below the land surface, and crossed by two bridges, the eastern one carrying the Athens-Patras National Road.

Several rulers of the region in ancient times (the Roman Emperor Nero among them) attempted to build a canal across the isthmus, though none succeeded. The Greek allies built a wall across the isthmus in 480BC to keep the Persians out, which remained in place until Venetian times. The Venetians and the Turks found it a useful source of stone and no sign of it survives.
*On the main Patras-Athens highway.*

## KÓRINTHOS (Corinth)
Modern Corinth, repeatedly levelled by earthquakes (the most recent in 1981) is a modern seaside town which can be bypassed en route to the ancient site. There is little of interest here, though the town has plenty of shops and a few restaurants.

The Corinth Canal, 23m wide and 6km long

Market day at Areópolis

# DEEP MÁNI

Deep Máni, a mountainous finger of land protected by cliffs and easily defended narrow passes, was never fully under Turkish control. The Maniot clans were virtually self-governing and spent their time feuding with each other from their tiny square castles when not allied in rebellion against Turkey. Feuds went on not only from village to village but between families in the same village, and rivals strove to build the tallest towers.

## AREÓPOLIS

Once resounding to the shouts and gunfire of the Mavromichalis clan, this now quiet village is where the War of Independence against Turkish occupation began.
*26km west of Yíthion.*

## KELEFÁ

The huge, empty grey shell of Kelefá Castle, built in the 17th century by the Turks to control the turbulent clans, guards the gateway to Deep Máni. To the north the village of Itilon stands beneath the grim peaks called the Pendadaktylos (the five-fingered).
*4km northwest from Areópolis-Yíthion road on a rough track (signposted). Unenclosed.*

## KITA

Once the largest and most powerful of the towered villages, Kita looks from a distance like a miniature city of skyscrapers, but most of its towers have fallen into picturesque disrepair.
*16km south of Areopolis.*

## KÓTRONAS

Ringed by steep rocky slopes, this out-of-the-way harbour village with a small stretch of east-facing pebbly beach sits at the end of a fjord-like bay.
*40km south of Yíthion.*

## PASSAVA

The battlements of the 13th-century Frankish castle, now in ruins, can be seen from the Yíthion-Areópolis road only with difficulty (see Inner Máni and Ákra Taínaron tour, pages 80–1).
*11km south of Yíthion.*

## PÓRTO KÁYIO (Porto Kaigio)

The tarred road ends here, at one of the

---

### WAR OF INDEPENDENCE

Areópolis, gateway to the Deep Máni, was renamed after Ares, the war god, to honour its role as the starting place for the War of Independence (1821–30). The belligerent Maniots exploded out of their mountain eyries to join the *klephts* (Robin Hood-like brigands) and the pirate captains of the Aegean in revolt. They were aided by 'Philhellenes', foreign volunteers determined to free Greece from the Turkish yoke and restore its golden age. Turkey was crippled by the destruction of its fleet at Navarino and in 1829 Britain, Russia and France brokered a treaty creating a Greek homeland in the Peloponnese, Athens and Attica, the Sterea Ellas and a handful of Aegean islands, but leaving the rest of Greece in Turkish hands.

prettiest unspoiled bays in Greece. Once famous for its game birds – its name means 'Port of Quails' – it is still a favourite with locals during the autumn hunting season. *65km south of Yíthion.*

## SPILAION DHIROÚ/DHIROU SPILIES (Dhirou Caves)

A 1.2km river flows through the Vlychadha Cavern, a wonderland of spires, cones, needles and stalactites. The tour by boat takes 30 minutes. The museum displays neolithic finds from the Alepotripa cave, still being explored. *7km west from the Areópolis-Yerolimín main road, signposted from Pirgos Dhirou (tel: 0733 52222). Open: June to September, daily, 8am–6pm; rest of the year, 8am–3pm. Admission charge. Museum open: daily, 8.30am–3pm. Separate admission charge.*

## TAÍNARON

South of Porto Kaigio the potholed road runs through rugged, semi-desert scenery to end abruptly above the site of the 5th-century BC Temple of Poseidon, in a cave said to be one of the entrances to Hades, the land of the dead. The cave, little more than a depression in the rock, now houses donkeys and nothing remains of the temple. To the right, past a tiny pebble cove, the rough path passes the remains of a circular mosaic floor, exposed to the elements. Follow the path southwest over the headland to the Taínaron lighthouse and the southern tip of Greece, where cliffs plunge to dazzling azure water. *7km south of Pórto Káyio.*

## VÁTHIA

Still ruinous but making a comeback thanks to tourism, the spectacular tower village of Váthia, atop a cactus-covered hill, is the best preserved of the Mani tower villages. Surrounded by bare hillsides, it is full of old houses and medieval bastions and keeps. *9km southeast from the port of Yerolimín.*

The river journey through the Dhirou caverns

The island fortress at Monemvasía, the Gibraltar of Greece

# THE EAST COAST

## ÁKRA MALÉA (Cape Malea)

Easternmost of the peninsulas of the southern Peloponnnese, mountainous Ákra Maléa (Cape Malea) points towards the island of Kíthira on the southern horizon. The cape's eastern side is rocky and inaccessible, and the main road ends about 11km south of Monemvasía.

## KIPARISSIA

The white villas and cottages of Kiparissia stand among the cypress trees which give it its name, above a sweep of pebbly beach. The imposing slopes of the Párnon massif rise almost vertically behind the village.
*40km north of Monemuasia.*

## LEONÍDHION

Precarious balconies overhang the streets of this pleasantly unchanged small town at the foot of a dizzyingly steep canyon running far into the mountains. Leonídhion stands 3km inland from its harbour and beach, the former a favourite with yacht sailors and the latter a magnet for holidaying Athenians.

Between the pebbly, 1km-long beach and the town is a delta of fertile farmland dotted with fruit trees, olive groves and colourful plantations of peppers, aubergines and tomatoes.
*68km south of Navplion.*

## MONEMVASÍA

The dizzying 300m-high rock of Monemvasía, 400m offshore, is a natural fortress, added to by Byzantine, Frankish, Venetian and Turkish builders. It gives its name to malmsey wine, exported from the Aegean islands to Europe by the Venetians.

The name means 'one entrance', and with its cliffs and ramparts Monemvasía looks like a tough proposition for any belligerent besieger. In fact, it was frequently conquered when the defenders ran out of water. Populous until the early 19th century, it was taken and sacked by the Greeks during the War of Independence and the last permanent resident of the cragtop fortress died in 1906.

The settlement on the rock and on the mainland opposite falls into three parts: the kastro, Pano Kastro and Yefira.
*100km southeast of Sparta.*

### Kastro (Castle)

The lower town, within the medieval walls, is a maze of arches, alleys, steps and tall 15th-century Venetian houses, many of them restored as hotels or holiday apartments. Strict rules ensure that houses are rebuilt in traditional style, and no vehicles can pass the iron-bound gates through the medieval walls. Even in high summer you can wander through cobbled lanes lined with crumbling walls and wild fig trees without meeting another soul, though in its medieval heyday it had a population of 30,000 and as many as 40 churches.

### Pano Kastro (Upper Castle)

The early medieval town on the flat top of the crag is a honeycomb of shattered walls and collapsed archways. The only intact building is the late 13th-century church of Ayia Sofia, with some interesting frescos.

### Yefira (Bridge)

The modern fishing and tourism town on the mainland takes its name from the causeway and bridge which connect it with the castle. Restaurants and cafés surround the harbour and there is a pebbly beach to the north. There is a sandier beach, with fine views of the castle rock, at Pori, 3km north of Yefira on the main road.

### PARALIA ASTROS

The shell of a Frankish castle on a headland overlooks a yacht and fishing harbour at the north end of a 2km crescent of sandy, pebbly beach. Behind the village, a mixture of 18th- and 19th-century stone houses below the castle and modern villas around the harbour, a sea of olives laps at the foothills of Parnon, 2km inland. Inland lies an immense freshwater lagoon ringed with reeds, a magnet for kingfishers, swans and wading birds.
*30km south of Návplion.*

### Kastro (Castle)

The 15th-century castle at Paralia Astros has outstanding panoramic views down the east coast, across the Argolikos Kólpos (Argolic Gulf) and the island of Spétsai (Spetses), and north to Návplion.
*On the hill above the town. Unenclosed.*

The Venetian bell-tower within the lower Kastro at Monemvasía

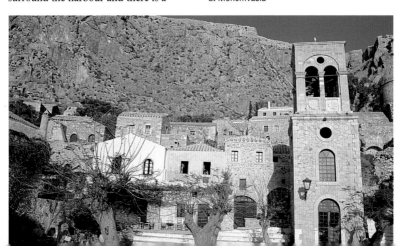

## THE EVROTAS VALLEY

### MISTRÁS (Mistra)

The ultimate medieval fairy-tale castle, with a complex of ruined domes, palaces and ramparts surrounding a pinnacle on the east flank of Taiyetos, above modern Sparta. Fortified by the Villehardouin princes to seal the pass above it, Mistra passed into Byzantine hands after the battle of Pelagonia (1259) and held out against the Turks until 1460, seven years after the fall of Constantinople. It was repeatedly besieged during the struggles for control of the Peloponnese in the 16th and 17th centuries, and during the War of Independence, when it was finally

Medieval Mistra

burned and abandoned.

The site is crowned by a fortress on a crag, with steps and paths winding through the ruined buildings below, several of which are being restored. The most important buildings are the frescoed church of Ayia Sofia, immediately below the castle; the imposing four-storey Palace of the Despots; and Perivleptos, Panayia and Ayios Nikolaos churches. Near the main gate, a small museum exhibits a collection of column pedestals and fragments.

*6km from Sparta, the lower Main Gate is 1km from the modern village of Mistras. The upper Fortress Gate is 2km further uphill (tel: 0731 93377). Signposted. Open: daily, except Monday, 8am–6pm. Admission charge.*

### SPÁRTI (Sparta)

Founded in 1836 by settlers made homeless by the destruction of Mistra in the War of Independence, modern Sparta shows little connection with the city-state which dominated the entire region from the 6th to the 4th century BC. Ancient Sparta depended for defence on the legendary courage and prowess of its warriors, not on fortifications, and, unlike their Athenian rivals, the Spartans built no great stone temples, monuments or public buildings. Modern Sparta is a pleasant enough market town set in breathtaking scenery, with the jagged, lunar summits of Taiyetos jostling for space on its western skyline.
*60km south of Tripoli.*

### Arkheologiko Mousio (Archaeological Museum)

Housed in an elegant neo-classical building in a statue-filled garden shaded by tall palms, the collection includes mosaics, marble reliefs from the 6th century BC, a bust of a Spartan warrior from 490–480BC, a colossal Hellenistic head of Hercules, and a collection of scowling votive masks from the nearby Sanctuary of Artemis Orthia.
*East side of Leoforos K. Palaeoglou, between Evangelistrias and Lykourgos (tel: 0731 25363). Open: daily, except Monday, 8.30am–3pm. Admission charge.*

### YERÁKI

The dramatic ruined fortress of Yeráki on its hilltop is visible far away across the

The hilltop castle at Mistra, the last outpost of the Byzantine Empire

flat bottom of the Evrotas valley, above the modern village of the same name. There is an awesome view of the saw-toothed Taïyetos, 20km west. The shattered shells of several small churches surround the castle walls.

*4km east of Yeráki village, 1km from main road. Unenclosed.*

## YÍTHION

Close to the mouth of the wide, fertile Evrotas flood plain, Yíthion dozes by a mirror-calm harbour sheltered by Kranai, the island where Paris and Helen spent their first night of passion together before fleeing to Troy. Elegant old mansions with wrought-iron balconies mount in tiers above the port, relics of its 19th-century heyday when its fleet of schooners carried all the trade of the region.

*48km south of Sparta.*

### Mousio Tzannetakis (Tzannetakis Museum)

This is a small museum situated in an 18th-century tower, devoted to the history of the Mani. Exhibits include books, writings and paintings.

*On the island of Kranai, reached by a causeway from the harbour esplanade (tel: 0733 22676/24631). Open: daily, 9am–1pm and 5pm-9pm. Admission charge.*

### Arkaiou Theatrou (Ancient Theatre)

Built by the Romans in the 1st century AD, the compact theatre has 13 tiers of seats.

*East end of Odhos Arkaiou Theatrou. Unenclosed.*

Mansions built by wealthy 19th-century shipowners line the harbour at Yíthion

## ITHOMI, KALÁMAI (KALAMATA) AND THE OUTER MANI

### ITHOMI (Ancient Messini/Messene)

A row of grim grey towers on a spur of Ithomi Oros (Mount Ithomi), remnant of a 10km ring of ramparts, guards the ruins of Ancient Messini, an agorá, theatre and stadium built in the 4th century BC. Messíni, destroyed after rebelling against Sparta, was rebuilt by the Theban ruler Epaminondas after his defeat of Sparta at Leuktra in 379BC. There is a fine aerial view of the site from the village of Mavromati, 300m above it. From the Lakonian Gate, 1.5km uphill from Mavromati, there is a panoramic view over the pastoral patchwork of the Messinian plain.

*11km from modern Messíni, and confusingly signposted Ancient Messini, Ithomi, Archaic Ithomi, Ancient Messini and Ithomi Archaeological Site. Unenclosed.*

### KALÁMAI (Kalamata)

The largest town in the southern Peloponnese with 40,000 inhabitants, Kalamata is of little interest to sightseers.

> **EARTHQUAKES**
>
> Southern Greece has been struck by earthquakes throughout history, which accounts for the ruinous state of many of the ancient temples. Kalámai (Kalamata) has been particularly unlucky, being rocked by quake after quake over the last two centuries. In September 1986 it was hit again. Much of the damage has been repaired with aid from the European Community, but the town still has a shell-shocked air.

The town was completely destroyed in the War of Independence and since then has been rocked by earthquakes several times, most recently in 1986.

### KARDHAMÍLI

This little town of sturdy 18th- and 19th-century balconied houses with its 2km beach of white pebbles and miniature harbour overlooking the Messiniakos Kólpos (Messinian Gulf) is the gateway to the Mani, a mountainous land of vendettas whose noble families built themselves miniature castles from which to defy their rivals. One of these quaint square towers, the stronghold of the Mourtzinos family, can be seen at the ghost village of Palaeo Kardhamíli (Old Kardhamíli) near by. It was built in 1808. Next to it stands a Byzantine church with an unusual stone spire decorated with a carved floral pattern.

*30km southeast of Kalamata.*
*Palaeo Kardhamíli is 750m from the west end of Kardhamíli, signposted Old Kardamíli.*

### STOUPA

A delightful, relaxed resort on a sheltered bay with a sandy crescent of west-facing beach, with Ákra Akritas on the horizon, backed by a dramatic landscape – the sheer, treeless and almost uninhabited slopes of the Taïyetos range.

*35km southeast of Kalamata.*

### THALAMES

The square-built stone houses and antique pantiled Byzantine church of Thalames perch on a steep limestone hillside among olive groves and cypresses. Below it the slopes plunge away to pebbly coves and hidden beaches.

*50km southeast of Kalamata.*

**Mousio Máni (Máni Museum)**
This gloriously eclectic and eccentric collection of tools, weapons, furniture, banknotes, coins, books, portraits and posters should not be missed. The ground floor houses cases of potsherds, glassware and rusting swords and muskets while the upper floor is decorated with naive posters depicting Greece's struggles for independence.
*On main street of the village, signposted (tel: 0721 74414). Open: daily, 8am–8pm; closed October to April. Admission charge.*

**TAÏYETOS ÓROS (Mount Taïyetos)**
Mount Taïyetos forms the jagged backbone of the southern Peloponnese, running from the centre of the province to form the peninsula of Ákra Taínaron. The western slopes of the massif are barren, but its eastern flanks, overlooking the Evrotas plain, are cloaked in fir and pine. Atop its highest peak, once sacred to Apollo, stands the shrine of Profitis Ilias (Prophet Elijah), the scene of a colourful annual festival (18–20 July, see Festivals). The ascent to the 2,407m peak can only be made on foot and should be attempted only by fit, experienced mountain walkers. The summits of the range are snow-capped as late as June.

Nine-kilometre long stone walls once surrounded the ancient city of Messini, protecting it from rival Sparta

# THE NORTH COAST AND ACHAIA

## ACHAIA CLAUSS

A charming mock-Bavarian castle in the hills is the headquarters of Greece's oldest winery. Founded in 1861 by Gustav Clauss (1825–1908), Achaia Clauss makes red and white table wines and dessert wines, all of which can be sampled and bought.

*5km from the centre of Patras, signposted (tel: 8075 312). Open: daily, 9am–7.30pm. Admission free.*

## CHLEMOÚTSI (Castle Tornese)

Round bastions and sheer walls surround the vaulted inner hall and courtyard of this hilltop stronghold. Built in 1220, it was the seat of Geoffrey II Villehardouin's princedom of Achaia, as this region is still called. From the ramparts, you can see the islands of Zákinthos and Kefallinia.

*86km southwest of Patras, 4km from Kilini. Open: daily, except Monday, 8.30am–5pm. Admission charge.*

## KALÁVRITA

This leafy mountain village has a special significance for Greeks. Near here, in 1821, Archbishop Germanos called for the beginning of the War of Independence. Many of the inhabitants were martyred by the Germans in 1943 on suspicion of harbouring resistance fighters. Kalávrita's main attraction is the narrow-gauge railway running through a deep canyon to Diakofto, on the Gulf of Corinth (see The Dhiakoptón to Kalávrita Railway tour, pages 82–3).

## KILLÍNI (Kilini)

A fishing harbour on the tip of a west-pointing headland, Kilini offers a long sandy beach and the opportunity of a day trip to Zákinthos.

## OLIMBÍA (Olympia)

The peaceful modern village of 900 people exists only to service visitors to ancient Olympia, the site of the Olympic Games for over 1,000 years. Most of the buildings on the archaeological site have been reduced to their foundations, but it is easy to picture the stadium packed with cheering crowds.

### Altis (Sanctuary)

The heart of Olympia and sacred to Zeus, the Sanctuary covered an area of 200 sq m. The Doric Temple of Zeus, its most important structure, was demolished in the 6th century AD by an earthquake, though its massive remains are still imposing. It was this temple that contained the huge statue of Zeus that was one of the Seven Wonders of the World. Some columns of the neighbouring Temple of Hera have been rebuilt.

Column bases of the Palestra at Olympia, training ground for the competitors

### Ergasteirion (Workshop of Phidias)
Built for Phidias, the greatest sculptor of classical times, who worked on his statue of Zeus here. In Byzantine times it became a church.

### Leonidhion
Donated in the 4th century BC by Leonidas of Naxos, the Leonidhion was a luxurious inn for the rulers and dignitaries who visited the games. The Romans added a central pool to its four wings of rooms around a courtyard.

### Mousio (Museum)
The most striking exhibits are the helmet of Miltiades, the victor of Marathón, found buried beneath the stadium as an offering to Zeus; the superb friezes from the Temple of Zeus, representing the legendary battle between the Lapiths and Centaurs; the statue of Hermes of about 350BC, discovered in 1877; and statues of Roman emperors.

### Palestra
A Hellenistic double colonnade surrounded this training arena, where wrestlers and other athletes sparred.

### Stadion (Stadium)
The grassy stadium with its 193m course seated 20,000 spectators. No women were admitted, except the priestess of Demeter, on pain of death.

*Archaeological Site (tel: 0624 22517), 2km from modern Olympia, clearly signposted. Open: Monday to Saturday, 7.30am–5pm; Sunday, 8am–5pm.*
*Museum (tel: 0624 22529), opposite archaeological site. Open: Monday, 11am–5pm; Tuesday to Friday, 8am–5pm; weekends and holidays, 8am–3pm.*
*Admission charge: includes site and museum.*

### PÁTRAI (Patras)
Greece's third largest city is the gateway to Greece for those arriving by sea from Italy. It was rebuilt after being virtually destroyed in World War II. The café-filled squares and avenues of the town centre are overlooked by a crumbling, 1,000-year-old castle.
*212km west of Athens.*

The cathedral of Ayios Andreas (St Andrew) in Patras

### Ayios Andreas
The largest church in Greece, built in 1979 to house the gold casket containing the head of the saint, who was executed by the Romans in Patras, and which was returned to Patras from St Peter's by Pope Paul VI in 1964.
*Platia Ayiou Andreou. Open: daily, except during services. Admission free.*

### Kastro (Castle)
The battlements of a 9th-century Byzantine castle with Frankish, Venetian and Turkish additions rise from the peak of a wooded hill close to the city centre.
*Southeast end of Odhos Ayios, Nikolaou. Unenclosed.*

# Inner Máni and Ákra Taínaron

The Máni is dotted with castles, Byzantine churches and ruined towers. The 136km route follows newly built roads and is well signposted. *Allow 8 hours.*

*Leave Yíthion by the coast road towards Areópolis, passing the long beach of Mavrovoúni and then winding through wooded hills.*

## 1 PASSAVA

The hilltop battlements of the 13th-century Frankish castle are

hard to spot from the road. Look out for the signpost to Khosiarion (Xosiario), 9km after leaving Yíthion. Park at the Country Tavern (signposted in English) and pick your way up a very rough track. Only the walls still stand. Allow 1 hour.

*A narrow pass ends in a fertile plain below the village of Vakhós (Vahos) and the bare flanks of Kouskouni.*

## 2 KELEFÁ

Signposted to your right, 4km off the main road on a rough track (park by the village cemetery and walk the last 1km), Kelefá's mighty walls sheltered a strong Turkish garrison.

*After 1km the main road emerges high above the west coast of the Máni, with the Messinian peninsula to the west.*

## 3 AREÓPOLIS

The 'capital of the Máni' is ringed with tumbledown houses and fallen walls, but many old mansions are being restored as second homes.

*The road south balances between desert mountains and sea cliffs on a fertile strip of olive groves and grainfields divided by dry-*

stone walls. At Pirgos Dhirou turn right
(signposted Spilaia Dhirou/Caves) for 5km.

## 4 SPILAION DHIROÚ (THE DHIROU CAVES)

Allow 25 minutes for the tour of the
Vlychadha Cavern and underground
river (see page 71).

*The main road bypasses a chain of half-
ruined tower villages like clusters of
miniature skyscrapers. At the hamlet of
Ayios Yioryios look seaward for your first
view of Tigáni. Turn right to Stavríon, a
4km detour, and park at the tiny collection
of towers 1km beyond. A donkey track leads
downhill to Tigáni. The walk is strenuous
and involves picking your way among
jagged boulders. Allow 1 hour.*

## 5 TIGÁNI

The clifftop castle gets its name, which
means 'frying pan', from the rocky
peninsula it stands on. The handle of the
frying pan is a natural causeway, making
it a superb natural stronghold.

*Return to the main coast road and turn
right.*

## 6 TOURLOTÍ

To the left, 1.5km north of Kita and
300m above the new road, the 9th-
century domed church of Tourlotí is one
of the prettiest of dozens of Byzantine
churches in the Máni.

## 7 KITA

The largest tower village, Kita was the
seat of the Máni's most powerful clans.
Tourism has brought some life back to
the half-ruined village.

*The sea is hidden by the Kavo Grosso
plateau. After 5km the road descends to the*

half-abandoned harbour of Yerolimin, then
winds through hills, passing through Alika.

## 8 VÁTHIA

The towers of Váthia house a Greek
National Tourist Organisation guest-
house (see page 177). A tiny pebbly
beach 1km below offers swimming.
*Continue towards the cape.*

## 9 PÓRTO KÁYIO AND ÁKRA TAÍNARON

The lovely lagoon is overlooked by a tiny
Turkish fort and is a favourite yacht
anchorage.
*Ákra Taínaron is 5km south and you must
walk the final kilometre to Greece's southern
tip (see page 71).*

*Backtrack to Alika and turn right,
cresting a pass 3km above Tsikkaliá
(Tsikalia). There are sweeping views of the
Lakonikós Kólpos (Laconic Gulf) and Ákra
Malea before the road plunges 300m to the
sea at Kokkala and its pebbly white beach.
It then follows the contours of the coast up to
Kótronas and turns inland to Areópolis.*

The barren peninsula of Tigáni is ringed by the
ramparts of a Byzantine castle

# The Dhiakoptón (Dhiakofton) to Kalávrita Railway

The narrow-gauge rack-and-pinion railway between Dhiakoptón, on the shores of the Gulf of Corinth, and Kalávrita offers the most spectacular train ride in Greece, passing through a series of tunnels in a narrow mountain gorge.

Originally drawn by tiny steam engines – one still stands at each of the two stations – the train is now driven by sturdy little French-built diesel locomotives which pull two carriages seating 68 people. First- and second-class seating is available. Six departures daily each way; no reservations needed.

*The 23km journey takes 68 minutes each way. Allow 3 hours (4 if visiting the Mega Spileon monastery).*

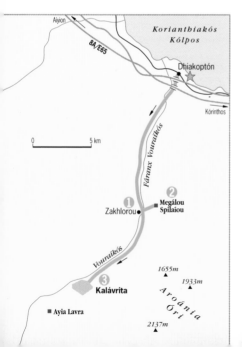

*Leaving Dhiakoptón the train rattles through lemon groves, passes under the busy National Road and enters the steep-sided Vouraïkós gorge.*

Towering grey and pink limestone crags and sheer cliffs pocked with caves and holes loom above the track as the train climbs laboriously through pine woods. As the going gets steeper the rack-and-pinion gear is engaged and the train weaves in and out of a series of gallery tunnels, moving at little more than walking speed.

## *1* ZAKHLOROU (ZAHLOROU)

After about 40 minutes the tiled roofs and white houses of Zakhlorou emerge from the chestnut and cherry trees. The train stops here briefly for passengers wishing to visit the monastery at Mega Spileon, which involves a steep, 45-minute walk.

## 2 MEGÁLOU SPILAÍOU (MEGA SPILEON)

Founded in the 8th century when its miraculous icon of the Virgin was revealed to two monks by a shepherd girl, the monastery was rebuilt this century after a fire and its exterior is dull. Inside, the icon is surrounded by gold gift-offerings, watches, chains and rings, and you can just make out the frescos painted on the sooty ceiling. The excellent small museum contains icons, holy relics and 18th- and 19th-century vestments, and is open daily, 8am–1pm and 5pm–sunset. Admission charge (small). Proper dress is necessary.
*Above Zakhlorou the slope is not steep and the train rattles at speed towards Kalavrita, beneath cliffs sculpted by erosion.*

Kalávrita station is the southern terminus of the Dhiakoptón railway

## 3 KALÁVRITA

The small town stands at the head of a fertile valley, 750m above sea level and

dominated by the saw-edged peaks of the Aroánia Óri (Aroania range). At the Monastery of Ayia Lavra, 7km from the town, Archbishop Germanos proclaimed the revolt on 25 March 1821 which became the War of Independence. The monastery, burned by the Turks in 1821 and the Germans in 1943, houses a small museum (open 8am–1pm and 5pm–sunset). The Koimisos tis Theotokou (Cathedral of the Virgin Mary) in Kalávrita's main square was also burned by both Turks and Germans. One of its two clocks is permanently stopped at 2.34pm, the time at which 1,436 villagers were massacred by the Nazis on 13 December 1943, an event also marked by a monument above the village. History aside, Kalávrita is a pleasant, quiet village with a cool *platia* shaded by trees in front of the cathedral.

Miniature locomotive on the Dhiakoptón railway line

# Stereá Ellás

$S$tereá Ellás (Sterea Ellas) is a narrow coastal strip bounded in the south by the calm waters of the Korinthiakós Kólpos (Gulf of Corinth) and dominated in the north by a series of thinly-populated mountain ranges. From east to west, these are Panaitolikón, Vardhoúsia, Gióna and Parnassós. In the north-west the Amvrakikós Kólpos (Amvrakic Gulf) takes a bite out of the coast and separates the region from neighbouring Ipiros (Epirus).

The sightseeing high point is the ancient sanctuary of Delfi (Delphi), second only to the Acropolis among the classical sites of Greece. There are medieval castles aplenty, too. Inland, the region displays striking mountain scenery, including one of Greece's handful of ski resorts, while on the west coast the Ionian Sea laps at some of the mainland's least-visited beaches. A major highway from Athens and Thebes passes through Levádhia (Livadhia), Arákhova and Delphi before meeting the coast at Itéa and skirts the Gulf of Corinth on its way to Andírrion, Mesolóngion and points north and west.

Ossios Loukas monastery has some of the finest Byzantine frescos and mosaics in Greece

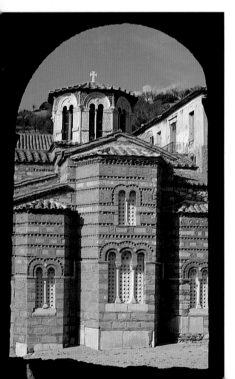

A gold mosaic decorates a doorway at Ossios Loukas monastery

# STEREA ELLAS

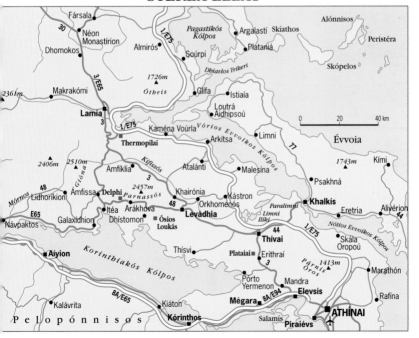

Fársala
30 Néon Monastírion
Dhomokos
1/E75
Pagastikós Kólpos
Argalastí
Skíathos
Alónnisos
Peristéra
Almirós
Soúrpi
Plátaniá
Skópelos
Dhíavios Trikeri
3/E65
1726m
Óthris
Glífa
Istiaía
2361m
Makrakómi
Loutrá Aidhipsoú
Lamía
3
1/E75
Kaména Voúrla
Vórios Evvoïkós Kólpos
Limni
Évvoia
Thermopílai
Arkítsa
0    20    40 km
2406m
2510m
Gióna
Amfíklia
Kifissós
Atalánti
Malesína
1743m
Kími
Lidhoríkion
Ámfissa
3
Khairónia
Kástron
Psakhná
Mórnos
48
2457m
Parnassós
48
Orkhomenós
Paralímni
Khalkís
E65
Delphi
Itéa
Arákhova
Levádhia
Limni Ilíki
Eretria
Aliviérion
Návpaktos
Galaxídhion
Dhístomon
Ósios Loukás
44
Nótios Evvoïkós Kólpos
Aiyion
Korinthiakós Kólpos
Thísvi
Plataiaí
Erithraí
Thívai
1/E75
Skála Oropoú
Pórto Yermenón
Mandra
Párnis Óros
1413m
Marathón
8A/E65
Kiáton
Mégara
8A/E94
Elevsís
Rafína
Kalávrita
Pelo?pónnisos
Kórinthos
Salamís
ATHÍNAI
Piraiévs

# DELPHI ROAD

## ARÁKHOVA

Though its steep-roofed, half-timbered
houses tremble to the passing of heavy
traffic on the main highway which runs
through the town, Arákhova is quite
peaceful. Off the busy main street, lined
with restaurants and souvenir shops
selling rugs and sheepskin coats, it is
pleasantly peaceful and its location –
above Delphi, commanding a pass over
the shoulder of 2,457m Parnassós –
affords fine views in all directions. With
bare hills above and below, it has a cool,
almost alpine climate and Athenians
come here to ski on the Parnon pistes
above the town as late as April.
*34km west of Levádhia.*

## KHAIRÓNIA/CHAIRONEIA
### (Heronia)

A gigantic marble lion guards the
battlefield where in 338BC the pikemen
and cavalry of Macedon crushed the
combined forces of the southern city-
states, led by Thebes. The 5.5m statue
marked the grave of the warriors of the
élite Sacred Band of Thebes, who fought
to the death. Greek guerrilla fighters in
the War of Independence smashed it
open, hoping to find treasure, but found
nothing. It was pieced together some 80
years later and re-erected. The town is
also the birthplace of Plutarch, the Greek
historian and philosopher (*c*.46–*c*.120).
*11km north of Levádhia.*

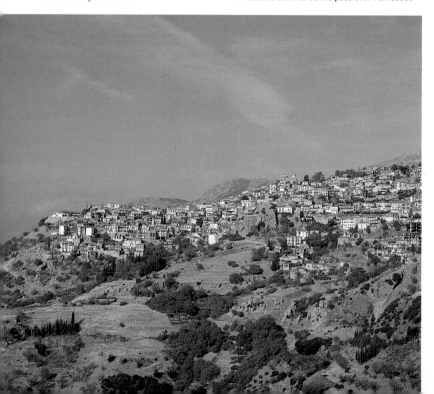

Arákhova commands the pass over Parnassós

## LEVÁDHIA

There is no sign today of the meadows from which this unkempt but not unappealing town takes its name. In medieval times Levádhia was the most important town in the region, thanks to its strategic site controlling routes between Athens and the west and north. Although a handful of the old Turkish-style houses with overhanging upper storeys and wrought-iron balconies survive, and the dome of a derelict mosque can be spotted at the corner of Tsogka and Stratigo Ioannou, for the most part Levádhia is uncompromisingly modern.

A clear, fast-running stream springs from a source below the limestone crag on which the town's 14th-century castle stands, and is crossed near its source by a hump-backed Turkish mule bridge. It takes about 20 minutes to scramble through pine woods to the dilapidated castle, but the climb is worth it for the view of Parnassós to the west and the fertile farmlands of the eastern plain. *190km west of Athens.*
*Frourio (Fortress), 750m from town centre, signposted. Unenclosed.*

## ORKHOMENÓS

Just outside the unassuming agricultural town of Orkhomenós are the ruins of the ancient settlement, a powerful city in Mycenaean times. The most prominent remnants are the theatre and, next to it, a collapsed Mycenaean chamber-tomb dating from the city's heyday in the 14th century BC. Climb to the top of the hill on which the acropolis of the city once stood for an extensive bird's-eye view of the ancient site.
*11km northeast of Levadhia; 1km east of the town centre on the road to Kástron. Open: daily, except Monday, 8.30am–3pm.*

## ÓSIOS LOUKÁS

The Byzantine church was completed in 1019 on the site of an earlier hermitage of St Luke the Styriote, who was celebrated for his miraculous healings and prophecies. It is built in the formal style, with a central dome over an eight-sided body. The best-preserved of the great Byzantine churches, it has 16 arched windows surrounded by mosaics of the prophets and surmounted by angels. The apse is dominated by a mosaic of the Virgin and Child. The exterior is a typical patchwork of brick and stone in the Byzantine manner.

Next to the main church is the Church of the Theotokos, where services are still held. On the gallery of the second floor of the monastic buildings opposite, note the wooden bar and metal chimes which are struck to call the monastery's handful of monks to prayer. *9km south of the main Levádhia/Itéa road, follow signs to Dhístomon, then to Ósios Loukás (tel: 3213571). Open: daily, except Monday, 8.30am–3pm. Admission charge.*

The monastic church of Ossios Loukas is the best-preserved of Greece's Byzantine churches

# Delfi

## (Delphi)

*T*he centre of the Ancient Greek world, the Delphi site is the most powerfully magnetic classical site outside Athens. Much of its charisma stems from its location, carefully chosen by its founders to amplify the awed emotions of pilgrims as they approached the sanctuaries and the oracle.

Close to the mouth of a deep gorge in the side of Parnassós, Delphi is ringed by massive peaks and looks south over a delta of olive groves which flows from the foothills down to the shores of the Gulf of Corinth. The amphitheatrical plan of the Sanctuary of Apollo is echoed by the 300m cliffs which loom above it.
*The archaeological sites are separated by the main Delphi-Arákhova road.*

### Ieros Dhromos (the Sacred Way and the main site)
The most fully restored buildings of the main site are the porticoed Treasury of

### THE ORACLE OF DELPHI
The earth-mother Gaia was worshipped at Delphi from the 14th century BC through priestesses who were intoxicated by fumes rising from fissures in the earth. With the advent of the Dorians, Gaia was supplanted by Apollo and the site became his greatest sanctuary. Apollo's mouthpiece was the Sybil or Pythia, whose tranced utterings in answer to pilgrims' questions were translated into verse by her priests. The answers, ambiguous as they were, were not forecasts but advice.

The treasury of the Athenians at Delphi

the Athenians; the votive offering of the Athenians, a Doric building erected in 490–480BC to commemorate the victory of Marathón; the 4th-century BC Temple of Apollo with six of its 50-plus Doric columns standing; the 2nd-century BC Theatre; and the 3rd-century BC Stadium. Just above the Treasury of the Athenians a very ordinary-looking boulder marks the location of the famed Oracle.

These and the foundations of other treasuries are connected by the Sacred Way, a broad, stepped road which zig-zags from the main entrance to the Stadium, from which there are fine views of the site and of the Temple of Athena, below the main road.

*1km east of the modern village of Delphi, above the Delphi-Arákhova road (tel: 0265 82313). Open: Monday to Friday, 7.30am–6pm; weekends and holidays, 8.30am–2.45pm. Admission charge.*

## Mousio Arkheologiko (Archaeological Museum)

One of the finest museums in Greece, containing fragments of friezes, *kouroi*, bronzes of griffons and sphinxes, ivory figurines and heads of Artemis and Apollo, and a splendid lifesize statue of a bull in silver and gold. Top billing goes to the Bronze Charioteer, the masterpiece of an unknown artist of around 478BC. The site was excavated by French archaeologists, and most of the museum labelling is in French and Greek.

*100m west of entrance to main archaeological site, signposted (tel: 0265 82313). Open: Monday, noon–6.15; Tuesday to Friday, 7.30am–6.15pm; weekends and public holidays, 8.30am–2.15pm. Admission charge.*

## Tholos (Rotunda)

Below the Sanctuary of Apollo stood two temples of Athena, a 6th-century BC Doric

The 3rd-century BC stadium and the columns of the Temple of Apollo at Delphi

building which was abandoned in the 4th century BC and replaced by a newer, smaller temple. Only the foundations of these remain. Between the sites of the two temples stand the three surviving columns of one of Delphi's most fully reconstructed relics, the Tholos. This circular 4th-century building was probably a shrine to Gaia.

*500m east of main archaeological site, below the Delphi-Arákhova road. Telephone, opening hours and admission charge as for main archaeological site.*

## Vrisi Kastalias (Kastalian Spring)

The sacred spring, a mere trickle of water for most of the year, emerges from a narrow gorge between the two cliffs which dominate the site of the Sanctuary. Here, pilgrims washed themselves before entering the Sanctuary. Two stone basins used for this ritual can be seen carved in the base of the cliff.

*100m east of the entrance to the Sanctuary of Apollo. Closed for stabilisation of rocks.*

# GODS AND HEROES OF

## APHRODITE

Born from the sea, Aphrodite was the goddess of love and beauty. Her most important temple on the mainland was at Corinth.

## APOLLO

Apollo was the god of male beauty and patron of the fine arts. His greatest sanctuary was at Delphi, but he was also worshipped at Corinth and Vassai (Vassae).

## ARES

The god of war and lover of Aphrodite.

## ARTEMIS

Twin sister of Apollo, Artemis the huntress is the goddess of chastity. Vravróna and Delphi were her most important temples.

Zeus hurling a thunderbolt

Frieze depicting the marriage of Athena and Herakles

## ASKLEPIOS

The god of healing and son of Apollo. His major shrine was at Epídhavros.

## ATHENA

The patron goddess of Athens had many aspects. She was the deity of wisdom, arts and crafts, and of victory. Her greatest temple was the Parthenon.

## DEMETER

Goddess of fertility, worshipped principally at Elevsís.

## DIONYSOS

The god of wine, joy and revelry, worshipped in Athens and on Mount Parnassós.

## HADES

The king of the dead, whose oracle was the Nekromantion at Efira (Efyra).

# ANCIENT GREECE

## HELIOS

The sun-god. Many of the tiny mountain chapels of Ayios Ilias (the prophet Elijah) may once have been his temples, an interesting play on the similarly-pronounced names.

## HEPHAISTOS

God of fire and metal, hence of smiths, and husband of Aphrodite. Worshipped at his principal temple, now called the Thission, in Athens.

## HERA

Hera was the wife of Zeus, greatest of the gods, and is the goddess of marriage. Her main temples were at Árgos and Olympia.

## HERMES

The messenger of the gods, and so the god of commerce, communication and eloquence.

## HESTIA

Hestia was the goddess of hearth and home.

## LETO

A minor goddess, lover of Zeus and mother of Apollo and Artemis.

## PERSEPHONE

The daughter of Demeter and wife of Hades, Persephone was the goddess of death and renewal. Worshipped with her husband at the Nekromantion.

## POSEIDON

The god of the sea, storms and earthquakes, second only to his brother Zeus, Poseidon's main shrines were at Athens and Cape Soúnion.

## ZEUS

King of the gods and ruler of the world, Zeus was worshipped principally at Olympia and Dhodhóni (Dodoni).

Poseidon

The extensive Venetian harbour fortifications of Návpaktos

# THE GULF OF CORINTH

## ÁMFISSA

A small medieval castle, the stronghold of the Catalan mercenaries who dominated this part of Greece in the 13th century AD, overlooks Ámfissa, on the shore of the 'sea of olives' which covers the plain below Delphi. North of the plain, the sharp-peaked 2,510m Gióna (Gionia) massif rises steeply. There are quaint 18th-century streets around the old *platia*, overlooked by the pine-clad castle peak.
*8km northwest of Delphi.*

---

### THE CATALAN COMPANY

Ámfissa was a stronghold of the Catalan Company, a force of mercenary soldiers from Spain who set out alongside the knights of the Fourth Crusade in 1204. When the crusaders sacked Constaninople in 1204 the Catalans gained the region betweem Ámfissa and Levádhia, where they built castles. They were vassals of the Frankish Dukes of Athens, but they turned on Duke Gautier de Brienne and on 13 March 1311 at the battle of Kifissos, near Orkhomenós, the Catalan infantry defeated his 700 knights by luring them into marshy ground. The Catalan Company vanished from history soon after with the recovery of the Byzantine Empire in Greece in the 14th and 15th centuries.

---

## ANDÍRRION

A squat Venetian fortress guards the busy pier of this port on the narrowest part of the Gulf of Corinth. On the south shore of the gulf, its twin guards the harbour of Rion.
*12km west of Navpaktos.*
*Ferries run at 15–30-minute intervals between the two, linking Patras and the Peloponnese with the northern mainland.*

## GALAXÍDHION

Galaxídhion is one of the gems of the Gulf coast, a charming town on a headland between two sheltered bays. Tall 19th-century mansions, fishing boats and seafood restaurants crowd the waterfront below a huddle of pretty balconied houses rising to the dome of a grand 19th-century church built by one of the town's many prosperous shipowners, all reflected in the mirror of the double harbour. If Galaxídhion had a beach it would be perfect; even without one it is one of the pleasantest stops on this coast.

_25km southwest of Delphi._

## ITÉA

Itéa offers the only beaches of any kind for around 30km in either direction, with a short crescent of pebbles at the east end of its eucalyptus-lined esplanade and a second stretch of grey sand and pebble beach just around the corner. Otherwise, Itéa fails to live up to the inspiring backdrop of Parnassós and Gionia behind it and the peaks of Killíni across the Gulf.

_12km south of Delphi._

## NÁVPAKTOS

Battlements and turrets surround the holiday-postcard harbour of this little port and scramble up through the town centre to enclose a substantial 15th-century Venetian castle among pine trees on the hill above.

Behind the harbour, a huge flagstoned square is shaded by pines and plane trees and cluttered with café tables. A busy modern town stretches either side of the old-fashioned centre.

_160km west of Levádhia._

---

### THE BATTLE OF LEPANTO

On 7 October 1571 a Turkish fleet of 200 galleys commanded by Ali Pasha sailed from Návpaktos – then called Lepanto – to do battle with the fleet of the Holy League, an alliance of Venetian, Spanish, Genoese, Neapolitan and Papal forces. These had been called together by the Pope to defend Christendom from Turkey's westward surge, and the fleet was commanded by Don John of Austria, bastard son of the Holy Roman Emperor Charles V.

Among the Christian combatants were Miguel de Cervantes (1547–1616), author of the comic epic _Don Quixote_, who lost the use of his left hand in the battle, and the Genoese commander Giovanni Andrea Dorea. Although outnumbered by the Turkish galleys, Don John's fleet shattered the century-old myth of Ottoman invincibility by destroying 200 Turkish ships while losing 10 of his own, and halted Turkish expansion westward for a generation.

---

The town of Galaxídhion prospered in the 19th century

## THE WESTERN STEREA

### AKHELÓÖS
The Akhelóös river, one of Greece's largest, meets the Ionian Sea in a wide fertile delta whose vast expanse of channels and reedbeds is gradually giving way to maize and cotton fields. The delta is a haven for waterbirds. Kingfishers streak along the riverbanks, egrets stalk among the salt-pans and fish traps lining the marshy shore, and storks nest in treetops and on the chimneys and telephone poles of local villages. The delta, a paradise for birdwatchers, is threatened by encroaching cultivation and by plans for further damming of the Akhelóös, whose northern reaches are already blocked by hydro-electric dams.

The Akhelóös river meets the sea in a vast spread of channels and reedbeds – a haven for waterbirds

*Access by dirt roads west of Katokhi, 21km from Mesolóngion, where the river's mighty main channel is crossed by the main Mesolóngion–Astakós road.*

### ASTAKÓS
Looking west to the island of Itháki (Ithaca), this tranquil harbour at the end of a long, narrow inlet dotted with desert islands offers little excitement, though a colourful sunset can be enjoyed from the comfort of a café seat on its taverna-lined esplanade.
*50km northwest of Mesolóngion.*

### MESOLÓNGION (Missolonghi)
Missolonghi's famous lagoon, a patchwork of fish farms and salt pans, is spectacular when seen from the causeway which links the mainland town with its island suburb of Tourlida, a haphazard collection of fishing shacks with a handful of summer-only fish tavernas. The historic town itself was much damaged in World War II.
*35km west of Andírrion.*

### Pili Exodhou (Gate of the Exodus)
Passing through what remains of the city walls, the gate is famed for the sortie made by 9,000 defenders of the city, women and children, in a desperate attempt to escape their Turkish besiegers in April 1826, during the War of Independence. They were betrayed, and fewer than 2,000 escaped to Ámfissa, 80km away. The last defenders blew up their powder magazine to take as many of their attackers with them as possible.
*Signposted.*

Astakós bay

**Iroon Kipos (Park of the Heroes)**
Next to the Gate of the Exodus, with modern statues of Byron and the Greek leader Markos Botzaris and other heroes of the 1821–30 war.

## MÍTIKAS
So many islands dot the Ionian Sea off Mítikas that this undiscovered one-street village with its 3km sweep of white pebble beach seems to be on a landlocked lake. Kalamos, the biggest of them, is only 500m offshore and a small ferry plies between the village and the handful of houses on the pine-covered island, where the battlements of a tiny 16th-century fortress overlook the bay.
*84km northwest of Mesolóngion.*

Lord Byron aged 19

## VÓNITSA
A huge castle squats above the silvery waters of the Amvrakic Gulf, overlooking the naturally sheltered harbour and esplanade at Vónitsa, a clutter of two- and three-storey Italianate houses and a stretch of pebbly beach. The 16th-century fortress was built by the Venetians to control the passage into the Gulf, an enormous mirror-like lagoon dotted with uninhabited islets.
*120km northwest of Mesolóngion The castle is unenclosed.*

**BYRON AT MISSOLONGHI**
The Romantic poet George Gordon, Lord Byron (1788–1824), is remembered all over Greece in squares and street names, his name Hellenicized as Vironos. Always an admirer of Greece and an enthusiastic supporter of Greek independence, he landed at Missolonghi in January 1824 determined to fight for the Greek cause and was elected its commander in chief. Before his complete lack of military experience could do any damage, however, he died in April of fever. Ironically, his untimely death helped to rally European opinion behind the Greek struggle. He probably did Greece more good as a dead hero than as a live commander.

# Arákhova, Delphi, Ámfissa and Galaxídhion

This tour takes in a cross-section of countryside from the pretty mountain village of Arákhova on the slopes of Parnassós to Galaxídhion on its bay of islands. *Allow 5 hours.*

## *1* ARÁKHOVA

Perched on the shoulder of the 2,457m high Mount Parnassós at a height of 900m, Arákhova has great views and in winter is popular with skiers visiting the mountain's pistes. In summer it is pleasantly cool.

*For 10km west of Arákhova the road snakes down the north side of a deep valley with olive terraces below and bare mountain slopes*

*above. After 8km you will get your first
glimpse of the Gulf of Corinth ahead, and
after a further 1km the columns of the
Temple of Apollo at Delphi come into sight.
Allow at least 3 hours for Delphi's sites and
museums (see pages 88–9).*

## 2 DELPHI
Modern Delphi exists solely to service
visitors to the ancient sanctuary. Its two
parallel main streets are packed with
hotels and uniformly mediocre
restaurants.
*The road hairpins down towards the sea
until, 5km below Delphi, it passes beneath
itself in a tight loop and bridge. Follow signs
for Itéa and Ámfissa. After 5km you reach
the fringes of the 'sea of olives' and continue
for 10km through the groves to Ámfissa.*

## 3 ÁMFISSA
This unassuming little town is crowned
by a pretty 13th-century castle among
pines on a crag. Built by Franks and
Catalan mercenaries, it incorporates
remnants of the earlier classical
acropolis. The walls surround the
remains of a keep, round tower, chapel
and barracks.
*Leave the town by Odos Ethniki Antistasi,
which runs from the south side of Ámfissa's
main square, and climb in zigzags for 5km,
leaving the olive-groves behind, and emerge
suddenly on bare hillside with the rocky peak
of Gionia on the northern skyline. The road
skirts the flank of the Gionia massif,
trending south towards the Gulf of Corinth.*

## 4 AYIA EVTHIMIA (AYIA
ETHIMIA)
Set among fields and almond trees, Ayia
Ethimia is an attractive old-fashioned
village of red-tiled stone houses. This
part of the drive is especially pretty in
spring, when the fields are vivid with wild

flowers, and in autumn, when the
almond orchards turn a brilliant red.

## 5 VOUNÍKHORA (VOUNIHORA)
The village is surrounded by a distinctive
maze of grey dry-stone sheepfold walls.
The road now climbs steeply over barren
slopes with fine views to the north and of
Parnassós with Delphi and Arákhova
perched on its flanks to the east.
*The whole Gulf of Corinth panorama comes
into view 2km beyond Vouníkhora and after
a further 3km you turn left, following signs
to Pendéoria and Galaxídhion in a series of
hairpins until you meet the main coast road
1km east of Galaxídhion. The turn-off to the
village is on the inland side of the highway
and passes beneath the main road.*

## 6 GALAXÍDHION
A substantial domed church, built in the
last century by one of Galaxídhion's
wealthy shipowners, surmounts this
pretty village on a headland at the mouth
of the Kólpos Itéas (Gulf of Itéa). With
its double harbour, fishing boats, yachts,
fish restaurants and waterfront
dominated by tall, elegant 19th-century
houses, Galaxídhion seems to belong
more to the islands than the mainland. It
lacks only a beach to make it perfect.

Wealthy shipowners' mansions from
Galaxídhion's 19th-century heyday

# Ípiros and Thessalía

## (Epirus and Thessaly)

*T*he two regions which make up the central part of the northern mainland could hardly be more different.

In the west, the Píndhos mountains which form the spine of Epirus conceal some of the wildest and most beautiful country in Europe, sheltering Greece's last remaining bears, wolves, griffon vultures and other endangered species. The Píndhos's eastern slopes descend steeply to the rolling farmlands of Thessaly, the richest agricultural land in Greece.

These are regions of climatic extremes, too. The Píndhos summits, reaching heights of more than 2,600m, are snowbound for up to five months, while Europe's highest summer temperatures have been recorded on the plains of Thessaly. Some of Greece's most picturesque mountain villages are to be found in the Zagória region of Epirus and on the Pelion peninsula of Thessaly. Other highlights of central Greece include the old-fashioned towns of Ioánnina and Metsovo and the cliff-top monasteries of the Metéora, and there are fine beaches on both Epirus's Ionian coast and Thessaly's Aegean shores.

Below, left: chestnuts are an important cash crop on the Pelion peninsula
Right: the Píndhos mountain range

# EPIRUS AND THESSALY

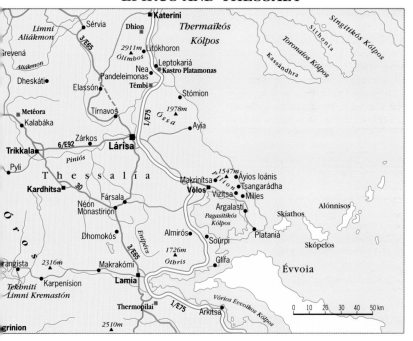

Limni Aliákmon
Grevená
Aliákmon
Dheskáti
Metéora
Kalabáka
Trikkala
Pyli
Kardhítsa
rangista
Tekhnití
Limni Kremastón
grinion

Sérvia
Dhion
Olímbos 2911m
Nea Pandeleimonas
Elassón
Tírnavos
Zárkos
6/E92
Lárisa
Thessalía
Fársala
Néon Monastírion
Dhomokós
2316m
Makrakómi
Karpenísion
Lamia
Thermopílai
2510m

Kateríni
Litókhoron
Leptokariá
Kastro Platamonas
Témbi
Ossa 1978m
Stómion
Ayiá
Piniós
Makrinítsa
Vólos
Vizítsa
Pílion 1547m
Ayios Ioánis
Tsangarádha
Miliés
Argalastí
Pagasitikós Kólpos
Almirós
Soúrpi
Plataniá
Glífa
Othris 1726m
Enipévs
1/E75
Arkítsa

Thermaïkós Kólpos

Síthonía
Toronaíos Kólpos
Singitikós Kólpos
Kassándhra

Skíathos
Alónnisos
Skópelos

Évvoia
Vórios Evvoïkós Kólpos

0  10  20  30  40  50 km

inhabited, some of them by a solitary monk or nun. Two – Ayia Triadha and Ayios Stefanos – are functioning monastic houses, while the rest are preserved as religious museums.

### Ayios Nikolaos (Saint Nicholas)
Ayios Nikolaos is a recently-restored 14th-century monastery whose 16th-century chapel is decorated with frescos of the Last Judgement by the Cretan painter Theophanes. They are all the more striking for their restoration.

### Ayios Stephanos (Saint Stephen)
Now a nunnery, Ayios Stephanos was founded in the 14th century and has two churches, a 14th-century basilica with frescos and a later 18th-century building. The museum houses manuscripts, embroideries and some striking icons.

### Ayia Triadha (Holy Trinity)
The 15th-century monastery may look familiar; the James Bond epic *For Your Eyes Only* (1981) was shot here. The building sits atop one of the tallest of the natural pillars.

### Mega Meteoron (Great Meteoron)
This is the grandest and most venerable of the monasteries, with a small museum in its 16th-century refectory and well-preserved frescos in the dome of its 15th–16th-century church.

### Ossios Varlaam
Ossios Varlaam also has a frescoed chapel and the prettiest flower-gardens of all the monasteries. Here, too, you can see the perilous-looking winch used in the past to haul up monks and visitors as

# CENTRAL THESSALY

### KALABÁKA (KALAMBAKA)
As you approach Kalambaka, the gentle contours and agricultural patchwork of the Thessalian lowlands start to rise towards the grand highlands of the Píndhos range. Behind the unexciting market town, a blank 555m cliff face rises, a landmark to show you are approaching the unearthly landscape of the Metéora.
*21km north of Trikkala.*

### METÉORA
Nothing prepares you for the scenic impact of this valley lined with soaring towers of rock, each crowned by a precarious monastery. The views over Thessaly and the valley of the upper Piniós are breathtaking. Only six of two dozen monasteries dating from the 14th century are open, and only five are

well as supplies. Its church of Ayioi Pandes (All Saints) dates from the 16th century and has perhaps the finest frescos of all the monastery churches, including scenes of the Last Judgemen⸀ and the life of John the Baptist.

## Roussanou

The monastery of Roussanou, with its red-tiled roof, is dizzyingly located on a crag which looks ready to topple away from the cliff face and is reached by a vertigo-inducing footbridge.

*The valley of the Metéora begins at Kastraki, 3km from Kalambaka. The trip taking in all six visitable monasteries is 17km.*
*For all monasteries: (tel: 0432 22278).*
*Open: hours can vary from monastery to monastery, but are generally 8am–1pm and 3pm–5pm, sometimes closed on holy days and religious festivals.*
*Separate admission charge for each monastery. Dress code: long trousers for men, skirts below the knee for women, long sleeves for both.*

## MÉTSOVON (Metsovo)

Local costume – typified by the clog-like shoes with red woollen pom-poms on sale in every souvenir shop – is dying out slowly, and you are most likely to see it worn on feast days. At 1,000m above sea level, Metsovo is bitterly cold in winter, so the colourful rugs and blankets which brighten Metsovo's main-street shops are no surprise. The view eastward over the fertile farmlands of Thessaly contrasts sharply with the hostile peaks of the Píndhos to the west. Above the town, the highest pass in Greece (1,705m) carries the main road between Thessaly and Epirus.
*90km nortrhwest of Trikkala.*

## Arkhondiko Tositsa (Tositsa Mansion)

The restored 18th-century mansion was the home of the wealthy Tositsa family, native philanthropists who also endowed the nearby Idhrima Tositsa (Tositsa Foundation).

Its exhibition includes traditional costumes and textiles.
*On the main street. Open: daily, except Thursday, 8.30am–1pm and 4pm–6pm. Admission charge.*

## TRÍKKALA

A dusty market town with a thriving old-fashioned bazaar area left over from its heyday as capital of the region under Turkish rule, Tríkkala stands on a low hill crowned by a crumbling Byzantine castle and is surrounded by farms.
*61km west of Larisa.*

The rocky pillars and pinnacles of the Metéora, which means, appropriately, 'in the air'

# PRIESTS, MONKS AND

The bearded village priest in his black robe is a familiar figure

The village priest with his black robe, stovepipe hat and beard is one of the chief characters of any Greek community. Most Greeks feel that to be Greek is to be Orthodox, and the Church helped to keep the flame of Greek language and culture alight during the long centuries of Turkish rule. It is still very much a living religion, and Greece sometimes seems to have more churches

than it needs. Even a small village may have two or three churches and chapels – Greeks who were successful overseas or in business have traditionally thanked their patron saint by building a church or chapel in his or her name.

The Greek Orthodox Church moved away from the Western Catholic Church over several centuries, the final split coming in 1074 when the Pope and the Patriarch in Constantinople excommunicated each other. Under the Ottoman Empire, Greece was cut off from the Christian West and the split became permanent. Clerics like Archbishop Germanos of Patras, who declared the start of the

# MIRACLES

War of Independence in 1821, were often in the forefront during the many rebellions against the Turks.

Oddly enough, the head (the Patriarch) of the Greek Orthodox Church lives not in Athens but in Istanbul (still called Constantinopolis by Greeks), the last living relic of the great Christian empire of Byzantium. Monks and abbots rank higher in the hierarchy of the Orthodox Church than priests and bishops, but married men may become priests – all those Greek names beginning with 'Papa' indicate a priest roosting somewhere in the family tree.

Sacred relics and centuries-old icons are a vital part of the Orthodox faith and are said to have miraculous powers. No church or chapel, however remote, is ever without its complement of flickering candles, kept alight by the devout.

The Church comes into its own at Easter, the biggest festival of the Greek year, when holy icons are paraded through the streets and solemn services are held by censer-swinging bishops draped in sumptuous silken robes.

## ICONS

The finest of Greece's ancient icons have an impact as strong as anything by Picasso. Icons – paintings of Christ, the Virgin, saints or angels – are Greece's direct link with the great Byzantine empire in its heyday. Some are more than a 1,000 years old, but for sheer beauty there is nothing to choose between these and icons painted as late as the 18th and 19th centuries. The style is strict, and the purpose is always to lift the spirit. Authentic icons are virtually impossible to buy, and taking them out of the country is against the law, but several modern icon artists such as Kostas Georgopoulos paint wonderful replicas which are faithful to the original. Georgopoulos uses up to 30 different materials, from silver and gold leaf to natural dyes mixed with egg yolk, animal glues, old hewn boards, and 10 different ageing chemicals.

The Sanctuary of Zeus at Dodona, the oldest sacred site on the mainland

# IOÁNNINA AND AROUND

### DHODHÓNI (Dodona)

The oldest sacred site on the Greek mainland stands in a remote valley among fields and sees few visitors. Dedicated to the Great Goddess from 2000BC before becoming a sanctuary of Zeus from around 1300BC, the most impressive feature is the theatre with its 45 tiers of seats, restored in the 19th century. Massive walls and column stumps outline the Temple of Herakles and the Sanctuary of Zeus.

*21km southwest of Ioánnina, 13km west of the main Ioánnina-Árta road. Signposted. Open: weekdays, 8am–7pm (5pm winter); weekends and holidays, 8.30am–3pm. Admission charge.*

### IOÁNNINA

Ioánnina's location on pea-green Limni Pamvotis/Límni Ioánninon (Lake Pamvotis), surrounded by rugged peaks, cannot be bettered. A tumbledown bazaar area, a 1,300-year-old walled town, and a handful of mosques and minarets surviving from Turkish times give the town an oriental air.

*469km northwest of Athens.*

### Arkheologiko Mousio (Archaeological Museum)

A well-displayed collection of bronze tools and weapons, stone and bone implements, and finds from Dhodhóni.

*Platia 25 Martiou. Signposted. Open: Monday, 12.30pm–7pm; Tuesday to Friday, 8am–7pm; weekends 8.30am–3pm.*

### Frourion (Fortress)

The fortress town is ringed by walls built in AD528 by the Emperor Justinian against the rampaging Goths. A tree-lined esplanade runs along the lake front. Enter the walls by the Glikidhon gate, off Dionysou Filosofotou just south of the café-filled square below the northeast bastion. Within, a derelict Turkish barracks stands beside a dusty parade-ground.

### Dimotikou Mousio (Popular Museum)

Rusting cannon and a pyramid of cannon-balls greet you as you enter the former mosque of Aslan Pasha. Some of the cannon bear the lion crest of the Republic of Venice or the double eagle of the Russian Tsars. There is a fine view of Pamvotis from the square outside the museum. Built in 1618 on the site of a church of St John the Baptist, the mosque was in use until 1922 and became a museum in 1933. Displays include relics and costumes of Ioánnina's Greek, Turkish and Jewish communities.

*Alexiou Noutsou. Signposted from the*

*entrance to the fortress. Open: daily, 8.30am–3pm. Admission charge.*

## Mousio Laografias (Museum of Folklore)

Silver jewellery, chased brass trays, and Sarakatsan embroidery and weaving are displayed with folk costumes in an old mansion with vividly painted ceilings.
*Mihail Angelou 42. Open: Monday to Wednesday, 10am–1pm. Admission charge.*

## Tsami Fethye (Victory Mosque)

The derelict mosque, built in 1430, stands amid ruins in a fortress within a fortress.
*Overlooking Platia Katsandoni. Closed to the public.*

## NISSI (Island)

Glass tanks full of live carp, eels, crayfish and crabs greet visitors to Lake Pamvotis's only island, a favourite trip for diners from Ioánnina. Some restaurateurs keep turtles, salamanders and even baby alligators – not to eat, but to catch your eye.

Five monasteries, the oldest dating from the 11th century and the most recent from the 17th, are dotted around the island.
*Boats go to the island from Ioánnina every half hour (hourly in winter) from the pier on Dionysou Filosofotou, close to the northeast corner of the fortress.*

## Moni Ayios Padeleimonas (Monastery of St Panteleimon)

Small exhibition of books and archives.

## Mousio Ali-Pasha (Ali Pasha Museum)

Within the monastery walls, in what were the monks' cells, a museum of etchings, watercolours and antiques

commemorates Ali Pasha, the Albanian warlord who ruled Epirus from 1788 until he was shot in 1822 for rebelling against the Sultan. You can still see the bullet-holes in the floor.
*Platia Monaxon Nektario-Theofanos. Open: daily, 8am–8pm. Monastery museum: admission free. Ali Pasha museum: admission charge. Signposted from the waterfront.*

## PÉRAMA SPILIÁ/SPILAION PERAMATOS (Perama Caves)

Greece's largest cave system, accidentally discovered in 1940, extends for 2km into the hillside, winding through grottoes full of twisted spikes and spires.
*In the centre of Perama village, 5km northwest of Ioánnina (tel: 0651 81521/81440). Open: daily, 8am–8pm (4pm in winter). Admission charge.*

The former mosque of Aslan Pasha in Ioánnina is now the town's Popular Museum

Fishing boats moored at the mouth of the Akheronda

# THE EPIRUS COAST

### AKHERONDA (Acheron River)

A strong-flowing icy stream, the Acheron emerges from a fissure in the mountainside 4km inland from the hamlet of Glyki. It reaches the sea as a wide, turquoise river at Amoudia, where it has created a 500m sandy beach behind which is a broad delta of fields and reedbeds.

*3km west of the main coast road.*

### AMVRAKIKÓS KÓLPOS (Amvrakic Gulf)

A huge, silvery lagoon dotted with uninhabited islands separates Epirus from Sterea Ellas. Shuttle ferries cross its 750m-wide mouth between Préveza and the southern shore. Off the northern cape on which Préveza stands, Octavian and Mark Anthony fought the sea-battle of Aktion (Actium) in 31BC (see Nikópolis). The north shore, between Préveza and Menídhi, is a region of salt-marshes and brackish lagoons which attract migrating birds, but has nothing to offer non-birdwatchers.

### ÁRTA

Árta was an important town in Roman and medieval times. Little remains of its former glory except a celebrated 18th-century Turkish bridge across the Arakhthos river, currently being restored. The 13th-century walls incorporate fragments of earlier classical and Hellenistic buildings.

*75km south of Ioánnina.*

### EFIRA NEKROMANTION (Necromanteion of Efyra)

In ancient times the Acheron, also known as the Styx, was thought to flow from the underworld and an Oracle of the Dead stood on what was then an island and is now a low hill surrounded by fields. Pilgrims passed through a labyrinth of corridors to question the priestess, who had to be at least 50 years old. Offerings to Hades and Persephone were lowered into a shrine below, believed to be the upper part of Hades' underground palace. A wall of giant blocks surrounds the site, where a small Byzantine church with frescos of the Virgin and saints stands above the chamber of the oracle. A small square Turkish keep is now the caretaker's office.

*1km from Amoudia on the main coast road, signposted (tel: 0681 41026). Open: daily, 8.30am–3pm.*

### IGOUMENÍTSA

The only reason for visiting this characterless seaport close to the Albanian border is to catch a ferry to Corfu or Italy.

*101km west of Ioánnina.*

### NIKÓPOLIS

Scattered over a vast area, brick and stone walls, gateways and the arches of an aqueduct rise from the woods and

fields. Two small archaeological sites are enclosed, but the most impressive part of Nikópolis and the best place from which to view the whole site is the theatre, accessible at any time. The stadium, opposite the theatre, is overgrown and indistinguishable to any but the most experienced eye. The site is powerfully evocative of lost glories. Built by Octavian, the future Roman Emperor Augustus, to mark his victory over Mark Anthony and Cleopatra at Aktion (31BC) the city was abandoned in 1040 after being sacked by the Bulgars.
*8km north of Preveza.*
*Archaeological site. Signposted. Open: daily, except Monday, 8.30am–3pm. Admission charge.*

Roman ramparts at the lost city of Nikópolis, abandoned in AD1040

### Kastro (Castle)
The walls surround an inner ring of battlements and a 13th-century keep where rusting cannon lie scattered.
*Open: daily, 8am–8pm (5pm in winter). Admission free.*

## PÁRGA
Once a Venetian harbour, Párga is a lively holiday resort. Rows of brightly painted houses climb from a crescent bay dotted with islands to a hill crowned by a Venetian castle. North of this headland stretches a 1km sandy beach. There are smaller beaches either side of the headland at the south end of the bay, and others can be reached by motorboats which run frequently throughout the day in summer.
*50km north of Préveza.*

## PRÉVEZA
There are adequate beaches a few kilometres northwest of town, but Préveza offers little else to the holidaymaker. The main road turns inland towards Párga, and shuttle ferries cross the mouth of the Amvrakic Gulf to the Sterea Ellas shore.
*125km south of Ioánnina.*

Rocky islands punctuate the bay in front of the whitewashed buildings of Párga

The Piniós river passes through the Vale of Tempe, a strategic pass since the earliest times

# LÁRISA, ÓSSA AND THE VALE OF TEMPE

## LÁRISA

A town of few charms, Lárisa's importance as a road junction in medieval times is reflected by a frowning medieval castle on a central hilltop overlooking the Piniós river, which flows through the town. Lárisa stood guard over routes north, south, east and west. Today, it is bypassed by National Road 1, which turns northeast from the city to enter the Vale of Tempe.
*318km north of Athens.*

## ÓSSA

Like a mountain in a child's story, Óssa stands alone, its often cloud-capped peak rising sharply from the cotton fields of the Thessalìan plain. Rising to 1,978m, Óssa is dwarfed by its giant neighbour, the 2,917m Olimbos (Olympus) not far to the north. A logging road, more suitable for four-wheel-drive vehicles than for saloon cars, runs from the hill hamlet of Spili over the shoulder of the mountain to the sea, with vertiginous

views of misty canyons, forest slopes, and the Olympus massif.

The Greek Alpine Society (EOS) maintains a mountain shelter closer to the summit for those who want to trek to the top of the peak.

---

**GODS V GIANTS**

While Zeus and the other Olympians were still consolidating their hold on the world after overthrowing Cronus and the other Titans, they faced a revolt by the serpent-footed Giants, brothers of the Titans. Led by Alcyoneus, the 24 giants tried to assault Olympus, the home of the gods, by placing Mount Pelion on Mount Óssa to make a stairway, but were defeated thanks to Heracles, who slew their leader, and Athene, who showed the Olympians a magic herb which made them invulnerable.

---

## STÓMION

Stómion is a quiet harbour-cum-resort

close to the mouth of the Piniós river, where lagoons, channels and reedbeds shelter storks, kingfishers, herons and other waterbirds. A sandy, deserted beach runs north for several kilometres. The green slopes of Óssa to the south and the bare, cloud-capped Olympus to the north make a breathtaking backdrop.
*40km northeast of Larisa.*

## VALE OF TEMPE

The Piniós river flows from its source in the Píndhos mountains across the plain of Thessaly before passing through the once-romantic Vale. A strategic pass since the dawn of time, the deep, 12km gorge in classical times formed a natural barrier between the Greece of the southern city-states and the wilder, less civilized lands of the northern Hellenes. It now carries National Road 1 as well as the main Athens–Thessaloníki rail line and is marred by fumes and noise. Prominently signposted, the Spring of Aphrodite and the Spring of Dafni, which flow into the Piniós, have been reduced to smelly culverts.

### Ayia Paraskevi

Midway along the Vale of Tempe, a large lay-by offers the chance to pull off the road and view the Piniós river, crossed here by a suspension bridge. A more attractive view of the river and the great valley is offered by the small motor cruisers which operate half-hour, 4km cruises on the river, departing when full (about every 30 minutes).
*On OE1 (National Road 1), 4km south of the tollbooth at the north end of the Vale of Tempe.*

### Kastro Platamonas (Platamon Castle)

The fortress founded in 1204 by Boniface de Montferrat, Duke of Thessaloníki, was added to by the Byzantines in the 14th and 15th centuries and later by the Turks. Squatting close to the mouth of the Vale of Tempe, it guards the strategic route between northern and southern Greece. The walls are some 7m high, with round bastions at each corner. The octagonal inner keep is being restored and is used for performances during the annual Olympus Festival.
*East of the main road on a hilltop opposite the modern village of Nea Pandeleimonas, signposted. Open: daily, except Monday, 8.30am–3pm. Admission charge.*

The Vale of Tempe, where according to myth the nymph Daphne was changed into a laurel tree by her earth-mother to save her from Apollo's amorous advances

The Vikos Gorge. Agility and a head for heights are essential requirements for the gorge trail

**OCHI DAY**

On 28 October 1940 the Italian ambassador presented General Ioannis Metaxas, then military dictator of Greece, with an ultimatum: allow Italian troops to move through Greece to attack the British in Egypt. Metaxas is said to have answered with one word, 'Ochi' (No), and 28 October, a national holiday, is still known as Ochi Day. The Italians invaded immediately, but were turned back by the outgunned but determined Greeks, who delayed an invasion until the arrival of the German forces in April 1941.

## THE NORTHERN PÍNDHOS

### DRAKOLIMIN

Close to the 2,000m contour, a clear tarn at the lip of a 500m sheer drop is the home of thousands of brightly coloured newts and fire-bellied toads. It is a stiff 8-hour round trip from Mikro Pápingo, calling for above-average fitness and good boots, but well worth it.
*5km east and 800m above Mikro Pápingo.*

### FÁRANX VÍKOS (Vikos Gorge)

The plunge into the 13km-long, 1km-deep gorge cut by the Voïdhomátis river is one of the most dramatic – and demanding – hikes in Greece. The walk takes a full day and is only for the very fit, as you must scramble over boulders and up steep zigzag paths.

In late spring, the gorge may be inaccessible as melting snow turns the Voïdhomátis into an ice-cold torrent. *The gorge runs northwest from Monodhendhri to Megalo Pápingo.*

### KALPAKION
### Polemiko Mousio Kalpáki (Kalpáki War Museum)

The museum's motley collection of elderly rifles, machine-guns, uniforms and other militaria commemorates Greece's against-all-odds victory over the Italian invaders here in the winter of 1940. Opposite the museum is a monument to General Ioannis Metaxas. *On the east side of the main north-south highway, 500m south of Kalpakion village, 35km north of Ioánnina. Open: daily, 8am–5pm. Admission free.*

## KÓNITSA

Bypassed by the main north–south highway, Kónitsa is a quiet, tree-filled, 19th-century town at the upper end of the vast valley of the Aóös river. Above it tower the peaks of Smólikas, Greece's second-highest mountain at 2,637m, and the Tímfi massif, rising to 2,497m at its highest.

*64km north of Ioánnina.*

## MONODHÉNDHRI

The stern grey limestone walls and stone-flagged roofs of Monodhéndhri perch on the very lip of the Vikos Gorge. If you do not feel up to walking the full length of the gorge, you can make the tiring but scenic descent to the river bed and back to Monodhéndhri in half a day. Several of the village's solidly-built traditional homes have been turned into comfortable guest-houses as part of the Greek National

---

### THE ZAGORIA

The lovely, dramatically sited villages of this mountain region are built and roofed with the same grey stone and seem to grow from the mountains which surround them. Zagória offers the best mountain trekking in Greece, with high ranges separated by deep canyons which are dry in summer but rushing torrents as the winter snow melts. Under Turkish rule, the Zagória villages won certain tax privileges, and many local men went abroad to work, sending money home to build the handsome houses and churches which adorn the mountainsides. Many of the 40-plus villages are deserted, but tourism (a newcomer to the region) is helping to bring them back to life.

---

The twin villages of Megalo Pápingo and Mikro Pápingo in the Zagória

Tourist Office's traditional settlements programme.

*45km northeast of Ioánnina.*

## PÁPINGO (Megalo and Mikro)

The twin villages of Megalo (Big) and Mikro (Little) Pápingo stand at the northwest end of the Vikos Gorge, dwarfed by the enormous, pitted crags of the Tímfi massif. In the saddle 500m above the upper village of Mikro Pápingo you can see silhouetted the Astraka mountain refuge, a tiring 3-hour walk up very steep paths. Megalo Pápingo is the most popular base for hiking and exploring in the Zagória.

*50–51km northeast of Ioánnina.*

The port of Vólos at the head of the Pagasitic Gulf, looked down upon from the Pelion peninsula

# VÓLOS AND PÍLION (PELION)

The northern part of the mountainous, boot-shaped Pílion (Pelion) peninsula is watered by many streams and wooded with beech, oak and chestnut and with pear and apple orchards. The toe of the boot is barren and rugged. Pelion is separated from mainland Thessaly by the Pagasitikós Kólpos (Pagasitic Gulf), which laps at sheltered beaches on the west coast of the peninsula. Lush forest covers the slopes of the east coast, which drop steeply to deep blue water and white pebble beaches. Pelion's substantial half-timbered mansions with their slate roofs and elaborate polished wood interiors are among the most beautiful village homes in Greece. Many have been restored thanks to the Greek National Tourist Office's traditional settlements programme (see page 177).

## ÁYIOS IOÁNNIS

A relaxed resort with a sweep of steeply shelving, east-facing sand and pebble beach below lush, tropical-looking slopes, Áyios Ioánis is popular with Greek vacationers.
*41km east of Vólos.*

## MAKRINÍTSA

The most accessible of Pelion's villages, Makrinítsa is also the most affected by tourism. Many traditional homes have been converted into guest-houses. The village stands above a deep valley, its eastern slopes greenly wooded but the western side, only a few hundred metres away, dry and bare.

An arcaded church of Áyios Ioánis Prodhromos (St John the Baptist) stands in a main square sheltered by three enormous plane trees. The urban smear of Vólos, 14km away, dominates the westward view.
*14km northwest of Vólos.*

## MILÍES/MILEAI (Milies)

The frescoed church of Áyios Michaelis o Taxiarchis (St Michael 'the brigadier') stands beside an expansive balconied square with breathtaking views over the green hills of Pelion and across the silver Pagasitic Gulf. Inside the church are apocalyptic murals of saints, angels, sinners and devils. Below the square a derelict railway station awaits the restoration of the Pelion narrow-gauge railway from Vólos.
*27km from Vólos.*

### Mousio Mileai (Milies Museum)

Exhibition of local costume and folkways.

*On the main street, above the square (tel: 0423 86204). Open: Tuesday to Sunday and all holidays, 10am–2pm; closed 10–20 March, June and September.*

## TSANGARÁDHA

Tsangarádha's scattered squares are connected by steep cobbled steps and rushing streams. This is the prettiest of the eastern Pelion villages, looking out over the steep forests towards the silhouette of Skiathos on the eastern horizon. Its landmark is an enormous plane tree, 18m round and said to be 1,000 years old.
*38km east of Vólos.*

## VIZÍTSA

At the end of a steeply winding road from the coast, Vizítsa is built around two huge flagstoned squares under the shelter of enormous plane trees and is full of the sound of running water. Villagers gather at café tables in the afternoon and evening to play backgammon and drink *tsipouro*, a fiery grape spirit.
*31km south of Vólos.*

## VÓLOS

Vólos, the gateway to the Pelion, is Greece's third port after Piraeus and Thessaloníki. A mainly industrial town at the head of the Pagasitic Gulf, it was rebuilt on a rigid grid pattern after being flattened by an earthquake in 1955.
*355km north of Athens.*

### Mousio Arkheologiko (Vólos Archaeological Museum)

Hundreds of Hellenistic tombstones, carved with everyday scenes, are the centrepiece of a collection which also includes Stone Age implements and Mycenaean pottery.
*N. Plastira 22 (tel: 0421 25285). Open:*

*daily, except Monday, 8.30am–3pm. Admission charge.*

### Mousio Theophilou (Theophilos Museum)

This mansion is decorated with vibrant primitive frescos of robbers, priests, pashas and warriors, the work of the self-taught painter Theophilos who spent much of his life roaming the Pelion.
*Off Eleftherias, Nea Vólos (tel: 0421 430 88). Open: 8.30am–3pm. Admission free.*

### Sidherodhromo Piliou (Pelion Railway)

The narrow-gauge tracks you can see weaving along Vólos's waterfront and out of town towards Pelion are a relic of the Pelion railway, built in the last century. Two tiny locomotives and their miniature carriages can be seen rusting in sidings at the main railway station.

Fresco of the Archangel Michael at the church in Milies which bears his name

# Villages of Zagória

The stone-built villages of the Zagória region with their grey-slabbed roofs stand among the most exciting mountain scenery in Greece. Tourism is a relative newcomer, encouraged by newly built roads. The region is traversed by deep canyons, crossed in many places by graceful arched bridges built without the use of mortar. Wildlife abounds. Look out for griffon vultures circling the high peaks and for tortoises crossing the road. *Allow 6 hours.*

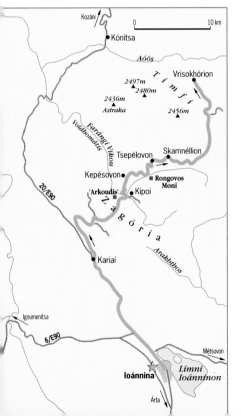

*The drive starts 18km north of Ioánnina, leaving the main Ioánnina-Kónitsa road at Kariaí and following the signposted road towards Tsepélovon. Continue to follow the Tsepélovon signs at each junction.*

## ARKOUDIS MEMORIAL

Twenty-six kilometres from the Kariaí junction, a roadside plaque commemorates the guerrilla leader Yioryios Arkoudis, 'killed by a Turkish bullet' here in 1906 when this part of Greece was still under the rule of the Turks.

A modern bridge crosses the confluence of two river beds 1km further on. A steeply arched old bridge stands next to it, between sheer cliff walls. You are now entering the heart of the Zagória canyon country. The river bed, dry for most of the year, becomes a torrent in winter and early spring.

*The road climbs for 8km towards Kepésovon, perched on the lip of the canyon.*

## KIPOI (KIPI)

Before reaching Kepésovon, you can turn right and detour for 4km to the village of Kipoi, to view the triple-arched

The three-arched bridge at Kipi is the finest of the Zagória pack-bridges

bridge crossing the ravine 1km west of the village.

Just after the Kepésovon turning, pull off the road and look across the gorge to where a little-used mule path zigzags perilously down the cliff face. These cobbled paths, most of which have fallen into disrepair with the building of modern roads, were the highways of the region. *Drive for another 5km.*

## RONGOVOS MONASTERY

The monastery and church of Ayios Ioannis are well worth the 10-minute walk from the road, even if a monkish caretaker is not in residence. The view into the canyon below is breathtaking. *3km beyond the monastery and 30km from the main Ioánnina-Kónitsa road, Tsepélovon is the biggest and most atmospheric of the Zagória villages.*

## TSEPÉLOVON

Two gigantic plane trees shade a flagstoned square, Platia Stratigou Tsakalotou Thrasyvoulou, and its three old-fashioned cafés. At one end of the square stands a six-sided stone clock tower built in 1868 and behind it is the attractive colonnaded church of Ayios Nikolaos, built in 1871 and lavishly decorated within. Many of Tsepélovon's older houses are derelict, but are being restored.

*From Tsepélovon the road passes through pine forests to Skamnéllion, then through alpine scenery for some 15km below limestone peaks, sparsely covered with pine trees, before dropping to the red-roofed village of Vrisokhórion.*

## VRISOKHÓRION (VRISOHORI)

Built on either side of a fertile, sheltered valley, the village is a mountain oasis of garden terraces and walnut trees among oak woods. The substantial arcaded church of Ayios Xaralampos with its carved stone doorway is typical of Zagória village churches.

*A bulldozed road, suitable only for four-wheel-drive vehicles and experienced off-road drivers, ends 3km from Vrisokhórion at the bottom of a steep canyon. When this book was being researched a concrete road bridge was being built with the aim of connecting Vrisokhórion with Kónitsa.*

# GOATS AND GOATHERDS

The tinkling of goatbells across a silent mountain valley is one of the unforgettably evocative sounds of Greece. Nobody whose car has been stopped and surrounded by a herd of goats being driven across the road will forget the smell, either.

The goat, like the forest fire, played its part in the deforestation of Greece, reducing most mountainsides to barren, rocky terrain that only a goat could love.

Like everything else in Greece, the goat is a political issue, with environmentalists condemning a 1980s government decision to allow grazing on national forest land devastated by fire – a move which may perhaps have encouraged firebugs to burn off still more trees for goat pasture.

The goat is still central to survival for many mountain villagers, and herders drive their flocks from lower slopes into the high peaks in summer to take advantage of pastures watered by melting snow.

Hill-walkers will meet goatherds in the most unpromising-looking locations, and their corrals of dry-stone walls, thorns, and corrugated iron (called *stanes* ) are useful landmarks in the Greek high country.

Many of the goatherds who pasture their flocks in the Píndhos mountains of northern Epirus are Vlachs, members of a dwindling ethnic minority who speak a language closely related to Romanian, and whose ancestors are said to have been Roman legionaries who guarded the mountain passes in ancient times.

Others are descended from the Sarakatsan clans, who until the early years of this century lived a truly nomadic existence. You can see their colourful rugs and embossed silver jewellery in many of the region's folk museums.

Goat meat rarely turns up on tourist menus, and even in Greek homes it is a dish for special occasions such as Easter and Panayiria, the feast of the Assumption of the Virgin (15 August).

Greek goats find a meal wherever they can

# Makedhonía and Thráki

## (Macedonia and Thrace)

*G*reece's northernmost provinces border Bulgaria, Turkey and the former Yugoslav republic of Macedonia, and their remoter regions are still comparatively untouched by the modern world.

Macedonia, hemmed in to the west and south by the great mountain ranges of the north Píndhos and Olympus, has a strong identity of its own. Its people are often taller and fairer than their southern compatriots and are often blue- or grey-eyed. Their huge province includes fertile valleys watered by Greece's biggest rivers, huge lakes, the highest mountain in Greece, the country's second city and – on the triple peninsulas of Khalkidhikí – a self-governing theocracy and some of the country's best and as yet totally unspoilt beaches.

Thrace, lying further east, clearly shows its Turkish heritage in the music, dress, arts and crafts of its large Muslim minority. Its flat coastal plain shimmers in the summer sun, growing bumper crops of grain, cotton and tobacco, minarets shoot skyward from many of its sleepy villages, and storks and pelicans haunt the reedbeds and lagoons along its coast. Of all the regions of Greece, Thrace is the least touched by tourism, depending for its livelihood instead on agriculture. In these flat farmlands the traditional two-wheeled donkey cart is still one of the most popular means of transport.

A combination of little-visited towns

---

### WHAT'S IN A NAME?

With the break-up of Yugoslavia, Greece claimed sole rights to the name Macedonia and did everything it could to block recognition of the province's northern neighbour, the former Yugoslavian republic of Macedonia, as the Republic of Macedonia. Though the campaign seems to have been lost, it is still a touchy subject and, like other topics which touch on the fierce Greek national pride, best avoided.

The commercial port of Kavala, surmounted by its Byzantine castle

and villages and some splendid rugged mountain country in the north of the region makes Thrace one of Greece's best-kept secrets.

# MACEDONIA AND THRACE

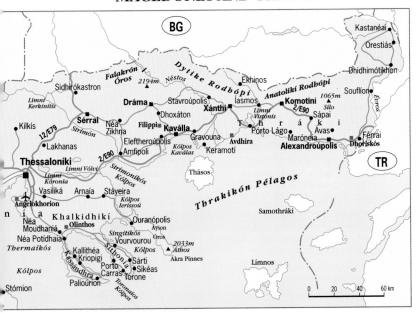

# EASTERN MACEDONIA AND THRACE

## AMFIPOLI (Amfipolis)

The fortifications of this impressive 5th-century BC city are being excavated and restored, as are the mosaic floors of its Christian basilica.

Between Amfipolis and the coastal highway, overlooking the Strimón (Strimonas) river, stands a monumental stone lion, pieced together in 1937 from fragments recovered from the river bed. It dates from the late 4th century BC. *Signposted north of the Kavala-Thessaloniki highway, 60km southwest of Kaválla (Kavala). Unenclosed.*

## ÉVROS DELTA

The Évros drains into a wide delta of salt lagoons and sluggish channels where seabirds, including pelicans, abound. *13–15km east of Alexandroúpolis. Turn off the main road at Loutra Traianopolis on to a network of dirt roads.*

## FILIPPI (Philippi)

The most impressive survivals of this town founded in the 4th century BC are the broad, paved expanse of the Roman agorá and the arches and columns of the Christian basilica, begun in the 6th century but never completed because it was too big to support its dome. The town is particularly famous because it was here that Octavian (the future Roman Emperor Augustus) and Mark Anthony defeated Brutus and Cassius, the murderers of Julius Caesar, in 42BC, and because it was at Philippi that the Apostle Paul established the first Christian community in Europe.

On the opposite side of the road is a theatre, carved out of the hillside in the 4th century BC and now used for performances in summer, and the remains of another basilica, built in about AD500. *18km northwest of Kaválla.*

## KAVÁLLA (KAVALA)

Turkish-style houses with shutters, tiled roofs and overhanging second storeys clutter the winding cobbled streets which ascend from Kavala's busy commercial harbour to its Byzantine castle. The Apostle Paul landed here on his first missionary journey to Europe, and it was here that Mehmet Ali (1769–1849) was born, who became Pasha of Egypt and whose last descendent as ruler of Egypt was King Farouk (abdicated 1952). *170km east of Thessaloníki.*

### Anapsihtirio Imaret (Turkish Almshouse)

A forest of domes and chimney-pots marks this derelict building above the harbour. Built to house the poor of the city by Mehmet Ali, its cool courtyard with its whitewashed arcades is now a pleasant café-bar adorned with relics of old Kavala. *Opposite junction of Theod Poulidou and Mohamet-Ali.*

### Arkheologiko Mousio (Kavala Archaeological Museum)

Finds include delicate polychrome glass vases, reliefs and mosaics from Amfipolis, gilded jewellery and a restored 250BC Macedonian tomb chamber. *Erithrou Stavrou (tel: 051 222335), at the western end of the harbour esplanade, in a small park, signposted. Open: daily, except Monday, 8.30am–3pm. Admission charge.*

### Kastro (Castle)

The Byzantine citadel was taken over and expanded by the Turks. An impressive aqueduct, which supplied the citadel and the town below with water, crosses the main Kavala-Alexandhroupolis road below the castle. *Open: daily, 9am–3pm. Admission free.*

## KOMOTINÍ

A quaint mixture of modern and traditional, Komotiní is a market town with a strong ethnic Muslim element. Look out for women in chador-like black dresses and headscarves and older men in soft skullcaps in the open-air market held every Tuesday. The bazaar area in the street either side of pedestrianised Venizelou is fascinating.
*113km east of Kaválla.*

### Mousio Morphotikou Omilou Komotinis (Museum of Folk Life and History)

Collection of domestic items and folk costumes, with fine examples of local wedding embroidery.
*Ayiou Yioryiou 13. Open: daily, except Sunday, 10am–1pm.*

### Yeni Came (Yeni Mosque)

The mosque and its graceful minaret stand next to a 19th-century clock tower bearing an inscription from the Koran.

Behind the mosque stand the headstones and tombs of a Turkish graveyard.
*Venizelou 83/Platia Ifaistou.*

## XÁNTHI

Xánthi's wealth traditionally came from tobacco trading, and its prosperity is reflected by the large mansions built by well-off tobacco factors in its old quarter, many now restored.
*56km east of Kaválla.*

### Laografiko Mousio (Folk Art Museum)

The museum is housed in a splendidly decorated tobacco baron's house with painted ceilings. Displays include weapons, copper and brassware, and gorgeous Sarakatsan rugs.
*Antika 7. Open: Monday, Wednesday, Thursday and weekends, 11am–1pm and 6.30pm–8.30pm. Admission charge.*

### Palaio Xánthi (Old Xánthi)

The old quarter, with its largely car-free cobbled streets and yellow and white stuccoed houses, stands above the modern town centre.
*North of Vasilissis Sofias.*

A restored tobacco trader's mansion in Xánthi's old quarter

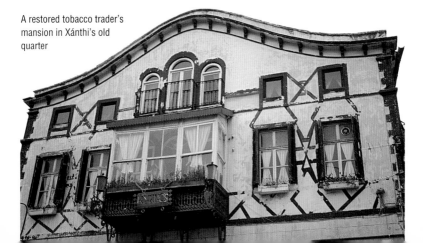

A 14th-century towered fortress guards the harbour at Ouranópolis

# KHALKIDHIKÍ

Shaped like a three-fingered hand, Khalkidhikí points south into the Aegean. The easternmost peninsula, closed to tourists, is Áyion Óros (Holy Mountain/Mount Athos), a semi-independent territory ruled by the abbots of its score of monasteries (see the Mount Athos tour, pages 130–1) and dominated by the sharp-edged peak of Athos, 2,033m high, on its southern tip.

Kassándhra, the furthest west of the three peninsulas and the closest to Thessaloníki's international airport is, not surprisingly, the biggest tourism puller, with a necklace of resorts catering to holidaymakers from all over Europe. It is worth spending one night on the west coast for the glowing sunsets, with the peaks of Olympus, Óssa and Pílion (Pelion) silhouetted on the opposite shore of the Thermaïkós Kólpos (Thermaic Gulf), some 50–60km away.

Sithonía (Sidhonia), the middle peninsula, is less developed and more rugged than its western neighbour. Thick pine forest alternates with bare boulders and the scars of forest fires. Sidhonia's east coast has some of the best and least crowded beaches in Greece. Its southern tip is barren and blasted by winter gales and summer heat.

## NÉA FÓKAIA

The small square keep of Ayios Pavlos (St Paul) guards a pleasant, east-facing sandy beach with three summer tavernas.
*8km south of Néa Potidhia on Kassándhra's east coast. The tower is not open.*

## NÉA POTÍDHAIA (Nea Potidhia)

The gateway to Kassándhra, where a narrow canal has been cut through the isthmus to allow yachts to pass through.
*80km southeast of Thessaloníki.*

## OLINTHOS

An extensive complex of walls and pits on a flat-topped hill marks the site of ancient Olinthos, destroyed by Philip II of Macedon, father of Alexander, in 348BC. He did a thorough job.
*North of the main road, 4km west of Néa Moudhaniá and 1km from the village of Nea Olinthos (tel: 0371 91280). Open: daily, except Monday, 8.30am–3pm.*

## OURANÓPOLIS

The departure-point for cruises around the Ayion Óros and for pilgrims heading for the monasteries is a bustling little port with a pretty location on the Singitikós Kólpos/Kólpos Ayiou Orous (Gulf of the Holy Mountain). You can

hire a boat to explore the small islands offshore. Ferries run frequently to Amoliani, the island opposite the harbour. A 14th-century fortress tower guards the harbour.
*10km south of the isthmus linking the Ayion Óros to the mainland.*

## PALIOÚRION (Paliouri)

A chain of beach resorts runs up the east coast of Kassándhra from Paliouri, close to the peninsula's southern tip. There are many good sandy beaches with a backdrop of pine-clad hills, and the scenery is outstanding.
*58km south of Néa Moudhania.*

## PETRALONA

Halfway between Thessaloníki and Kassándhra are the beautiful stalagmite and stalactite caves of Petralona, with colours ranging from pure white to deep red. The caves were inhabited in palaeolithic times, and contain the earliest known traces of man-made fire, dated to 700,000 years ago.
*North of Eleohoria, on the N. Kalikratitia – N. Moudhaniá road. Open: Tuesday to Sunday, 8.30am–3pm. Admission charge.*

## PORTO CARRAS

A self-contained complex of four enormous, obtrusive and charmless hotels overlooking a yacht marina, riding centre and golf course.
*Midway along the west coast of Sidhonia.*

## SÁRTI

A small resort popular with holidaymakers from Thessaloníki, Sárti stands by a sandy beach at the mouth of a green valley. Lots of tavernas and discos indicate an active nightlife in summer.
*On the east coast of Sidhonia, about 30km from its southern tip.*

## SIKÉAS (Sikias)

A triangle of farmland forms a fertile oasis of fields and orchards hemmed in by low, jagged hills behind a long curve of sandy, little-visited beach.
*On the east coast of Sidhonia, about 20km from the southern tip.*

## TORONE (Toroni)

Toroni could not be more different from its big neighbour. This tiny resort has 2km of sandy beach on a wide west-facing bay, with a backdrop of barren, rocky hills.
*5km south of Porto Carras.*

## VOURVOUROU

Vourvourou is set on a shallow, almost landlocked lagoon overlooking a calm bay with a scattering of tiny islands. There are sandy beaches either side of the small village.
*On the east coast of Sidhonia, close to its northern end.*

Yachts at anchor in Porto Carras marina on the Sidhonia peninsula

# THESSALONÍKI

Greece's second city was largely destroyed by fire in 1917 and struck by an earthquake in 1978, so it comes as some surprise that so many ancient and medieval buildings survive. Built on a long crescent bay at the head of the Thermaïkós Kólpos (Thermaic Gulf), it is a lively city, with smart shops, lots of good restaurants and fashionable cafés, and an energetic nightlife.

Bronze *krater* (wine cauldron) from the 4th century in the Thessaloníki Archaeological Museum

*Enter the old quarter at the Dingirle Koule, at the northeast end of Zografou.*

## APSIS GALERIOU (Arch of Galerius)

The 4th-century arch was built at the crossroads of Roman Thessaloníki to honour the Emperor Galerius. It stands beside one of the city's busiest streets and is being restored.
*Corner of Egnatia and Gounari.*

## AKROPOLIS (Acropolis)

Sections of the city's 4th-century ramparts, extended and reinforced by the Byzantines in the 14th century and the Turks in the 15th, partially enclose the old quarter. The most imposing remnants of the medieval fortifications are the Dingirle Koule (Chain Tower), a twin of the Lefkos Pirgos (White Tówer) on the seafront, and the recently restored section of walls between the Pirgos Palaiologos and the Pirgos Andronikos towers, dating from the 14th century.

## ARKHEOLOGIKÓ MOUSÍOU (Archaeological Museum)

The stupendous finds from the royal Macedonian tombs at Vergína (see page 129) are the central attraction of this fine museum. The workmanship and materials testify to the wealth and sophistication of ancient Macedon. Among the most striking are the tiny ivory heads of Philip II and Alexander, beautifully wrought gold jewellery, the embossed gold funerary chests and delicate ornamental wreaths, the bronze, silver and gold shields and cauldrons, and the skeleton of Philip II.
*Junction of d'Esperey and Stratou (tel:. 031 830538). Open: Monday, 11am–5pm; Tuesday to Friday, 8am–5pm; weekends and holidays, 8.30am–3pm. Admission charge.*

## ÁYIOS DHIMÍTRIOS

The church, originally built in the 5th

The White Tower on the waterfront is Thessaloníki's most prominent landmark

century but extensively rebuilt since then, is the largest in Greece. It contains the relics of St Dhimitrios, the city's patron saint, who was executed by the Emperor Galerius at that spot in AD306. *Upper side of Platia Dikastirion (tel: 031 270008). Open: daily, except Monday, 8.30am–3pm. Admission free.*

## ÁYIA SOFIA

Like Ayios Dhimitrios, this 8th-century church became a mosque with the Turkish conquest. Now a church again, its dim candlelit interior is decorated with painted domes, restored trompe-l'œil mosaics and richly ornamented screens.
*Midway along Egnatia, between Egnatia and Tsimiski. Open: daily, closed 12.30pm–5pm. Admission free.*

## ÁYIOS YEÓRYIOS/AYIOS YIORGIOS (Rotonda)

The squat, massive building was intended to be the tomb of the Roman Emperor Galerius, was converted into a church in the following century, and became a mosque under the Turks.
*Filippou, 50m north of the Apsis Galeriou (Arch of Galerius). Temporarily closed for restoration.*

## BEDESTAN (Old Market)

The Ottoman-period market area off Venizelou is a chaos of stalls and shops selling everything under the sun. Noisy and colourful, it is a photographer's delight. Go early in the morning to catch it in full swing.

## LAOGRAFIKO-ETHNOLOGIKO MOUSION MAKEDHONIAS (Folklife-Ethnological Museum of Macedonia)

A collection of costumes, artefacts, and

The doorway of Thessaloníki's 8th-century church of Áyia Sofia

photographs illustrating the vanished folk art and life of northern Greece, housed in a 19th-century mansion near the waterfront. There is an interesting display on the traditional *karaghiosis* shadow-puppet theatre.
*Vass. Olgas 68 (tel: 031 830591). Open: Monday and Wednesday, 9.30am–5.30pm; Tuesday, Friday and Saturday, 9.30am–2pm. Admission charge.*

## Levkos Pirgos (White Tower)

The 35m circular tower on the waterfront was a bastion of the Byzantine city walls, rebuilt by the Turks in about 1430, and used mainly as a prison. It houses an excellent Byzantine museum with some very striking icons, tombs, mosaics and frescos. The top storey houses a pleasant, cool café whose rooftop terrace offers a fine view of the town and the harbour.
*East end of Leoforos Nikis (tel: 031 830538). Open: Monday, 11am–5pm; Tuesday to Friday, 8.30am–5pm; weekends and holidays, 8.30am–3pm. Admission charge.*

# FISHERMEN

**N**o Greek harbour is complete without its complement of tiny, brightly painted fishing boats and lengths of crimson-dyed net spread out to dry.

Look closely at the prow of many of these little vessels and you will see, cut into the wood, a diamond-shape – a stylised modern version of the painted eye with which the ancient Greeks decorated their galleys.

Most fishing is done at night, and flotillas of one-man craft (sometimes towed behind a larger vessel) usually

Catch of the day.

set out at sundown, to come puttering back with their catch at first light.

Some 5,000 years of intensive fishing have taken their toll of the Aegean's stocks, and Greek boatmen have long used everything from fine-mesh nets to fish-traps and tridents.

In more recent times, dynamite became a potent and popular way of maximising results, and it is not uncommon to meet fishermen who have lost a hand through a mishap with explosives.

With such a comprehensive approach, it is hardly surprising that the catch is increasingly small and mostly made up of tiddlers. Nets full of whitebait, sprats and mackerel are common, but the prized *barbounia* (red mullet) commands a far higher price.

Bigger fish like tunny and swordfish are often caught off the southern Peloponnese, in the deep waters of the Steno Kíthiro (Kithira Channel).

Boats fitted with powerful acetylene lamps are used to attract squid into a circle of nets, while octopus are caught with a trident or a formidable triple hook on a hand-line.

Greece's lakes, too, have their fishing fleets. On Límni Ioánninon (Lake Pamvotis), Límni Kastorías (Lake Kastoria) and the Límni Préspes (Prespa lakes), as well as on the reservoirs formed by Greece's many hydro-electric dams, local fishers set out after carp and other freshwater fish in black-tarred punts.

And on Greece's beaches, fishers of another kind trawl for a different catch: young Greek men who spend their summers in romantic pursuit of female tourists are called *kamaki* – 'harpooners'.

Fishing boat at anchor

Fresh from the Aegean

# WESTERN MACEDONIA

## DHION

Highlights of the most impressive site in Macedonia are the marble and mosaic floors of the baths, the Sanctuary of Isis with copies of the original statues, and a length of the cobbled road which led to Olympus.

*115km south of Thessaloníki. The site is 2km east of Dhion village (tel: 0351 53206). Open: weekdays, 8am–6pm; weekends and holidays, 8.30am–3pm. Admission charge.*

## Mousio (Museum)

The museum has a rich and well-displayed collection of statues, coins, jewellery and everyday objects and an excellent explanatory video programme.
*In the centre of Dhion village. Signposted. (tel: 0351 53206). Open: Monday, 11am–6pm; Tuesday to Friday, 8.30am–6pm; weekends and holidays, 8.30am–3pm. Admission charge.*

## KASTORÍA

Surrounded on three sides by its lake, Kastoría is one of the prettiest towns in Greece. It grew wealthy on the fur trade,

As the highest mountain in Greece it was only natural that the gods should choose Mount Olympus for their home

and though the beavers which gave it its name *(castor* is Latin for beaver) have disappeared from the area, many small factories still make up the distinctive patchwork fur garments for which the town is known. Grand 19th-century fur-merchants' mansions stand on the slope overlooking the lake, southeast of the modern town centre.
*210km west of Thessaloníki.*

## Koumbelidhiki Panagia

The most important of Kastoría's antique churches has striking exterior frescos of Salome and John the Baptist. Decorative brickwork, interspersing geometric rows of brick with masonry, is a feature of all Kastoría's Byzantine churches.
*Off Caravagelli. Closed for renovation.*

## Laografiko Mousio Kastorias (Kastoría Folk Museum)

On the ground floor of this fur-trader's mansion are barrel-filled cellars, a green courtyard with the kitchen and a copper still. The upper floors have elaborately decorated woodwork, polished floors and painted ceilings.
*Kapetan 10. Open: daily, 8.30am–6pm. Admission charge.*

## Mousio Byzantikon (Byzantine Museum)

The museum's collection of glowing crimson and gold icons is one of the best in Greece. Unfortunately, all texts and explanations are in Greek.
*Off V. Iperiou, next to the Xenia hotel. Open: daily, except Monday, 8.30am–3pm. Admission charge.*

## LÍMNI PRÉSPES (PRESPA LAKES)

Megali Préspa (Great Prespa) and Mikrí Préspa (Little Prespa) are a refuge for pelicans, storks, egrets, spoonbills and cormorants. Around them stand a handful of villages which seem to have been barely touched by the 20th century.
*190km northwest of Thessaloníki.*

## ÓLIMBOS ÓROS (Mount Olympus)

The tallest mountain in Greece (2,817m) and the legendary home of the gods dominates Macedonia and the north from most angles. The peak is usually covered in cloud by midday, adding to its air of mystery (see Climbing Mount Olympus, page 140).

## PÉLLA

The ancient capital of Macedonia, Pélla was also the childhood home of Alexander the Great. Mosaics of warriors in battle, stag hunts, and the abduction of Helen by Paris (see page 59) have been perfectly preserved under layers of silt. Also worth seeing are the columns of the Colonnade of the Court. Excavations are continuing, and a viewing-tower gives you a bird's-eye view of this extensive Macedonian site.

The museum, on the opposite side of the road from the site, has an excellent collection of marbles and some lovely fluid pebble-mosaics and terracotta statuettes.
*On the main road between Thessaloníki and Yiannitsá (Yianitsa), 39km west of Thessaloníki (tel: 0382 31160/31278). Open: daily, except Monday, 8.30am–3pm. Admission charge covers site and museum.*

## VERGÍNA

The tombs identified as those of Philip II of Macedon and other members of his family make this the most significant site unearthed this century. Above ground, the remains of the royal palace include a magnificent mosaic floor with stylised floral and geometric patterns. Below it, the magnificent marble-lined royal tombs with their great stone sarcophagi cannot fail to impress, though the treasures of the tombs – and Philip II's remains – are in the Thessaloníki Archaeological Museum. A smaller tomb, beneath an unsightly metal roof, is between the palace and the village.
*Anaktora (Palace): near Palatitsia, 2km from modern Vergína, signposted. Tombs: on the outskirts of Vergína, signposted (tel: 031 830538). Open: daily, except Monday, 8.30am–3pm. Admission charge.*

Kastoría and its lake

# Áyion Óros (Mount Athos)

Mount Athos, the Holy Mountain, has been ruled by its monks since the 10th century. Special permission from the Ministry of Northern Greece is required to visit the 45km-long peninsula, and women – and even female animals – are banned. Around 1,500 monks now live in the 20 monasteries.

Each monastery is ruled by its abbot and each is built in a distinctively different architectural style. Some perch on the slopes of the mountain, others stand beside natural harbours.

The monasteries of the west coast can be clearly observed from the cruise ships which sail daily from the small port of Ouranópolis, just north of the frontier between the Holy Mountain and the outside world.

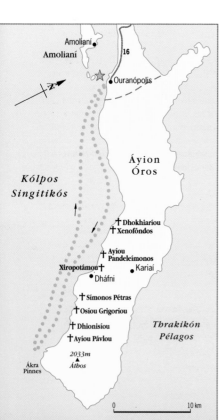

Snacks, drinks and camera film are sold on board. Boats must stay at least 500m offshore, so a zoom lens and binoculars are useful. Tickets are sold in advance by agencies on the Ouranópolis harbour-front, and the trip takes 4 to 6 hours. A multi-lingual commentary (English/ German/Greek) is provided.

*Leaving Ouranópolis the boat cruises southeast along the barren coast of the peninsula.*

### DHOKHIARÍOU (DOHIARIOU)
Easily spotted by its crenellated defence tower, this monastery on the seashore was built in the 10th century. It now has around a dozen monks.

### XENOFÓNDOS (XENOPHONTOS)
Named after its 10th-century founder, St Xenofon, the fortress-like building overlooks a long pebbly strand.

The 14th-century monastery of Dhionisíou near the peak of Mount Athos

Damaged by pirates and fires, it has frequently been rebuilt and is a patchwork of styles.

### AYÍOU PANDELEÍMONOS (AYIOS PANTELEIMONAS)

Most striking and colourful of all, with scarlet walls and green onion-domes, each surmounted by a gold orb and cross, the present monastery was built by Russian monks in the late 18th century.

### XIROPOTÁMOU (XEROPOTAMOS)

High on a ridge above the coast, Xiropotámou overlooks the tiny harbour at Dháfni. One of the most modern monasteries, it has been rebuilt a number of times over the last three centuries after a series of disastrous fires.

### DHÁFNI (DAFNI)

Below Xiropotámou, Dháfni is the peninsula's official harbour and entry-point for pilgrims. The mountain's only road runs from the port to Kariaí (Karies), the administrative capital of Mount Athos.

### SÍMONOS PÉTRAS (SIMONOPETRA)

Perched dizzyingly on its crag, Simonos Pétras is unmistakable, a seven-storey building which seems to grow straight out of the cliff.

### OSÍOU GRIGORÍOU (GREGORIOU)

Another clifftop eyrie, Grigoríou is dedicated to St Nicholas and is the smallest of the Athos monasteries. With binoculars you can clearly see its cheerfully colourful red-tiled roof and blue balconies overlooking the sea.

### DHIONISÍOU (DIONYSIOU)

The fortress-like 14th-century building is easily recognised by its tiers of white and pink balconies, 80m above the sea. The interior contains some fine frescos.

### AYOU PÁVLOU (AYIOS PAVLOS)

High above the sea, Ayiou Pávlou is a dour stone building cradled by outcrops of the peak of Mount Athos.

### ÁYION ÓROS (MOUNT ATHOS)

While the whole peninsula is known by this name, the peak itself is at its southern tip. Its steep slopes drop sheer into the sea and the summit towers to a height of 2,033m.

*From the southern tip, the boat returns to Ouranópolis.*

### AMOLIANÍ

Most excursion boats stop at this small island, about 20 minutes from Ouranópolis, where a pretty harbour offers a choice of tavernas. There is a beach about 10 minutes' walk from the harbourside.

Ministry of Northern Greece, Platia Dhikitiriou, Thessaloníki. Permission to visit the holy mountain is usually granted only to Orthodox pilgrims or scholars with a special interest in Greece.

# ALEXANDER THE GREAT

Separated from the warring city-states of the southern mainland by mountain ranges, Macedon was thought of by civilised Hellenes as a near-barbarous land.

But the disastrous Peloponnesian War (431–404BC) between Athens and Sparta drew in all the cities of the south and spelt the beginning of the end of their era.

As their political, military and economic power waned, Macedon became a power to be reckoned with.

At the battle of Khairónia in 338BC, (see page 86), Philip II's Macedonians shattered the combined forces of the southern cities, using radically new tactics. Against the swords and shield-wall of the south, Philip threw a phalanx of pike-wielding infantry backed up by heavy cavalry.

Commanding the cavalry wing was his 18-year-old son, Alexander. Two years later, following Philip's assassination, he became king and began the meteoric career which made him a legend.

Alexander had been groomed in the warrior skills of Macedon and in the finer arts of civilised Greece, the philosopher Aristotle having been his tutor, but he is remembered above all as a brilliant general.

A year after his father's death, Alexander crushed a revolt by the Thebans and sacked their city, consolidating Macedon's control of the Greek mainland.

In 334BC he invaded Asia Minor, defeating a Persian army on the River Granikos, and six years later all Persia was his. Pushing east, he took Sogdiana (Uzbekistan), Bactria (Afghanistan) and reached India, but his exhausted soldiers

Two images of the youthful Alexander: (left) a marble bust and (right) a mosaic from Pompeii

refused to go further.

Returning to Persia in 324BC, he planned to forge Persia and Greece into one empire, but met strong opposition. Before he could overcome it, he died of fever. He was 33 years old.

His empire quickly collapsed as his generals set up kingdoms for themselves in the east, though Macedon remained the major power in Greece until Rome defeated its last independent king, Perseus, at Pydna in 167BC.

# GETTING AWAY FROM IT ALL

It was a land of scintillating diversity,
a cornucopia of riches.
It was almost part of the mainland,
but not quite. It was an island,
but an island apart from the rest.
And it was only two hours from Athens.

SARA WHEELER
*An Island Apart (1993)*

Spetsai's tiny beaches and pretty houses are a stone's throw from the streets of Athens

# ARGO-SARONIC ISLANDS

Frequent fast hydrofoils bring the beaches and pretty villages of these attractive islands close to Athens. Flying Dolphins/Ceres Hydrofoils provide services to and from the islands and their offices are situated at Akti Themistokleous 8, Freattys 185 36 Piraeus (tel: 4280 001). Journey times from Piraeus range from half an hour to 2 hours.

## AÍYINA (Aegina)

The largest of the Argo-Saronic islands and the closest to Athens, Aegina is a favourite weekend resort of Athenians wanting peace and quiet. Visit Aegina to swim, eat at seafood tavernas, and visit the temple.

### Naos Aphaia (Temple of Aphaia)

The Doric temple to Aphaia, protectress of women, retains most of its 32 columns.

*On the hilltop close to the northeast tip of the island (tel: 0297 32398). Open: Monday to Friday, 8am–5pm; weekends, 8.30am–3pm. Admission charge. 40*

## ANGÍSTRION

A tiny island with one little fishing-harbour-cum-resort, Angístrion seems much more remote than it is. Only a few hundred metres from Aegina, its beaches are usually much less crowded. Come here to do nothing except swim, sunbathe and relax.

*30 minutes from Aíyina by boat.*

## Ídhra (Hydra)

Rows of whitewashed mansions rise above a port crowded with fancy yachts and cruisers as well as the inevitable fishing boats. There are no roads outside the village, but there are coves and pebbly beaches for swimming within walking distance of the village.

*1 hour and 40 minutes from Athens.*

## Póros

A stone's throw from the mainland, the village is a multicoloured clutter of houses and the harbour bustles with hydrofoils and ferries. There are good beaches on the mainland opposite, and small boats shuttle to and fro every few minutes.

## Spetsai

Spetsai sits at the mouth of the Argolikós Kólpos (Argolic Gulf) a short hop from the mainland. The village is an attractive mix of 18th-century shipowners' mansions and neo-classical 19th-century buildings, surrounding two harbours, the older fishing port and the newer harbour where ferries and hydrofoils dock. Much of the island is covered by pine woods and there are pleasant walks and good beaches. *2–2½hours and 30 minutes from Athens.*

## ÉVVOIA (Evia)

Greece's second-largest island is only a couple of hours away from Athens via frequent ferry services from Rafína and Marmári and Káristos, a small resort near the south tip, which has an enormous pebble beach, a ruined Turkish castle, and lots of seaside tavernas. You can also get to Evia by car, as a swing bridge connects it to the mainland at Khalkís (Khalkidha) (see map on page 47).

## LEVKÁS

This delightful Ionian island is connected to the mainland by a long causeway. There are beautiful white beaches on the west coast and an archipelago of uninhabited islands dotted around the sheltered waters of the east coast (see map on pages 98–9).

## SKÍATHOS

The pine-covered island of Skíathos has some of Greece's finest sandy beaches, and its beautiful island capital with its Italianate clock towers and red-tiled houses is a package-holiday favourite. *Daily hydrofoil services from Vólos in summer.*

## THÁSOS

Thásos is a huge, pine-covered island only an hour by the frequent ferry service from Kaválla. It has excellent sandy beaches.

Sunset over Póros. The coastline to the north is inaccessibly mountainous

Glossy ibis (*Plegadis falcinellus*) is one of the rarer birds in Greece

# BIRDWATCHING

The rivers and wetlands of the Greek mainland offer some of the finest birdwatching in Europe.

## AKHELÓÖS

The vast expanse of the Akhelóös delta is one of the finest birdwatching areas in Greece. The river reaches the sea through a maze of channels, among reedbeds, lagoons, cotton and maize fields and stands of eucalyptus. The shoreline is a marshy patchwork of lagoons, salt-pans and shallow, muddy bays. Kingfishers, larks and wagtails infest the river channels, and nearer the shoreline you can expect to see herons, egrets, many gull species, cormorants and terns.
*About 30km from Mesolóngion (see page 94).*

## ANGELOKHORION

The salt-pans at Angelokhorion, near Thessaloníki, attract Mediterranean gulls, slender-billed gulls and Audouin's gull in spring and autumn, as well as many kinds of wader and tern. You may also spot Cory's shearwater flying close inshore.
*Near Ayía Triás, southeast of Thessaloníki.*

## ÉVROS

The mud-flats and salt-marshes of the Évros delta attract waders of all kinds, herons, storks, pelicans, cormorants, plovers and larks.
*About 30km east of Alexandhroupoli (see page 120).*

## LÍMNI MIKRÍ PRÉSPA (Lake Mikri Prespa National Park)

Pelicans, pygmy cormorants, egrets, ibises and storks haunt the reedbeds of the remote lake. Huge flocks of jays can often be seen in the beech woods surrounding the lake.
*35km north of Kastoría (see page 129).*

## LÍMNI VISTONIS (Lake Vistonis)

Salt-pans and a lagoon lie south of the causeway which cuts Lake Vistonis in two, carrying the main road.
Another causeway leads to the island church of Ayios Nikolaos, which is an ideal vantage-point for spotting ibises, egrets, pygmy cormorants, pelicans and herons.
*Midway between Xánthi and Komotiní (see page 120–1).*

## MESOLÓNGION

The lagoon at Mesolóngion with its fish hatcheries and salt-pans attracts curlews and many other waders, avocets, black-winged stilts, terns and gulls, and Kentish plovers.
*(See page 94–5.)*

## NÉSTOS RIVER

Look out for herons, terns, gulls, waders

and (very rarely) flamingoes among the lagoons just north of Keramotí, close to the mouth of the Néstos river.

*East of Kaválla. Follow signs to Gravouna, then Keramoti.*

Right: Stork's nest on a telephone pole
Below: Long-nosed viper (*Vipera ammodytes*)

## WILDLIFE

The wild mountains of Greece are home to some of Europe's last wolves and bears, though you are most unlikely to see them. Wolves are claimed to be on the increase in the northern mountains and are ruthlessly hunted, getting the blame for attacks on flocks which are more likely to be the work of dogs. Bears are rare and very shy.

The same hill country which shelters these vanishing predators is also the home of the spectacular griffon vulture and the lammergaier vulture, two of Europe's largest raptors, and of harriers, buzzards and golden eagles.

A variety of snakes, including vipers, smooth snakes and grass snakes, are common, and killed impartially whether venomous or not. Rocky hillsides and stone walls are the haunt of many species of lizard, including several species of wall lizard and the larger, more vivid green lizard and the distinctive eyed lizard. Geckos are found clinging to walls after dark and often gather around electric lights which attract the insects they feed on. Terrapins congregate in ponds and rivers, where they like to bask in sunny locations on banks and logs.

Land tortoises are found everywhere but are commonest in the Píndhos Óros (Píndhos mountains) and are all too frequently seen squashed on the road.

# FLOWERS & BUTTERFLIES

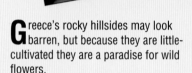

**G**reece's rocky hillsides may look barren, but because they are little-cultivated they are a paradise for wild flowers.

Much of the country is deemed suitable only for goat pasture, and wild flowers are left to flourish without interference.

In addition, Greek farming is still piecemeal, allowing wild plants to thrive in fields, orchards and olive groves alongside cultivated plants.

The best time to see Greece in bloom is in spring (as early as March in the southern Peloponnese or as late as June in the north) when hillsides and plains are ablaze with red, yellow and purple. Wild orchids are abundant, as are cistus, anemones, poppies, irises, gladioli, vetches, crocuses and many others. Purple and blue morning glories cover ruined walls, and every watercourse is marked by the pink flowers of oleander. Even after the lower regions have been scorched dry by the summer sun, the high slopes of Taïyetos and Píndhos where melting

snow prolongs the spring may be a happy hunting ground.

Greece's climate and soil suit many species of orchid. As early as February you can hope to spot the giant orchids (*Barlia sp.*) and some varieties of bee orchid in the southern Peloponnese, and mountain-loving helleborine orchids may be found on north-facing slopes as late as July.

Unfortunately, European Union subsidies are encouraging many Greek

Far left: Hummingbird hawk moth (*Macroglossum stellatarum*)
Left: the Scarce swallowtail butterfly (*Iphiclides podalirius*)
Below: Giant orchid (*Barlia robertiana*)

farmers to experiment with more intensive cultivation. As a result, crops in parts of the mainland are becoming less varied, reducing the opportunities for wild flowers to flourish.

The range of food plants available and the limited use of insecticides make Greece a butterfly heaven, and the vivid colours of butterfly wings are all the more readily spotted against the greys and browns of dry summer landscapes.

Among the most exotic butterfly species are the huge, zebra-striped scarce swallowtail (*Iphiclides podalirius*), the southern swallowtail *(Papilio alexanor)*, and the plain tiger *(Danaus chrysippus)*. On hillsides, look out for the many different species of fast-flying fritillaries, and in fields and road verges watch for the flashing wings of more than a dozen species of blues.

The day-flying hummingbird hawk moth is a common denizen of flower gardens and fields, unmistakable because of its long, curling tongue and its ability to fly backwards with fast-beating wings. Its night-flying relatives, the huge poplar hawk moth, lime hawk moth and oleander hawk moth, are often drawn to unshaded lights after dark.

The Olympus trail zigzags steeply through pine woods and treeless peaks

## CLIMBING ÓLIMBOS ÓROS (MOUNT OLYMPUS)

Greece's mightiest mountain has nine peaks of more than 2,600m. The highest, Mitikas, reaches 2,917m.

Allow three days and two nights for the climb. Enter Ólimbos National Park from the village of Litokhoron, near the foot of the mountain and drive, walk, hitch-hike or take a taxi to Prionia at 1,100m. From here a well-trodden trail zigzags steeply through pine woods to the Greek Alpine Club's Refuge A, a 3-hour hike. The refuge, at 2,100m, sleeps 90 people in bunk-bedded dormitories. Simple but filling meals are available.

Start for the summit immediately after breakfast, following a trail marked by metal arrows to Olympus's third-highest summit, Skala.

Do not attempt the final 200m separating Skala from Mitikas without an excellent head for heights and some climbing experience. On one side of the ridge between the two peaks there is a vertical, 500m drop. On the other, the path is no more than a series of holds.

Skolio, the mountain's second-highest peak, is an easy 750m walk from Skala. Allow 7 hours for the round trip from Refuge A to the summit and back.

Nights on Olympus are chilly and the days cool. The refuge provides blankets, but you should take a sweater and windproof jacket. Other essentials include a water-bottle, good boots, and dried fruit or chocolate.

*Book accommodation in advance. Ellinikos Oreivatikos Syllogos Litokhoron (Greek Alpine Club of Litokhoron), Kentriki Platia, 60200 Litokhoron (tel: 0532 81944). Open: May to October, 8am–noon and 4pm–6pm. Katafigion A (Refuge A) (tel: 0352 81800). Open: May to October, 6am–10pm.*

## CRUISES

Among the most popular cruises are those taking in the delightful villages of the Kikhlades (Cyclades) islands. Cruises can be as short as one day or as long as a week, and can be arranged through any Athens travel agency or through major hotels.

**Dolphin Hellas Cruises**. *Akti Miaouli 71, 185 37 Piraeus (tel: 4512 109).*
**Epirotiki Lines**. *Akti Miaouli 87, 185 38 Piraeus (tel: 4291 000).*
**Sun Line**. *Iassonos 3, 185 37 Piraeus (tel: 4523 417).*

### YACHTING

There are dozens of yacht charter companies in Greece, most of them based in and around Athens. Yachts can be chartered with or without a licensed crew. The weather is suitable for sailing from April to October, though in August the strong Meltemi wind can keep boats in harbour for up to three days at a time.
*A list of yacht charter companies is available from the Greek National Tourist Office (see Directory, page 189).*

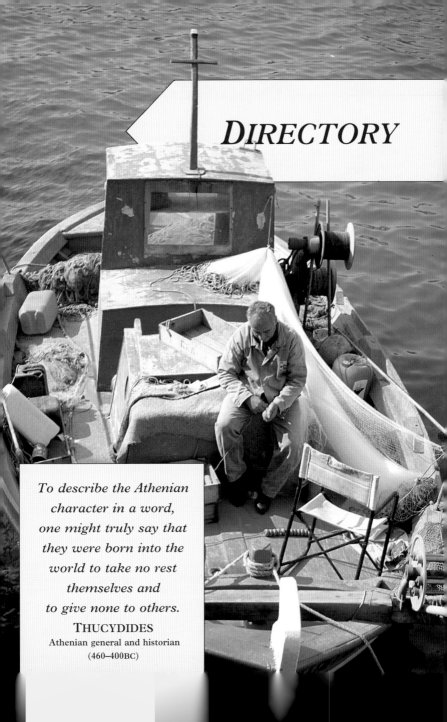

To describe the Athenian
character in a word,
one might truly say that
they were born into the
world to take no rest
themselves and
to give none to others.

**THUCYDIDES**
Athenian general and historian
(460–400BC)

# Shopping

*T*here are bargains to be found, especially in Athens. If you are shopping for distinctive regional products – such as rugs and blankets from Arákhova or silverware from Ioánnina you may find them cheaper in Athens than in the villages in which they are made.

Shops traditionally open between 8am and 1pm, close until around 5pm then reopen until about 8pm, though in Athens many souvenir shops stay open all day and late into the night. Most shops close on Sundays except in resort areas.

### Antiquities and imitations

Genuine antiques and icons require an export permit (rarely granted), and in any case are very thin on the ground. Beware of fakes. The major archaeological museums licence a range of accurate and attractive replicas of ancient statues, vases, jewellery and other finds, and these are a much better buy.

### Beads and bangles

Brightly coloured ceramic beads, necklaces, gold and silver-plated bracelets, and the black and blue glass beads traditionally believed to ward off the evil eye make cheap and cheerful gifts. *Komboloi* or 'worry-beads', carried by many Greek men, are sold very cheaply in souvenir stores and at every street kiosk.

### Clothing

Good buys include cotton sweaters. Thessaloníki, a centre of textile manufacturing, is the cheapest place in Europe for leading-brand denim jeans, shirts and jackets.

### Flokati rugs

Huge, shaggy rugs of wool tufted on to a woven backing may be in natural, unbleached wool or dyed in a variety of vivid colours. Still widely used in Greek homes, they are sold throughout the country.

### Footwear

Boots and shoes are well made and affordable. The best buys are to be found in main-street stores where Greeks shop.

Hand-made embroidery is a dying art and one of the best buys you can make

The sandals sold in tourist markets rarely wear well.

**Herbs**
Oregano, marjoram and thyme are among the better-known varieties, and prices are much lower than in your supermarket at home. Herbal teas are also widely sold in produce markets.

**Jewellery**
Jewellers abound, in smaller provincial capitals as well as in Athens, selling gold and silver jewellery based on ancient designs or on more modern interpretations. Prices reflect the value of the material, and while silverware may be cheaper than elsewhere in Europe, gold can be more expensive. Craftsmen in Ioánnina still make silver filigree work, sometimes decorated with turquoise. Antique silver buckles and belts can sometimes be found, but there is no guarantee of authenticity.

**Leather goods**
Leather handbags, satchels and travelling bags made solely for the tourist market are sold in markets everywhere. Prices are low and get lower with bargaining, but workmanship is not always first rate. Examine seams, straps and buckles before buying.

**Museum shops**
The official shops at major museums sell fine copies of ancient works. They cost little more than the poorer imitations sold in tourist shops, but are much better value.

**Tax-free shopping**
Value added tax at 18 per cent is charged on anything you buy. Tax-free shopping is available to visitors from outside the

Traditional worry-beads (*kombolói*) make cheap and cheerful souvenirs

European Union at selected shops in Athens and other major cities and resorts. A full list of shops offering VAT refunds to non-EU residents is available from: **Tax Free Club**, *Customer Service Office, Nikis 10, 105 63 Athens (tel: 3225 569 or 3240 802).*

**Textiles and traditional handicrafts**
Woven wool bags, blankets and rugs in bright colours and fine cotton embroidery and lace are among the best souvenirs you can buy. The National Welfare Association's handicraft programme, aimed at keeping Greek traditions alive, provides up to 5,000 women with equipment, designs and raw materials and sells their work through shops in Athens and elsewhere. *National Welfare Association, PO Box 1094, 10110 Athens (tel: 325 0524).*

The Kolonaki district offers the smartest shopping in Athens

# SHOPPING IN ATHENS

Adhrianoú, which runs in a crescent through the Plaka, offers gift-hunters a rich choice of ceramics, T-shirts, scarves, hats, sweaters and leather goods made for the visiting shopper. Smart Athenians shop for clothes, shoes, jewellery and accessories elsewhere. The main downtown shopping areas are around Syntagma and Omonia, and in fashionable Kolonaki.

Similar types of store still tend to cluster together, oriental-style, on the same streets, so you will find a big choice of jewellers' stores on Voukourestiou and around the corner on Venizelou. There are more jewellers on Mitropoleos, which runs west from Syntagma and is also a good place to look for clothes, shoes and rugs.

## BOOKS
**Compendium**
English-language books, magazines, travel guides and maps.
*Nikis 28, Syntagma (tel: 3221 248).*
**Eleftheroudakis**
Multilingual books, magazines, maps and guides.
*Nikis 4 (tel: 3231 401), Sinopis 2 (tel: 7708 007), and Kifissias 294 (tel: 6878 350).*

## FLOKATI RUGS
**Karamichos-Mazarakis Flokati**
Handknotted rugs to new designs as well as traditional flokati.
*Voulis 31–33 (tel: 3224 932).*
**Yannis Michalopoulos**
*Mnisikleous 8 (tel: 3240 384).*

## HANDICRAFTS
**National Welfare Organization** shops sell handwoven rugs, embroidery, lace and other arts and crafts from all over Greece.
*Voukourestiou 24, Ipatias 6 (inside the Hilton) and Vasilissis Sofias 46 (tel: 325 0524).*

## JEWELLERY
**Athiniotakis**
*Voukourestiou 20 (tel: 3636 539).*
**Andreadis**
*Voukourestiou 24 (tel: 3608 544).*
**Lalaounis**
Designs in gold and silver based on ancient motifs.
*Panepistimiou 6 and Voukourestiou 12 (tel: 361 1371).*
**Zolotas**
With Lalaounis, the best-known of the Athens gold and silver sellers.
*Stadiou 19 (tel: 3240 871).*

## MUSEUM SHOPS
**Mousio Benaki** (**Benaki Museum**)
Greek handicrafts, textiles and jewellery. A good place to shop for gifts.
*Koumbari 1 (tel: 361 1617).*
**Mousio Ethniko Arkheologiko** (**National Archaeological Museum**)
Copies of many of the museum's finest exhibits.
*Patission 28 (tel: 8217 717).*
**Mousio Goulandri Kykladhiki Texni** (**Goulandris Museum of Cycladic Art**)
Accurate copies of the marvellous 5,000-year-old Cycladic figurines.
*Neofytou Douka 4 (tel: 723 4931).*

## SHOES

Look for branches of the city-wide Mouger, Moschoutis or Petridis chains in main shopping areas.

## MARKETS IN ATHENS

### Ifaistou (Ifestou)

The original venerable Flea Market on Ifestou is a mixture of trendy clothes and shoe-stores, and glory-holes where you can buy anything from a postman's battered leather satchel to an army surplus parachute or a World War I artillery shell crafted into a beaten-brass flower vase. One long-established shop has a line in helmets which ranges from copies of those worn at the Battle of Marathón in 490BC to German and Italian headgear from World War II. Another sells antique prams, toys and carved animals from fairground carousels. The Flea Market is also a good place to buy hiking and camping gear. The best day to visit is Sunday, when the market spills over into surrounding streets and becomes a happy hunting ground for bargain-seeking Athenians.

*Next to Monastiráki metro station.*

### Kendrikí Agorá (Central Market)

The Kendrikí Agorá (Central Market) is a photographer's heaven, though the squeamish may find the meat market section, with its racks of carcases and innards, a bit hard to take. The fish market, with stall after stall selling seafood from tiny whitebait to huge grouper and tunny, is spectacular. In surrounding streets are shops and stalls selling dried herbs and nuts, sweets, fruit, vegetables, game and household goods. The market cafés in the pre-dawn hours are a favourite rendezvous for Athenian nightlifers who have outlasted the city's bars and clubs. The market opens at first light.

*10 minutes' walk from Monastiraki metro station, on the corner of Athinas and Evripidou.*

### Pandrosou (Pandhrossou)

Both sides of Pandhrossou are packed with shops selling smart leatherwear, fashion jewellery and replica antiques, and there is not a flea in sight. Most of the new shops take major credit cards.

You can find almost anything in the Plaka flea market

## MARKETS AND SHOPPING AROUND GREECE

Away from Athens and the main holiday resorts, the stalls of the *laiki* (popular) market, where local people shop for fruit, vegetables and household supplies, are great places to shop and wander. The *laiki* is usually held several mornings a week in a main square or street. You can find out when and where at the local *dhimarkion* (town hall) or police station. Bargains include linen and embroidery,

enamelled pots and pans, tiny coffee cups and – in recent years – Russian-made watches, cameras and binoculars peddled by Greek refugees from the former USSR. Village hardware stores, usually on or near the market square, are great places for souvenirs such as hammered brass and copper trays, goat-bells, striped blankets or walking sticks.

Several Greek towns have a special reputation for locally made products. Arákhova is known for its wool rugs,

Ioánnina for its silverware and Kastoría for its patchwork furs. Here and elsewhere, one shop is much the same as its neighbour and a walk down the main street will give you a good idea of what is for sale and how much it costs. Prices will be much of a muchness around town. Bargaining is common, but do not expect to beat the asking price down by more than about 10 per cent. Cash always commands lower prices than credit cards.

### Arákhova

Coarsely-woven wool rugs and blankets dyed in earthy reds, orange and black are made locally and sold in stores along the main street, along with shepherds' twisty staffs and carved olive-wood kitchen ware.

### Delphi

Modern Delphi's two main streets are packed with shops selling replicas from this and other archaeological excavations. Quality varies. The best bear the seal of approval of the National Archaeological Museum in Athens.

### Ioánnina

A delightfully ramshackle bazaar area of medieval-looking workshops and stores lies just inland from Dionysou Filosofotou and the walled old town. For Ioánnina's famous silver filigree, visit the many jewellers' shops on Nissia, the island just offshore.

### Kastoría

The lakeside city has been famous for its furriers for more than 2,000 years. Their speciality is piecing together garments

As elsewhere in the world the local market is the cheapest source of fresh produce

from scraps of fur, and most of their work can be bought as cheaply in Athens as from the workshops here. Beware, too, of buying garments made from the fur of endangered species. Though technically illegal, this trade continues to flourish. Buyers can be fined and their purchases confiscated by Customs on their return home.

### Komotiní

An old-fashioned maze of streets northeast of Platia Ireni, the main square, houses a picturesque bazaar area and a bustling arcaded produce market. The antique shops along Venizelou, the pedestrianised main artery of the quarter, are piled with antique inlaid furniture, Turkish hookahs, lamps, vases and candlesticks – as well as with plenty of obvious fakes.

### Olympia

**Museum Art of Greece**, *Leoforos Kondhíli (tel: 0624 22573)*, is outstanding not only for its fine replicas of statues and bronzes but also for its quality copies of Byzantine icons.

### Thessaloníki

Thessaloníki's bazaar area – a rectangle bounded by Egnatias, Dhragoumi, Aristotelous and Tsimiski – offers the best street shopping in Greece. It is also a great place for photography, with stalls selling everything from live fish to fake designer watches. Look for these and other bargains on Venizelou and Ermou, or for colourful stalls selling fruit, vegetables, meat and seafood in the huge central market.

The **Thessaloníki Archaeological Museum** shop sells excellent replicas of exhibits and antiquities from this and other Greek museums.

# Entertainment

*E*ntertainment in Greece embraces everything from the tragedies of Sophocles to the traditional music and dances of rural Greece, which are performed not only for tourists but for the Greeks' own enjoyment.

In Athens, several English-language newspapers and magazines (daily, weekly and monthly) have entertainment pages which list current performances. They include: *Athens News* (daily), *Athenscope* (weekly), *Athens Today* (monthly, free), *The Athenian* (monthly), *Greek News* (weekly). Elsewhere, your best bet is the local tourist office (see page 189), the *dhimarkion* (town hall) or, in holiday resorts, a travel and ticket agency.

## CINEMAS
In major cities you can catch recently released US and European films with the original soundtrack and Greek subtitles. The video and television boom has forced many local cinemas in smaller towns to close.

### Athens
**Achilles**, *Patission 140 (tel: 8656 355)*.
**Alexandra**, *Patission 79 (tel: 821 9298)*.
**Athina**, *Patission 122 (tel: 8233 149)*.
**Athinea**, *Haritos 57, Kolonaki (tel: 7215 717)*.
**Atlantis**, *Vouliagmenis 245 (tel: 9711 511)*.
**Attikon**, *Platia Ay. Konstantinos (tel: 4175 897)*.
**Avana Assos Odeon**, *Kifissias 234 (tel: 6715 905)*.
**Elly**, *Akademias 64 (tel: 3632 798)*.
**Orphis**, *Vouliagmenis 141 (tel: 9019 724)*.
**Palace**, *Platia Pankratiou (tel: 7515 434)*.
**Plaza**, *Kifissias 118 (tel: 6921 667)*.

### Thessaloníki
**Alexandhros**, *Ethnikis Aminis 1*.
**Aristotelion**, *Ethnikis Aminis 2*.
**Esperos**, *Svoulou 22*.
**Makedhonikon**, *Ethnikis Aminis/Filikis Eterias*.

## CLASSICAL MUSIC
Classical music concerts take place frequently in Thessaloníki and Athens.

### Athens
**Athens Concert Hall**, *Vasilissis Sofias, 11521 Athens (tel: 7225 511 and 7221 1169)*.
**Ethniki Lyriki Skini (National Lyric Theatre)**, *Akadimias and Charilaou Trikoupis (tel: 360 0180)*.
**Goethe Institut**, *Omirou 14–16 (tel: 3608 111)*.
**Hellenic American Union**, *Massalias 22 (tel: 3629 886)*.
**Pallas Theatre**, *Voukourestiou 1 (tel: 3228 275)*.

### Thessaloníki
**Kratiko Theatro**, *Odhos Pavlou Mela/Platia Lefkou Pirgou (tel: 031 223785)*.
**Vasilio Theatro**, *Odhos Pavlou Mela/Platia Lefkou Pirgou (tel: 031 261677)*.

## CULTURAL EVENTS
Several annual drama festivals aim to preserve Greece's ancient dramatic

heritage side by side with modern productions and interpretations of the classical playwrights. Nobody with an interest in classical drama or in modern music, opera, ballet and dance should miss the simultaneous Athens and Epídhavros Festivals, held every year from mid-June to the end of September. The success of this twin event has encouraged the production of annual cultural festivals in other parts of Greece. Exact dates for each year are available from the Greek National Tourist Office (see **Practical Guide**, page 189).

### Athens
For the annual **Athens Festival**, contact the Athens and Epídhavros Festival Box Office, Stadhiou 4 (tel: 3221 459/3223 111). Mid-June to late September.

### Delphi
The **International Symposium on Ancient Greek Drama**, which includes theatre, music and dance performances and visual art exhibitions. June to August.
*European Cultural Centre of Delphi (tel: 7233943).*

### Epídhavros
The annual **Epídhavros Festival**: performances of classical plays from the 5th century BC. Mid-June to mid-September. Held in the ancient Theatre of Epídhavros.
*Epídhavros Festival Box Office (tel: 0752 22691).*

### Ioánnina
The **Ioánnina Festival**: classical and modern theatre and traditional dance. July to August.
*The ancient theatre at Dhodhóni (tel: 0651 20090).*

Shadow puppet. Sadly shadow plays are becoming increasingly rare in Greece

### Kaválla
**Festival of Philippi** and **Thásos**: classical drama in the theatre at Filippi (Philippi) and on the island of Thásos. July to August *(tel: 051 223504).*

### Thessaloníki
**Dimitria Festival**: classical and modern drama, music, ballet and opera performed by Greek and foreign companies.
October *(tel: 031 286519).*

# MUSIC

Traditional Greek music is a mix of Eastern and Western influences. Greeks are fond of modern pop, but the wailing minor keys and unfamiliar rhythms of their own songs and dances have a strong flavour of the older, more oriental Greece. The most familiar music to visitors – played for the dance you are most likely to be invited to join – is the *sirtos*, a follow-my-leader circle-dance for any number of dancers. Typical instruments all over Greece include guitar, lute, fiddle and tambourine, with or without the accompaniment of various wind instruments typical of each region.

*Bouzouki* or *rembetika* music was brought to Athens by Greek refugees from Turkey in the 1920s and became fashionable among wealthy Athenians who would ostentatiously applaud the musicians by smashing their dinner-plates. The surviving *bouzouki* clubs of Athens are expensive and only for real enthusiasts. If you go, remember that smashing the crockery is an expensive kind of applause – you have to pay for the breakages.

Traditional ballads often recall the heroes of the epic struggle to throw off

wind instruments, including the *gaida*, a local version of the bagpipe, a shrill oboe called the *zournas*, and a type of flute called the *kaval*. Unlike the stately circles of Epirus, the regional dances are rapid and energetic, with much fancy footwork.

The typical folk music of the Peloponnese is the lively *palea dhimotika* ballad, driven along by guitar, fiddle and tambourine and recounting tales of daring, victory and defeat.

the Turkish yoke and many dances are re-enactments of historic incidents. In the north, these ballads include the mournful *kleftiko* of Epirus, celebrating the deeds of the *klefts*, mountain bandits who, like Robin Hood, are also remembered as heroes of the national resistance.

The music of Thrace and Macedonia features a number of unique

Greek bagpipes (*gaida*)

## DANCING

Dancing is a part of any celebration, even the most impromptu, for Greeks are still very much in the habit of making their own amusement.

Even among the fashionable youth of Greece, an evening spent dancing to the latest electronic beat may well end in the small hours with a traditional *sirtos*.

You can sample an evening of the kind of traditional entertainment Greeks enjoy at any *exoxiko kentro* (country centre). These are usually some kilometres from the nearest town, offering city-dwelling Greeks a nostalgic evening of home cooking, wine from the barrel, powerfully amplified traditional music, and dancing – both by performers and the audience.

One of the best places to sample Greek music and dance is at the **Dora Stratou Dance Centre**, *Théatro on Filopapou in Athens (tel: 3244 395)*. The late Dora Stratou was single-handedly responsible for saving much of Greece's musical heritage. She recorded many tunes and dances which had never been written down and were in danger of vanishing with the generation of villagers who remembered them. Her work rekindled interest in folk music, and the Dora Stratou troupes perform dances from all over the mainland and islands, not only at their own open-air theatre in Athens but at festivals throughout Greece and worldwide. The theatre is open nightly from May to September. Tickets are usually available on the night of the performance, or can be booked through agencies, main hotels, or from the theatre.

## DISCOS

Tourism has combined with the Greek love of any kind of dancing to ensure that every holiday resort has an oversupply of discos and dance clubs. These start to warm up around midnight, play the latest dance hits at maximum volume and change name, ownership and venue virtually every season. Many are no more than an open-air dance floor, bar and sound system overlooking the beach. There is little to choose among them – pick whichever nightspot takes your fancy. Admission to clubs and discos is usually free, but drinks are more expensive than in an ordinary bar. Bigger indoor clubs with dry ice and dance music can be found in Athens and Thessaloníki, but most of them close during the summer, when their DJs and many of their clientele head for the bright lights of the islands.

**Athens**
*Absolut Dancing Club*, *Filellinon 23 (tel: 3237 197)*.
**Aerodhromio**, *Pergamou 25*.
**B-25**, *Vouliagmenis 328*.

Greek women traditionally wore elaborately embroidered costumes and magnificent necklaces to dance on feast days and at weddings

Greek dancers in traditional costumes at the Dora Stratou Dance Centre

### Thessaloníki

**Barbarella**, *Leoforos Mikras (1km from the airport – bus No. 78).*

### SOUND AND LIGHT

The Acropolis Sound and Light Show is viewed from seating on the Pnyx *(see page 37).*

*Tickets from Athens Festival box office (see below) or at the entrance on the Pnyx (tel: 9226 210). Operates daily, except Good Friday, April to October. Programmes: English, daily, 9pm–9.45pm; French, daily, except Tuesday and Friday, 10.10pm–10.55pm; German, Tuesday and Friday, 10pm–10.45pm.*

### TELEVISION AND VIDEO

The television is a fixture in every small rural *kafeneon* or taverna. The national TV channels ET1 and ET2 broadcast a steady diet of imported British and US films, programmes and soap operas which are subtitled in Greek. Satellite TV is spreading fast and is offered by most business hotels and many larger resort hotels. Many hotels and bars in the more popular international holiday resorts also offer a nightly programme of video movies, sports and music programmes from around the world. There is no charge for these – the idea is to lure you into the bar.

# CAFÉ SOCIETY

The Greek café has undergone a quiet revolution in recent years. It is still the mainstay of local nightlife, but it is no longer restricted to older men. In most towns and villages the evening starts with the *volta*, a twilight stroll along the waterfront or around the *platia* by old and young – from wizened patriarchs and proud grannies showing off their latest grandchildren to dapper teenage dandies eyeing potential partners. Then the generations separate. Older women return home while their husbands settle down for an evening in a favourite old-style *kafeneon* to drink ouzo or coffee and talk politics over cards or backgammon. Meanwhile, the younger generation will hop from one bright new café-bar to the next. Bar-hopping can mean no more than moving to the next table – most cafés huddle together by the harbour or around the main square, and it takes an educated eye to figure out which outdoor tables belong to which bar. Owners of these glossy new establishments favour exotic names like Apocalypse, Bikini Red, Tequila Sunrise or No Name. An equally exotic selection of fancy imported liquor is always proudly on display behind the gleaming bar, but young Greeks are as likely to drink iced coffee – which is just as well, since the motorcycle is their favoured transport. And although the old *kafeneon* is traditionally an exclusively male domain, younger Greek women (like their boyfriends) head for the café-bars to see and be seen.

Café society: old and new

# Festivals

*T*he dates of many Greek festivals are set by the Orthodox calendar, and most of them celebrate one of the hundreds of Orthodox saints, some of them familiar in the West, some of them unique to the Orthodox Church. Many of the festivals are more or less private family affairs, with church services followed by a special meal served at home, but some are bigger and more public celebrations with parades, fireworks and public feasts in which the whole community may join. Because so many Greek village families have been separated by migration to the cities or overseas, the biggest and most emotional celebrations are those like the Assumption of the Virgin Mary (see below), when all the members of the scattered family return to their ancestral home.

### 1 January
Ayios Vassilios (St Basil), the Greek equivalent of Santa Claus, comes not on Christmas Day but New Year's Day.

### 6 January
Epiphany is mainly a religious festival when village wells, springs and the baptismal font of the village church are blessed. At some seaside locations young men traditionally dive for a blessed crucifix, but this custom is dying out.

### Lent
The three-week period of Lent is marked by feasting, carnival and parades,

reaching a peak seven weeks before Easter (see pages 158–9). The biggest and noisiest celebrations are at Patras, where the carnival features a fancy-dress parade, dancing and music. There are celebrations and events too in Athens and Thessaloníki.

### 25 March
The Feast of the Annunciation is also celebrated as Independence Day (a bit prematurely as the date marks the beginning of the War of Independence in

Celebrating one of Greece's many Orthodox festivals

1821, not the eventual recovery of all the territories of modern Greece more than a century later).

## 23 April
Ayios Yioryios, the patron saint of shepherds, is honoured at village churches in the Píndhos mountains and elsewhere. One of the more accessible celebrations is at Arákhova, on the slopes of Parnassós.

## April–May
Make your arrangements well in advance if you plan an Easter visit as all of Greece – and Greeks from all over the world – converge on their family's village and transport and accommodation are at a premium. Easter in Greece is celebrated according to the Orthodox calendar and can be up to three weeks ahead of or behind the Western Easter. Exact dates for Easter and other moveable feasts can be obtained each year from the Greek National Tourist Office (see **Practical Guide**, page 189).

## 1 May
May Day is both a traditional holiday on which people gather armfuls of brightly coloured wild flowers to make wreaths which hang above the door until midsummer, and a day of celebration and demonstration for Greece's strong left-wing parties.

## 18–19 July
Profitis Ilias (the Prophet Elijah) is honoured at his chapel on the highest peak of Taïyetos and at other mountain chapels.

## 15 August
Apokimisis tis Panayías

(Assumption of the Virgin) is second only to Easter in importance. Transport and accommodation can be hard to find, because Greeks return to the family village not only from the cities but from overseas. It is a great family celebration, with food, drink and dancing often until daybreak, and well-behaved visitors will be made welcome.

## 26 October
Ayios Dhimitrios, patron saint of Thessaloníki, is celebrated here and elsewhere with extensive sampling of the first of the summer wine.

## 28 October (Ochi Day)
Only the Greeks could celebrate as a national holiday their entry into a war which devastated their country, but celebrate it they do. It commemorates General Ioannis Metaxas's laconic negative response to the Italian ultimatum of 1940 – 'Ochi' (see page 110). Parades, music and dancing mark the event.

## 25 December
Christmas in Greece is not the major festival or commercial event that it is elsewhere. It is an important religious occasion and is marked by special church services, but there is little public celebration.

## 31 December
Children traditionally make the rounds of the village or neighbourhood singing carols, and adults get together with neighbours or family.

Traditional dress for
Independence Day

# EASTER

Easter in a Greek village is a never-to-be-forgotten experience. The biggest event of a crowded festival calendar, it combines solemn religious ceremony, emotional family reunions, and plenty of public song and dance. Most Greek festivals are first and foremost family affairs, celebrated in the home, but Easter spills out into village streets and cafés. With the weather often at its best, and everyone in a holiday mood, Easter is a great time to visit. Winter is over, and the busy summer season has not begun.

For Greeks living abroad, it is a time to go back to their roots. For their children, brought up in the USA, Canada or Australia, it may be the first taste of the very different lifestyle of a Greek village.

A far less commercial event than Christmas in English-speaking countries, Easter is impossible to avoid. The week's sacred events at cathedrals and churches throughout Greece are broadcast continuously on radio and television, and you will hear the solemn Gregorian chants of the Orthodox Church issuing from every place of worship. Bishops and priests abandon their everyday black for the gorgeous, gold-encrusted robes and jewelled crowns worn only for the most sacred occasions. In many places, ancient icons are carried in procession, and outside the churches the air is heavy with incense. Public worship begins on the evening of Good Friday and reaches a climax the following day with midnight mass, the lighting of thousands of candles to reaffirm the Resurrection, and an eruption of

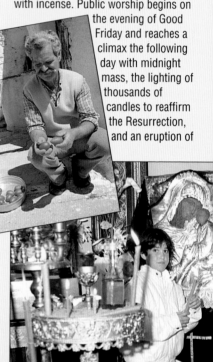

fireworks. Easter Sunday traditionally begins with the breaking of the Lenten fast and a lamb or goat is roasted whole for Sunday lunch. Traditionally, red-dyed hard-boiled eggs are handed out as a special Easter delicacy. General merry-making with friends, family and neighbours continues through the day and late into the night. Village-wide hangovers on Monday morning are not uncommon.

Easter is a mixed time of sombre religious ceremonies and boisterous family gatherings
Far left: red-dyed eggs are a special Easter treat
Below: Easter cakes

# Children

$G$reece welcomes children warmly and there are very few places anywhere where they cannot be taken. Couples will frequently be cross-examined as to whether or not they have children and if not, why not? Greeks regard children as an unmixed blessing, and crying babies or the fractious late-night behaviour of tired youngsters will be tolerated in village tavernas and cafés.

The National Gardens in Athens offer an escape from the city traffic for children and parents

### Food

Food should not be a problem, even if your children are picky eaters who insist on a chips-only diet. These are on every Greek menu, as are other plain and familiar dishes such as fish, burgers, and salad. Canned soft drinks are universally available, as are most well-known brands of sweets and chocolate bars, ice-cream and ice lollies. Sticky Greek cakes and desserts from the *zacharoplasteion* (pastry shop) are also a hit with young children. Greece is above all a country where life is lived outdoors almost all year round, and Greek youngsters are raised on a free-range basis with the whole village and its surroundings as a playground. Visiting toddlers can easily join in.

### The seaside

The main attraction for families visiting Greece is the beach, and sea and sand are the focus of most family resorts. Greece's seas have little or no tide, so the sea is always at your doorstep and is almost always calm enough even for young children to swim in safety. Sheltered, gently-shelving sandy beaches ideal for families with small children can be found on the Khalkidhikí (Chalkidiki) peninsulas in Macedonia (see pages 122–3), in the southern Peloponnese at Koróni and Methóni (see pages 64–5) and Stoupa (see page 77), and in Argolis at Tolón (see page 58).

### Things to do

Children with an interest in wild flowers and wildlife will find Greece a delight, with dozens of birds, lizards, tortoises and turtles, butterflies and other insects to identify and watch. Those with an interest in marine life will find the clear waters of inlets and harbours as full of sea creatures as any marine aquarium, and will be fascinated by the varied haul unloaded by fishing boats each morning. The end of any Greek village pier always attracts a gaggle of junior anglers, and simple hook-and-line kits are sold in all village shops.

Pedaloes, canoes, and other simple watersports equipment are for hire at all summer beach resorts, and older children can use them with confidence in

Greek youngsters have the run of the village and the taverna

shallow waters and enclosed coves. Although Greek waters have virtually no tides, they do have inshore currents so caution must be used. Bicycles for children and adults can also be rented at some resorts.

Children with an interest in history will find that the ancient sites, medieval castles and deserted fortresses of mainland Greece offer a fascinating 'hands-on' lesson in the past, and younger children will enjoy scrambling to the highest tiers of the ancient theatres. Running races in the millennia-old stadium at Olympia or Delphi can be a welcome release of energy after the journey. In the unlikely event of poor weather, a visit to one of the many folklore museums with their displays of traditional costumes, kitchenware, tools, weapons and jewellery will keep children entertained.

Purpose-built facilities and entertainment for children are rarely provided. Most villages have a small playground, though old-fashioned wood and metal swings and roundabouts are potential hazards for smaller children. Some larger resorts and hotels have separate swimming pools for toddlers, and many package tour operators offer fun-clubs, child-minding and babysitting services (see **Practical Guide**, page 181).

Sandy Greek beaches offer children hours of pleasure

# Sport

*T*he great sporting passions of Greece are basketball and soccer, which are watched avidly both live and on television and are enthusiastically played at all levels. It is a small village indeed which does not have a dusty football pitch on its outskirts and a basketball pitch in its schoolyard or outside the village hall.

Basketball has become a national passion, rivalling football

Basketball has outstripped soccer in the popularity stakes, partly because the national team performs strongly in international events, but the Greek soccer team's success in qualifying for the 1994 World Cup in the USA helped to rekindle enthusiasm for soccer. You will see graffiti acclaiming the top Athenian team, Panathinaikos (PAO), not only all over Athens but all over the country.

## BASKETBALL
**Greek Basketball Federation,**
*N Saripolou 11, Athens (tel: 8244 125).*

## SOCCER
Matches are played regularly on Sundays at 5.30pm in season (October to April) and tickets are available at each team office.
**Greek Soccer Federation,** *Syngrou 137, Athens (tel: 9336 410).*
The most important national venue for football and other sporting events is the Peace and Friendship Stadium, *Nea Faliron, Athens (tel: 4819 513).*

## SPORTS FOR VISITORS

### GOLF
Greece has the ideal climate for golf, especially in spring and autumn, but there are only two courses on the mainland which approach international standards.
**Glyfadha Golf Club**
The only high-quality golf course in Greece is in the seaside suburb of Glifádha (Glyfadha), with an 18-hole course, dressing rooms, sports store, restaurant and bar. *12km from central Athens, signposted (tel: 8946 820).*
**Porto Carras**
The Porto Carras resort complex, Khalkidhikí *(tel: 0375 71221).*

### RUNNING
The heroic first Marathon run (see page 50) is re-enacted twice a year, for seeded athletes in April and for all runners in October. Details from **SEGAS** (Greek

Sports and Athletics Federation), *Syngrou 137, Athens (tel: 9359 302).*

## SKIING
Skiing is increasingly popular in Greece, and although Greek slopes do not rank with the best in Europe they are certainly among the cheapest. The ski season begins in mid-December and continues until the end of April, when you can combine a day's skiing with a holiday on the beach or touring. The main ski centres are at Parnassós, near Delphi (see page 86 and 96–7) and on Pelion (see pages 112–13).

**Parnassós Ski Centre**
*24km from Arákhova (tel: 0234 22689).*
**Pelion Ski Centre**
*27km from Vólos (tel: 0421 25696).*

## TENNIS
There are tennis courts on a number of the beaches managed by the Greek National Tourist Office and at many major resorts. For further information, contact **EFOA** (Greek Tennis

Association), *Omirou 8, Athens (tel: 3230 412)* or the **Athens Tennis Club**, *Vasilissis Olgas, Athens (tel: 9232 872).*

## YACHTING
Yachts of all sizes are available for charter from Greek marinas, with or without skipper and crew. With hundreds of coves and beaches accessible only by sea, uninhabited offshore islets and hideaway harbours, Greece is the best yachting country in the Mediterranean. A list of yacht charterers is available from the Greek National Tourist Office (see page 189).

**Hellenic Sailing Federation**, *Akti Navarchou Kountouioti, Kastella, Piraeus (tel: 4137 531).*
**Yacht Club of Athens**, *Karageorgis Servias, Mikrolimano, Piraeus (tel: 4127 757).*
**Naval Club of Thessaloníki**, *Themistokli Sofouli 112 (tel: 031 414521).*
**Porto Carras Naval Club**, *Neos Marmaras, Sithonia (Sidhonia), Khalkidhikí (tel: 0375 71381).*

Ski season on Mount Parnassós lasts from December until early April

Greek waters provide perfect conditions for windsurfing

## WATERSKIING

Waterskiing facilities are available at all holiday beaches in summer and there are waterski schools at most major resorts. For further information, contact the **Greek Waterskiing Association**, *Stournara 32, Athens (tel: 5231 875).*

## WINDSURFING

Greece's waters, with their reliable breezes, are perfect for windsurfing and boards are for hire at every beach resort. A number of international events are held each year. For details, contact the **Greek Windsurfing Association**, *Filellinon 7, Athens (tel: 3230 068).*

# ADVENTURE SPORTS

Greece's mountain landscapes are an adventure playground offering an exciting and extensive range of activities above and below ground, in the air and on the water.

## CAVING

The limestone rock of mainland Greece is riddled with long cave systems and underground lakes and rivers. Many of these have been opened up to visitors under the management of the Greek National Tourist Office, but kilometres of caverns still remain to be explored. **Hellenic Speleological Society**, *Mantzarou 8, Athens (tel: 3617 824).*

## CLIMBING AND TREKKING

Greece's mountains are wonderful for walkers, offering relatively gentle routes which can be completed in one or two days as well as much more demanding itineraries. Mount Olympus, the highest mountain in Greece and the second highest in the Balkan region, is a surprisingly undemanding ascent and from May to mid-October is within the abilities of most reasonably fit walkers, with well-marked trails and dormitory accommodation in several mountain refuges. Allow three days for the ascent and descent, with two nights' stay in a mountain refuge (see page 140). Another relatively easy trek, which can be completed in one day, takes you to Drakolimin, a mountain lake on the slopes of Tímfi Óros (Mount Timfi) in the Píndhos range (see pages 110–1). In the same region, the spectacular Vikos Gorge offers a demanding one- or two-day hike for fitter walkers. In southern Greece, the ascent to Profitis Ilias, the highest peak of the Taïyetos range, is still more demanding. The Greek Alpine Club, which manages refuges on all these mountains, publishes a range of guides and detailed route maps and can advise on mountain conditions, equipment and when to go.

Rock climbing is growing in popularity, but the soft, crumbly limestone of most Greek mountains is not ideal climbing rock, attractive though it looks.

Basic mountain safety rules must be obeyed even on shorter walks, as the mountains are thinly populated and a sprained ankle far from help can spell disaster. Take plenty of water, and make sure that someone knows where you are going and when you expect to be back. Nights on the higher slopes are chilly even in high summer, and you will need proper walking boots – not just trainers – for more serious trekking. Other essentials include a water-bottle and water sterilising tablets.

EOS (Greek Alpine Club) maintains refuges with dormitories on the main trekking routes. On Olympus, these are staffed and serve simple meals. Elsewhere, they are usually unstaffed and you must get the key from the local EOS office in the nearest village. The EOS also supplies information, bulletins and maps.

**Ellinikos Orivatikos Sindhesmos (EOS)**, *Karageorgis Servias 7, Athens (tel: 3234 555).*

## HANG-GLIDING

The bright-coloured delta wings of hang-gliders can often be seen circling over the steep ridges of the Píndhos mountains near Ioánnina (page 104–5) which create great up-draughts.

**Delta Wing Gliding School**, *Apollo 44, Piraeus, Athens (tel: 5247 516).*

## SCUBA DIVING

Until recently the Greek authorities have held diving in deep suspicion, fearing the theft of antiquities from seabed sites. Key

underwater archaeological sites have now been thoroughly mapped and remain off-limits, but you can learn to dive at Vouliagméni and at Várkiza, near Athens (see page 49) and there is more extensive diving off the coast of Sidhonia (see pages 122–3). Rules for divers are strict and include a ban on touching, removing or even photographing any antiquities you find and on spear-fishing with scuba gear. Visibility in Greek waters is usually excellent, but there is less underwater life than you might expect – the result of thousands of years of intensive fishing.

**Hellenic Federation of Underwater Activities**, *West Airport Terminal Post Office, 16604 Ellenikon, Athens (tel: 9819 961).*

A rock climber pits his skill against the pinnacles and precipices of the Metéora

# Food and Drink

## WHAT'S ON THE MENU?

The best Greek food is the simplest: fish straight from the boat, vegetables fresh from the field served as salad with wild herbs and olives or in stews. Most restaurants offer multilingual menus. The translations can be as opaque as the original Greek, inviting you to sample 'smashed bowels in roasted spit' or 'one brain salad'. Puzzling them out is half the fun ('one brain salad' is just that – a sheep's brain served cold atop a bed of lettuce). You will sometimes be invited into the kitchen to choose your meal, while in the smallest restaurants you just take pot luck or make do with omelettes, chips and salad. Only in the smartest restaurants will food be served course by course.

*Meze*, a selection of dishes served simultaneously, is a Greek culinary tradition, and in smaller restaurants everything often comes at once or in an unexpected order – chips, for example, often arrive first as a kind of appetiser.

## Fish

Fish is priced according to weight and category. You choose your fish from the kitchen, where it is then weighed and the price calculated before filleting. Seafood is popular but pricey, with delicacies like *barbounia* (red mullet) and *melanouryia* (no translation) at the top of the price range. Swordfish (*xifias*) steaks are always available and moderately priced, usually coming in enormous portions. At the cheaper end of the scale are *marides* (whitebait), *goupes* (sprats) and *kalamares* (fried baby squid). *Astakos* (langouste, though usually translated as lobster) is expensive by local standards, though most visitors will think it good value. Unfamiliar seafood dishes include *oktapodhi* (octopus) served in a variety of ways, either cold as a snack, grilled, or in a stew with rice or pasta.

In northern Greece, with its many lakes, you will find freshwater fish like carp and eel on the menu along with crayfish, lake crabs and frogs' legs.

Fresh fish is always on the menu in Greek harbour towns and holiday resorts

Octopus is a Greek favourite but an acquired taste for visitors

*Moussaka* (lamb or veal cooked in layers of cheese and aubergine), *yiouvetsi* (beef stewed with noodles in a clay pot), *kotopoulo* (roast or grilled chicken) and *souvlaki* (veal, lamb or pork cooked on a skewer) appears on most menus. In the north, a spicy sausage called *spetsofai* is often served in a stew with vegetables. More familiar meat dishes include grilled lamb chops or pork cutlets, and *keftedhes* (meat balls in sauce). Chips are the favoured accompaniment to meat dishes.

## Vegetable dishes

The 'traditional' Greek salad is a meal in itself, featuring heaps of tomatoes, onion, cucumber, green peppers, and olives drowned in oil and flavoured with dried herbs. It is known as *horiatiki* only in

tourist restaurants, where it is usually served crowned with feta cheese (if you don't want cheese, ask for *salata hores feta*, salad without cheese).

Dishes like *gemista* (tomatoes or green peppers stuffed with herb-flavoured rice) and *dolmades* (stuffed vine leaves) may or may not contain meat. Vegetable-only dishes include *vriam* (ratatouille), and a variety of pulses including *fakes* (lentil stew), *gigantes* (stewed broad beans), *mavromati* (boiled black-eye beans served cold with coriander) and *fasolakia* (green beans stewed with tomatoes). Cold dishes include *tsatsiki* (yoghurt flavoured with cucumber and garlic).

A slab of strong-flavoured feta cheese is the heart of a hearty Greek salad

Stuffed tomatoes and peppers are a village staple and a treat for vegetarians

Meze snacks traditionally accompany a mid-morning glass of aniseed-flavoured ouzo

## PLACES TO EAT AND DRINK

Greeks eat late, and dinner is the big meal of the day. In resorts where tourists outnumber locals, restaurants have adjusted to the foreign habit of eating early in the evening. If your first choice of restaurant is full, you will almost always find others, just as good, next door or near by. Dress codes are virtually non-existent for both men and women; generally, a clean shirt for men and anything other than beachwear for women is acceptable anywhere and most outdoor resort restaurants are accustomed to serving daytime clients in bathing suits.

Greek eating-places fall into a number of categories. Virtually all serve alcohol at all times (except on election day) but some offer a full menu, others only snacks, pot luck, or specialities. Most restaurants stay open late – Greeks set on a night out will dine at 10pm, stay till after midnight, then go on to a bar or nightclub. In summer,

*Rizokalo* (rice pudding flavoured with cinnamon)

almost all dining is al fresco, except in major cities.

### Bar

Places described as bars or 'pubs' are usually smart, shiny and relatively expensive, serving cocktails and imported liquors and beers to a younger clientele and often open only after dark. In busier resorts, an early-evening 'happy hour' often attracts a noisy clientele. Bars usually serve only soft drinks, alcohol and iced coffee.

### *Estiatorion* (Restaurant)

Open for lunch and dinner, the *estiatorion* is where Greeks go on family occasions. In major cities, restaurants can be quite formal but in resorts they are usually friendly and relaxed and offer the widest choice of meals and drinks.

### *Kafeneon*

The *kafeneon* is the nearest thing Greece has to a neighbourhood bar or pub. Open all day and usually past midnight, it serves coffee (Greek or instant), Greek spirits, beer and *retsina*, often with a plateful of snacks such as sunflower seeds, cubes of cheese, or slices of sausage. It is a centre of village social life (or in big cities the focus for a block of shops or apartments) and many older men spend much of their day at a café table over tiny cups of coffee or glasses of *ouzo*.

Baklava from the corner pastry shop is only for those with a really sweet tooth

## *Ouzeri*

The *ouzeri* serves *ouzo* (of course), wine, beer and coffee, almost always accompanied by *meze*, a series of substantial snacks which can add up to a light meal.

## *Psarotaverna* (Fish Restaurant)

The *psarotaverna* specialises in seafood, usually overlooks the harbour, and is probably the most expensive place to eat. The menu will include the full gamut of fish and crustaceans, but few alternatives.

## *Psistaria* (Grill Restaurant)

For carnivores only, the psistaria serves grilled meat of all kinds. The grill is usually up front, and like the *psarotaverna*, few alternative dishes are offered.

## Taverna

A catch-all term for an unpretentious restaurant where you eat what is in the pot that day, washing it down with jugs of wine, the *taverna* is to be approached with caution. In out of the way corners of Athens and Thessaloníki there are delightful old tavernas where you can eat the best meal of your Greek holiday at a very affordable price. In busy holiday centres, however, anywhere calling itself a taverna is likely to be a tourist trap pure and simple. As a general rule, if most of your fellow diners are Greeks you are in for a treat; if they are foreigners, think twice.

## *Zacharoplasteion* (Pastry Shop)

If you have a sweet tooth  the *zacharoplasteion* is the place for you. Selling sweet pastries and sticky cakes to take away or eat at pavement tables, it also serves Greek and instant coffee and soft drinks.

Local diners at an old-style taverna in the city of Thessaloníki

Inside an old-fashioned restaurant on Monastiraki

## RESTAURANTS

You can eat well in even the smallest of Greek villages. Most of them have more than their fair share of cheap and simple tavernas. In most resorts and country towns there is little to choose between one eating-place and its neighbour, so stroll along the harbour or round the square and pick whichever takes your fancy. Eat where the Greeks eat and you will find the food better, cheaper and more varied than in restaurants catering only to holidaymakers. Few restaurants in Greece are worth a special visit, and those as much for the view or the atmosphere as for the food. We have listed restaurants in Greece's three main cities, as well as a handful of other places which stand out from the crowd.

The following table is an indication of restaurant prices. The D (for drachma) sign indicates the cost of a three-course meal for one without wine. A half-litre carafe of *retsina* or beer costs around 350 drachmas, a bottle of red or white wine between 1,500 and 2,000 drachmas. Only the most up-market city restaurants accept telephone reservations (or even have a telephone). Prices may increase in drachma terms by up to 20 per cent a year, so only a rough price guide can be given.

| D | under DR3,000 |
| DD | under DR4,500 |
| DDD | under DR6,000 |
| DDDD | over DR6,000 |

### ATHENS
**Apotsos DD**

This long-established *ouzeri* hidden in an arcade off Venizelou (Panepistimiou) is decorated with antique posters and is a lunchtime favourite with Athenians.
*Venizelou (Panepistimiou) 10.*

**Bakalarakia D**

The Athenian version of a fish and chip restaurant. Specialities include battered cod and *skordalia*, a dish made with mashed potatoes and garlic.
*Kidhathineon 41.*

**Eden DD**

The best vegetarian restaurant in Athens, with meatless moussaka as well as many traditional meat-free dishes. Closed Tuesday.
*Flessa 3 (tel: 3248 858).*

**Fish restaurants DDDD**

The small fishing harbour of Mikrolimano is surrounded by the best (and most expensive) fish restaurants in Athens.
*Take a taxi (about 10–15 minutes from the city centre) or take the metro to Nea Faliron.*

**Gerofinikas DDDD**

Grand, old-fashioned restaurant specialising in game and in rich Eastern-influenced dishes. Booking advisable.
*Pindharou 10 (tel: 3636 710/3622 719).*

**O Platanos DDD**
An outdoor grill-restaurant beneath an
enormous plane tree. *Closed Sunday.*
*Dioyenous 4.*

**Taverna Dhimokritous DDD**
The menu at this attractive restaurant in
a lovely neo-classical building is more
extensive than most.
*Dhimokritou 23 and Tsakalof.*

**Theophilous DDD**
This venerable taverna, decorated with
frescos, opened in 1899. In the heart of
the Plaka.
*Vakhou 1 (tel: 3223 901).*

**IOÁNNINA**
**Nissi**
Choose from a score of outdoor
establishments serving freshwater fish
and shellfish on Ioánnina's restaurant
island. Most are on Monaxon Nektario-
Theofanos, a small, tree-shaded *platia.*

**MONEMVASÍA**
**To Kanoni DDD**
Elegant restaurant in a restored 17th-
century mansion, overlooking the roofs
of the fortified medieval town.
*Kastro (tel: 0732 61387).*

**PATRAS**
**Evangelatos DDD**
Situated near the waterfront with views
out to sea.
*Ayiou Nikolaou 7 (tel: 277772).*

**Ippopotamos DDD**
Up-market restaurant on Patras's
pleasantly old-fashioned central square.
*Platia Yioryiou 1 (tel: 270095).*

Athens has elegant traditional restaurants as
well as cheerful tavernas

**Psari DD**
Simple fish and grill taverna.
*Ayiou Dhimitriou 75.*

**STOUPA**
**To Fanari DDD**
On the headland just west of Stoupa, the
restaurant has mind-blowing views back
across the Messinian Gulf.

**THESSALONÍKI**
**Krikelas DDD**
The city's grandest and busiest taverna.
*Gramou Vitsi 32 (tel: 414690).*

**Limaniotis DDD**
An atmospheric seafood restaurant with
live music in the evening. Near the
harbour.
*Navarhou Votsi 1–3.*

**Olymbos Naoussa DDD**
Lunch-time restaurant with specialities
including *midia tiganita* (fried mussels),
elegant surroundings and a view of the
sea. On the waterfront.
*Nikis 5 (tel: 275715).*

**Stratis DDDD**
A very popular restaurant with
outstanding seafood. Reservations
recommended.
*Nikis 19 (tel: 234782).*

Ouzo comes under many labels, but it always tastes of aniseed

## BEVERAGES

### Beer

Almost all the beers sold in Greece are strong lagers, brewed locally under licence and always served ice-cold. Common brands include Amstel, Henninger, Heineken, Kaiser and Kronenburg, all around 5 per cent alcohol by volume and usually sold in 550ml bottles. Imported beers such as Beck's are often sold in smarter bars, and brands such as Guinness and Newcastle Brown Ale may be found in some resorts.

Prices vary widely and depend not so much on what you drink as where you drink it. A small bottle of imported beer in a neon-lit cocktail bar may cost three times as much as a large bottle in a local tavern.

### Brandy

Locally made brandy – sometimes described as *koniak* (cognac) – comes in three-, five- and seven-star quality. Sweeter than French brandies, it makes a pleasant after-dinner drink. The best known brands include Cambas and Metaxa.

## Coffee and tea

_Kafes elliniko_ (Greek coffee) comes black and thick, in thimble-sized cups, and is always served with a glass of water. If you like it without sugar ask for _sketo_; if you like extra sugar ask for _glikou_. Most Greeks drink it _metrio_, with one measure of sugar. Instant coffee is universally known as Nes. If you want it hot ask for Nes _zesto_ or you may be given _frappe_ – iced instant coffee. _Tsai_ (tea) is available almost everywhere and is invariably made with British Lipton's tea-bags. If you like your tea or coffee with milk, ask for it _me gála_.

## Imported and local spirits

Imported liquors such as Scotch, bourbon, vodka and gin generally cost considerably more than the locally made versions, most of which are destined to be cocktail ingredients. Measures, however, are always generous.

## Ouzo

Sunset is the customary time to take your Greek aperitif, though _ouzo_ can be (and is) drunk at any hour of the day or night. A clear, sweet, aniseed-based spirit, it is always served with a glass of water and usually with ice. It turns cloudy when water is added.

## Retsina

_Retsina_ or 'resinated' wine was formerly stored in earthenware jugs proofed with pine resin, which gave it a distinctive flavour. Today, resin is added artificially. It is an acquired taste, but one worth acquiring, and is by far the cheapest of Greek wines when sold in 550ml bottles. In many villages the taverna will sell retsina _apo to bareli_ (from the barrel) by the carafe and this is always well worth sampling.

## Soft drinks

All the well-known soft-drink brands are available throughout Greece. Although Greek farmers dump surplus oranges by the roadside, freshly-squeezed orange juice (_ximo portokaliou_), available in most holiday resorts, is remarkably expensive.

## Tsipouro

A clear and lethal spirit made (like Italian _grappa_) from the skins and pulp left over after pressing grapes to make wine, _tsipouro_ is sold in miniature bottles in village tavernas all over the northern mainland.

## Wine

Greece makes a range of red, white and dessert wines, all of them affordable and none of them outstanding. In general, white wine (_krasi aspro_) is a better bet than red wine (_krasi mavro_). Boutari, Cambas and Tsantali whites and reds are acceptable. Several small boutique wineries, including Hatzimihali and Lazaridhi, make better and more expensive wines, and are worth sampling if you can find them. Wines maybe categorised as either _ksero_ (dry) or _glyko_ (sweet).

Greek wines vary, but some of the best come from barrels like these

# Hotels and Accommodation

*F*inding somewhere to stay is almost never a problem in Greece. There is accommodation to suit all pockets in all but the very smallest villages, and even in these you may find the local shopkeeper is willing to rent a spare room (or, in summer, a camp bed in the garden or on the roof). Bear in mind, though, that almost all pensions and hotels in summer holiday resorts close in mid-October and do not re-open until April. You will also find it tricky finding accommodation at Easter (see pages 158–9) and Apokimisis (see page 157) when millions of Greeks return to their ancestral villages. Book well ahead for these dates.

In theory, Greek accommodation is strictly controlled and licensed by the government. The reality is rather different. Nobody knows exactly how many rooms are available for rent each summer, as local entrepreneurs are continually adding more rooms and apartments, and in practice prices are determined not by the authorities but by market forces. If you turn up before or after the main holiday season you will find hoteliers much more willing to negotiate than in mid-summer. Most accommodation renters will take 10 per cent off the standard rate if you stay for three or more nights.

Accommodation is easy to find. Older hotels, built just before or after World War II, usually cluster around the main square of provincial towns or, in harbour towns, along the waterfront. In smaller villages and resorts, look out for signs offering rooms in privately run accommodation. These usually read 'Rent Rooms' or (for German visitors) '*Zimmer Frei*'. Until the 1980s, such accommodation was usually in the spare bedroom of a family home. These days, it is more likely to be in a purpose-built block with solar-heated hot water and en suite or shared shower and toilet.

In seaside resorts much of the holiday accommodation is in bright, newly built apartments with fully equipped kitchens. These are booked up by holiday companies in high season, but are often available at very reasonable rates in spring and autumn and are excellent value if you plan to stay in one place for a while.

Gythion Hotel, Yithion

Poolside at the Athens Hilton

All licensed accommodation is divided into categories A to E, with separate listings for hotels and for pensions and apartments. Rooms are rated not on quality but on the facilities available (a scruffy old-fashioned hotel with telephones and television in the rooms and a mediocre restaurant will be rated higher than a bright new one without such services). Hotels and pensions are also being built faster than they can be inspected and listed, so many attractive new properties have no rating. The system should be treated with caution. Most accommodation is on a room-only basis, and where breakfast is offered it is rarely worth the DR900–1,200 extra you pay.

Prices vary considerably depending on the season, and can increase by up to 20–30 per cent a year. When this book was researched a twin room with en suite facilities cost from around DR4,500 in a small family-run pension to DR45,000 in a top Athens hotel. A C-class hotel (equivalent to 3-star) cost between DR10,000 and DR15,000. D- and E-class hotels, many of them built between the wars, are usually very cheap and central but shabby and run-down. Few visitors will want to use them.

Most accommodation in seaside resorts closes between the end of October and the beginning of April.

❖

THOMAS COOK
*Traveller's Tip*

*Travellers who purchase their travel tickets from a Thomas Cook network location are entitled to use the services of any other Thomas Cook network location, free of charge, to make hotel reservations.*

Hotel Malvasia, Kastro, Monemvasía

## APARTMENTS

Self-catering apartments are available in many holiday resorts, either as part of a package holiday or (in spring and autumn) for independent travellers. They usually have two bedrooms, with a lounge area which can be converted into a third bedroom, and a kitchen equipped with two-ring electric cooker, fridge, pots, pans, glasses, crockery and cutlery.

## CAMPSITES

Campsites can be excellent value, especially if you are touring by car. They offer secure parking and camping spaces usually shaded by poplar and plane trees, and facilities usually include a simple restaurant, mini-market, communal showers with constant hot water, and a laundry area. Most campsites are on the coast, next to some of the best beaches in Greece, but there are also sites at places like Olympia and Delphi, many of them

with swimming pools. Prices are comparable with the cheapest rooms. Sites to be avoided include those in the Athens area, most of which are unkempt and ill equipped.

*A list of campsites in Greece is available from the Greek National Tourist Office.*

## HOTELS

Hotels are classified from A to E, with most A-class properties in the Athens region. C-class hotels, the largest category, are found at all resorts and tend to be big, bland and busy in high season, echoing and empty the rest of the year. D- and E-class hotels, found in larger towns, are cheap but usually grubby and run-down.

## PENSIONS

Small, family-run pensions, usually with around a dozen twin-bedded rooms, offer some of the best-value accommodation in Greece, especially off-season. Most of them are recently built, offering rooms with en suite facilities. Solar heating is universal, so do not expect hot water too soon after sunrise.

## STAYING IN STYLE
The only international-name luxury hotels in mainland Greece are in Athens, most of them on Platía Sýntagma in the city centre or on Leofóros Syngroú. Most have open-air pools as well as business centres, room service, and a choice of expensive restaurants and bars.

## TRADITIONAL SETTLEMENTS
The Greek National Tourist Office operates a Traditional Settlements programme which aims to breathe new life into dying communities and to preserve some of the best of Greek vernacular architecture by converting traditionally built homes into comfortable guest-houses, installing modern facilities without changing the style of the building. These are not cheap (rates compare with B- and C-class hotels) but are worth every penny for their atmosphere and location among some of the most spectacular landscapes and most picturesque villages in Greece. There are traditional settlements in the Mani and in Monemvasía in southern Greece, in several of the villages of the Pelion peninsula in Thessaly, and in the Zagória villages in Epirus.

Most provide room-only accommodation. Reservations are essential. Further information from the Greek National Tourist Office (see page 189).

## VILLAGE ROOMS
In some villages, old-style 'village rooms'

are still rented in family homes, where the beds are likely to be elderly and the price may seem disproportionately high. To balance this, you will get a glimpse of local life and as many cups of Greek coffee as you are willing to drink.

## VILLAS
Luxury villas, some with their own pool and landscaped grounds, are available at some up-market resorts such as Vouliagméni on the outskirts of Athens, and are easiest to find as part of a package holiday. Most travel agents should be aware of tour operators offering villa packages.

## YOUTH HOSTELS
Old-fashioned, crowded, dirty and usually burdened with tyrannical rules and regulations, Greek youth hostels are no cheaper than many privately-rented rooms or older D- and E-class hotels. Many so-called 'youth hostels', especially in Athens, are privately run and have no connection with the International Youth Hostel Association. They are best avoided.

The Hotel Grande Bretagne, Athens

# On Business

*D*espite the artificial boost given by European Union cash injections, Greece's economy remains the most problematic in the EU. Privatisation of a cumbersome public sector was suspended with the election of the PASOK government in 1993, and business is burdened by inefficient bureaucracy. When this book was researched, even EU citizens who wished to work in Greece required a work permit, and getting it involved touring a number of offices, testing for HIV, and a psychiatric evaluation.

Shipping, tourism and agriculture dominate the Greek economy. The shipping industry is in the hands of a relatively small number of private and parastatal companies, but small, family-run operations predominate in farming and tourism.

Many Greek executives are educated in the US, Britain and Canada, and almost all speak fluent English and are familiar with the needs of their overseas colleagues. A new breed of executive sees Europe, rather than the Anglo-Saxon countries, as its role model.

With the collapse of Communism and Soviet influence over its northern Balkan neighbours, Greek business has taken an active interest in the fledgling market-led economies of countries like Bulgaria, Romania, Hungary and even Albania, where the Greek drachma has become the favoured foreign currency. Both Athens and Thessaloníki are well positioned to take advantage of shifts in the Balkan business climate, and the Greek government and business community are keen to forge links with the new economies.

## ACCOMMODATION

Major hotel chains including Hilton International, Inter-Continental, Marriott and Novotel have properties in Athens. The capital's two top hotels, the Grande Bretagne and the George V, are both on Syntagma, the city's central square. Greece's major home-grown hotel groups, Astir Hotels, Capsis Hotels and Elektra Hotels, are the best bet for accommodation in regional business capitals such as Thessaloníki and Patras.

## BUSINESS ETIQUETTE

Greek business etiquette is relaxed. Punctuality is appreciated, but turning up late for a meeting is not a mortal sin. Normal business wear is jacket and tie for men (a suit is not essential) and skirt or dress for women. Not all Greek offices are air-conditioned, and in summer many executives may dispense with jacket and tie in favour of an open-necked, short-sleeved shirt and slacks. Shake hands on meeting and on parting. Note that many offices close between midday and 4pm.

## BUSINESS TRANSPORT
### City to city

Olympic Airways operates an extensive inter-city network. Flights should be reserved before you arrive in Greece as they are often overbooked. Air taxi and helicopter charter services are available from Athens and other major airports.

Rapid express trains run between Athens and Thessaloníki (6hr 13min) and Athens and Patras (3hr 26min), but trains to other points are too slow for the business traveller. Inter-city express buses, which are fast, modern and air-conditioned, offer an alternative.

### In the city

Taxis are the most convenient way of getting around big cities but finding one unoccupied can be a problem in Athens. Ask your hotel to book a taxi for vital journeys. Car rental is widely available through international and local companies but few business travellers will want to wrestle with the complexities of Greek one-way systems, city traffic and navigation. Chauffeur-driven cars, the best option if within your budget, can be hired through major hotels and car hire companies.

### Communications

The Greek telephone system is antiquated and inefficient and you may have to try repeatedly to get through to the number you want, especially in Athens. Operators are usually helpful and competent in English. Fax facilities are widely available, even in small towns and family-run hotels, and sending a fax message is often easier and less time-consuming than making a phone call. International courier services are also available in Athens, Thessaloníki and Patras.

### Conference and exhibition facilities

Greece offers extensive facilities for conferences and exhibitions and is a popular incentive travel destination. Accommodation rates for conference and incentive groups visiting outside peak season are very competitive.

The best conference and exhibition venues are in major international hotels, which are more likely to be able to

provide adequate pre-event planning, better communications and more efficient back-up services during the event.

Greece's biggest exhibition centre is in Thessaloníki and offers highly professional event organisation and extensive facilities.
**Hellexpo**, *Egnatia 154, 546 36 Thessaloníki (tel: 23 92 91 or 29 11 11)*.

### Media

Two English-language magazines, *Greece's Weekly* and *Odyssey*, are useful sources of background information for the business traveller. *Balkan News*, launched in 1993, covers business topics in Greece's former socialist bloc neighbours.

*Greece's Daily*, a news preview distributed by fax, provides news and analysis ahead of the Greek and international daily press.
*Balkan News, Greece's Weekly* and *Greece's Daily* are published by Balkan Press Ltd, *Alevra 4, 156 69 Papagos, Athens (tel: 6548 208)*.
*Odyssey*: Zephyr Publications, *Alopekis 20, 106 75 Athens (tel: 725 3995)*.

## SECRETARIAL AND TRANSLATION SERVICES

Bilingual secretarial services and translation facilities can be arranged through the business centres of most leading hotels in Athens and Thessaloníki but are not widely available in smaller cities.

# Practical Guide

**ARRIVING**

**By Air**

Athens International Airport is the main gateway for charter and scheduled flights to points throughout Europe and worldwide. Thessaloníki International Airport is the northern gateway. Charter airlines fly to Kalámai (Kalamata) and to Préveza between April and October.

Domestic flights are often overbooked. If you plan to fly within Greece, book your flights before you leave home and remember to reconfirm.

Facilities at Greek airports are basic. Car rental companies, taxis, and municipal and private airport shuttle buses offer a choice of transport from Athens International Airport into the city. Elsewhere, the choice is between municipal buses and taxis.

Athens International Airport has two terminals: the western terminal is reserved for Olympic Airways international and domestic flights, and the eastern terminal for all other airlines. A shuttle service operates between them (8.30am–8.30pm). Some airport taxi drivers will overcharge unwary visitors. Insist that the meter is switched on and check that the figure '1' is illuminated, indicating a normal fare. The figure '2', indicating a double fare, should show only between midnight and 6am or for travel outside the city boundaries, which does not apply to the airport.

**By Land**

The crisis in the former Yugoslavia cut the most convenient overland route to Greece. Road and rail travellers can use ferries from Italy (see below) or travel through Hungary, Romania and Bulgaria.

The *Thomas Cook European Timetable*, published monthly, gives up-to-date details of most rail services and many shipping services throughout Europe and will help you plan a rail journey to, from and around Greece. It is available in the UK from some stations, any branch of Thomas Cook or by phoning 0733

268943. In the USA, contact: **Forsyth Travel Library Inc.**, *9154 West 57th Street (PO BOX 2975), Shawnee Mission, Kansas 66201 (tel: 800 367 7982 toll free).*

### By Sea
Frequent ferries connect Igoumenitsa and Patras with the Italian ports of Ancona, Bari, Otranto and Brindisi.

### Passports and Visas
Passports are required by all except European Union citizens, who may use national identity cards. British visitors may use a one-year British Visitor's Passport or a full passport. A maximum stay of six months is permitted. Citizens of the USA, Canada, Australia and New Zealand may enter for up to 60 days without a visa. Travellers from South Africa will need a visa. Travellers who require visas should obtain them in their country of residence, as it may prove difficult to obtain them elsewhere. In the UK, the Thomas Cook Passport and Visa Service can advise on and obtain the necessary documentation – consult your Thomas Cook travel consultant.

### CAMPING
A list of campsites is available from the Greek National Tourist Office (see **Tourist Offices**, page 189) and from **Association Greek Camping**, *Solonos 102, 10680 Athens (tel: 362 1560).* Camping outside official sites is technically illegal, a rule which is widely ignored.

### CHILDREN
There are few special facilities for babies or older children except where provided by packag~ :our companies for their clients. S _rvices provided by holiday comp°.iies often include babysitting for

younger infants, playgroups for toddlers and activity groups for younger children. Baby milk, food and nappies for infants are available in tourist resorts at most mini-markets and elsewhere from the *geniko emporion* (general store) or from pharmacies.

### CLIMATE
Winters are mild and short, with temperatures at their lowest (around 10°C, much colder in the mountains) and rainfall at its highest. By March, days are warmer and April and May offer changeable weather with the possibility of rain balanced by the likelihood of sunshine. Rain rarely falls between June and late September. Midsummer temperatures average more than 30°C. Heatwaves in July and August often bring temperatures of 40°C and above. September temperatures average 25°C and can exceed 30°C.

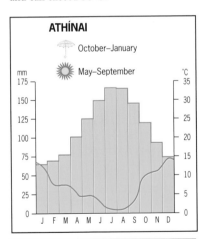

**ATHÍNAI**

October–January

May–September

**WEATHER CONVERSION CHART**
25.4mm = 1 inch
°F = 1.8 × °C + 32

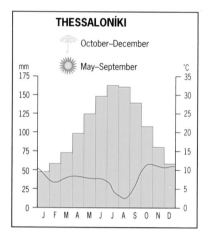

**THESSALONÍKI**

October–December

May–September

Temperatures drop noticeably through October, but even in December you can often sit outdoors wearing only a light jacket or sweater.

## CRIME

Visitors are rarely crime victims. Even Greece's big cities are among the world's safest. That said, normal caution should be exercised. Look after money, travellers' cheques, credit cards and other valuables.

## CUSTOMS REGULATIONS

Normal EU rules apply. Non-EU visitors may bring in 200 cigarettes, 50 cigars or 250g of tobacco, one litre of spirits, two litres of wine or liqueurs, 50ml of perfume and 250ml of cologne.
It is forbidden to export antiquities and works of art found in Greece.

## DISABLED TRAVELLERS

Facilities for disabled travellers in Greece are poor. Hotel lifts are often too small for wheelchairs and ramps are extremely rare. Pavements – where they exist – are often uneven. Hilly archaeological sites and steep village streets and steps pose special problems. All arrangements should be checked in advance and needs spelt out. Organisations which may be helpful include **Lavinia Tours**, *Egnatia 101, Thessaloníki 54110*, and the **National Association for Rehabilitation of the Handicapped**, *Hassias, Nea Liossia, KA 1322 Athens*.

## DRIVING
### Accidents

*1* If possible, set up warning signs. In theory, all cars must be equipped with a reflective warning triangle. Not all hire cars are.
*2* If someone is injured, the accident must be reported to the police (see page 184). Passers-by in such cases are required to stop and assist. It is advisable to contact the police as a precaution, even if the only damage is material.
*3* If you can, write down the names and addresses of other drivers involved, make and licence plates of vehicles, and the names of any witnesses. Write down the date and time of the accident and if possible take photographs from several angles.
*4* Under no circumstances admit liability, sign any statement of responsibility, or lose your temper.

### Breakdown

The Automobile and Touring Club of Greece (**ELPA**) provides tourist information (tel: 174) and road assistance (tel: 104) 24 hours a day.

### Car hire

Rental cars are available from inter-national car hire chains in major cities and resorts and from independent local operators. Renting a car in Greece is expensive and you will find it cheaper to make arrangements through an international chain such as Holiday Autos, Budget, Eurodollar, Europcar, Hertz or Avis before leaving home. Rental cars are often over-used and under-maintained – check tyres, brakes and steering before leaving the depot. Full collision damage waiver, personal accident, bail bond and liability insurance is essential.

Even major chains often exclude damage to the underside of the vehicle or the tyres from their collision damage waiver provisions. Make sure you have adequate liability insurance to cover such damage.

### Documentation

A full British or other EU driving licence is valid for driving in Greece. Most other nationalities require an international driving licence. This can be obtained before you leave home or in Greece from the Automobile and Touring Club of Greece (**ELPA**). You will need your national driving licence, passport and a passport-size photograph. In 1993, **ELPA** charged DR1,500 for this service.

### Drink-driving

Blood alcohol content of more than 0.08 per cent is a criminal offence, blood alcohol of between 0.08 and 0.05 per cent a civil offence, and penalties are severe. The best advice is to avoid alcohol altogether when driving.

### Fines

Police may impose fines for motoring offences on the spot but may not collect them. The fine must be paid at a Public Treasury office or a bank within 10 days.

### Fuel

Petrol costs around the European average. Lead-free fuel is widely available. It is forbidden to carry petrol in a can in the vehicle. Few petrol stations accept credit cards. Petrol stations are not usually self-service.

### Navigation, maps and road signs

Romanised spellings of Greek placenames vary. The differences, however, are not so great as to make a name unrecognisable. On main roads, signs are in the Roman alphabet as well as the Greek one. Off the beaten track, signs are often only in Greek, and you will need a working knowledge of the Greek alphabet to find your way (see page 22).

### Rules of the road

Speed limits (often ignored) are 50kph in built-up areas, 80kph outside built-up areas and 100kph on motorways. Seatbelts must be worn where fitted. You can be fined for not carrying a warning triangle, fire extinguisher and first-aid kit (many rented cars lack these).

### Toll roads

Greece's main toll highway is Odos Ethnikos 1 (National Road 1) between Athens and Thessaloníki, which is overcrowded and under-maintained, with stretches of dual carriageway giving way to stretches of potholed single-track. A second major toll highway connects Athens with Corinth, where it splits, heading south to Tripoli or west to Patras. Tolls are cheap, but unless you are in a hurry the toll roads should be avoided.

### ELECTRICITY

Voltage is 220 volts AC. You may require an adaptor for the round two-pin sockets in use in Greece. Power cuts are not uncommon.

## EMBASSIES AND CONSULATES
### Australia
*Mesoghion 15, Athens (tel: 7757 650/4).*
### Canada
*Gennadiou 4, Athens (tel: 7239 510/9).*
### New Zealand
*Semitelou 9, Athens (tel: 7710 112).*
### United Kingdom
*Ploutarchou 1, Athens (tel: 2780 006).*
### USA
Embassy: *Vasilissis Sofias 91, Athens (tel: 7212 951/9 and 7218 400/1).*
Consulate: *Nikis 59, Thessaloníki (tel: 266121).*

## EMERGENCY TELEPHONE NUMBERS
### Athens
Medical emergencies: 166
Tourist Police: 171
Fire: 199
### Elsewhere in Greece
Ambulance: 166
General Emergency Number: 100
(manned by the police and dealing with crime, fire and medical emergencies)

The Thomas Cook Worldwide Customer Promise offers free emergency assistance at any Thomas Cook Network location to travellers who have purchased their travel tickets at a Thomas Cook location. In addition, any MasterCard cardholder may use any Thomas Cook Network location to report loss or theft of a card and obtain an emergency card replacement as a free service under the Thomas Cook MasterCard International Alliance.

## HEALTH
Up-to-date health advice can be obtained from your Thomas Cook travel consultant or direct from the Thomas Cook Travel Clinic, 45 Berkeley Street, London W1A 1EB (tel: 0171 408 4157), which is open for consultation without appointment, 8.30am–5.30pm, Monday to Friday, and can give vaccinations and supply medical advice.

There are no mandatory vaccination requirements and no recommendations other than to keep tetanus and polio vaccination up to date. Vaccination against hepatitis A and typhoid is also recommended if you intend to travel to some of the remoter areas. AIDS is present. Food and water are safe.

All EU countries have reciprocal arrangements for reclaiming the cost of medical services. UK residents should obtain forms CM1 and E111 from any UK post office. Claiming is a laborious and long-drawn-out process and you are only covered for medical care, not for emergency repatriation, holiday cancellation, and so on. You are therefore strongly advised to take out a travel insurance policy to cover all eventualities. You can buy such insurance through the AA, branches of Thomas Cook, and most travel agents.

## MEASUREMENTS AND SIZES
Greece uses standard European measurements and sizes (see page 185).

## MEDIA
The English-language newspapers *Athens News* (daily) and *Greek News* (weekly) give a quirky insight into national news and views. The bi-monthly glossy magazine *Odyssey* takes a more thoughtful approach. British, US and European newspapers are on sale in Athens and in most holiday resorts the day after publication. English news bulletins are broadcast daily on the ERT2 radio station (98KHz) at 2pm and 9pm. The BBC World Service can be

picked up on 9.41, 12.09 and 15.07MHz.

## MONEY MATTERS

The Greek currency is the drachma (DR). Coin denominations include 10, 20, 50 and 100 drachma and notes in 100, 500, 1,000 and 5,000 drachmas. Most major currencies, travellers' cheques and Eurocheques can be exchanged at banks, post offices, bureaux de change and travel agencies. The latter two charge a heavier commission but are open when banks and post offices are shut. Banks and post offices are generally open 8am–2pm on weekdays only, but hours may vary.

Credit cards are accepted only in the larger and more expensive hotels, shops and restaurants. MasterCard and Visa are the most widely accepted.

Thomas Cook travellers' cheques free you from the hazards of carrying large amounts of cash and in the event of loss or theft can quickly be refunded. Sterling cheques are recommended, though cheques denominated in US dollars and other major European currencies are accepted. Major hotels, many restaurants and shops, ticket and travel agencies, and car rental offices in main tourist areas accept travellers' cheques in lieu of cash.

The following branches of Thomas Cook can provide emergency assistance in the case of loss or theft of Thomas Cook MasterCard travellers' cheques. They can also provide full foreign exchange facilities and will change currency and cash travellers' cheques (free of commission in the case of Thomas Cook MasterCard travellers' cheques).

*Karayeorgias Servias 4, Sindagma, Athens.*
*Thomas Cook Bureau de Change, Othonos Amalias 25, Patras.*

### Conversion Table

| FROM | TO | MULTIPLY BY |
|---|---|---|
| Inches | Centimetres | 2.54 |
| Feet | Metres | 0.3048 |
| Yards | Metres | 0.9144 |
| Miles | Kilometres | 1.6090 |
| Acres | Hectares | 0.4047 |
| Gallons | Litres | 4.5460 |
| Ounces | Grams | 28.35 |
| Pounds | Grams | 453.6 |
| Pounds | Kilograms | 0.4536 |
| Tons | Tonnes | 1.0160 |

To convert back, for example from centimetres to inches, divide by the number in the the third column.

### Men's Suits

| | | | | | | | |
|---|---|---|---|---|---|---|---|
| UK | 36 | 38 | 40 | 42 | 44 | 46 | 48 |
| Rest of Europe | 46 | 48 | 50 | 52 | 54 | 56 | 58 |
| US | 36 | 38 | 40 | 42 | 44 | 46 | 48 |

### Dress Sizes

| | | | | | | |
|---|---|---|---|---|---|---|
| UK | 8 | 10 | 12 | 14 | 16 | 18 |
| France | 36 | 38 | 40 | 42 | 44 | 46 |
| Italy | 38 | 40 | 42 | 44 | 46 | 48 |
| Rest of Europe | 34 | 36 | 38 | 40 | 42 | 44 |
| US | 6 | 8 | 10 | 12 | 14 | 16 |

### Men's Shirts

| | | | | | | | |
|---|---|---|---|---|---|---|---|
| UK | 14 | 14.5 | 15 | 15.5 | 16 | 16.5 | 17 |
| Rest of Europe | 36 | 37 | 38 | 39/40 | 41 | 42 | 43 |
| US | 14 | 14.5 | 15 | 15.5 | 16 | 16.5 | 17 |

### Men's Shoes

| | | | | | | |
|---|---|---|---|---|---|---|
| UK | 7 | 7.5 | 8.5 | 9.5 | 10.5 | 11 |
| Rest of Europe | 41 | 42 | 43 | 44 | 45 | 46 |
| US | 8 | 8.5 | 9.5 | 10.5 | 11.5 | 12 |

### Women's Shoes

| | | | | | | |
|---|---|---|---|---|---|---|
| UK | 4.5 | 5 | 5.5 | 6 | 6.5 | 7 |
| Rest of Europe | 38 | 38 | 39 | 39 | 40 | 41 |
| US | 6 | 6.5 | 7 | 7.5 | 8 | 8.5 |

## NATIONAL HOLIDAYS

(see also Festivals, pages 156–7)
*Note that Easter and associated moveable feasts are determined by the Greek Orthodox calendar. Dates for Easter can differ from the Western Easter by up to three weeks.*
New Year's Day (1 January)
Epiphany
Shrove Monday
Independence Day (25 March)
Good Friday
Easter Sunday
Easter Monday
Labour Day (1May)
Day of the Holy Spirit
Assumption of the Virgin Mary (15 August)
Ochi Day (28 October)
Christmas Day (25 December)
St Stephen's Day (26 December)

## OPENING HOURS

**Banks** See **Money Matters** page 185.

### Museums and Sites

Opening hours given by official sources often bear no relation to those in force at the site or museum, which may change without notice. Most sites officially close at 3pm. Some major sites in Athens stay open longer. Winter hours for these sites are usually shorter than summer (1 April to 31 October) hours.

### Shops

Traditionally open from 8am to 1pm and from around 5pm to 8pm, but shops catering to tourists usually stay open longer. Most shops outside tourist areas close on Sunday.

## ORGANISED TOURS

Organised tours arranged by travel agencies in Athens can be an affordable way of seeing a number of sights outside the city if you have no transport of your own. Drawbacks include those of travelling with a group. Travel agencies and tour operators at popular resorts also offer a range of tours to sights and beauty spots near by.

## PHARMACIES

A green cross marks the *farmakio*. Greek chemists have some medical training and can give advice and prescribe medicines for common ailments. Pharmacies open during normal shop hours and are closed on Saturdays and Sundays.

## PLACES OF WORSHIP

Sunday services at most Orthodox churches are held from around 7.30am and last for some hours. Decently dressed (long trousers and shirt sleeves for men, below-the-knee and arm-covering dresses for women) visitors may attend.
Churches of non-Orthodox denominations are found only in Athens, where they include:
Anglican: church of Ayios Pavlos (St Paul) at Filellinon 29
Roman Catholic: church of Ayios Dionysios (St Denis) on Omirou
American inter-denominational: church of Ayios Andreas (St Andrew) on Sina.

## POLICE, see Emergency Telephone Numbers.

## POSTAL SERVICES

Most larger villages have a post office, distinguished by its prominent circular yellow sign. They are normally open during morning shop hours, but city-centre post offices are also open Saturday mornings. It can often be quicker to change money at a post office than at a bank. Stamps (*grammatosima*) are also sold at kiosks and postcard shops.

Parcels for posting must be inspected by the post office clerk before sealing. Air-mail letters take three to six days to reach the rest of Europe, five to eight days for North America and slightly longer for Australasia. Cards take much longer.

## PUBLIC TRANSPORT
### Athens Metro

A single line runs from Kifissia in the north through the city centre (Omonia and Monastiraki are the most convenient stops) to Piraeus. Trains run every 15 minutes, from 5am to midnight. Buy your ticket from a machine or ticket booth and validate it as you enter the platform.

### Buses

**Inter-city buses** are cheap, frequent and fast. Athens has two long-haul bus stations. Buses for Évvoia (Evia), Delphi, Ámfissa, Lárisa, Levádhia, Trikkala and the Metéora go from Liossion 260 (*take municipal bus 29 from Amalias, opposite the National Gardens*). Buses for all other destinations go from Kifissou 100 (*take bus 51 from the corner of Vilara and Menandhrou, near Omonia*).

**Municipal buses** within Athens and Thessaloníki display their number and destination on the front. Tickets can be bought before boarding from ticket booths near main stops or from a *periptero* kiosk. Stamp your ticket in the machine by the door on boarding.

### Ferries

Piraeus, the port of Athens, is the main gateway to the Aegean islands. Many nearby islands and points on the Peloponnese coast are served by hydrofoils, some of which go not from

the main Piraeus harbour but from Zea Marina, about 3km away. Make sure you know where your boat leaves from. Up-to-date timetables are published monthly by the Greek National Tourist Office (see page 189). Ferries also sail from Rafina (see pages 50–1). Many mainland towns have services to nearby islands. They include:

Alexandroúpolis (*to Thásos, Samothráki*)
Astakós (*to Itháki, Levkás*)
Igoumenítsa (*to Corfu, Paxí*)
Kavala (*to Thásos, Samothráki*)
Killíni (*to Zákinthos, Kefallinía*)
Patras (*to Corfu and other Ionian islands*)
Thessaloníki (*to Thasos, Samothraki, Sporades group*)
Vólos (*to Sporades group*)
Yíthion (*to Kithira, Andikithira, Crete*)

You can change money at banks, bureaux de change, travel agencies and post offices

## Taxis

Taxis are cheap and are good value even for long journeys, especially if you are travelling with friends. They should be metered, and most taxi drivers are friendly, honest and helpful (but see **Arriving**, page 180, for possible problems of overcharging). Drivers may pick up other passengers going in the same direction: this will not reduce your fare. In Athens, an empty taxi is often hard to find.

## Trains

Trains are cheap but slow, with the exception of the express trains between Athens and Thessaloníki, which take 6 hours 15 minutes. Main routes run between Athens and Thessaloníki (with international connections) on the northern mainland and Athens and Corinth, Patras and Kalamata in the Peloponnese. The most spectacular rail journey in Greece is between Dhiakofton and Kalávrita (see pages 82–3).

## SENIOR CITIZENS

Older visitors accustomed to cooler climates may find Greece's fierce midsummer heat unbearable. You may prefer to travel before mid-June or after mid-September, when the weather will be warm but not punishing. Just as Greeks love children, they also respect older people. On the other hand, they also expect them to fend for themselves – for example, when boarding a bus – and in a country where queueing is unknown this can be trying.

## TELEPHONES

The easiest way to call is from a metered phone in a street kiosk. You pay at the end of the call. Many shops and small hotels also have metered phones, as do campsites and travel and ticket agencies in resorts. Few of them allow calls using AT&T or similar charge cards. Metered phones are also available in booths at offices of OTE (Greek Telecommunications Organisation). These are cheaper, but hours are less convenient.

Dialling codes from Greece are:
Australia:   0061
Canada and the USA:   001
New Zealand:   0064
UK and Ireland:   0044
International operator:   161

In this book, local area codes are included in all telephone numbers except in the Athens and Thessaloníki sections. Dialling codes within Greece for the three major cities are:
Athens: 01
Patras: 061
Thessaloníki: 031

## TIME

GMT + 2 (+ 3 in summer). Clocks change in spring and autumn on the same date as other EU countries, but the time change does not always coincide with other countries such as the USA.

## TIPPING

Service is included in restaurants but it is normal to leave small change on the table as an additional tip. This is also usual in bars and cafés. There is no pressure to tip in hotels but a small tip will be welcomed. Inflation makes it impossible to be more specific; in 1993 a tip of DR100 was acceptable, a tip of 500 excessive. In taxis, 'keep the change' is normal practice.

## TOILETS

Standards vary enormously but have improved dramatically in recent years.

Toilets in cafés and tavernas are usually better than public facilities. Greek plumbing is narrow-bore and easily blocked, and in most place you are requested not to flush toilet paper but to put it in the waste bin provided. Only the latest modern hotels are exceptions.

## TOURIST INFORMATION

The Greek National Tourist Office (GNTO) has offices worldwide and provides a range of information which includes hotel listings for all parts of the country, up-to-date transport schedules, and information on archaeological sites, exhibitions, festivals, and other events.

**Abroad:**
**Australia**
51–7 Pitt Street, Sydney NSW 200 (tel: 02 241 1663)
**Canada**
1300 Bay Street, Main Level, Toronto, Ontario M5R 3K8 (tel: 416 968 2220)
1223 Rue de la Montagne, Montreal, Quebec H3G 1Z2 (tel: 514 871 1535)
**United Kingdom**
4 Conduit Street, London W1R ODJ (tel: 071 734 5997)
**USA**
645 Fifth Avenue, New York NY 10022 (tel: 212 421 5777)

168 North Michigan Avenue, Chicago IL 60601 (tel: 312 728 1084)
611 West 6th Street, Suite 1998, Los Angeles CA 90017 (tel: 213 626 6696)

**In Greece:**
**Athens**
Karayeorgi Servias 2 (tel: 01 322 2545) (in the National Bank building on Platia Syntagma)
**Delfi (Delphi)**
Vass. Pavlou-Friderikis 44 (tel: 0265 82900)
**Ioánnina**
Nap. Zerva 2 (tel: 0651 25086)
**Kaválla**
Filellinon 5 (tel: 051 228762/231653)
Platia Elevtherias (tel: 051 222425)
**Navplion**
Platia Iatrou (tel: 0752 24444)
**Olympia**
Praxitelous Kondili (tel: 0624 23100)
**Patras**
Iroon Politekhniou, Glifadha (tel: 061 420303)
**Thessaloníki**
Mitropoleos 34 (tel: 031 222935)
**Vólos**
Platia Riga Fereou (tel: 0421 23500)

The Athens Metro system is elderly but is also a quick and cheap way of getting around

## ACKNOWLEDGEMENTS

The Automobile Association wishes to thank the following organisations, libraries and photographers for their assistance in the preparation of this book.

**MARY EVANS PICTURE LIBRARY** 15, 60b, 62/3, 63a, 90/1, 95; **ROBERT GAULDIE** 64b, 113, 139a; **HILTON INTERNATIONAL** 175; **TERRY HARRIS** 5, 24, 25, 135, 142, 146, 149, 159b; **THE MANSELL COLLECTION LTD** 14a, 14b, 59, 132a, 132b; **NATURE PHOTOGRAPHERS LTD** 136 (P R Sterry), 137b (E A Janes), 138 (K Blamire), 139b (A Cleave); **SPECTRUM COLOUR LIBRARY** 119.
The remaining photographs are held in the AA Photo Library and were taken by Terry Harris with the exception of the cover and pages 19, 33, 34b, 37b, 38, 39b, 40, 43, 47, 48, 52, 56, 58, 60a, 61, 62/3, 65, 66, 67, 69, 72, 75a, 75b, 88, 104, 105, 123, 125, 140, 174, 177, taken by Richard Surman, and pages 150b, 151b, 151c, 157, 160, 161a, 179, taken by Peter Wilson, and the spine taken by Tim Larsen-Collinge.

The author thanks the following companies for their help in providing transport and accommodation in Greece: British Airways; Holiday Autos; Intercontinental Hotels; and Virgin Atlantic Airways.

**CONTRIBUTORS**
**Series adviser:** Melissa Shales   **Designer:** Design 23   **Copy editor:** Ron Hawkins
**Verifier:** Joanna Whitaker   **Indexer:** Marie Lorimer